The Other Boy

THE OTHER BOY

Heidi Field

TULE

The Other Boy

ONE

Blair

SIX IN THE morning seemed far too early to be trudging down the garden to my darkroom, the cacophony of birdsong reminding me that the still, cool dawn belonged to the wildlife, not to humans. If my client wasn't insisting on seeing the contact sheets from yesterday's shoot before lunchtime, I'd still be snuggled in bed beside Scott, but she was representing one of the biggest names in fashion, so pandering to her every whim was worth it—for my career and my bank balance.

I bunched my curls into a messy bun, tightened the knot on my dressing gown, and flicked on the safelight in the darkroom. Stepping inside, I inhaled the pungent metallic scents of the photography chemicals, not unlike the heady smell of gasoline and an odour that filled me with pleasure and comfort. I'd been in here till after midnight last night, giving the contact sheets a good five hours to dry. I reached up and began unclipping the sheets and slipping them into plastic sleeves.

That second glass of wine before bed was a bad idea. My mouth was dry and my eyes felt heavy and sore. The shoot yesterday had been one of the worst of my career. The client was a tyrant. I could barely take a shot without her bellowing at the models, fiddling with the lights, or telling me how I should be doing my job.

I had twenty years of experience in this business, and my photos had graced the covers of some of the world's most famous magazines and been used to market many of the biggest brands in the fashion industry. Yesterday's client had treated me like I was a novice who was hard of hearing. I cricked my neck to the left and right trying to release the tension that was already building up at the thought of another exhausting day with this woman.

A gentle knock at the door. I ignored it. Another. Scott and Jamie both knew better than to disturb me when the red pilot light switch was illuminated. It wasn't that I needed the safelight right now, or that the contacts would be damaged in any way, but simply that I was tired and on edge and wanted to be left alone to organize the contact sheets in peace before racing off to the train station.

The handle of the door slowly turned, and the door opened an inch. "You need to come inside, BB. Now."

I yanked open the door to find Scott standing in the alcove. He looked worse than I felt; his olive skin was several shades lighter, his wavy dark hair was all over the place, and his eyes were wide and unblinking. An uncomfortable feeling flittered about in my stomach, and I couldn't swallow.

I gripped the doorframe. "What's going on? You look terrible. Are you alright?"

Scott took my hand. "The police are here. About Jamie."

My body felt light as a feather as I walked with Scott across the lawn. The pretty birdsong had ceased, and the trees that lined our garden stood still as statues. I floated through the kitchen and into the lounge as if I wasn't properly connected to the world, fear building inside me, pulling me out of myself.

A dewy morning light filtered in through the bay window of our spacious front room, and I noticed a car drive slowly past the gate at the end of our drive. Two police officers sat on our large sofa. They seemed small, somehow, their bodies awkwardly sunk into the cream leather, our colourful cushions engulfing them, the cozy piece of furniture at odds with their officious demeanour. Their uniforms matched the thin stripes in the wallpaper on our feature wall, but this morning, the contrasting glitter strips seemed to have lost their sparkle.

I sat beside Scott on the other sofa, opposite the officers, the oak resin coffee table like a vibrant river between us. I smiled, but my lips wobbled at the edges so I bit my cheek. I'd never spoken to a police officer before. Never had one knock on the door. They looked at each other, at me and Scott, around the room.

What was it Jamie had done? He was out yesterday when I got back from work, and I didn't hear him come home. I'd tried to stay up, but I was exhausted. I began to list all the things that might get him in trouble with the police. Probably drinking and causing a disturbance. Maybe he'd sprayed graffiti somewhere, taken his art into the public domain. He was a good boy, insular. He wouldn't do anything bad. Just normal, stupid teenage stuff, I guessed. They were probably here to rap him on the knuckles, give him a shock to keep him on the right path.

Scott gestured to the older male officer and then the

younger female. "This is Officer Jelani and Officer Shah."

The older officer took off his hat, revealing thick black hair neatly cropped and swept to the side. "Please call me Mika."

I swallowed. "So, what's Jamie done?"

Mika made eye contact with me and Scott, then paused for a moment. "A body has been found in Peasedale Forest. We have reason to believe that the body is your son. We would like to take a DNA sample to confirm the identity."

We all sat in silence. It was like the world had gone into slow motion, like we had been extracted from reality and were hovering in a vacuum, unable to speak or move.

Scott put his hand on my knee and squeezed. I looked down at his hand, his wedding ring, the wrinkles on his skin and the blood vessels tinged blue beneath.

"You've made a mistake," he said. "Jamie is upstairs in bed. Why don't you go and wake him up, BB?"

The room expanded, the walls moving farther and farther away from me, and my body felt like lead. I couldn't move. A body? They found a body in the woods somewhere, and they think the body is Jamie.

I stared at Mika, looking for a sign that he had said the wrong thing by mistake. "A dead body?"

He nodded. "Yes."

A dead body. In the woods. Who they think is my boy.

Scott moved his hand to my shoulder. "Blair?"

I snapped my head around to face Scott. "Did you see him last night?"

Scott clenched his jaw. "Just go upstairs and get him, and then all this will go away."

He was so pale; his whole body was shaking. I'd never seen him like that before, and it terrified me. I stood up. My legs felt so weak, I had to reach for the doorframe as I left the sitting room. My heart was thudding in my chest, and I had to swallow to hold back the bile that was creeping up into my throat. I hadn't heard Jamie come home. I hadn't heard Minnie bark, which she always did every time one of us came in. I stopped at the bottom of the stairs and looked at the hooks on the wall in the hallway. Jamie's coat wasn't hung there. His shoes weren't on the rack underneath. His house key wasn't in the saucer or discarded elsewhere on the dresser. There was no mud on the limestone tiles. Oh god, please don't let this be happening.

I took the stairs one at a time. The carpet muffled the sound of the creak that the seventh step made. Jamie had learned to step over it when he got back too late, hoping not to disturb me, but I always heard him. Maybe he had just been extra quiet last night. I'd had two glasses of wine. I gripped the banister as I went, sweat from my palms making my hands slide along the polished chrome handrail.

I stood outside Jamie's bedroom door and listened, willing him to make a noise, a groan, a cough. I leant closer, desperate to hear the sound of his phone playing something. Twisting the handle, I pushed open the door. Please let him be in there. The door swung open and I stared at his bed, his untouched bed, still as pristine as he had left it the day before. I couldn't take a deep breath, only shallow gulps, making my head swim. Racing to the bathroom, I threw open the door and looked in the shower cubicle. No Jamie. I checked the spare room, too. This was wrong. All wrong.

What the police said about a body, about it being our son, they had to be wrong.

I stumbled down the stairs and back into the siting room. "He's not there, Scott. He's not there. I can't find him."

Scott leapt up and barged past me, looking for Jamie in the dining room and the kitchen. He even went outside; I could hear him yanking open the shed and shouting for Jamie in my darkroom. When he returned, his face was grey, sweat matted his hair and he was stroking the stubble on the sides of his cheeks. "Where the hell is he?"

Mika stood up. "I'd like to get a DNA sample and send it to the lab. The quicker we do that, the sooner we will know if the body is your son."

Scott felt in his pockets. "I'll call the school. Find out who he's been hanging around with. He probably stayed at a mate's house last night."

Mika nodded sympathetically. "Does he do that a lot?"

Scott looked at me and then Mika. "No. No, he doesn't." He raised his hands in the air. "look, can we just take a breath? Stop a second? Surely we can just come to the morgue and identify the body. You must have a solid reason to think it's our son, right? So, let's just go and see for ourselves."

Mika gripped his hat in both hands and held Scott's wild, searching gaze. "We received an emergency call from Jamie's phone last night. The body we found is not suitable for visual identification. There is significant trauma. Did Jamie have any specific markings on his body—a tattoo, scar, birthmark?"

Significant trauma. I didn't want to think about what that meant. I couldn't let my mind go there. This would all turn out to be a mistake, I was sure if it. Jamie would walk through the front door any minute.

Scott ran a hand through his now damp hair. "He had a scar on the outside of his left calf from falling off his scooter, shaped like a boomerang, about an inch long."

I reached for Scott's hand and squeezed. "It's not Jamie. I know it's not him."

Mika gestured toward the stairs with his hat. "Could you take officer Shah upstairs so that she can get the sample? A toothbrush or hairbrush."

Officer Shah was shorter than me and half my age, with beautiful light brown skin and the kind of thick, straight chocolate-coloured hair that I had always coveted. She had a presence about her that made me nervous, her bright eyes and soft features hiding a far sharper demeanour. She was watching me, judging, trying to decide if I was genuine, if I was keeping secrets.

As we headed upstairs, I heard Mika and Scott talk about Jamie's friends, where he might have been the night before, and the reasons why he might not have come home. I wasn't sure if Scott knew the right answers. I wanted to go back down and help him, but I didn't know the answers either. What would the officer think of us, not knowing where our fifteen-year-old son had been after school yesterday?

Jamie's room smelled of him, his strong teenage body odour mixed with a hint of deodorant and those incense sticks. I glanced around, hoping to see something that would give me a sign as to where he was, that he was okay. Officer

Shah bagged up Jamie's hairbrush and took his toothbrush from the sink in the corner of his room. It was so surreal, like a dream, and I wanted so desperately to wake up.

TWO

Scott

A Day Later

I'D DRUNK SO much coffee over the last twenty-four hours that I couldn't focus, I had the shakes, and my head was throbbing. Blair was sitting opposite me at the kitchen table, staring at her mobile. Staring at that emergency message from Jamie's phone, sent at 11:53 on Monday evening. I got the same message: *Emergency SOS. Jamie called emergency services. Jamie has listed you as an emergency contact.* The next message, sent a few minutes later, showed his location. Somewhere remote in Peasedale Forest.

The police had responded and found a body, but as yet, no sign of Jamie's mobile phone. The search continued yesterday and they found more bodies, although the information we were given was minimal. They couldn't go telling members of the public details about a crime until they had hard evidence proving that those members of the public were relatives of the victim. And, even then, they needed to be sure those relatives weren't involved. We were under strict instructions not to talk to anyone, including family.

Being on the other side of a police investigation was a strange and daunting experience, and no amount of experience as a crime reporter could have prepared me for how isolating it felt. Our world had stopped, and the walls of our house were closing in, crushing us, sucking out all the oxygen from the air.

Waiting to hear if our son was dead made my insides curdle. Cold toast sat in the rack untouched, the butter knives clean, and the lids still firmly on the jam and honey jars. That was breakfast—yesterday. Neither of us had eaten a crumb.

Blair pushed her mug of coffee across the table toward me. "I can't drink anymore. I don't know if I'm coming or going, and I think if I stand up I'll pass out."

"We need to eat. This is crazy. There's no way that body is Jamie. He must have lost his phone or it was stolen. Whoever had it got themselves into some trouble and used it to call for help. I bet Jamie has no idea what's going on and is hanging out with his mates and playing truant from school."

"What mates, though? We went over and over this so many times yesterday. Have you ever met any of his friends? Has he ever spoken about them to you? You're assuming he has friends, but I've seen him sitting on that swing in the park all on his own so many times, and Christ knows where he goes or what he does when we're not back from work till late."

"He's home, painting and eating dinner. He's always leaving those microwave meal packets lying around or the empty plate from the food you leave for him."

"Was Frank sure he hadn't seen him? Frank's always at home."

"I went round to talk to him twice yesterday, and he's

sure that the last time he saw Jamie was when he left for school on Monday morning. I shouldn't have spoken to him at all. Not until the DNA results. The police didn't want us talking to anyone just to ensure nothing would get leaked to the media. And I can assure you that someone in the office will already have gotten wind of something going on. Police and forensics lugging equipment into a forest will draw attention from some nosy members of the public, and before you know it there'll be a media onslaught."

"Why is it taking so long? Surely they can get a DNA test done faster than this. They've found a dead body, for pity's sake."

"Officer Shah said that they had found more than one, remember, so that could slow down the test results. She said that the police had expanded the crime scene, which would mean a lot more forensic evidence."

"We could just go and look at the body. Then we'd know for sure it wasn't Jamie and the police wouldn't be wasting any more time on us."

"It doesn't work like that. They'll need to do a postmortem, and that will only take place after the body has been removed from the scene. Forensics only gets one chance to gather evidence, so moving the body will only happen when they are satisfied there isn't anything else to find. We'll have to wait for the DNA results."

My body was numb, my head in investigative journalist mode. I knew what was coming, what the world was about to see, the newspaper articles and television coverage, the dissection of the lives of all the victims and their families, followed by the ensuing hunt for the killer. I'd read between the lines as Officer Shah had tried to give us as little information as possible, her job as a police officer taking precedent over her responsibilities as the family liaison. Whatever had happened in Peasedale Forest was big, and for some reason, the police thought our son was a part of it.

Blair dropped her head into her hands and dissolved into gut-wrenching sobs. "I can't do this. I can't lose him. It can't be Jamie. Please don't let it be him, Scott."

I soared around the table and swooped in on Blair, enveloping her in my arms and resting my head on hers. "DNA tests come back negative all the time. It won't be Jamie. The police have got it wrong. I know they have."

Blair lifted her head and buried her face in my shoulder. "This is insane, inhuman. Making us wait. Leaving us like this."

"let's go outside and get some air; it's stifling in here."

I lifted Blair off her chair and walked her out into the garden, sitting her on a wicker lounger and laying a fleece rug over her body. She slumped into the cushions and pulled the rug up to her chin, staring up into the grey sky. Even the outside felt heavy, the clouds low, barely moving, as if the sky itself was going to cave in on us. She was right. This was inhuman, letting us agonise over the possibility of our son's murder, and there was no way I could sit and wait any longer. The fresh air in my lungs only made me more jittery as I listened to cars diving along the road, birds chirruping, someone mowing or hedge-cutting, getting on with life as if nothing had changed.

I marched back inside, determined to get some answers. Grabbing my phone from the kitchen table, I hit the speed-dial button for Mika.

"Officer Jelani speaking."

"It's Scott. Scott Bagby."

"We're just outside."

"About time."

The doorbell rang.

My shoulders loosened as I rushed along the hallway to the door. Mika had sounded alert, formal. Not the tone of a man about to give two parents the devastating news of their fifteen-year-old son's death. I flung open the door and stepped aside to let Mika and Officer Shah inside. They both had their hats in their hands.

Officer Shah looked past me. "Where's Blair?"

"Outside. This way." I led them along the hallway, through the kitchen, and out of the bifold doors to the garden. "I guess you want to give us the news together. Blair, honey, the officers are here."

I couldn't stand still. My body was fizzing with nervous tension, so I rocked from foot to foot, my hands clenched.

Blair threw off the blanket and leapt up, slipping her hand into mine, her gaze flitting between Mika and Officer Shah. "It isn't him, is it? Please tell us it isn't him!"

Mika took a slow breath, and my heart started beating so hard in my chest that I thought it might break through my ribs.

Mika looked at us both, made eye contact, and then shook his head. "I'm so sorry. The DNA test was a match. The body found yesterday morning is your son."

Blair made a sound that I will never forget, a wail so haunting that even Mika turned pale. Blair collapsed onto the decking, her fists balled into her hair, screaming and screaming and screaming. I couldn't move. I couldn't speak or think or breathe.

THREE

Blair

A Week Later

S ITTING IN THE lounge, staring at the television, I felt like a prisoner in my own home. A pack of salivating journalists were practically camped outside our gate.

We weren't the only family being held hostage by the press. There were twelve other victims, all boys between the ages of eight and fifteen, Jamie being the oldest. They were tortured and killed in a ramshackle hunting cabin in Peasedale Forest and buried a short walk away in an area of woodland no bigger than our downstairs. The bodies were found in differing states of decay; some had been buried for years. The press had gotten hold of the story, and the details and speculation were at a fever pitch, with the desperate parents of missing boys coming forward in droves. My boy was in the centre of a serial killer's mess, a man the media had nicknamed the *Pied Piper of Peasedale*, a man still at large.

Jamie had been his last victim, killed only a few hours before the police arrived in the forest. Our sweet son's body was still warm when they found him. That was the hardest part to hear. I hadn't been able to see him, touch him, kiss his lips, or say goodbye since we were given the news. His corpse was now laid in a morgue, refrigerated like a cut of meat.

We had been given snippets of information by Mika and Officer Shah, but I spent most of my time watching the news, stories of the murders of thirteen boys in Peasedale Forest coming thick and fast. I listened and watched and absorbed everything that was being broadcast, everything that was said about my boy, but I didn't feel anything. Nothing. I didn't feel a single emotion. I was numb, I wasn't hungry or tired or hot or cold, and I couldn't see the point of doing anything, none of those pointless ways in which we fill our time—working, cleaning, cooking, washing. What was it all for?

SCOTT WAS LIKE a frenetic hornet, buzzing around the house, desperately searching for something, constantly on the phone calling everyone he could think of to ask about Jamie: when they last saw him, who he was with, what he was doing. I could see it was driving him crazy. He'd disappear into the garage to use the gym equipment and come out soaking in sweat. He'd crash around in Jamie's bedroom, empty out cupboards and reorganise them, and cook up elaborate meals in the kitchen and then throw them out because neither of us could stomach them. I had to turn up the television to block him out.

A photograph of Jamie hung above the fireplace in the lounge. I sat back and stared at his happy face, his untidy shock of red curls, his bottle-green eyes and pale freckled skin. He had a lopsided grin, always a little awkward in front of the camera. I needed to see him again, hold him, smell him. I wanted the police to knock on the door and tell me that they got the DNA test wrong, messed it up somehow, got confused with all the other bodies and forensic evidence, tell me it wasn't Jamie's body they found after all.

Scott came into the lounge and turned up the lights. The blinds had been shut since Jamie's body was identified, and we skulked around the house avoiding the windows and the doorbell. Scott handed me a tray with a plate of mac and cheese and a glass of milk. He left the room and returned with his own tray of food, cheese on toast with tomatoes and Worcester sauce, and a lemonade. We were picking food that Jamie had loved, food that reminded us of him, with familiar smells and flavours that brought back memories.

Scott took a bite of his toast and flicked through the channels. "After we've eaten, we're having a bath. We both stink."

I sniffed my armpit through the dressing gown that I had sobbed, slumped, and slept in for the last week. "I'm just not ready to get myself together. It's too soon."

"I know. I agree, but what are we doing? Watching the endless gory details about our son's murder and his killer, hoping that it's all a terrible nightmare? We need to find out what happened. Why our boy was murdered by this monster. What we missed. I need to know."

The screen flashed with the headshots of the thirteen boys. A woman appeared standing in front of police tape in Peasedale Forest. She was holding a microphone, her cropped grey hair damp, her cerise shirt unbuttoned at the top.

Scott tapped the mute button. "If we can't see Jamie, then we can at least see where he died."

I paused, about to spoon in a mouthful of macaroni. "Go out there?" I pointed my spoon in the direction of the window. "Past them? They'll eat us alive."

"We can go around the back, through Frank's garden. We'll go in disguise. Beanies, T-shirts, and jeans. You can tuck your hair up. I think we should go to Peasedale, to the forest. Maybe it'll give us some clue, some insight into what Jamie was thinking. Maybe we'll feel closer to him if we go to the place where he died."

It was a crazy idea, but as soon as Scott mentioned it, I wanted to go. I needed to see those woods, see that shack. Jamie would never go to a place like that, and it would be obvious to us if we saw the woods that the body they were saying was Jamie couldn't possibly be him. Maybe we would even find him hiding in the forest somewhere, or hurt, unable to find help. We just might stumble across his phone and something on it would prove that it wasn't him who made the emergency call. Maybe there would even be a photograph or a message telling us where he was.

I pushed my plate of food aside and got up. "Come on then. Let's go. Dark clothes and beanies. See you out back in five minutes."

I rushed upstairs to pull on some fresh underwear, my black jeans, and one of Scott's black T-shirts. I tied my hair up tight on top of my head with a few grips to keep any stray curls in order."

Scott was standing by the back door with two beanies in

his hands and a backpack. "I've texted Frank, and he's waiting by the back gate. We can take his car, too. You'll have to hide in the back footwell until we're past the paparazzi."

I grabbed the backpack from Scott, and he locked the back door. He had packed a torch, snacks, water, a portable phone charger, and a first-aid kit. Sneaking through Frank's side door, our kindhearted neighbour ushered us into his garage. He was a big man, in his late fifties with long salt-and-pepper hair and a beard, and he loved his tools and outdoor adventures. We often joked about how he would have made a great addition to the A-Team.

When we were safely in his car, me on the floor wedged behind the front seats, Frank opened his electric front gate from inside the garage at the same time as the electric garage door. The press barely had time to turn before Scott sped out of the driveway and up the road. When the coast was clear I climbed into the front seat and pulled on Jamie's maroon beanie.

We sat in silence as we drove the two-and-a-bit-hour drive up to Peasedale. The police had reached the shack via a service station on the main road that led into the town. We'd seen the chaos at the service station on the television and had no desire to throw ourselves into the lion's den, so Scott decided we should stop on a quiet road before reaching the garage and make our way into the woods from there. We wouldn't avoid the scrum of the investigation, media, and growing crowds of inquisitive members of the public, but at least we'd have a little time to get acclimatised to the location before we joined the fray.

Peasedale Forest was dark and unwelcoming, nothing like the tourist trap of our local forest, Kingsholt, with its wide paths, bicycle trails, playground equipment sculpted out of the trees, and large café, park, and picnic area—not to mention the high ropes and Segway hire operation. No, Peasedale was for the solitary walker, the hermit seeking sanctuary away from other humans—people who had something to hide.

We pushed through tall bracken, stepped over and round brambles and low branches, weaved through thick, moss-laden tree trunks. Scott had his phone out looking at the map, but we didn't need it; the noise from the hustle and bustle at the scene and the constant stream of members of the public coming and going drew us in. We blended into the crowds of reporters and nosy onlookers all scrabbling for the best view behind the police tape.

There was little to see; tents were blocking the view of the places where the bodies were found, and screens encircled the shack. Men and women in their forensic suits were bagging up evidence, taking photographs, and poking yellow number cards into the ground while the police held back the crowds. There was a smell that snuck up my nostrils and lingered, a musty tang that made my top lip curl. What on earth would Jamie be doing in a place like this? Everything about it felt wrong, unsavoury, frightening.

Someone touched my shoulder. I jumped and spun around, expecting to see a camera flash in my face, my identity revealed, and a sudden onslaught of ravenous reporters.

"Let's move this way." It was Scott. He took hold of my

upper arm and guided me along the line of people toward the shack. "I don't know why I thought this would be a good idea."

The people around us were talking about the boys and the killer. Trying to make sense of what happened, conjecturing about the killer's motive, wondering why the boys would have come all this way to this horrid place. What was wrong with them; what was going on with their families? It was awful to hear, the inferences people were making about me and Scott and how we drove Jamie here, and how his troubled life led him to make such a terrible choice. I couldn't bear it. I clamped my hands over my ears and looked at Scott. His eyes were wild, his teeth clenched.

Someone turned to us, shaking her head. "They were all so young. What kind of parents don't know where their kids have gone or what they're up to?"

Scott took hold of my wrist and pulled me away from the mayhem. "We should go home. This was a mistake. We should let the police do the investigating."

He was shaking so much, I put my arm around his waist. "Okay. Let's go."

Heading back to the car, my skin prickled and the back of my neck felt cold. Scott kept turning back and then marching forward, each time his pace picking up. Light started to filter through from the road up ahead, and I could just make out our car in the distance. Scott paused, holding out his hand to stop me from taking another step. I looked across at him. His head was craning to the side. I followed his gaze. There was a loud crack.

I snatched a breath. "What was that?"

"I think someone has been following us. Maybe someone recognised us."

I stared hard into the woods. "A reporter?"

Scott didn't reply. I couldn't think who else it could be. Then a dreadful thought flashed into my head. They hadn't caught the killer. Maybe he was here, watching everything. Watching us.

"Oh my god, Scott. Do you think it's him, the killer?" My whole body turned to ice, and I shivered.

Scott grabbed my hand and started to run to the car, dragging me along with him. I thought I could hear footsteps behind us, crunching over the undergrowth, but I didn't look back. Scott pulled the car keys out of his pocket with his free hand and clicked the lock. The rear lights flashed, and we slammed into the car, scrabbling for the door handles. As soon as we were inside, Scott locked the doors and started the engine.

I looked back as Scott pulled out into the road, but I couldn't see anyone. "Who do you think it was?"

"Fuck knows, but I wasn't about to hang around and find out."

FOUR

Scott

A Month Later

ALONE IN THE dining room, trying to swallow down a microwave curry, I stared at the television screen that came out from its stand high up in the far corner of the room. The *Pied Piper of Peasedale* was still all anyone was talking about, heading up every news show and dominating the papers and social media. Stories of how he had mutilated his victims, raped them, kept them alive to torture them, their last days spent in petrified agony. Not Jamie, though. Our boy's suffering was short-lived; he was missing a toe and a finger, a tooth was found in his stomach, and there were marks on his wrists and ankles matching the shackles on the torture board in the shack, but in comparison to the other bodies found, there was minimal damage, he wasn't sexually assaulted, and his death came quickly, the coroner's report recording the cause of death as a single stab wound to the chest.

Jamie's experience at the hands of this monster didn't fit the killer's MO, and that was making the police and the press ask uncomfortable questions. Why was he not tortured and raped like the other boys? How did he manage to send an emergency message? Did he have a different relationship with the killer? The other parents had rallied, spilling out details of their boys to reporters, questioning why their innocent sons had found themselves deep in a forest in an abandoned shack. Their interviewers posed the idea that they must have been coaxed there, perhaps by another boy, an ally to the killer, an accomplice even. I spat out the mouthful I had been chewing for the last two minutes, pushed my plate away, and switched off the television.

I was about to go up to Jamie's bedroom for what felt like the hundredth time and search for a clue about what happened, evidence that would make him as much of a victim as the other twelve, when there was a tap on the sliding doors. I looked up and saw Mika and Officer Shah peering at me. Frank was with them, looking the same as he did every day, his gardening gear and floppy grey hair giving him that outdoorsy carefree appearance. Our kind neighbour had been ushering the officers around the back of his house and through the side gate to avoid the press, who remained resolute outside our gate. He waved and then disappeared. I left my plate on the dining room table and went to the back door to let the officers in, and we sat in the kitchen, always in the same chairs. Apparently, the same-seats thing is because we have developed a small personal territory around a familiar seat that makes us feel comfortable. I guess anything that would make our situation more comfortable was a bonus.

Officer Shah also always asked the same question when she came to the house. "Where's Blair?"

I pushed my hair out of my eyes, aware that I looked a state, and gave my usual answer. "In Jamie's room. Probably asleep on his bed."

Officer Shah didn't ask me to go and get her; she just nodded.

Mika cleared his throat. "The killer has been arrested."

"What? You've caught him?" An urge to drive straight to the station, barge my way in, and rip the bastard's limbs off swept over me like a tsunami, the hatred I could feel for another human being sending my pulse into overdrive. I stood up and paced around the kitchen, taking deep breaths to try to alleviate some of the rage.

Mika kept his eyes on me but remained seated at the table. "He gave himself up, Scott. Walked right on into Peasedale Police Station. His name is Gunner Piper, a local Peasedale resident. He has confessed to the murders, given a DNA sample, and is prepared to talk to the police."

I gripped the edge of the worktop, needing to hold onto something solid as my head whirled. The man who murdered my son was alive, healthy even, and he walked into a police station and admitted to his crimes. Like some fucking celebrity wanting his fifteen minutes of fame.

"Prepared to talk to the police? As if he's doing you a favour?!" I walked to the sink and turned on the cold tap, splashing some water on my face and running my fingers through my hair.

This wasn't what I envisioned. I wanted to change the law and give him the death penalty. I wanted to bring back stoning. I wanted him to be publicly hung, drawn, and quartered, and I wanted to be the executioner. He was the *Pied Piper of Peasedale*, a violent, depraved murderer.

"Gunner Piper." I spat out the words. "Gunner Piper."

"Why did he kill my boy?" Blair was standing in the kitchen doorway, a ghostly look about her, eyes bulbous and raw from all her crying.

I wanted to go to her, hold her, scream with her, but I was afraid that if I moved, even a twitch, my rage would be let loose and I would destroy everything in my path until my hands had ahold of Gunner Piper's throat so that I could squeeze the life out of his body.

Instead, I stood at the sink, staring into the plughole, and shook. Officer Shah led Blair to a chair and busied about making a cup of coffee. "Gunner Piper will be interviewed, and we need to establish that the evidence fits with his account of what happened. There won't be a court case, just a sentence hearing."

Mika got up and put a hand on my shoulder. "He'll go to prison for the rest of his life."

Officer Shah handed Blair a coffee. "Why don't you take it outside, Blair? Get some fresh air?"

Blair followed Officer Shah outside. I watched them through the window as they headed out to the bench by the roses.

"You could always join the group that the other parents have set up," Mika said, his hand still gently gripping my shoulder. "It helps to talk to other people in a similar situation."

"We're fine. We don't want all that. It's hard enough for Blair to take in what's happening without having to listen to all those other parents. Besides, what would we say? We couldn't tell the police anything useful; we didn't have a clue what Jamie was doing in those woods or who he was with.

We thought he was home or in the park—painting, listening to music, lazing about like other teenagers. What would they think of us, not knowing where our son was or what he was up to? Besides, Jamie wasn't treated like the other boys. He was different somehow. No, Blair doesn't need all that."

Mika walked across to the window and watched Blair and Officer Shah. "And you, Scott, what do you need?"

I sat back down, dropping my head into my hands. "I need my boy back. I need that monster to pay for what he did. I need Blair." Slamming my palms into the table, I looked up at Mika. "What I don't need is the press hounding us, fake stories about Jamie's life being splattered over the tabloids, or the other parents telling us how we should be dealing with our grief. And I sure as hell don't need all this speculation about an accomplice."

"Fair enough." Mika secured his hat on his head and wandered out into the garden.

Mika wasn't our friend. He wasn't even on our side. He was a police officer, and his job was to find the truth and make the criminals pay for their crimes. He couldn't make any of this go away just because that's what Blair and I wanted. I followed him outside and nodded my goodbye as he and Officer Shah made their way through the side gate into Frank's garden.

Blair and I sat outside on the bench for the rest of the day. She drifted in and out of sleep, her head resting against my shoulder, while I stared into space, wondering about Gunner Piper.

It was Minnie whining at the back door that drew me out of my inertia. The light had long gone, a full moon illuminating the garden and turning the furniture and trees into eerie shadows. Minnie wanted her food and her bed. I nudged Blair, and we both plodded inside, Minnie skulking along behind us and sitting in her basket waiting for her bowl to be filled. She missed Jamie, too. Scooping up Minnie's bowl, I took it into the utility room and filled it with two handfuls of dry food; I couldn't be bothered with the meat and fussing about with the can.

When I returned to the kitchen, Blair was gone. I checked in the lounge before making my way upstairs. She hadn't even turned the lights on. As I neared Jamie's bedroom, I heard Blair talking, her voice low and hushed. Hovering outside the door, I leant in and listened. I couldn't make out words, just mumbles, as if she was having a conversation with someone.

Without making a sound, I opened the door and stepped into our son's room. Blair was standing by the window peeking through Jamie's blind, one of the slats lifted with her forefinger, a slither of moonlight streaking the bottom half of her face. Being in Jamie's room had become a strange experience, familiar but empty, everything a trigger: his bed that hadn't been slept in for a month, his school uniform strewn on the floor that last day he was alive, the posters and postcards and picture frames that all held memories of happy times. It wasn't the memories that jabbed at my decimated heart but the fact that there wouldn't be any new ones.

Blair pushed her face closer to the blind. "I can see him, you know. And he knows it. I don't know why you didn't tell me about him. I would have listened. Maybe I could have helped."

Clearing my throat to signal my intrusion, I walked up behind Blair and rested my hands on her hips. I leant my head forward next to hers, brushing our cheeks together, to get a look through the crack. "Who are you talking to?"

She didn't respond.

"Who can you see out there?"

"Him." She pointed out past the gate and the road to the park.

I squinted and peered into the dark. We had picked this house for its charm and its location in a town named Thadley. The house itself was positioned alongside Thadley's two-hundred-and-ninety-acre medieval deer park; our home was a fifteen-minute walk from the primary and secondary schools, an easy cycle into town, and we could see the kids' play area from our upstairs windows. The park itself was comprised of open grassland, a golf course, a cricket club, a river, streams, and ponds. Who wouldn't want to raise a family in such an idyllic setting? How quickly our paradise has become our purgatory.

Light from the streetlamps filtered out toward the play area, but there was no one about. I looked beyond the glow of the lamps but couldn't see anyone. Since the story broke about Jamie's death, the local residents had avoided the park, and parents were clinging tightly to their children, keeping their teenagers inside after dark, the stranger-danger fear at its max. They wouldn't stay away much longer, though. The news of Gunner Piper's arrest would become the next big story, and daily life would resume, everyone safe in the knowledge that the murderer was behind bars. Details of his gruesome crimes would filter out into the world over the coming months as he milked his celebrity status. Most serial killers kill for enjoyment; Jamie managed to get one who also wanted attention. A wave of anger rippled through my body, making my skin prickle.

I noticed some movement in a car parked across the road from our gate, a flash of a phone light, no doubt a determined reporter hoping to harass one of us on a late-night walk or photograph us doing something scandalous in the early hours.

I moved my arms further around Blair's shrinking waist. "I don't see anyone."

"He's right there. Staring straight at us."

"Where exactly? Who is this man?"

"I'm not sure he is a man. He looks about the same age as Jamie. He's always hanging around in the park, looking."

"Always?" The last thing I wanted to do was to mistrust Blair, but there really wasn't anyone there.

"Who were you talking to before I came in?"

"Jamie. Who do you think?"

"Jamie isn't here, BB."

"Of course Jamie's here. He's always here."

I squeezed my cheek against my wife's, what was left of my heart sinking in my chest. "Come on, let's get you in the bath. Go and get your clothes off, and I'll meet you in the bathroom."

Blair left the room, and I pulled up Jamie's blind for a better look out of the window. It was difficult to see any detail in the darkness; I could only make out the swings and slides, a dark area that was the sand pit, and the fence that enclosed all of the play equipment. I fanned my gaze beyond the play area, but nothing drew my attention. Maybe whoever it was Blair saw had left before I got a chance to see them. Maybe there was no one there at all. If she was imagining talking to Jamie then she could well be imagining a stalker. She needed to see a doctor, that was clear. I was out of my depth with everything, but as soon as Blair was more stable, as soon as we were coping better, I'd find out all I could about Gunner Piper and why he did what he did to my son. Just as soon as we were both ready to face it.

When I got to the bathroom, the only light Blair had switched on was the one that shone on the cylindrical mirror above the sink, its blue glow creating a mix of purple shades against the pink decor. Blair loved vibrant colours; not a single room in our house was contemporary grey or cream or white. She was sitting naked in our cerise roll-top tub with its dragon feet, looking like a sad, beautiful mermaid, her red curls billowing over her shoulders. Her skin was almost translucent against the baby-pink tiles. I lifted the drapes that hung like theatre curtains separating the bath from the toilet, sink, and shower cubicle and knelt to seal the plughole and turn on the taps.

Blair leant back against the sloping end of the tub and turned her head toward me. "I wonder what Gunner Piper looks like? Do you think he'll tell the police why he killed all those boys? How he killed them? He must have a very kind face for the boys to follow him all the way into those woods to that dingy cabin."

I held my hand under the running water until the temperature was just right. "A wolf in sheep's clothing."

Blair slid a little further into the tub. "The devil in disguise."

I lifted the shampoo bottle from the white wicker table beside the bath. "A snake in the grass."

I began to wonder who exactly we both meant by the wolf, the devil, and the snake. Was it Gunner Piper or the mysterious boy Blair thinks she saw or someone else?

Blair slid under the water, submerging her head and pushing her hair back from her face as she emerged. I squirted some shampoo on my hands and began to lather it into her hair. This was as close as we could get right now, and caring for Blair was the only thing keeping me sane.

Minnie started barking, and the sensor lights outside flashed on, flooding the bathroom with light. The reporters had never ventured beyond our gate, always keeping a respectful distance, although their camera lenses managed to reach right inside our house.

I rinsed off my hands in the bathwater. "I'll just go down and see what Minnie's barking about. Probably a fox."

Blair's mention of a man or a boy watching us had put the wind up me. I checked the locks on all the doors and windows and had a good look outside. I let Minnie out of the kitchen into the rest of the house, and she ran straight to the door that led from the hall to the garage. I unlocked it, switched on the garage light, and walked around my car. The high window in the outer wall of the garage was shut and locked, and nothing in the garage had been disturbed. The shelves were tidy as always, the gym equipment at the far end was as I'd left it earlier in the day, the bikes hung on the near wall as they always did. Minnie stood below the window barking for a while before giving up and wandering back to her bed growling.

When I went back into the bathroom, Blair was standing by the open window. "I told you he was here, didn't I?"

"Who?"

"Jamie."

FIVE

Blair

Six Months Later

I T TOOK ME ten minutes to scrape off the red 'B' of Bitch. There was no way I was leaving this filth on the garage doors for all the neighbours to gawk at on their way to work. My sweet son wasn't *Gunner's Bitch,* and spraying the words on my house was cruel and ugly and a lie.

I dunked and scrubbed, splashing suds all down my pyjamas, each stroke of the wire brush producing that uncomfortable screech of metal against metal. I used to love the smell of fresh paint, but as I scoured away the bleeding letters, the stench churned my stomach. Pausing, I leant back against the door, inhaling the fresh, crisp dawn air. The sun was slow to rise this morning. Everything was still. Even the birds didn't dare to chirrup.

I heard the clink and crunch of Scott's footsteps against the shingle.

"Nothing like an early-morning outdoor activity to start the day." My devoted husband appeared from the side of the garage carrying our other wire brush.

"I'm using my left hand. Trying to even myself up. My right arm ached for days after the last time, and now my right bicep is definitely bigger." I flexed my right arm to

34

show off toned muscle.

Scott cocked his head and raised his eyebrows to show he was impressed. "Maybe you should take up arm wrestling."

I watched him shift his brush to his left hand, dunk it in the bucket, and start working on the paint, his solid arm erasing the letters in half the time it was taking me.

I realised that our Great Dane had not followed Scott outside. "Where's Minnie?"

"Undecided about the early start. I left the door open for her." He paused for a second. "I don't suppose you'll let me paint over it this time?"

I resumed my scrubbing. "Nope."

I had been so proud of our home after all the renovations, but now, the neat exterior of 22 Cedars Road, with its clean lines and light colours, only served to highlight the red spray paint. The foul language. Its toxic insinuation. This was supposed to be the home we welcomed our daughter-in-law into, where we wanted to make memories with our grandchildren, a place to fill with photographs of all of our son's adventures as he grew into a man and made his way independently out into the world.

Scott shook his brush, garnishing the driveway with scarlet flecks. "You know, it's probably already been posted on social media."

I noticed Jamie leaning against the far end of the garage door. I smiled at him. His apparition didn't scare me anymore. He had a glazed look in his eyes. His hair was dull, the auburn curls limp and crusted with dirt.

"Doesn't matter if you scrub it off or cover it up, Mum. Every time you look at that door, you'll see what they wrote

35

about me."

I looked over at Scott to see if he showed any indication that he could see or hear our son, but he didn't. He just kept plunging and scouring.

"Whoever's doing this will get bored eventually," he said.

He was one of life's waiters, hoping that eventually, everything would sort itself out if he was patient enough. Watching, delaying, gathering information. It's what made him such a good journalist. It also made him infuriating.

"That's not the point, though. Jamie wasn't that man's bitch, was he?"

Scott dropped his brush into the bucket and took off his dressing gown, throwing it over the gargoyle that stood tall and menacing beside the porch. I watched him, knowing that I wouldn't get a response. He was deliberately ignoring my question. I knew why. He thought it was a stupid thing to ask. He had no doubts about our son's innocence. In Scott's mind, there was absolutely no way Jamie had anything to do with the monster who took his life.

We had rehashed the conversation a hundred times—every word our son spoke, every gesture he made we had examined and discussed, trying to find the answers to who Gunner Piper's elusive accomplice might be and whether our son was involved in some way. Gunner Piper hadn't mentioned an accomplice when he gave accounts of his murders, but every time he had been asked outright about it, he'd remained silent. Never a denial. The press had loved the intrigue, and the haters had pointed their fingers at our boy.

Scott worked on the 'G' until he had taken off all the paintwork from that part of the garage door. Angry scratch marks revealed the dull grey metal underneath the paint.

"Do you remember our spray-painting phase?" he asked. "We kept at it for the best part of a year. Drove your parents nuts. Your dad let us use his back fence after that second fine. We only stopped on your fifteenth birthday because we decided we'd grown out of it."

I loved him for trying to lift the mood. I hated him for not falling apart like me. "Mum made me wash the cars and do the dishes for a month. We never wrote bad stuff, though. I did the bubble writing. Love and peace, mostly. And you did food."

"How great were my hot dogs?"

It was exhausting pretending to be upbeat. I don't know how he kept going. Dragging my thoughts away from Jamie took all the strength I had.

My arm ached, but I liked the discomfort—it kept me focussed. "It makes sense that there was an accomplice, though. I mean, no kid would go anywhere with a man that looked like Gunner Piper, would they?"

Scott swapped the brush into his right hand and made a start on the 'u'. "What about Boke Bridge? Brenan's older brother and his homemade cider? Remember? We spent half the night making friends with that homeless guy who wore an eye patch. The hole still gives me nightmares."

"It's not the same. Gunner Piper was evil. And we can only imagine how he got that dreadful scar." I paused mid-scrub, my hand resting on the garage. "We should move. We can't live like this. Why would someone do this to us when they don't even know the truth?"

I bashed the brush against the door. I wanted to scream

and shout and tear the garage down so that everyone could hear. I wanted the world to know that my son was just a victim. Like all the other boys. But how could I convince the world if I couldn't convince myself?

Scott turned me toward him and squeezed my shoulders. "Stop, honey. It's okay. We're going to get through this. I promise. Why don't you go back inside and I'll finish up here."

I could feel the tears welling up again.

I swallowed them away and shook my head. "What help am I sitting inside? This is about our *son,* and I'm going to put it right."

Jamie was picking at the "h" with his thumbnail. "It's going to take more than a wire brush and some elbow grease to put this right, Mum."

I desperately wanted to answer my sweet boy, but Scott had already taken me to the doctor three times after over-hearing me talk to Jamie's ghost. I had sufficient medication to sedate a small army, and I took just enough of it to satisfy my husband and keep my hallucinations under the radar. It was the only way I was going to keep my wits about me. I'd never find the other boy if I was sky-high or verging on comatose.

Minnie came lumbering around the side of the house, barking and howling, her lanky Great Dane limbs launching her awkwardly into the air with every clumsy leap. The big goof knocked over the bucket of water as she charged past me and Scott toward the gate. I spun around and just caught sight of someone disappearing into the trees on the far side of the road.

"Did you see that?"

Scott was picking up the bucket. "She's not exactly in stealth mode. And she just soaked my shoes."

"Across the road. I thought I saw someone."

Scott let out a long breath. I knew what he was thinking. But I wasn't making it up. It wasn't my mind playing tricks. It wasn't the medication, either. I saw someone. Just like I had before.

He dropped his brush in the bucket and reached down for mine. "The kids did what they came to do. I shouldn't think they'll be back again tonight. You have been taking your meds, haven't you?"

I stared into the darkness beyond the gate, willing the intruder to show himself. "There was somebody there. In the trees."

"I'll get more water." Scott walked off to the back of the house.

Scott didn't even look over. He just scooped up my brush from the ground and walked round the back. Minnie was standing on her back legs, front paws hooked over the top of the gate, Scooby-Doo style. There *was* a person there. They were standing in the shadows before they ran off, almost as if they wanted me to see them.

It was him.

Again.

SIX

Scott

LEAVING BLAIR IN bed the following day, drowsy from the myriad drugs I had coaxed down her, I took a trip to Peasedale. Gunner Piper's hometown. Had I been reporting this story, I would have thought *The Pied Piper of Peasedale* was a genius nickname; instead the moniker made my skin crawl. All I saw was the celebrity status it had afforded him, the place it gave him in the history books, his ranking on the serial killer lists. I suspected that more people in this country knew the story of the serial killer Pied Piper better than they knew the fairy-tale one.

I had kept quiet for the last six months. I kept my reporter's hat tucked away, let the police do their jobs, and let the press have their stories, giving myself and Blair time to grieve. I had hoped we would find some peace knowing Gunner Piper was locked away, that his confessions would bring an end to the mystery of our boy's final hours. Instead, Blair has lost herself in a miasma of hallucinations and medications, while I have been petrified by the idea of stirring up a hornet's nest if I go searching for answers, destroying my wife and my marriage with a truth neither of us could handle.

My inertia had done us no favours. Yesterday, I decided,

was enough. I needed to start doing something to find out what really happened to Jamie, what the police failed to discover, and what Gunner refused to divulge, our boy's death being the only one that the monster hadn't talked about.

I wanted to start at the beginning, which meant starting with Gunner. Where *he* began. His one surviving relative was a brother, who lived in Peasedale, working in the same factory where he worked. The man, Hunter Piper, had faced his fair share of media scrutiny, but I wanted to see him face to face. God knows what I was going to say to him, but I hoped that he would have something for me, something that he hadn't shared with the police, something that he didn't think was relevant but might just shed some light on why Jamie was his brother's final victim.

Reaching the turnoff from the motorway that led to Peasedale, the town was everything I expected. A town built on industry: cramped, grey, some superficial regeneration masking the high unemployment rates and low-wage families who barely survived here. On one side of the highway, the town could be seen in all of its industrialised glory, manufacturing clearly taking centre stage, with the residential areas squeezed uncomfortably between the factories. On the other side was the forest: thick, dark, and disturbing.

Driving into the town, I thought I might have passed through a hidden portal and been dumped back into the end of the last century. The town centre was dominated by a drab nineteen seventies shopping centre, grey concrete buildings, more multistorey car parks than it seemed was necessary, bleak generic office blocks, and garish nightclubs.

No one was bettering themselves in a place like this; their only hope would be to escape.

Located on the edge of the town was the sheet-metal fabrication plant, a surprisingly smart building with a curved roof and tinted-glass panels, surrounded by well-kept trees and grassy areas. I turned into the car park, found a solitary space in the far corner, and lowered the window. The air smelled thick and toxic.

This was the building where my son's killer had worked his whole career. Thirty years of feeding sheets of metal into a machine. His brother was the security guard. Surely a brother he worked alongside for nearly three decades would have some answers for me. I took a long deep breath, trying to slow my heart rate and calm my nerves. My throat was so dry I couldn't swallow; my hands remained firmly gripped to the steering wheel despite my wanting to release them, and my mind was filled with images of my son's cold, grey body.

I needed a little Dutch courage, so I opened the glove compartment and pulled out the unopened bottle of whiskey I bought at the off-licence the night before. I unscrewed the cap and took three big gulps. It burned the back of my throat and, mixed with the flavour of liquorice that lingered in my mouth from the packet I ate on the journey up here, the taste was far from pleasant. I waited for the alcohol to kick in, loosen me up, take the edge off my darkening mood. Nothing. I took three more large gulps and waited some more.

A security guard approached. It was *him*. I thought I might have had time to prepare myself, meet him on my terms, but he was coming toward me with the tenacity of a bloodhound on the trail of wounded prey. I quickly swigged the bottle again, my eyes watering as the sharp tang hit my taste buds. I didn't care that the guard could see me. What was he going to do about it? I replaced the lid and tucked it back into the glove compartment. My hands started to shake. This was not how I had pictured the meeting.

The man marching toward me was the spitting image of his brother: a man in his late forties, wiry, tattooed, with a mop of wispy sand-coloured hair. They could have been twins. I wanted to rip this man's throat out with my bare hands, tear his limbs from his body, make him pay for what his brother had done.

The guard knocked on the window. I pressed the button and let it down a few inches so that his eyes were framed in the opening. The eyes were the last thing that Jamie would have seen, those pinched blue eyes, and that scar. This man didn't have a scar.

"Can I help you?" the guard asked.

He was a heavy smoker, easy to spot: yellowed teeth, gravelly voice, and a stale, musty aroma that seeped in along with the factory fumes. I could feel sweat trickle down my spine.

"Yes," I replied.

I really hadn't thought this through properly. The guard stared into the car, his eyes searching around, and then he sniffed, a short sniff and then a longer one. I reddened at the incrimination of my breath.

"Either you're here for a meeting or an interview, or I'm gonna need to call the cops."

"Meeting," I said, lowering the window further and smiling. "You look familiar."

"Oh, here we go! You a reporter? Piss off!"

"No, I mean, yes, I am a reporter, but that's not why I'm here."

This was going all wrong. I unclipped my seatbelt and flung open the door.

The guard stepped back, his eyes narrowing as I swung my legs out of the car.

"You need to get back in the car," he said.

As I pulled myself to my feet and shut the door behind me, the whiskey hit. My head spun.

"What the hell is going on?" the guard asked, pulling out a walkie-talkie from his coat.

"I want to talk, that's all, just talk." I held up my hands in defence, but as the guard approached me, my fists clenched.

"I'm gonna need someone in the car park, and call the police," he barked into the walkie-talkie. Then he clipped it back on his belt and eyeballed me.

He took a step forward, his nose inches from mine. I wasn't intimidated, just angry. His fusty breath seeped up my nostrils. His beady eyes bored into me. Was this how Jamie felt? I shoved him away. It felt good watching him stumble.

He steadied himself. "What the fuck?"

Adrenaline and whiskey surged through my veins.

"Hit me," I said.

"What?"

I bounced from foot to foot. "Go on. Hit me." Who did I think I was, Rocky Balboa?

He looked at me like I was being ridiculous, which, in hindsight, I was. Then he laughed. It was like a red rag to a bull. I swung for him. Caught him clean across the jaw. My knuckles stung, but the adrenaline rush was electric. He wasn't laughing anymore.

What happened next was out of my control. I was powerless. My rage had taken over. I swung; he swung. There was blood. Mine or his, I didn't know. I could feel my heart bashing at my chest. There was a searing pain that stung my nose and eyes. It all happened so fast.

Each punch I took was like an energy boost. I wanted more. More of the pain. More of the release. More. I swung again. He was quick. He knocked my hand away and jabbed me in the ribs. I lost my breath for a few seconds. The smack of his forehead against mine sent both of us staggering backward. The world went into slow motion.

As I steadied myself on the bonnet of the car, my legs were kicked from under me, and I went down, knees first. Before I knew what was happening, I was facedown on the tarmac with the guard kneeling on the back of my legs, pinning my right arm behind my back. The bravado I had felt only seconds before had evaporated.

How, on earth, was I going to explain this to Blair?

A police siren rang out, and a patrol car pulled up. Two officers jumped out of the vehicle, lifted me to my feet, and pushed me flat against the bonnet of the patrol car, cuffing my wrists behind my back. My whole body was shaking.

The guard stepped back. "Another bloody reporter. This one's drunk."

My head did feel funny, although it was hard to tell if

that was because of the alcohol or the possible broken nose.

"I didn't intend to start anything. It was an accident," I said to the officer.

"Doesn't look like an accident."

"I can explain."

"You can do that at the station."

The policeman guided me into the back of the patrol car. The other officer was talking to the security guard, who was wiping blood from a cut just above his eyebrow. I didn't feel better. The pain in my body was no match for the agony in my heart.

With my forehead against the glass, I stared at the guard. The brother of my son's killer. The guard became *him*, smiling back at me, gripping onto Jamie, *his* hand clenched onto my boy's black hoodie, *his* scar half-closing his right eye, my son sobbing. Forensics had found urine and faeces stains on Jamie's trousers.

I threw up in the back of the police car. Whiskey/liquorice puke.

AFTER A SIX-HOUR detainment, which I used to sleep off the alcohol, I explained myself to the officers and was released with a caution. Luckily, the guard had no intention of pressing charges and had asked that the whole incident be forgotten, which I took as a sign of guilt—or pity.

I cleaned myself up in the toilets of the motorway rest stop and bought a new shirt, throwing the blood-stained one away. Listening to my favourite rock album, I drove home, volume up, window open. The bass pumped through my body, the fresh air whipping around the car, giving me goose bumps, and I pressed my foot hard on the accelerator as I sped along the motorway at ninety miles an hour.

It was nearly midnight by the time I arrived home. I expected Blair to be tossing and turning in bed wondering where I was. I fumbled in my pocket for my keys, and as I pulled them out, they slipped through my fingers, falling between the step and a gargoyle. It was too dark to see where they landed, so I took out my phone, flicked on the torch, and dropped to my knees to search.

Our outside lights had been smashed and the gargoyles damaged when the graffiti began. I figured I'd fix it when everything had settled down, when Gunner had confirmed that Jamie was not his accomplice and the police investigation proved the same. Neither Gunner nor the police had said anything to dispel the rumours about our son—nothing to confirm them either, but that meant nothing to the press. Social media had rallied the haters and made Jamie their target.

I couldn't keep waiting for all this to just go away before we rebuilt out lives. The next day, I would order new lanterns and bulbs and replace Blair's gargoyles. It was time I pulled myself together. I had worked so hard for all this. I owed it to Blair to keep everything shipshape and ready for her to enjoy when she was feeling stronger, regardless of whatever I found out about Jamie.

The top of the stable door opened. Minnie lifted her front paws over the lower door, rested her giant Great Dane head on her paws, and looked at me with her small, solemn eyes. Blair appeared beside her, stroking the dog's head as she studied me.

"Scott? What are you doing down there?" My wife's mass of curly red hair framed her head like a halo of fire.

Blair had always been so robust. Keeping up on our early morning runs, lifting weights with me in our home gym at the back of the garage, holding her own with all the gardening equipment and DIY tasks. We had been an impressive couple, both having just turned forty, highfliers in our careers with energy levels and figures to match. I'd done my best to stay fit these last six months, the gym a form of respite, an opportunity to push myself hard and briefly suppress my inner pain with physical exertion. Blair had let everything go. She was disappearing, mentally and physically. Some days it was hard to look at her.

"I'm de-mossing the paving slabs." I felt the jagged edge of the key digging into my kneecap.

"You need vinegar. I saw it on YouTube."

Jangling the keys in the air, I carefully rose to my feet. I unlocked the bottom door and Minnie nudged it open with her big soft snout. She jumped up at me for a hug, her face level with mine, her paws over my shoulders. After a brief embrace and the obligatory wet kiss, I pushed Minnie down and stepped toward Blair, taking her face in my hands and kissing her tenderly on the lips. Her pale, freckled skin was soft and warm in my palms. She smelled like she had just stepped out of the shower. I put my arms around her and held her tight, wishing we were okay still happy. I didn't want to let go.

She cuddled me back, resting her head on my chest, the

weight of her body sinking into mine. We enjoyed the moment. Our brief connection. Holding each other. A few seconds of respite from the pain. I inhaled the sweet smells of her favourite citrus shampoo and vanilla perfume and felt her soft auburn curls brush against my cheek as my arms enveloped her too-thin frame. Then her feet began shuffling, her weight moving from one to the other, her hands patting my back. She was done. A fleeting hug was all we could manage. She stepped back and let me go, my body instantly feeling heavy and unsteady. I gripped the doorframe with one hand as I stepped into the hallway.

Reaching forward, Blair pushed my floppy curls out of my face. "You look worse than you did after that camel bit you."

I put my hand on top of hers as she gently touched the scar that ran down the front of my ear.

"I got into a fight." Holding my ribs, I wriggled off my shoes.

Blair dropped her hand and frowned. "Ted finally had enough of your terrible jokes, huh?"

"I really did get into a fight," I said, remembering the rush of adrenaline when I landed my first punch and the shock and sting of taking a hit.

"What with this time, a paving slab or a doorframe?"

"A human being. A seven-foot, stacked, irate human being. With knuckle dusters."

"Okay, tough guy, you got into a fight. Well, I hope it was worth it."

She was unusually chipper, and the fact that she was still up and dressed set off a warning siren in my head. I didn't have the energy for a challenging exchange or an emotional outburst.

Don't get me wrong, I loved the no-nonsense Blair. I loved that she didn't believe me about the fight. Because I'm not that man, never have been. I'm a turn-the-other-cheek kinda guy, a talk-my-way-out-of-anything chap. But, today, I wasn't that guy and I hadn't felt like my usual steady self in quite a while.

She kissed me tenderly on my bruised eye. "Do you remember when that boy—what was his name, Kester something-or-other?—wanted to fight with you to decide who should take me to the end-of-year social? I punched him on the nose for you because he was in the year below, and you didn't think it was a fair fight."

"Kester Hendersen," I said. "Didn't his mum marry the chemistry teacher?"

She helped me take off my coat and then hung it on the hook by the door before disappearing into the kitchen. I could smell fresh toast and pancakes; the lights were on in every room downstairs and there was music playing. The corridor seemed to stretch ahead of me like a scene from *The Shining*. I drifted quietly into the kitchen as Petula Clark blasted out our special song, "Downtown," and stood motionless in the doorway surveying the scene before me.

Blair stood over the hob, spatula in hand.

"Fancied a midnight feast?"

Blair turned and smiled at me. "Jamie always loved pancakes for breakfast. With lemon and sugar and banana. Oh, I need to get bananas."

"It's the middle of the night, BB." She was looking so

sexy in a pretty blouse, pyjama bottoms, and a provocatively high pair of stilettos. "Quite the outfit you've got on."

The table was neatly laid with three plates, three bowls, and three mugs, a jug of milk and another with orange juice, a full toast rack, granary and white slices, and three egg cups with eggs in. Blair lifted a pancake from the pan to a plate already piled high. The smells in the room were wonderful.

"Jamie gave me this top last Christmas, remember?"

"Did you take your meds today?"

My wife's grief was brutal for both of us, snatching away her reality, toying with her memories, and sullying every relationship she had, but the worst of it was this part, the hopelessness. I could do nothing to fix it. I couldn't put this right.

She paused, hovering the spatula over the pan as if she had just been turned to stone.

"BB?"

"I don't know how to live without him." She tried to flip the last pancake, but it had stuck to the pan. "Now look what I've done!"

She began scraping at the crispy mess as a smell of burning wafted from the pan. I walked over to her, pried her hand away from the handle of the pan, and switched off the hob.

She stood before me with the spatula in her hand. "I don't want to take life one day at a time. I don't want a life without Jamie. Don't you understand? What life is there if our son isn't in it with us?"

I wrapped my arms around her. "We have each other. We can get through this together."

She dropped the spatula and let her head fall onto my chest. "How? How do we get through this? He's never coming back. Never."

"No. He isn't. But we're still here, and he would want us to keep going. He'd want us to be happy again. Together."

"I miss him so much."

"Me too."

Blair's body began to shake as she sobbed into my shirt. I could feel a wet patch forming as her tears soaked into the material. I had tears of my own to shed, but I was afraid to let any more out in case I couldn't stop them. What if I never stopped crying? Then where would we be? Jamie wouldn't want that for us.

Our song was on repeat, and as it reached the final chorus, I thought about our first kiss at the school social, Petula serenading us from the speakers. We were sixteen, a year older than Jamie was when he died. He was still so young, tall but scrawny like I was at that age, with so much to discover about himself and the world. He didn't get to complete his final year of secondary, never took that first set of important exams, never made it to his first school prom. I'll never know if he got a first kiss. The pain in my heart felt so real, so tangible, as if it was splitting apart. I swallowed back my tears and gritted my teeth. I wasn't going to cry; I couldn't fall apart. Blair needed me to stay strong.

SEVEN

Blair

RELIEVED TO HAVE arrived at Sketchy's Inks tattoo parlour after a laborious train ride and a confusing trek through Peasedale with its ugly tower blocks and littered alleyways, I waited by the funky pillar-box-red reception desk. The wall behind it was a colourful graffiti mashup. I liked it. I tapped the bell on the counter but no one arrived, so I took a seat on the blue leather sofa on the opposite side of the room facing the desk, a rectangular glass table in front of it laden with magazines and files. My stomach rumbled, and I wished I'd packed something for lunch. I had hoped to arrive early and stop at a café, but the train delay put pay to that. Of course, if I hadn't had an appointment to get to, the journey would have gone without a hitch. Maybe they'd offer me a biscuit and a cup of tea.

I slid off my shoes and let my toes stretch out against the cool tiles. It smelled metallic and lemon-fresh in the studio— someone had been overzealous with the bleach—and the familiar buzzing sound of the tattooist pen came from the other side of a door at the back of the room, sounding like a swarm of angry bees on the move. I could see my reflection in a long mirror attached to the wall beside the desk. I'd lost weight since Jamie died. Too much.

A girl walked through the front door, setting off the bell as it opened and closed. She was in her late teens, possibly early twenties; it was always difficult to tell with girls, especially when they used *that* much makeup. She had long purple hair, piercings in every conceivable fleshy part of her face, eyes like Marilyn Manson, and wore black lipstick. Her thigh-high boots clomped against the shiny black-and-white tiled floor, and a chain from her nose ring to her ear jingled as she moved. She had a wrap, a bag of crisps, and a smoothie in her hand. Jamie was always asking for money to buy himself meal deals for lunch on his way to school.

The girl approached me and smiled. "Can I help you?"

"Yes. I've booked in for a tattoo."

"Blair, right? So, what are we doing for you today?"

"Just a name on my wrist—Jamie," I said, pulling out the slip of newspaper I'd concertinaed and slipped into the back pocket of my jeans before I left home.

As I unfolded the clipping, it tore a little along one of the folds. It had been in and out of my pocket more times than I could remember and was beginning to fray and fade. I had plenty more, though. I'd kept at least thirty copies of the article.

"I'll get you the menu of fonts and sizes," the girl said.

"I have a picture." I held up the piece of paper. "The font is called 'souvenir.' I checked online."

I studied the girl's face. She must have seen this picture on the television or in the newspapers. She glanced at the clipping. Her left eyebrow raised ever so slightly, and her mouth twitched.

"She definitely recognises it." Jamie stood behind the

reception desk, his black hoodie pulled up over his head, hiding his face. "Perhaps word has got round, rumours of a crazy woman asking about the murderer of those boys?"

"I'm not crazy!" He always seemed to pop up when I was feeling a little anxious.

"Not at all," the girl said. "People have names tattooed in all sorts of places."

I smiled awkwardly, snapping my gaze back to her. She clomped off through the door at the back. Jamie was sitting at the other end of the sofa thumbing through a file of tattoo designs, his hood now away from his face. I liked having him around.

I settled back against the cushions to study the photographs of decorated body parts that covered the back wall. One of the shots caught my attention. It was a foot and ankle with a delicate vine weaving around from the big toe to the lower calf. The vine blurred, the skin turned grey, and the two smaller toes disappeared, leaving jagged open wounds and loose bits of flesh. I stared at the toes, trying to decipher what instrument severed them: scissors, a knife, hedge cutters possibly, or teeth? Was the person alive when the toes were cut off? I wondered what drove someone to do that to another person.

"Would you like to come through?" the girl asked, holding open the door at the back of the room.

I looked over at the reception desk as I crossed the room. Jamie was gone.

The girl took me along a short corridor past a door on the left and in through a door on the right. She beckoned me to a chair in the centre of the room behind a small table with another chair opposite it and a trolley with all the bits and bobs a tattooist uses.

"I'll just get Twigs." The girl left the room.

"Dad's not going to like you doing it again." Jamie sat in the seat across from me.

"Well, it's not your father's wrist!"

A door clicked open and a large, hairy man walked into the room. I looked up and smiled. The man settled himself in the now-empty chair across from me. He fiddled with the equipment to his left.

"Unusual name that, Blair. Where's it from?"

Twigs. A bearded biker, complete with face tattoos and a studded leather jacket, working in a pristine shop named Sketchy's Inks, wearing a pair of square-rimmed glasses.

I let myself sink a little further into my seat and un-clenched my toes. "Scotland. My father is Scottish. I was raised there."

Twigs pulled on some disposable gloves, cleaned and dried the skin on my wrist, and then stuck on a temporary tattoo of the name *Jamie* for me to check. I stared at my wrist. It was perfect. Exactly the same as the other three. The anticipation of the needle and that scratchy feeling made me a little lightheaded.

"Ready?" asked Twigs.

I took a deep breath. "Ready."

"You're gonna regret this, Mum!" Jamie stood behind Twigs, leaning over his shoulder to see my wrist.

"So, this ya lad's name or ya beau?" Twigs switched on the tattoo pen.

A giggle burst out of my mouth.

"My boy," I said.

"First time, or are you a seasoned inker?" He let his glasses drop to the end of his nose so that he could peer at me over the top of them.

I flushed. Was he flirting? "I've already had three other names tattooed."

I used my free hand to pull up my trouser leg to reveal a 'Jamie' on my ankle, then I dropped my jumper over my shoulder to expose another 'Jamie' above my left shoulder blade.

"The other one's at the base of my back."

Twigs pushed his glasses back up and lifted the tattoo pen.

"Lotta Jamies you got there. Same kid, or couldn't you think of a better name for the other three?"

I laughed too loudly. Who has the same name tattooed all over their body? Jamie was right; Scott would be furious that I was doing it again. He didn't understand why. Maybe the wrist was a bad idea, but I couldn't think of where else on my body I could get it done. My knee? Forehead? Perhaps the sole of my foot would have been more sensible. Oh well, too late now.

"I'm a foster mum," I said. "I have a habit of being sent boys called Jamie. Must have been a popular name in the last decade."

"You really think he's gonna buy that, Mum?" Jamie was standing across the room, a small notepad in his hand. He was sketching.

"Foster mum, huh? Well done, you—hard job that! All those tortured little bleeders with shits for dads and wasters for mums."

"Not all," I replied, trying to validate the pretence. "Some parents just had a lot of bad luck, you know—health issues, money worries."

"Shit happens, right?"

"Yes, indeed, shit most certainly does."

The pen whirred, and Twigs began tattooing 'Jamie' onto my wrist. The sting was sharp and made me feel woozy.

"Have you ever tattooed a list of names along someone's arm?"

Jamie shook his head. "Oh, that was subtle."

Twigs kept his head down, focussing on his work. "Any particular someone?"

"A man. With a scar across one eye. Small blue eyes. Looks like a pitbull. Wrinkled brow. Squashed nose. Thinning, sandy-coloured hair."

"You're wasting your time, Mum. You should just pay for the tattoo and leave." Jamie disappeared.

Twigs finished the tattoo before he spoke again. "Thought it would be the coppers asking about him. They never did, mind." He pushed his glasses up his nose and lifted the newspaper clipping that I had left on the table. "My colleague, Jason, did his tattoos. I remember seeing the scarred man a couple of times. Jason left a while back, just after all the boys were found. You're one of the mums, huh? Janis recognised you. Bit of a fascination with serial killers that one."

"Nothing is fascinating about a depraved, violent man who preys on teenage boys." I decided not to be so friendly to Janis when I got up to leave.

"Was he ever with anyone else?" I asked Twigs as he covered my wrist with clingfilm.

"Yep. Always had a lad with him."

I opened my bag, pulled out my purse, and removed a passport photograph of Jamie, his unkempt red curls and pale skin making him look like a mad scientist.

"What about this boy?" I showed Twigs the photo.

"Couldn't you at least have found a more flattering picture? My acne's horrendous in that one." Jamie was back, fiddling about by the ink pots. "Why don't you do your next tattoo in a different colour?"

I looked over to him and tutted.

Twigs was studying the photograph. "Difficult to say if it was him. I never got a good look at the kid. He was wearing a black hoodie like that one." He tapped his finger against the photograph. "Pulled so low over his head, I couldn't see the lad's face. Could've been him. Could've not."

I started shaking. Had Jamie been to this very tattoo parlour with the man who killed him? Why? Why would my son do that?

"You don't know it was me. He doesn't recognise my face. It could have been any of the boys. Any one of his thirteen victims. All teenage boys wear black hoodies, Mum. It's an essential wardrobe item at my age."

Twigs removed his glasses and smiled at me. It was too late for comfort. I could already feel the chanting coming on, and I was powerless to stop it. "Jordan. William. Leon."

"You alright, love?" Twigs asked.

I felt faint as small black spots began to dance around in my field of vision. I tried to look away, but the black spots moved with me. It was disorientating. A rushing sound like the roar of an engine filled my ears. Then something slammed into the back of my head. I was in darkness. It was silent. My body was floating.

I heard a voice, way off in the distance, and my head felt as if it was resting against something hard and cold. The strange whooshing sound returned. My body felt as if it was falling. A bright light was switched on, making me squint and turn my head. A man was bending over me—hairy, big. I tried to sit up, but my head pounded, and I had to swallow several times to stop myself from vomiting.

Slowly the world returned: the lemon bleach scent, the cold tiled floor, Twigs hovering above me. Janis helped me to sit up and sip a glass of freezing-cold water. It stung my teeth and made me shiver as the icy liquid ran down my throat and into my stomach. My head cleared.

Janis held the doors open while Twigs led me back out to the sofa in reception. "Looks like you've had a long day. If I call you a cab, can you remember where you live?"

"Twenty-two Cedars Road, Thadley."

"Didn't think you were from around here. I'll get you a tea and some chocolate biscuits while you wait." Twigs disappeared into the back room to get the tea and biscuits, and Janis called a taxi from the reception desk.

When the cab arrived, I thanked Twigs and handed him some cash. I didn't wait for change.

Slumped into the back seat of the taxi, I held my bag in my lap and smiled at the reflection of the driver in the rearview mirror. "Twenty-two, Cedars Road, Thadley, and I don't care how much it costs."

"It's a ways to go in a cab, Miss. You sure I can't take you to the station? I'll have to charge for my return journey too. Half a day's pay right there."

"Fine. Whatever. I don't want to take the train again." I just wanted to go home. Get out of this place and far away from it.

"Alright, love, if you say so."

I rested my head against the cab window. The day outside was grey. Rain spat at the window, obscuring my view. The taste of sweet biscuit lingered in my mouth, and my wrist felt uncomfortable, slightly numb and sore. Underneath a double layer of clingfilm was the tattoo. 'Jamie.' Shit! Why had I done it again? I know why. Because a hairy man named Twigs told me he'd seen a boy wearing a black hoodie. The boy was with the killer. Maybe it was my boy.

The last time I'd seen Jamie wearing his black hoodie was when we were on the train on the way home after watching a musical. I couldn't remember what it was that we saw. Jamie had lowered his head onto my shoulder and fallen asleep. Why was he so tired? There had been a row. Jamie hadn't come home till late the night before. Scott was livid. I'd cried.

Where had Jamie been? He wasn't himself. He'd been quiet, sleepy, hungry. His fingernails were clogged with muck.

EIGHT

Scott

MINNIE ALERTED ME to the car pulling into the drive, and when I opened the door I was met by a flustered Blair rummaging in her bag. I'd been worried sick when I got back from work and found that she wasn't in, but the last thing I wanted to do was to make her feel bad for getting out of the house. It was a step in the right direction, and I was sure she would have a perfectly valid reason for being home after dark.

"What are you looking for, honey? Are you alright?"

"I'm fine," she said, pushing past me.

I reached out to help her with her coat, but she shrugged me off and pulled it tight around her chest.

"Okay then, coat staying on, huh?"

Blair was quiet, sheepish, avoiding eye contact.

I closed the door behind her. "So, where have you been today?"

A car horn honked.

Blair stared at the floor. "The driver needs paying. I didn't have enough cash and misplaced my cards."

She tugged her sleeves down to hide her wrist, but I'd already clocked the tattoo. The sleeves weren't long enough to hide it. I kept my mouth shut and squeezed the back of my neck to relieve some tension. I couldn't believe she had done it again. She began searching through the pockets of the other coats hung on the rack. I had no idea what was going on in her head right now, but I was going to find out, right after I paid the cabbie. I grabbed my wallet from the hallway drawer and went outside.

I almost choked when the driver told me the cost of her ride. Why on earth didn't she take the train? I stormed back into the house slamming the door behind me. I was fuming. I couldn't fathom why she was behaving like this.

"Peasedale? What for this time? That was a three-hundred-pound cab ride! I had to do a bank transfer!"

Blair ignored me and carried on searching the pocket of our coats. "I think I need my gloves; my hands are cold."

"Gloves? Indoors?"

"Yes, please."

She pushed her hands into her jacket pocket and looked up at me with sad, crazy eyes. Where had my bright-eyed, feisty wife gone? Part of me wanted to shake her, but part of me wanted to bundle her up into a hug and never let go.

"Since when did you start suffering from Raynaud's disease?"

Blair snapped her head toward the stairs. "When did you start using such big words?"

I looked over at the staircase. I couldn't be sure if she was talking to me or some figment of her imagination.

"You must have heard of Raynaud's. Didn't you have a photographer friend who suffered from it? Always wearing those fingerless gloves and complaining about the air-con? Why don't I just rub those hands warm for you?"

She stepped back as if I was a hot stove that just caught fire. She really didn't want to show me that tattoo. I'd play along for a while. Let her get inside, warm up, calm down.

"Gloves it is, then." I disappeared into the cupboard under the stairs. "Any particular gloves?"

"Jamie's yellow ones, with the footballs on the finger-tips."

When I came out of the cupboard, Blair wasn't in the hallway. I hadn't heard her take the stairs, so I looked in the kitchen.

She was standing by the kitchen sink sipping water from her palm.

"I could only find one of Jamie's gloves. Do you want me to get you a glass?"

She shook her head and held out her hand.

I held out the glove and as soon as she reached for it, I grabbed her hand and stepped closer to her. Lifting her other hand, the one she was holding down by her side, I pushed up the sleeve of her jacket to expose yet another tattoo of 'Jamie,' this time on the inside of her wrist. Snatching her arm away, she pulled on Jamie's yellow glove and tugged the jacket sleeve back down. Why didn't she just talk to me? Tell me she wanted to do this to herself and explain why. I'd understand. At least, I'd try to.

"Not again, BB. Why did you need to do it again?"

There we were, in the kitchen, standing opposite each other, me holding her wrist, our eyes locked like two kids in a staring competition. An invisible wall between us. A standoff. I had laid the table for a candlelit dinner, dimmed the lights, and set the love songs CD Jamie had given us for our anniversary playing in the background. This was not how the evening was supposed to pan out.

How stupid to think we could have a romantic dinner like a normal couple.

Heading off for work this morning had felt like the right thing to do. Blair was taking her tablets and was busy in her darkroom for the first time in ages. When I got home and she wasn't there, I thought it was a sign that she was getting better, moving forward, healing a little. Dinner was supposed to be a small pat on the back for us both. How could I have read it all so wrong?

Her body was rigid. She lowered her eyes, fixing her gaze on my hand and her wrist. I couldn't let her go, not until she had given me an explanation. She had done it again. Got herself yet another tattoo, this time our son's name emblazoned on her wrist. What was she going to do, tattoo his name all over her body? She hated tattoos. My god. Gunner Piper had the names of the boys he killed tattooed up the inside of his arm, and this one would remind her of that monster every time she saw it. At least the others were out of sight, on her back, hidden under her sock.

I didn't mind tattoos. I loved that it was our son's name. But this was the fourth time she'd done it, and I had no doubt it wouldn't be the last. Was she punishing herself? Was she punishing me? Had she forgotten about the other tattoos? My god, was she so delusional that she had no idea what she was actually doing?

I took a breath and lifted her chin so that I could look in her eyes. "I love you, you know. I'm right here if you want to talk to me." My mouth was so dry, I had to swallow hard before I could get any more words out.

She jerked her head to the side to shake me off. I stroked her cheek with the back of my hand. She was so lost. I wanted to rub the tattoo away and forget all about it. But I couldn't. I'd see it while she ate, when we cleaned our teeth, when she lifted a cup of tea or glass of water. I'd see the damn thing every day for the rest of our lives, and it wasn't Jamie it would make me think of. It was *him*. She'd done this because of *him*.

I released her wrist and put my hands gently on her shoulders to try to coax her into communicating with me. "This is the fourth time, BB. What are you going to do, cover your whole body in his name?"

Her big green eyes filled with tears. "I'm going to sit by the fire; I'm cold." Slipping free of my grasp, she snaked off to the lounge.

I kicked a kitchen chair into the table. The candle fell, spilling wax onto the polished oak tabletop. Brilliant! Now I'd have to spend an hour scraping that off and revarnishing. I had laid the table so fastidiously, wanting everything to be perfect for our dinner. What a waste of time that was! I felt like sweeping my arm across the table and launching the whole damn lot onto the floor, smashing the plates onto the slate tiles, sending the cutlery clanging and clattering across the floor, shattering the glasses against the kitchen units.

I didn't do that. Instead, I lifted my shoulders back and followed my wife into the lounge. She was cross-legged on the floor in front of the fire, staring into the flames. Why was she ignoring me?

"Talk to me, honey. Tell me what's going on. How can I

help you if you won't talk to me?" She was taking so many damn drugs, I'm not sure she even knew who the hell she was anymore.

"Blair! Please. Explain to me why you did that to yourself so that I can understand. I want to understand. I want to be there for you. I can't do that if I don't know what's going on in your head."

She turned her body to face me, her eyes red with tears. "I was looking for something. For the place where Gunner Piper got his tattoos. I thought that someone there might know about him, about the boys, about why he did what he did. I thought I might find out something about Jamie."

"We've done this three times already. Why would you find out something about Jamie? What could you possibly find out?"

She was looking for ways Jamie was connected to Gunner instead of reasons why he wasn't. Like she wanted to prove his guilt rather than his innocence. There was no evidence linking Jamie to a tattooist.

"Maybe he told someone something about our boy. They talk to you, the tattooists. Same as the hairdresser. It's easy to get carried away and share all sorts of things with them."

I sat on the rug next to Blair, pulled off her glove, and interlocked my fingers with hers. Gunner Piper was an evil, depraved psychopath, but he wasn't an idiot. He had shared exactly what he wanted with the police. His family and friends had no idea about the secret darkness in his life. He was not a man who would let something slip to a tattooist.

"And did you? Did you find out anything this time?"

Minnie plodded into the room and climbed onto the

sofa, resting her head over the arm nearest the window. Blair snapped her head to the side and shushed as if she was distracted by someone else, but there was only Minnie.

"Well? Did you?"

"I did."

"What? You did?"

She looked over her shoulder again, tutted, and looked back at me. "It was the parlour where *he* got his tattoos. Twigs did my tattoo. He said that his colleague did Gunner Piper's tattoos and that he remembered seeing Gunner a couple of times, always with a boy in a black hoodie."

"We already know he made friends with the boys. Gave them drink and food and weed to lure them to his cabin."

"I showed the tattooist a picture of Jamie. I thought he might be one of the boys they'd seen."

"Was he?"

"The boy always had his head down and hood up."

"One boy or different boys?"

"Didn't say."

"Jamie wouldn't go to a tattoo parlour with a strange man. He didn't do drugs. He didn't drink. He didn't have tattoos. He wasn't like that."

"Maybe there *was* an accomplice. Maybe Gunner had help. Another boy? The boy who watches the house? The one who went to the tattoo parlour? If I can find the boy in the hoodie then perhaps he can tell us what really happened to our son."

"They found all the boys, BB. All that accomplice rubbish is just the media stirring things up. And as for the boy that watches the house... I've looked outside every day and never seen him. Just like I don't see Jamie." I stroked her hand and took a few long breaths. "What if we tear ourselves apart chasing ghosts, BB?"

Hadn't I gone looking for answers too? Ended up in a fight? But at least I found something real, tangible, a living human being with a connection to the killer rather than a figment of my imagination or a hunch.

I could see the desperation in her eyes, pleading with me, a futile hope that she was clinging onto so that she didn't drown in her own sorrow. "Nothing you find will bring him back."

She lifted my hand to her mouth and kissed my palm. "We can put things right. You can help me find the truth!"

I held her face in my palm and tilted my head to the side. "What if we don't like what we find? What if the truth isn't what we want it to be? What if it makes everything worse? What if we end up feeding the media's vilification of our son? Do you really want to take that risk? Look what it's doing to you already. The meds, the tattoos... You're not eating or sleeping; you're talking to a hallucination."

Blair covered her ears. Her face twisted. Eyes scrunched shut. "STOP IT! STOP IT!"

Minnie lifted her front legs onto the back of the sofa and began howling. I looked between her and Blair. Christ! What was happening to us?

I took a deep breath. "Minnie. Get down." She walked around the sofa, unable to relax.

I pulled Blair into a hug, both of us slumped into each other on the rug in front of the fireplace. "We can't go on like this. We need help. *You* need help."

She hugged my arm tight against her body. "I need Jamie. I need to find the other boy. I need to know what really happened. I need to...to find out if Jamie was involved."

This wasn't right. She wasn't right.

"Did you take your tablets today?"

She got up and left the room. For a moment, I thought she had walked out on me. Had enough. I was expecting to hear the bath running or the front door slam, but she returned moments later with her bag gripped tight in her hands. She sat back down on the rug beside me and emptied the contents onto the floor.

"What are you doing?"

Blair began rummaging through her belongings. "I want to show you that I took my tablets. That they're not here." She spread makeup, tissues, keys, her purse, and all sorts of other bits and pieces onto the rug.

"Okay, okay. I believe you." I didn't, though.

Her hands were shaking. Eyes wild and full of panic.

She kept turning her head to the side, conversing with her phantasm. "Leave it. I know what I'm doing. I don't need your help, thank you very much."

There were no tablets in her bag. I got up and went into the kitchen to check the pill pot. Also empty.

"Did you take them, honey, or did you throw them away?" I held out the pill pot with the empty compartment as I walked back into the lounge.

Blair was on her hands and knees collecting her things and dropping them back in her bag.

"I took all of them. Every single one. In one big gulp. Satisfied?"

"You took them all at once? Jesus! What were you trying to do, kill yourself?" I knelt back down to help her.

"Leave me alone," she said, pushing me away.

She looked across to the other side of the room. "Well, I'm not feeling like being very nice right now."

She was getting worse. I thought time healed. One minute we were comforting each other, the next I felt like her carer, and the next we were at loggerheads, as far away from each other as two people could be.

I sat back on my knees and watched her scrabbling around on the floor conversing with the ether. "I'm hurting too, you know. I lost Jamie, too. I need you, BB. I need us."

Blair paused, her head down, hands hovering over her bag. "I don't know what to do anymore."

Minnie stood by the window, whining. "How about we take Minnie for a walk?"

"Sure." Blair let the items in her hands fall to the floor.

I picked up Jamie's glove and turned it over in my hands, picturing him wearing them on one of our early morning winter walks around the park in the days when he still liked spending time with me. "I assume this will be going back on?"

Blair took the glove and pulled it on, hugging her hand to her chest. "Thank you."

I stood up and held out my hand to help her to her feet. "I'll get the lead and boots."

THE NEXT MORNING, I woke to the distant sound of Minnie

bark-howling. Blair's side of the bed was empty, the sheets cold. My wife didn't do early mornings out of choice. Something was amiss. I sat up, rubbed my eyes, and listened. No shower running or kettle whistling or toilet flushing. I couldn't hear the sound of the outside tap or the screech of a wire brush against the garage doors. Only Minnie, her distress relentless. The barking and howling interspersed with a desperate whine. Something was wrong. And if I let that racket go on too long, I'd be getting a call from one of the neighbours. I pulled on my dressing gown and raced downstairs to investigate, my senses on high alert.

"Blair? Blair!"

She didn't respond. What if she was hurt? Or worse? The sudden thought of losing her, too, hit me hard, and for a moment I couldn't breathe. She was so fragile, so lost. Following the commotion out through the kitchen and utility room to the open backdoor, I found Minnie in the doorway facing the garden, her body trembling with the effort of her wailing. Scanning the garden, I saw Blair crouched on her knees near the roses by the left-hand fence. Her nose was inches from the lawn, and she was raking her hands into the dirt. She was alive. I took a deep breath and let it out slowly to allow myself to calm down.

The sun was up; the roses always caught the first rays. There was a light breeze, and the birds were in full song hidden in the trees at the bottom of the garden. We had a bird table and birdbath that we had neglected these last six months, but the birds were still hopeful that one of us would remember them and fill the feeders. I made a mental note to do that later, once I got Blair back inside and cleaned up.

"Blair," I called as I walked over to her. "What's happened? What's wrong, honey?"

Her hands were caked in mud, her pyjamas too. She wiped her forehead, smearing black earth across her face.

"I can't remember where he put it," she said. "It's around here somewhere. Do you remember? He spent ages digging the hole and carefully covering it over once he'd dropped it in. I've tried to find it, but it just isn't here."

There were several deep holes in the lawn. Blair had clearly been digging for a while.

"How long have you been out here?"

Several hours at least.

"Ten minutes," she said.

I bent down and took hold of her filthy hands. "If you tell me what it is you're looking for, maybe I can help."

"You know. His time capsule. We had a ceremony and everything. I don't know why, but I woke up thinking about it this morning. I remember buying him the tin and digging the hole, but I've forgotten what he put inside."

"I'd forgotten all about that. Let me think. I'm pretty sure he put in some of those football cards, a ten-pound note in a sealed bag, which he put in in case of an emergency, and his favourite chocolate bar that I have no doubt will be nothing more than a foil wrapper now. And a letter."

"How old was he?"

"He was eleven, wasn't he? It was just before he gave up the football. That's why he put all his favourite cards in there. He buried it next to your yellow roses so he wouldn't forget where he put it."

Blair picked up the trowel and crawled over the grass to

the yellow rosebush, its last flower of the year beginning to droop and brown at the edges.

I followed her over and knelt beside her. Minnie had come too and was now sitting on the other side of Blair, watching intently as she began digging.

I tried to help, scooping away earth with my bare hands. "Where are the gardening gloves?"

She waved her trowel in the air behind her. "I lost them somewhere."

I looked around the garden and saw something sticking out of one of the other holes. "Hang on, I think I can see them."

Sure enough, they were dropped down a hole that was elbow-deep. One glove was resting across the top of the hole and the other was wedged deep down. It must have come off as she pulled her hand back out. I could barely squeeze my arm in to retrieve it.

Pulling them on, I joined Blair, and together we excavated the area of the garden where Jamie's time capsule was buried. It was still there.

I held the capsule out to Blair. "Would you like to open it, or shall I?"

"Can I?"

I handed it over, and she brushed away the dirt to reveal the eight screws that secured the lid. "We need tools."

"If my memory serves me correctly, Jamie put them in a labelled jar in the shed."

I left Blair as she was cleaning off the tin. The jar with the Allen key and spanner was on the bottom shelf in the shed where Jamie had left them, the label faded but still readable. 'Time Capsule' was all it said. As I carried the jar out to Blair, Minnie raced back inside the house barking maniacally. Moments later, the doorbell rang.

"I'll get that. You can make a start on the capsule." I handed Blair the jar and went to open the front door.

Minnie had given up her guard dog act by the time I opened the top section of the door. There was no one on the other side. I looked up the drive, but there was no one there either. The gate was shut. No sign of a car leaving. Then I noticed a leaflet on the front step. I opened the bottom of the door and picked it up. It was another of those grief retreat flyers. We'd had flyers like this for groups, retreats, coffee mornings, and counselling dropped through our letterbox countless times over the last six months. There certainly wasn't a shortage of well-meaning people out there eager to help us through our grief. That was the yin and yang of life. With every hater blaming Jamie and branding him an accomplice, there was an altruist wanting to share our pain and heal our souls. I left the leaflet on the dresser with the others and headed back outside to see how Blair was getting on with the capsule.

She was holding the cylindrical tin upside down, staring at something in her palm. "Look!" She lifted her hand to show me.

"It's a key." I picked it up and inspected it. "Was it in the tin?"

"It was the *only* thing inside." Blair shook the capsule to prove her point.

"What about the cards and the letter?"

"Just that key."

"Jamie must have dug it up, emptied it, and put in this key."

Blair had tears streaming down her cheeks. "I wanted to read his letter."

"Come on, honey, let's get you inside and cleaned up. We can work out where the key belongs after we're dressed and had something to eat."

I couldn't think of why Jamie would want to bury a key or what on earth the key was for. And what the discovery of a secret key and an empty time capsule would do to Blair's delicate mental state was anyone's guess.

NINE

Blair

I T WAS OUR favourite spot in the pub, tucked away in the corner right beside the front window where we could watch all the shoppers coming and going.

"I'll go and order, shall I?" Scott said, taking the menu and walking up to the counter. "Will you be okay here for a few minutes? I'll just be up at the bar."

"Yes. Fine." I studied the menu. "I think I'll get a brownie with ice cream for pudding."

Jamie appeared in the seat opposite me, dirt smeared across his face, his hair matted and glistening with sweat. "I think you should have the apple pie for a change."

I looked up. "You would love sharing my brownie. And why do you look such a mess?"

A woman sat at the table next to us, glanced around, and then whispered to her companion.

"You can't keep talking to yourself like this, Mum," Jamie said. "It makes people feel uncomfortable."

I couldn't care less how other people were feeling. They weren't my responsibility. I was talking to my son.

"You're avoiding my question." He was so like his father.

"Why are you asking me now? You never asked me when I was alive. Didn't even mention it to Dad. You were too busy with your photos, or maybe you were too scared to ask."

He was right, of course. I was always busy, and part of me hadn't wanted to know what he was up to. Part of me sensed that I wouldn't like his answer. I dropped my eyes and focussed on my fingers, trying to pick out the dirt that was wedged into the tiny grooves of my engagement ring. "I should have asked before."

Jamie didn't respond. I didn't need to look up to know that he was gone. I turned my attention to the bar, hoping to see Scott making his way back to the table. He was by the till talking to a barman. He turned and smiled at me. I smiled back.

Out of the corner of my eye, I spotted a boy walking toward the toilets. A black hoodie covered his head and hid his face. He turned in my direction, paused for a moment, and then disappeared past the bar and off in the direction of the men's restroom. I froze. I couldn't breathe. Was that the boy I'd been seeing outside our gate? The one doing the graffiti?

Easing my chair back, trying not to draw attention to myself, I got up and headed to the back of the pub, passing the bar as I went. My heart was pulsating in my neck. I wanted to find out who the boy was and why he looked in my direction. Did he want me to follow him?

"Blair?" Scott called out as I hurried past.

I turned around, flashed a smile at my husband, and swept some stray curls off my face. "Just going to the toilet."

"Okay, see you back at the table." Scott picked up our drinks and walked back through the pub to where we had been sitting.

I pushed open the door to the men's toilets. Both cubicles were wide open and empty. A man stood with his back to me, peeing into a urinal.

"Has a teenage boy come in? Black hoodie? Just a minute ago?"

The man zipped up his trousers and turned around, his face flushed. "Not seen anyone," he said, hurrying out of the room without washing his hands.

That all-too-familiar knotting feeling filled my stomach. What was I doing?

"I think you took the wrong door," a tall man said as he shimmied past me and walked up to the urinal. "The ladies' toilets are next door."

There was a strong smell of earth and decay. "Sorry," I said, backing out and letting the door swing shut.

The boy definitely walked in this direction, and there wasn't anything else back here other than the fire exit. I went into the ladies' room, locked myself in a cubicle, closed the toilet lid, and sat down. Jamie had left before answering my question. About the mud. Why was he so muddy? Was it Jamie I saw passing the bar to the toilets, or that other boy? I remembered something about a key. I needed to think. Get some air. Pull my thoughts together.

Scott would be wondering what I was doing, but finding that boy was more important. Back outside the toilets, the noise of the pub was disorientating. It was never a pleasure coming to the pub on the weekend. Always so busy. Everyone making the most of their time away from work. I much preferred the peace and quiet of home. I scanned the tables. Scott was sitting by the window engrossed in his phone. I wouldn't be long. Just a few minutes. He wouldn't even notice I'd gone. Not wanting to push past the queue of people waiting at the bar, I snuck out the fire exit at the back of the pub.

The whole of town seemed clogged up. A truck trundled along the road, its engine roaring as it passed by. Something caught my ankle. It hurt. I whirled around to see a woman with a buggy walking away. I would have told the woman to look where she was going if she hadn't marched off so fast.

I glanced up and down the high street. I couldn't see Jamie anywhere. Up ahead, the pedestrian lights turned green and the man began to flash. I ran up to the crossing and raced across as the man turned red, a Land Rover honking at me whilst I was still feet from the pavement. *A little patience wouldn't hurt!*

An elderly lady pulling a tartan shopping trolley ambled past staring at me. Did I know her? I smiled and tucked a wayward curl behind my ear, but the old lady didn't smile back. I looked up and down the high street. Every time I thought I saw a teenage boy with a hoodie, the crowds engulfed him. I decided to go left. To the department store. I always needed something from in there. If the boy had wanted me to follow him, it made sense to go somewhere I was familiar with.

A group of teenagers tumbled past, chatting loudly, taking up most of the pavement. I moved to the side, watching the group go by. One of them was wearing a hooded top, the hood hanging down revealing a shock of blond hair. Was that him? The boy from the pub? He didn't turn around.

Someone bumped my shoulder. I thought I could hear

my name being called. A car revved its engine as it drove past, making me jump. I took a deep breath. Coming to town when it was like this was no fun. I should have come in earlier.

I hurried into the department store. I might as well pick up some pillowcases while I'm here, I thought. It won't take a minute, and the beddings are on the second floor, so I'll be able to scan the whole store on my way up.

"Mum?"

I looked around but couldn't find Jamie in the crowd.

"You're getting yourself all conflustered, Mum. Take a breath. Chill."

I felt a hand slip into mine. Jamie was standing beside me.

I squeezed his hand tight. "What does conflustered even mean?"

He laughed. "It's what you're doing right now. Where are you going and what are you doing? Where's Dad?"

My hand dropped to my side and Jamie was gone again. Conflustered, indeed! I was getting something. Pillowcases. I turned a circle to get my bearings. There were never enough signs in department stores. Not like the supermarkets. I went up and down the escalators twice before I found the bedding at the back of the shop. The white pillowcases were on the top shelf. Typical. I pulled down a pack of two white pillowcases.

They'll do, I thought, tucking them under my arm.

A phone rang. It was mine. I pulled my mobile out of my pocket and a picture of Scott flashed up on the screen. I hadn't been that long, had I?

"Where are you?" he asked.

"Buying pillowcases."

"I'm in the high street looking for you. Why did you leave the pub?"

"The pub? Oh."

"Where are you now?"

"The department store."

"Right. Stay there. I'm coming to get you."

The boy obviously wanted to unnerve me. He didn't want to be found. I couldn't tell Scott. He'd think I was making it up again, losing my mind, seeing things that weren't there. I wanted to go home. I rushed to the exit and as I reached the automatic sliding doors, someone swept past me. It was the boy again.

"Look where you're going," I called out.

The boy left the shop, leaving behind a stench of tobacco and sweat. As I stepped out into the street, an alarm sounded.

"Will you be paying for those, madam?"

I spun around. "I'm sorry?"

A woman stood inches away from me, her eyes boring into me, her neat grey crop and ample bosom reminding me of a history teacher I'd clashed with at the end of secondary school. The teacher had been friends with Scott's mum and made no secret of the fact that she thought I wasn't good enough for him.

"Yes, she will." Scott appeared, scooping his arm around my waist and sweeping me back into the store.

There he was, like always, my knight in shining armour. Taking the pillowcases from under my arm, Scott walked with me to the till and paid. The assistant handed me a bag with my pillowcases inside.

Outside the shop, Scott interlocked his fingers with mine and kissed the back of my hand. "So, shall we go back to the pub for lunch or just head home?"

I wanted, so badly, to tell him about the boy, but I knew he wouldn't understand. I looked up and down the street and spotted the boy scurrying along the pavement in the direction of the car park. "Home. Definitely home."

I marched ahead of Scott, trying to keep up with the boy. Maybe he was going to wait by our car. Perhaps he wanted to tell us something about Jamie.

"Slow down. It's not a race." Scott grabbed my arm. "Wait up. The car isn't going anywhere."

No, but the boy was. The green man at the pedestrian crossing started flashing, and the beeping sound signalled the lights were about to change. Whipping my head around, I saw somebody running across the road at the last minute. It was the boy. He had his hood pulled up. Snatching my arm out of Scott's grip, I dashed across the road. A car horn sounded. I turned my head. There was a screech of brakes. I tried to run faster to get to the pavement on the other side of the road.

I heard Scott shouting. "Blair! *Stop!*"

Another screech of brakes.

The pavement was a couple of steps away. I was going to make it. The boy had darted off down a side street. The car didn't stop moving. I felt a thud as my hip collided with the front of the car. I wasn't running anymore. My body flipped around and for just a second, I saw the car's windscreen. A face with wide eyes on the other side of the glass. Like a slow-motion scene in a movie. My head hit something, and then my body was thrown onto the ground.

I lay still, disorientated. I could see the sky. There was a nasty smell of burning rubber. The tarmac felt warm against my palms. My head went fuzzy. I could hear people talking and shouting. My whole body felt like it was on fire. Every bit of it hurt. Faces were looking down at me. Scott's face was there.

"Lie still, honey. Someone's calling an ambulance. I'm right here."

I listened for Jamie, but the only sound was my heart-beat.

TEN

Scott

I T HAD BEEN a long night, and my shoulders loosened a little as I turned the corner into Cedars Road. I needed a shower and food and sleep. There was blood on my jeans and shirt and my curls were greasy clumps, making my scalp itch. I wanted to be stretched out on a rack to pull all the tension from my body.

My fists clenched around the steering wheel when I saw the scramble of vans and cars parked haphazardly outside my house. I hit the brakes and pulled up on the kerb for a minute to think. I'd had the heads-up from a few work mates that a video of Blair and the car accident had made its way onto social media. My boss had called to ask if they could run a short article about the incident, knowing that someone was bound to connect the dots soon enough and connect us to the Pied Piper of Peasedale. A career as a reporter had taught me that the best form of defence was to attack, so I agreed to the story, but it looked like a quiet sit-down with a colleague was no longer in the cards.

Part of me wanted to get out of the car and tell them all to piss off and leave me alone; part of me wanted to laugh at my naivety. I mean, Blair was not difficult to recognise at just over six feet, with striking red curls and pale freckled skin. She stood out from the crowd, and Jamie had inherited his mother's looks. The dots had quite clearly been connected, and my boss was not the only editor keen on the latest story generated by Gunner Piper's notoriety. Serial killers were newsworthy. Especially those who killed children.

Approaching our driveway, a handful of reporters emerged from their cars, cameras at the ready. I was about to take my chances and get out to open the gate when Frank appeared. He was wearing his old walking boots, water-resistant khaki hiking trousers, and an olive-green short-sleeved shirt with only the bottom four buttons done up. Along with his shoulder-length, wavy grey hair and bushy beard, he looked more suited to the Canadian Rockies than our over-manicured corner of Thadley. He was ten years older than me, but right now he looked a whole lot younger and fitter. He swung open the gate and I drove in. He had trouble wrestling the gate shut and herding the paparazzi back, but he wasn't the kind of man to be beaten.

As I stepped out of the car, cameras flashed, and a cacophony of questions were shouted at me. I decided to face the onslaught head-on.

Frank walked back to meet me, blocking my way back up the drive. "They've been here a few hours. Why don't you go inside? Those vultures will get bored eventually."

"You know, I'm one of those vultures." I rested my hand on his shoulder and smiled.

"Doesn't make it right." He shook his head. "How's Blair?"

"Comfortable. Confused. She's not been getting the right help."

The reporters continued to snap away and call out, so I took a deep breath and walked toward the gate. "You don't need to come with me, Frank. No need to get your ugly mug in the papers, too."

"Maybe I want my fifteen minutes of fame!" He walked beside me, head up, chest forward. "I'll play bodyguard. You don't look like you could fight off a mosquito right now."

I had no doubt the imminent newspaper and online articles would have plenty to say about my clothes, hair, and general state of disrepair, but that's how I looked after my wife ran out in front of a car in the middle of a busy high street, and the reporters would have to make of it whatever they liked. I was done caring. They'd already labelled my son an accomplice and my wife was in crisis, so there wasn't a lot more they could destroy.

Frank's eyes were pinched, his brow furrowed, as he scowled at the crowd. It wouldn't have surprised me if he turned into a grizzly bear and began slashing at our antagonists with six-inch claws. I liked that about him. He was as soft as a marshmallow inside, but you wouldn't believe it if you were one of the paparazzi right now.

I touched his arm and gave him a reassuring nod. "I recognise a couple of the faces. Let's hope they're feeling gentle."

Reaching the gate, we stopped and waited for the men and women behind the gate to stop shouting questions. Frank gestured to them to keep quiet.

I took a breath. "Blair is grieving. Her mental health has suffered. She made a mistake today in town, and I'm not entirely sure why she ran across the road when she did. She hit her head and had a nasty gash that needed stitching. She'll be in hospital for a few days recovering from a concussion. There's no story here. She made a mistake, that's all. She wasn't trying to run out in front of a car; she just thought she could get across before the lights changed."

I had no idea what she had been thinking before she ran across the road. Most likely chasing after ghosts again. All I knew for sure was that she was confused, she'd left the pub, picked up some pillowcases, and needed to get away from the hustle and bustle of town. Frank took hold of my shoulder, led me back to the house. A few of the reporters threw questions after us, but I didn't bite. There was no big story to unearth, and my statement was all they were going to get. No doubt the papers the next day would run a story about the mother of the boy they had labelled as the accomplice being so tormented with shame, she was trying to kill herself. It would blow over.

Unlocking the front door, I heard Minnie yowling from the kitchen. "She'll need a walk."

Frank followed me inside. "I'll make us a cup of coffee, and then I'll keep you company for a quick once round the park. We don't want that pack of wolves harassing you again, and I could do with some fresh air. Been at my desk all day and didn't make it out for my usual morning run."

"Thanks, Frank."

"No worries. You and your wife have been through so much."

Frank flipped on the kettle and rooted around the kitchen for coffee. I pulled out two thermos mugs and then went to the back door to retrieve Minnie's lead.

We walked to the park, letting Minnie off the lead when we reached the pond. She wasn't a swimmer, but she loved to bark at the ducks and steal sticks from the dogs who had swum out to fetch them and then obediently brought them back to their owners.

"You're not dressed for a day in the office, Frank."

"Job came in early this morning and I decided to get going on it straight away. These small residential projects don't take me long, not like the big industrial projects I used to do. I miss designing the big assembly-line manufacturing facilities, but working from home, freelance, and without the stress or pressure, suits me better."

"I've tried to explain to Blair that the reason you have such an immaculate home and garden is due to your architect's eye for precision and detail."

Frank chuckled. "You noticed."

"Blair noticed. She has told me on many occasions that I should make more effort to make our place look as good as yours."

"I don't have anyone to look after, not since Mila passed. It's just me and the house. I guess that's why I set up the Neighbourhood Watch. I like to keep an eye on the street. Make a note of any unusual activity. Mila used to be extra vigilant about strangers. Her job as a continuity supervisor meant she noticed anything and everything that was amiss. Guess it rubbed off on me."

"Have you ever seen anything suspicious? Caught any burglars in the act?"

"Nope. A few comings and goings but nothing untoward. Your lad was a secretive kid, though. Took advantage of having two working parents. Reminded me of my own upbringing."

"Secretive how?"

"I saw him hiding something in your flowerbed one afternoon, a few weeks before he went missing. Told your wife. She said he was always doing mysterious things."

I whistled to Minnie, who was harassing a rather terrified-looking dachshund. "It was his time capsule. We dug it up the other day. He'd emptied it out and put a key in it. No idea what the key opens."

"I often saw him with that tall lad. Jace—I think that was what he called him. Heard them talking one morning after you and Blair had left for work. The two of them were climbing into your garage via the window. I went round and asked what they were up to, and they gave me a story about a lost key and forgotten homework. Didn't leave the house till the afternoon. I did mention it to Blair."

A boy. With a name. Perhaps it was the same boy Blair kept mentioning. She obviously knew about him—this Jace, whoever he was—but I didn't remember her ever talking to me about him. On the one hand, it was good to know that Jamie had a friend, one he had been seen with and brought to the house, but on the other hand, hearing that they were playing truant from school and trying to break into the house through the garage wasn't so great. Maybe Blair did tell me and I'd just forgotten, although it wasn't an insignificant piece of information about our son.

"You okay there, Scott?"

"I was trying to remember if the school contacted us about Jamie not turning up for school. It could have been an inset day or bank holiday, but then why wouldn't he have told you that?"

"I don't think taking the odd day off school is anything to worry about. Boys need to take a few risks and break some rules now and then." Frank had a few big gulps of his coffee.

"I remember, on the way to school one morning with my best friend Leith, we decided to take a detour to the abandoned farmhouse. My mum found us a couple of hours later after a call from the headmaster. We were knee-deep in the nearby stream searching for frogspawn. I had to wash the car and clean the house for a month."

"He still turns up, every now and then. Jace. Hovers around by the gate. I guess he misses your boy. He was there today, watching the press."

"What?"

Frank had seen this boy, recently, since Jamie's death. It had to be the same boy Blair was seeing, which meant it was an actual living, breathing human, not a figment of her imagination. I hadn't wanted to question what or who she was seeing, but whenever I looked outside, there was no one there, and she was talking to our son's apparition. What did this boy want? If he was just missing Jamie, why didn't he just knock on our door? Maybe he would have some answers for us; maybe he saw what happened. He could have been the person who made the emergency call from Jamie's phone; maybe he was involved in Jamie's death.

Frank nudged my arm and laughed at Minnie as she blundered from dog to dog, hoping to coax one into a game of chase. Most found her size intimidating and either hid behind their owners' legs or threw themselves, legs akimbo, on the ground at her feet. They didn't see the goofy lovable klutz that she really was. I have replayed the day of Jamie's murder so many times, and on each occasion I imagined him taking Minnie with him and her acting as his bodyguard, scaring off Gunner Piper and saving his life. She wouldn't have done that, of course; she'd have tried to be Gunner's friend and most likely gotten herself killed, too.

My body felt heavy and drained of energy, my head swirling with ideas for how to find this mysterious boy who was lurking around our house. "Let's head back. I need an early night."

Frank paused, staring across the pond. "Whenever you want to talk, Scott, or just have some company on a walk, I'm just next door. I know I haven't lost a kid, but I do understand grief."

"Thanks, Frank. I appreciate that."

The hospital called as we headed out of the park. Blair was asking for me.

"I'm sorry, Frank, I'm going to have to get a move on."

Frank clipped Minnie onto the lead. "You go ahead. I'll take care of the dog for a few days if you'd like. Blair showed me where you keep a spare key for emergencies. Happy to take Minnie out for walks and feed her. I'll enjoy the company."

"That would be great, Frank, thanks."

I jogged home and got straight into the car, the jumble of photographers and reporters backing out of my way as I opened the gate and drove away. Frank wouldn't be far behind, and he'd close the gate for me.

Back at the hospital, I found Blair lying in the bed, her

head turned slightly to the side. She looked small and fragile, the bedsheet up to her shoulders, one arm outside, with a cannula in her hand. There was a bald section on the back of her scalp where the cut on her head had been stitched.

Hospital rooms always feel like transitioning rooms. Something changes about a person and the relationship you have with them that can't be undone. There is a loss of something other than dignity and physical function. It feels like a transaction of sorts, not just the healing of an injury and the acquisition of scars but a shift in the dynamics between the patient and the family. The accident and Blair lying helpless on the hospital bed would always be in my memory, and it weakened her, made her more vulnerable, bound her to me a little tighter because she needed me in a way that she hadn't before and I could see how empty my life would be without her.

My chest tightened and I had to swallow back tears. How could I have let this happen? I was right there with her. Why didn't I grab hold of her? Why didn't I see what she was about to do? I kissed her gently on the cheek and sank into the chair.

"Hey, BB."

Opening her eyes, she stretched her fingers toward me.

I slid my hand into hers. "Oh, honey, I love you so much. I'm so sorry this happened. I'm so sorry I took you into town for that stupid lunch, and I'm sorry I didn't stop you from running after that car. I shouldn't have let go of you."

Her beautiful blue eyes had lost their sparkle. "I just…"

She was trying to swallow, the skin on her lips taut, pulling at the deep red cracks. I lifted her head and helped her to sip some water, plumping her pillows so that she was a little more upright.

"I just want to be with Jamie." Tears instantly pooled in her lower lids.

I didn't think my heart could break anymore, but piece by tiny piece, it was crumbling away.

I rested my forehead on hers. "Me too, honey."

I needed to find that boy. I needed to know what he knew about our son and Gunner Piper. I needed to get the answers before my heart turned to dust and there was nothing left of me and Blair to fight for.

ELEVEN

Blair

M Y EYELIDS FELT as if they were made of treacle as I peeled them open. I must have drifted off. Scott was still sitting beside me, and the light in the room was so bright it illuminated his head as if he were an angel with a halo. He had a sad smile on his face, not the wide, bright smile he used to have. Before.

"There you are," he said.

My head was throbbing, and I could feel a dull ache in other parts of my body—my left hip, left elbow, and both knees. My skin was prickling and my body shook with a shiver that ran from my head to my feet. I pulled my lips apart and breathed in a sticky breath. I tried to speak, but the sound I made was barely audible. I tried again.

"Seb. James. Theo. Noah. Tristan. Ralph. Stanley. Christopher. Nicholas. Jordan. William. Leon."

A young male nurse, tall and slender with soft features, small dark eyes, and wavy brown hair injected something into my hand. "She keeps reciting those names. I've talked to the consultant. Someone from the crisis team will be down to see her soon to give her a psychiatric evaluation."

Another psyche evaluation. More mental health tests. I'd done this with the doctor already. I had tablets. Scott should tell them I just needed someone to talk to. Someone who would listen to me. I'd like to talk to him, but he wanted to fix me. I didn't need fixing; I didn't want to stop seeing Jamie. I just wanted to understand what happened to my boy, how it happened, why it happened. The more I thought about Jamie, the more muddled my memories became—events overlapping, merging. I couldn't connect anything or form a timeline of his behaviour, just a jumble of flashbacks that tormented me.

My mind couldn't grip hold of anything tangible, as if it was floating around looking for a way back inside me. Scott pushed some stray curls off my face and looked up at the nurse. "Our son was killed. He was one of The Pied Piper's victims. Those are the names of the other twelve boys he killed, and each name is tattooed along the inside of Gunner Piper's arm from wrist to elbow. Of all the images to embed in Blair's brain, that tattooed list of names seems to have made the greatest impression."

The nurse paused and shook his head. "How awful. No wonder she ran out in front of that car."

Why were they talking about me instead of *to* me?

I tapped a finger against my mouth. "Water, please."

Scott helped me sip some water, and my mind squeezed itself back into place. "I can hear your conversation perfectly well, you know. I'm not crazy or deaf, and I didn't try to run in front of a car. It was an accident. I was trying to get across the road, quickly."

The problem was, I just couldn't stop thinking about that man with his tattoos and all those dead boys and the other boy hanging around the house. And then there was

Jamie, popping up all the time. It was confusing me. I couldn't think straight. Maybe it was all the pills the doctor had given me.

I looked up at the nurse as he wrote the readings on my medical monitoring equipment on the notes on his clipboard. "Jamie wasn't on the list."

The nurse finished and then sat on the edge of the bed and stroked my arm. "I can't imagine how dreadful it's been for you."

Tears trickled down my cheeks and dripped off my chin, but I didn't wipe them away. I didn't try to stop them; I needed to let them out. Being comforted by a stranger, albeit a nurse who was caring for me in hospital, was a special kind of compassion. He didn't want anything in return; he wasn't mending his own broken heart at the same time. It was a one-way street, and I was the beneficiary.

"I'll be back later to do your next checks." He squeezed my hand before leaving the room.

Scott was still there. Still smiling at me. I think I'd feel better if he shouted at me, told me I was stupid for what I did, pushed me for a reason as to why I behaved in such a reckless way. I guess he was all out of ideas. We were done with shouting, silence, sobbing, and pretending. What else was there for us to try? He promised me yesterday that he'd find a clinic for me to visit for some grief therapy. Somewhere away from home for a little while. Away from him. Just to get my head together and to give him some rest. I needed help, and he needed space to process what was happening and to grieve himself.

I lifted myself a little more upright and Scott helped me

sip some more water. "Did you find somewhere for me to go?"

His face hardened as he looked down at our hands. "I made a few calls earlier while I was driving home. The clinic the doctor suggested has a spot. It's not too far away, so I can come and visit whenever you like. I've just booked you in for a couple of weeks to start with. See how you go."

"Thank you. I won't be under your feet, causing trouble, and you can get on with work. I don't feel safe at home on my own and everywhere I look, Jamie is there. I can't tell what's real and what isn't."

Scott pushed his hair off his face and sat back in the chair. "You know what is and isn't real. You've just been spending too much time in your head, overthinking everything. We're grieving. Differently. I wish I could help you."

I leant forward. "You're welcome to readjust my pillows."

Scott plumped the pillows. "You know what I mean."

"I want to talk to you, but you always change the subject. I want to talk about Jamie, about who he was and why he died."

"He was killed by a monster. Lured by an evil man who coaxed and manipulated innocent boys. It could have been any boy." Scott took a big gulp of water.

"What if it wasn't that simple? What if there was more to it?"

"What if there was? I get it, I really do. I want to know exactly what happened to him and why, and I think you might even be right about there being a boy who was hanging around the house. Frank has seen him. But, honey,

I'm afraid that you're too fragile to go searching for the truth at the moment. What happens the next time you run out into the road? This time it was a head injury and superficial cuts and bruises. Next time I could lose you. I need you to be well, strong, able to handle the truth without putting yourself in danger."

"Okay, I get it. I'm not coping and I do need help, but then we are finding out what happened to our son. What about that key? That was strange, don't you think? Finding that key in his time capsule? I searched the house, but I couldn't find that puzzle box he had."

"Puzzle box?"

"You bought it for his eleventh birthday. Remember? It took him ages to open it, and he refused to use the instructions. I thought that might be where the key belonged."

"That's what you were turning the house upside down for. Why didn't you say?"

"Because I knew that you'd take me back to the doctor for even more pills, and I already can't think straight."

"Fair enough. I would have done that, and if I had then maybe you wouldn't be in here."

"Will you look for the box?"

"I haven't seen that box in years. I'll look for it, though, and if it's in the house, I'll find it."

There was a knock at the door and a porter wheeled in a trolley with the dinner trays. "If there's one good reason to get well, it will be to get out of here so that I don't have to eat any more of the food."

Scott pulled the table across the bed in front of me and took the tray of food from the porter.

I smiled at the young girl who was staring awkwardly at me. "Thank you." I guessed that having the mother of the boy accused of being a serial killer's accomplice in your hospital must be big news.

Jamie stood beside the trolley looking at the other trays of food and scrunching up his nose. "I made you famous, mum."

Scott lifted the lid. "I wonder what delights you have been served this evening."

I stared at the meagre offering. "My favourite. Macaroni and cheese and jelly."

We both laughed. Jamie was gone.

I ate a small mouthful of the food and grimaced. "Jamie wasn't a stupid boy, you know. He had some street smarts. Unlucky just doesn't feel right. Did he go to that shack willingly, do you think? Was he drugged by someone else and dragged there? Somebody must have the answer."

"Gunner Piper certainly isn't giving us anything. He's offered up so much detail for the other boys. It doesn't make sense. Maybe we'll never know."

I forced in my mac and cheese while Scott sat silently watching me. The last thing I needed was to have him think I was starving myself. I had no appetite, but if I wanted to get better and find the truth then Scott was right—I needed to be well and strong.

When I finished, I looked up at Scott. "You want to find the truth as much as me—I know you do. I just don't understand why you're holding back. Isn't it eating you up inside that you don't know why your son went with that man and ended up in that shack? The not knowing is killing me. You can't let a story go when it's for work."

Scott got to his feet and walked to the window. "I've been too busy worrying about you—talking to yourself, running after ghosts, throwing yourself in front of cars. I also don't want to be chasing dead ends for the rest of our lives."

"I'm not talking to myself. I'm talking to Jamie."

"It isn't him, though, is it? It never will be."

"I didn't mean to run out in front of a car. I thought I saw that boy."

"What does he look like, this other boy?"

"Jamie's height, I guess. Broader though. I haven't seen his face as he's always wearing a hoodie and his head is down."

"That's not much to go on."

"Our son changed. He was such a funny boy. Enjoyed playing football. It was that school. Everything changed when he started at that school."

Scott shook his head. "He grew up."

"It was more than that. He didn't talk to me so much. Hid things. Blanked me, blocked me, and bullshitted me."

"He became a preteen and then a teenager, that's all."

"He started talking back to me."

"He was becoming his own man. With his own thoughts and opinions."

"There was more to it. It was that boy. The one in the hoodie."

We let an awkward pause hang in the air. This was a roundabout we couldn't seem to get off. He knew what I was talking about, he just wasn't ready to admit it."

I slumped back in the bed. "I think I'd like to rest now."

Scott settled me under the sheets and moved the table to the side.

I watched Scott pull on his coat. "Why don't you ask Frank for some help with Minnie? He knows where the spare key is. He's offered to look after her before."

"Already done that. I saw him when I got back. He walked round the park with me."

I was glad he had Frank to talk to. Frank was a good neighbour, never afraid to talk about how he was feeling after Mila died. Maybe he would draw some of that buried emotion out of my husband.

Scott kissed me on the forehead. "A few more days in here and then I'll be able to take you to the clinic."

"Pack me a bag."

"Of course. Love you."

I waited for Scott to leave, then I waited a little longer, drifting in and out of sleep until the nurse switched off the lights and I could hide in the quiet of the night. My mind wandered, and a hidden memory replayed in my head.

A memory of Jamie coming home late.

Scott was away.

I was sitting on the stairs when Jamie opened the front door and crept into the hallway. "Where were you, Jamie? What have you been doing?"

He took off his shoes. "Leave it, Mum. Just leave it."

I folded my arms and stared at him. "I can't leave it. I don't know where you go with that other boy. I don't know who he is or where he lives. I don't know what you get up to."

Jamie turned and faced me. "Why do I have to be getting

up to anything? We just chill. Talk. It's no big deal." He pushed past me and stomped up to his room.

I remembered the mud on his shoes, the dirt under his nails, and the smell of earth and rot. The memory faded, but there were more like that, hidden away in my mind, when Jamie had come home late dragging muck into the house. I reached for the water cup by my bed, took a sip, and then slid back under the covers and lay staring at the ceiling. This wasn't my bed. It wasn't where I wanted to be. It was cold and I felt exposed, the walls were bare, nothing was interesting to look at, and my head hurt where the lump was.

What Jamie got up to *was* a big deal. Big enough to get him killed.

TWELVE

Scott

D RIVING BLAIR TO the clinic two days later was tough. I settled her in, kissed her goodbye, and said I would come and visit when she was ready. The ball was in her court. I drove away feeling like I had let her down. I couldn't help her, couldn't understand what was going on in her head, so I left her in there hoping that someone else could fix her.

I arrived home alone. Jamie was gone and now Blair. The last couple of days had been exhausting, so I dragged myself up to bed and slept for the best part of twenty-four hours. When I finally surfaced, I was grateful to discover that Frank had taken Minnie out for a walk and fed her. For the next few days, I just about managed to zombie around the house, barely eating, not washing, and ignoring my phone.

It was daytime when the doorbell rang. I was asleep again. Dozing, at least. In and out of dreams. My mind restless, my body lethargic. My stomach would have rumbled if there was anything in it, but it was so empty there wasn't even enough air inside me to let out a gripe, let alone a grumble.

The doorbell rang a second time. I dragged myself out of bed and loped down the stairs, hoping the invader would get fed up with waiting. No such luck! The bell rang again. I stood and waited on the bottom step. Maybe they'd give up after the third try. Even Minnie was too downcast to keep up her usual barking. The letterbox flicked up.

"Scotty!" a voice shouted through the gap, lips pressed against the metal opening. "Scotty, beam me up!"

"Captain K?" It was the nickname I called Leith MacIsaac, my oldest friend. "No way!"

I should have guessed he'd turn up. Never fails to be there for me in a crisis.

"Yes way! Now let me in; I'm sweating my baws off out here and need a beer!"

We were huge *Star Trek* fans back in the day, and the nicknames stuck. I smiled and patted Minnie on the top of her head before letting Leith inside.

"Scotty, mate, what the hell! You look like a Talosian." A skinny alien with an oversized, veiny head. The likeness was sketchy at best.

"Seriously, you're so goddamn scrawny. Jeez, mate, looks like I got here in the nick of time," he said, pulling me in for a hug.

"Why are you here?"

"To save you from total meltdown by the looks of it. Come on, shower! I'll make lunch—if you've got any food in the fridge—and then we'll take the mutt out. Smells like she's been improvising with her toilet habits."

"That could be me."

Leith marched me upstairs to the bathroom, turned on the water, and waited with his back turned until I got into the cubicle.

"I'm in," I said when he didn't move.

"Let the cleanup begin," he said. "You know, the greatest danger facing us…"

"Is ourselves," I said. "Aye, aye, Captain." I felt a smidge brighter.

After wallowing under the hot water until my skin wrinkled, I emerged smelling of vanilla and cocoa beans. Back in my bedroom, pulling on fresh clean clothes, I discovered that my trusted friend had stripped my bed. Downstairs, he had cleared away the dirty mugs and plates I'd discarded around the house and had a look around in the kitchen cupboards.

Leith pulled out a chair for me. "You smell human again. Now you need to eat."

He handed me a plate piled high with vegan burgers, baked beans, spaghetti, and a side bowl of pear halves.

"Wow! You've outdone yourself this time," I said, sitting down and scooping up a spoonful of beans. "Mm. You even heated these up."

"Your cupboards are pretty bare. Anyway, we managed very well on cold beans during the Indian leg of our gap year, thank you very much, and if I remember rightly, without them you'd have shit yourself inside out."

"Really helpful anecdote there while I'm eating, thanks. I also remember that my Delhi belly turned me into a human leaf blower after you made me eat beans for a month."

"Oh, mate, you were hurting." Leith began to laugh uncontrollably. "Your farting was out of control. By far the funniest month of my life."

His laugh was infectious and before I knew it, I was laughing along with him. Thank the stars for a best mate. I wolfed down my lunch and then we headed to the park with Minnie for some fresh air.

"So…" Leith began as we sat on a bench overlooking the perfectly round, manmade pond in the centre of the park, two swans gliding happily across and a raft of ducks fussing about by the near bank.

I almost felt normal.

"How are things with you and Blair?" he asked.

Well, that feeling didn't last!

I sat back and took a deep breath. "I don't know where to start."

"You've just gotta start gassing. We'll do it like a Q and A to get the ball rolling. Where is she, by the way? Squirrelling away in her darkroom, by any chance? Still resisting the digital revolution?"

"She's in a residential clinic. She isn't coping. Talks to herself—well, to Jamie actually. Churning stuff over and over in her head until she doesn't know where she is or what she's doing."

"Last time we spoke, you were back at work and it sounded like things were improving."

"I thought they were, but all that stuff about Jamie being an accomplice is still plaguing us, and Gunner Piper is spewing out details about all the other boys except ours. We've been woken by kids writing graffiti on the garage doors. Then, last weekend, Blair ran right into the path of a moving vehicle. Spent a few days in hospital with a concussion and asked me to find somewhere for her to go for a couple of weeks to get some therapy. The whole episode was so surreal. I still can't believe it actually happened."

"What the hell was she thinking?"

"God knows! She's taking a bunch of medications for anxiety, depression, PTSD, insomnia, paranoia, psychosis—I couldn't keep up in the end. The long and short of it is she didn't know what she was doing. Christ, she's even had Jamie's name tattooed on her body four times, dug holes all over the garden looking for his time capsule, and can't stop raving on about some boy wearing a black hoodie."

"What a fucking mess, mate!"

"Mess is an understatement."

"So, what next? What's the plan?"

"Plan?"

"To sort all of this out."

"No plan. She's in the clinic until she's well. I don't think there's a quick fix here, just a long hard slog to recovery."

"And what about you?" Minnie bounded up to Leith and dropped a stick at his feet, which he threw into the pond. "You're a bottler. We all know that. Maybe you need to talk to someone, too. What about all those leaflets I saw on your sideboard?"

"Not really my thing. The distraction of work helps."

"Forgive me for being so bold, but I was surprised, with all the crime stories you've covered, that you haven't wanted to look more closely into Jamie's death. Not even dip your toe in the water. If it was my boy, I'd want to know everything there was to know about him. About Gunner Piper, the other victims, why the monster wasn't stopped sooner."

"In the beginning, Blair and I were in shock. The grief was debilitating. We did go out to Peasedale Forest when the story first broke in the press, hoping to find some answers, but that was a disaster, with members of the public blaming our parenting for what happened to Jamie, and I was paranoid we were being followed. Honestly, I felt out of my depth, too close to the crimes to be able to investigate them with the right perspective. When Blair started seeing Jamie, I didn't know what to do. I dragged her to the doctor and tried to take care of her, but she disappeared inside herself and shut me out. Or I shut her out."

"So, there's nothing you can do? No avenue you haven't explored? The Bloodhound has finally lost the scent, huh?"

"I've done some digging, talked to friends and neighbours and the school, but I never found anything worth following up. There is a boy out there somewhere who I think was a friend of Jamie's—Blair's seen him hanging around and so has our neighbour—but every time I go looking for him, he's gone. If an entire police force can't give me the answers I want, with Gunner Piper behind bars and cooperating with them, what the hell am I going to be able to do?"

"Jeez, mate, that's not the Scott I know! That newspaper of yours didn't name you The Bloodhound for nothing. The truth will set you free, isn't that the saying?"

"What if it doesn't? What if the search drives us both mad? What if the truth just makes everything worse?"

"You always told me Jamie was a good lad—quirky, artistic, but with his head screwed on. So, how did he end up falling victim to Gunner Piper? I read all the articles, watched the news. He wasn't a boy who was easily led."

"Why don't we talk about you for a bit? You must have

upset somebody recently."

"Very funny. Now don't change the subject."

Minnie returned and dropped the stick again, along with a pool of wet drool, in my lap. I threw it back into the pond and got to my feet. "We found a key. Hidden in Jamie's time capsule. Blair thought it might belong to his puzzle box, but she couldn't find it. I promised her I'd turn the house upside down and if it was there, I'd find it. Maybe that's the next piece of the puzzle. And, of course, there's the other boy."

Leith stood up and whistled to the dog. "A mystery to unravel. Well, a hidden key seems like a great place to start. Let's go and find that box!"

THIRTEEN

Blair

I SAT ON my bed in the characterless room I had been assigned at the clinic and tried to picture Scott: his black floppy hair, big wide smile, and asparagus-green eyes. I'd done a vegetable test against them when we were both seventeen; asparagus was the closest match. I wish he was here now, his arm around me as I rest my head against his broad, muscular chest, breathing in the sweet, spicy scent of his aftershave.

Scott always made me feel safe, even when Jamie came along and the world I thought I felt comfortable in became a very dangerous place for my tiny baby. He walked with me while I pushed the buggy, sat with me while Jamie fed, and even drank his beer sitting on the toilet while I had a bath during those first few befuddling months. Whenever I had a crisis of confidence, he'd kiss me and tell me that I was the best mother our little boy could wish for. And on the worst of days, when Jamie pushed all my buttons, the dinner burnt because I was wrestling the whirling dervish into the bath and ranting like a crazy lady, he'd come through the door with a dazzling smile that instantly lifted my spirits.

"You look like you've had a much harder day than me, honey," he'd say. "I'll take over from here. Why don't you run yourself a bath."

He managed to look like the dad that got it right without breaking a sweat. I missed him already, and I'd only been here three days. I thought this would be the right place for me, but I was struggling to acclimatise. The rooms smelled medical, the furniture was hard and irritated my skin, the food was bland, and I hadn't plucked up the courage to talk to anyone yet. The only modicum of comfort was an intricate carved picture of a lady sitting beneath a weeping willow that hung on the wall opposite my bed.

"TIME FOR GROUP therapy, Blair."

The announcement startled me, making me jerk my head backward, giving me a brain freeze. A tall, older woman stood in the doorway, a kind smile on her face, her grey hair in a short, angled bob. I hadn't met her yet. Her name badge read 'Kami.'

"Deep breath, Mum. You'll be great." Jamie leant against the doorframe next to the nurse.

I ignored the phantasm of my son. I knew that he was just a figment of my imagination. The meds were supposed to be dealing with that, but Dr. Ortiz had said that Rome wasn't built in a day and my recovery would take time and effort. I had enjoyed my first session with him. Talking to a psychologist was a lot easier than I had expected.

I followed Kami to a sparse, clean room, housing a circle of six blue, comfy chairs, a motley band of misfits, and a man with a clipboard. I took a seat, smiling at the two women sitting on either side of me. The woman on the left smiled back; the woman on my right sat wringing her hands and staring at her feet.

There was a low twitter of chatter. A memory of Scott and the asparagus test wafted in and out of my mind. A childish giggle floated about, unreachable. My head felt fuzzy and tight. I hated the idea of group counselling and all the morbid sharing we were about to be forced to do. I had managed to avoid every bereavement therapy group and grief retreat that had been offered, but time hadn't healed my heart or my head, and I knew that I had to give this a try, not just for me but for Scott, too. I took a deep breath and placed my hands in my lap. I was as ready as I'd ever be.

"Let's introduce ourselves for the benefit of our new arrival. I'm Nigel," said the man with the clipboard.

The group obliged with names.

I was last in line. "I'm Blair."

"Good. And would you like to tell us all a little more about yourself?" Nigel sat back and crossed his legs.

I gripped the side of the chair. I wanted to get up and leave, but I didn't know where to go. I felt exposed and vulnerable and very much out of my comfort zone. I wasn't a big talker. Not in this way, at least. Avoiding the gawps of the group, I focussed on the end of my sandals, where my toes poked out. I wiggled them.

"I'm a fashion photographer. I live in Thadley with my husband and our…our Great Dane."

Something glinting at me by the window caught my eye. I looked up and saw Jamie grinning at me, one hand fiddling with something around his neck.

"Go on, tell them. Nigel knows already. He just wants you to say it."

He wasn't real. I looked away from him. The group was silent. Watching me.

I lifted my head and looked at Nigel. "I had a son. His name was Jamie. He was killed."

The woman on my left put a hand on my knee. "Well done. We've all lost someone, Sweetie."

I had lost my son in the most terrible way. I wasn't the same as these women. I wasn't. My breathing was loud and fast. Sweat was dampening my hairline. I could feel the chanting bubbling up inside me. I held my breath trying to hold it in. I didn't want to talk about Jamie. Not now. Not here. Not like this. I let out my breath, and the chanting blurted out before I could hold myself together. "Seb. James. Theo. Noah. Tristan. Ralph."

I slammed my hand over my mouth.

The woman to my left looked up. "Are you alright?"

"Thank you, Leoni," Nigel said, writing something on his clipboard. "Take a breath, Blair. You've talked this through with Dr Ortiz, haven't you? Why don't you tell us who the boys are?"

Nigel placed his clipboard on his lap, rested his hands carefully on top, and smiled at me. It was the same smile I'd seen on the faces of all those police officers. It was a sorry sort of smile.

Everyone stared at me.

"Blair?" Nigel prompted.

The room was silent. It was no use; I was going to have to give them something.

"They're the names of the boys they dug up. In the woods."

"Go, Mum!" The glinting flickered again by the window as if something shiny was reflecting the sun, but Jamie had gone.

"What happened to the boys?" asked Nigel.

I took a deep breath. "They were murdered."

"Ha! I can't believe you just said it!" Jamie's voice sounded farther away.

Nigel sat forward, elbows on his knees. "I know that was hard."

The woman on my right reached across and took hold of my hand. It was time. I knew that it was time. I wanted to talk about my son and now I was somewhere where the people around me were prepared to listen.

I sat taller, my hand clasped in my lap. "Jamie was murdered by Gunner Piper. The Pied Piper of Peasedale. Some people think Jamie was his accomplice. He wasn't. It was the other boy. The one in the hoodie. And I'm going to find that boy and get the truth out of him."

I looked around the room. Listened. Jamie was gone, but whatever was around his neck still glinted at me. An image of him on holiday flashed into my mind. Something dangling from his neck caught the sun and made me squint. I wanted to ask what it was and where he got it, but he kept tucking it away beneath his T-shirt.

I put a hand up to my neck and a shiver ran through my body.

FOURTEEN

Scott

Pub of choice was The Hornet's Nest, known for its late close, club vibe, and younger clientele. We were not going out for a few pints and a heart-to-heart; we were going to get wasted and relive our youth. I had hoped to sit and smoke my last spliff with Leith that night, but it wasn't in the drawer where I put it for safe keeping. Not that it mattered because my oldest buddy had the same idea.

After our heart-to-heart in the park, Leith had decided that we should begin our search for the puzzle box the following day, after a night out so that we could have some fun first. Blair always said that compartmentalising was Leith's superpower. He could never stomach too much of the serious stuff at once, and I agreed that a breather from everything that had happened would be good for me.

We sat in the overcrowded smoking area of The Hornet's Nest, cheek by jowl with pissed, scantily clad, barely legal girls and a swarm of horny, lairy lads. The lads were obnoxious to the point of rudeness, their drink and testosterone-fuelled bodies too much for them to handle. I had flashbacks of our younger years. Did Leith and I really behave like that?

Smoking weed, it appeared, required no skulking or secrecy in this crowd of high-seeking youngsters as we were engulfed in a fog of pungent fumes, which felt more like being inside a giant bong than outside under a thin awning.

For a few hours, we relaxed, laughed, and, much to the amusement of the younger generation, danced-ish. It was more a drunken throwing of one's limbs, hopefully somewhat in time with the music, ideally without knocking over a fellow dancer or falling over ourselves. Leith failed on all counts, backhanding a thick-built skinhead and then falling facedown at the feet of the aforementioned skinhead's female dance partner.

"Conquest is easy. Control is not," Leith pronounced as he rose to his feet. "More whiskey!"

At the bar, I just about made myself understood above the noise, and despite the effects of way too much alcohol, I returned to the dance floor, armed with two large whiskeys, to find Leith gurning, which was very possibly a grin that he'd taken too far. It was difficult to tell at this point in the evening. Right on cue, The Firm's "Star Trekkin'" came on, the DJ kindly introducing it. "Here's one for the boomers."

Actually, we were in the Generation X category, but what did it matter? Boomers, Gen X, Millennials, who gives a toss? A good tune is a good tune.

"YA CANNAE CHANGE THE LAWS OF PHYSICS!" we shouted in unison. We downed our whiskeys and went berserk, clearing much of the dance floor and finding our way onto tens of smartphones, no doubt being instantly uploaded onto a host of social media sites. Did I care? Hell no. I was having a ball, letting loose, free as a fucking bird. By the end of the track, we were jumping up and down, shout-singing the words to the song like a couple of middle-aged pissheads, which, at that moment, we were.

The next thing I knew, Leith grabbed the skinhead's girl-friend by the hand and spun her around before pulling her toward him for a dance, the old-fashioned way. She wasn't impressed. I reached for my inebriated friend's arm, intending to pry him off the affronted girl, but the skinhead got there first. The girl was roughly slung across the dance floor by her beau, leaving Leith face to face with a snarling, red-faced vengeful boyfriend.

Before I had a chance to intervene, Leith was shaking the guy by the hand and apologising profusely. I'm not sure I'd ever seen him quite so sheepish. Explaining how he had only wanted a dance with a pretty girl and what a lucky guy the boyfriend was. Telling the now amused skinhead how happily married he was and that he meant no harm.

Confrontation successfully averted, we left the club and headed home. We stopped for a kebab and found ourselves back in the park, sprawled out on the bench, scoffing our midnight snack just like in the old days.

Leith polished off his last mouthful and wiped his lips on his sleeve. "Do you remember when you asked Blair to the prom? I thought you two would never work out. She was so driven. Too ambitious for you, I reckoned."

"Yeah, I remember. I guess her ambition was infectious."

"You sure as hell caught the bug. Made a real success of yourself."

"Thanks."

"I'm so sorry for what happened to your boy. I know I've said it a hundred times. But I really am. Devastated for you both. Can't really blame Blair for losing it. Freya still can't talk about you two without crying her eyes out."

"We'd love to see her. I know Blair would like to talk to her. She doesn't really have friends down here. Bit of a loner as a freelance photographer. Freya's the only other person she's ever been close with."

"Blair will get better, I know it. She's strong. What you two have together is great. She needs you as much as you need her. Give her time."

"Time. The more time she has, though, the more she thinks about this idea of an accomplice. She got those tattoos of Jamie to try to find out about him. The worst of it is, I know she's right. I believe that there is another boy out there, but instead of helping her, I'm pushing her away. I'm so damned frightened of what we'll uncover about our son."

"If you think she's on to something, you owe it to her and yourself to follow it up. If she's willing to face the truth then you should be right there with her."

"I don't know. Leith, our boy was murdered. If someone out there knows exactly what happened, if someone else was involved, then they are dangerous. Me prodding about for answers could put us at risk, Blair, at risk. And I can't lose her, too."

"Makes my blood boil."

"If there is an accomplice out there, of course, I want to find him. I want to meet him, face to face, and drag the truth out of him. Then I want to skin him alive. But, then what? It won't bring Jamie back, and what will it do to Blair? I want answers and I want to protect my wife, but I can't do both."

"Maybe she doesn't need protecting. From the truth, at

least."

We wandered home, our heads buzzing from the loud music, our legs wobbly from the alcohol. For a few hours, I had managed to put Blair and Jamie and our broken family in the back of my mind and have fun. Leith and I had talked sport, cars, work, current affairs, and music. We danced, drank, and laughed.

I drifted unsteadily along the streets with Leith, the heavy burden of guilt and shame and failure feeling lighter in my alcohol-induced haze. I could see why people became secret alcoholics. It gives you distance from reality—the troubles still there but just out of reach.

As I lifted the latch on our gate, reality came crashing back into focus. Something had tripped the motion-sensor lights, and the disturbance had clearly upset Minnie, whose howling could be heard from the end of the driveway.

"It's probably a fox," I announced to Leith, although my gut was telling me otherwise. "I'll just do a quick sweep around the house."

"I'll go inside and calm that hound down. You got the key?" Leith held out his hand.

I fumbled around in my pocket, found the key, and handed it to him. We split up. It was late, around one in the morning; the road was quiet, houses dark. I made my way around the house, no idea what I was looking for. I walked carefully, trying not to make any noise, not because I didn't want to disturb an intruder but because I didn't want to be seen by a potential prowler who might be carrying a deadly weapon. Since Jamie's murder, all those 'what if?' scenarios had become terrifyingly tangible.

It was pin-drop silent. No birds, no breeze, no distant car noise. All I could hear was my breathing and my heart, which was thumping away in my chest and getting louder and faster with every step I took. There was light coming from the kitchen window at the back of the house and Minnie had stopped howling, so I figured that Leith was successfully inside and being licked to within an inch of his life. The garden was empty. I checked the shed and Blair's darkroom, but both were shut and bolted, and there was no sign of either being opened or damaged.

I continued round to the back of the garage. There was a familiar smell. A strong, pungent odour. Weed. It hung in the air and got stronger as I made my way round to the side wall. My feet crunched on something. I looked down. There was broken glass and the butt of a joint. The window was broken.

Then I heard feet on gravel. Running. My body responded before my brain had fully engaged; I charged around the end of the garage to the driveway. A figure was heading at a high speed toward the gate. I followed. The figure scrambled over the gate and ran off to the left, toward the river. I heard Leith calling my name as I threw myself over the gate and chased after the person fleeing from my house.

The gibbous moon provided just enough light for me to keep the trespasser in my sights. I wasn't a runner, but I was gaining ground. My quads were burning, my chest on fire, but I kept running as fast as I could. We sped down the bank toward the waterway. Whoever I was chasing wasn't heading for town; they were heading for the woods. I had to get to them before they reached the trees or I'd lose them.

The river looked like shiny treacle, the water barely moving. There was a bridge not too far along. My body was screaming at me to stop, get air, give in, but I pushed on. I was getting closer. One last burst of effort and I'd have them. Whoever I was chasing was also slowing. They must have realised I was nearly on them because they turned abruptly and launched themselves into the river.

It was deceptive, the river, deeper than it looked, the stones on the riverbed loose and dangerous. I paused at the edge of the bank, watching as the escapee stumbled and fell. I pulled out my phone and switched on the torch. I had been chasing a boy, a young boy, not yet a teenager. He gasped for air as he tried to stand, his wet clothes dragging him down, making him lose his balance again.

Dropping my phone on the bank, I strode into the water. It was freezing. I was immersed up to my waist. The calm surface of the river hid a strong current that pulled at my legs. The boy was struggling, panicking, splashing around as he tried to swim. I waded toward him and grabbed at his clothes until I had hold of him under his arms.

"I've got you. I've got you. You're alright. Settle down. I'll get you to the bank."

He stopped flailing about and let me drag him out of the water. Leith and Minnie had caught up with us. Leith helped heave the boy out of the water first then came back to help me. Minnie sat on the bank watching us and keeping her distance.

The boy and I lay on the bank shivering for a few minutes.

"You can't stay here. You'll both freeze." Leith took my

hand and pulled me up.

The boy rolled onto his front and lifted himself onto all fours, coughing up the river water he had inhaled. I picked up my phone and shone my torch at him. It wasn't a face I recognised.

"What were you doing at my house?"

"Nothing." The boy sat back on his knees.

"You broke the garage window. Were you trying to break in?"

The boy got to his feet. He looked around. "I don't know anything about a window."

Leith grabbed the boy's arm. "Let's just take him home and call the police."

The boy jerked his arm from Leith's grip and stepped backward. "No. Don't. Don't call them, please. My mum'll kill me."

He looked scared and small as he hugged his shivering body. I felt sorry for him. He had gotten himself caught up in something that went out of control.

"Why don't you just tell me what you were doing at my house and then we can forget any of this ever happened?"

"You're kidding!" Leith threw his hands in the air and turned his back on the boy.

I still had my phone facing the boy, the torch light glaring at him.

I took a picture of him. "There. I've got you on camera. I'll collect the butt of that spliff and the broken glass, too. If you tell me what's going on and swear to never step foot near my home again, we'll call it quits."

The boy looked at me with defeat in his eyes. "I just had

to find something. Some pictures and a notebook. I was just supposed to search a boy's bedroom. I never made it inside. You came back while I was trying to get in through the window. I was gonna wait till you went in the house, then leave, but you came round the back, so I had to run."

Minnie was twitchy. The night noises had her on high alert. I put a hand on her head to calm her. Was this boy the one Blair was talking about? The one Frank had seen outside our house? They described the boy as tall. Always wearing a hoodie. If anything, this boy was small for his age.

"Who asked you to find these pictures and this notebook?"

"I don't know. I mean, I don't know his name. He gave me a hundred quid, told me the address, and said he'd give me another hundred when I gave him the stuff."

"What did he look like?"

"Tall. He had his hoodie up. Black hair, I think."

"Where were you going to meet him to hand over the picture and books?"

"He said he'd find me. That's all I know. Can I go now?"

"Do you know what it was about? What was in the pictures or the notebook?"

"He didn't say. Just to get inside, find the stuff, and get out. I didn't ask any questions. I just took the money."

"What's your name?"

He paused. "Kevin. It's Kevin."

I was so cold, my legs and feet were going numb. "I don't want to see you near my home ever again, Kevin, do you understand?"

I turned and walked away, Leith and Minnie beside me.

I didn't look back.

Leith clipped Minnie on the lead as we walked. "I'm glad you got that picture of him and his name. You might just want to find him again."

My wet clothes were heavy and freezing, and all I wanted to do was get home and get dry. "What do you mean?"

"You know. To use him. As bait. To find out who that other boy is and what he wants with your son's stuff."

"That's a bit too Poirot, even for you, isn't it?"

"Do you want answers or don't you?"

"What I want is a hot shower and a good night's sleep."

"Fine. But tomorrow we're going to find whatever it is that boy was searching for, and if it doesn't give you any answers then we're going to find Kevin and he's going to lead us to whoever it was who paid him to burgle your house."

Leith wasn't wrong. If we find the notebook and photographs, they might well give us some answers about Jamie's death. They could leave me with more questions. Maybe Kevin can lead us to this other boy.

Leith opened the gate and I padded through, my clothes now stuck to my skin, my fingers and toes completely numb. "Fine. Tomorrow we'll search, and then we can talk about Kevin."

FIFTEEN

Blair

SITTING IN THE corner of the community room looking out of the window, I tucked my hands into the pockets of my old cardigan. My mother had knitted it for me when I was pregnant with Jamie. It was far too big, but it was warm and snuggly and reminded me of those early days of motherhood when I was so exhausted all I could do was curl up on the sofa with my new baby, dozing and feeding him, my head a fog.

I had worn it every day for the first month after Jamie's body had been dug up. Scott had packed it in my clinic bag along with all of my favourite comfy clothes. He paid attention. Perhaps more than I had given him credit for. I had been angry at him for not being around enough, not noticing what was going on with Jamie. Only, I wasn't angry with him, not really. I was angry with myself. I had been too busy with work. I was the one who had kept things from Scott. How was he supposed to know what was happening with his son if I never shared anything with him? I had spent too much time telling him Jamie was fine because I didn't want to admit that he wasn't and that it might be my fault.

I sank my hands deep into the pockets of the cardigan and wrapped it tight around me. Something small, hard, and sharp was wedged into the seam in the bottom corner of the right pocket. I pulled out the object and stared at it as it sat in my palm. I turned it over with my finger, felt its smooth edges and sharp point.

It was one of Jamie's teeth.

It had been handed to me in a clear Ziploc bag. Scott had insisted. Threatened to put something about it in the paper. It was our boy's tooth, not evidence to be locked away. It was only one tooth, after all. The rest were still in Jamie's mouth, but this one had been found in his stomach. He must have swallowed it when it was knocked out. Was it loose? Was that why it fell out? Perhaps not; perhaps it was tightly embedded in his jaw and a great force was needed to dislodge it. The tooth used to be part of my boy's smile. When was the last time he smiled?

"Fancy a game of Scrabble?" The woman who had held my hand in group therapy stood before me, clutching a Scrabble box, a hopeful smile stretched across her face. She was in her sixties, I guessed, more grey than brown in her bobbed hair, dark circles around her wrinkled eyes, and deep laugh lines. She was short, lean, with a downward curve of her shoulders, as if she had spent her life stooped over a sewing machine or perhaps putting together intricate electronic circuits. She had a look in her eyes like she was taking in every detail of my face down to the very last pore.

I snapped my fist closed and held the tooth in my pocket. "I'm not really a games kind of girl."

"There's not a lot to look at out the window. Forecast is drizzle all day. Maybe a game will take your mind off whatever it is you're churning around up there." The woman tapped the side of my head. "I'm Everlee, in case you'd forgotten."

Doctor Ortiz had told me to engage with people. Share my thoughts and feelings. There was no point in being at the clinic if I wasn't going to make an effort. Besides, if I wanted to get out of here and find that boy, I needed to figure out how to eliminate Jamie's ghost or at least convince everyone else that I had.

I smiled back at Everlee. "Okay, then."

Keeping my hand in my pocket, clutching my son's tooth, I followed Everlee to a table. "Shall I get us a cup of tea while you set up?"

Everlee opened the box and pulled out the board. "Yes, please. White, no sugar. And I'd love some of those chocolate bourbon biscuits."

My first word was B U R Y, my second was E A R T H, my third was E M P T Y. Scrabble wasn't doing anything to clear my mind of my son.

"So, tell me about this other boy and why your Jamie has been accused of being his killer's accomplice?"

I nearly choked on my tea.

Everlee put the letters she was holding back on the stand and rested both of her hands on the table. "Sorry. Bit blunt, huh? I can't go outside. Bloody fool I am. My son is having to waste his hard-earned money so that I can be in here and try to talk my way out of my kooky head. My husband and I live in the middle of the countryside. His name was Nikola. He had terminal cancer. He didn't tell me, though. Instead, he hung himself from a tree at the bottom of our garden. Selfish bugger could have picked a different way out. Every time I step out of the damn door, all I hear is the creak of the rope against the branch as Nikola's body swings back and forth. If I look at a tree, any tree, without fail, there he is. Head flopping to the side, arms limp."

We had something in common. I wondered if that was why Everlee had sought me out. Had she worked out that I was seeing Jamie?

"Why did Nikola hang himself?"

"I liked you the minute you opened your mouth. You're a say-it-straight girl. I like that. No beating around the bush. Nikola and I lived a good life: clean, healthy. He had plans to retire and travel, write, and earn another degree. He watched his dad die slowly and painfully. I guess he wanted to save me from watching him deteriorate in the same way. His swinging ghost looks at me sometimes and says, 'I did it for you, Ev.' Bullshit. Selfish is what it was. Denied me that last part. Caring for him. Helping him to go out gracefully."

This woman was angry, too.

"I guess you're working with Doctor Ortiz on your resentment toward Nikola."

Everlee looked up and grinned. "I'm trying. Not ready to forgive him just yet. Problem is, I've become a prisoner in my own home."

Jamie leant over my shoulder. "You can make S P O O K."

I looked down at my letters. "You really pick your moments."

Everlee looked quizzically at me. "Not talking to me then, were you?"

Jamie appeared beside Everlee. "You're good to go with

S P O O K, Mum. She can't use the triple letter score; she's got a rack of vowels."

I shook my head. "No, I wasn't. He's watching our game."

Everlee pushed her chair back, stood up, and downed her mug of tea. "How about you keep me company on a walk around the grounds and I'll keep you talking, and we can try and banish our demons together?"

Jamie rolled his eyes as he stepped away from the table and swept his arm out in front of him, gesturing for us to leave. I liked him popping up now and then, but I knew I couldn't spend the rest of my life conversing with an illusion. It was a manifestation of my grief, nothing more.

I ignored Jamie and focussed on Everlee. "If you're sure you're up for it."

"In at the deep end. Doctor Ortiz is a wonderful man, but his process is slow."

I glugged my tea and followed my new friend out of the clinic.

As the glass doors to the outside world slid open, Everlee hooked her arm through mine. "Right. Let's do this."

I wasn't sure if going rogue was the right course of action. People's minds can be fragile. What if this did Everlee more harm than good? We had only taken a few steps when my companion's bravado began to fail.

I paused. "Tell me what's going on."

"I can hear the creaking. It's in the distance."

"Do you want to go back inside?"

"No. Dr Ortiz said there was a reason I was seeing Niko-la. That my mind was looking for something that I needed to move forward. I want to find out what my mind is trying to unlock." Everlee cleared her throat, and we walked on toward the copse at the end of the garden.

Perhaps my mind was trying to tell me something about Jamie. Maybe there was something more to these visions than just grief. A tall, proud oak stood at the start of a pathway that led into the trees. That was the tree we were heading for. I felt Everlee tense, her arm clamped onto mine.

"What is it?"

"The tree. Nikola."

The tree was now only a few feet away. I couldn't see anything hanging from any of the branches, but Jamie was leaning against the trunk, staring up.

"At least I'm not a corpse, swinging like that."

Sometimes his humour was a little dark. "I don't think that's appropriate."

Everlee stopped walking, jerking me to an abrupt halt.

I extracted my arm from Everlee's grip. "So, you're seeing Nikola up there with the creaking soundtrack of the swinging rope and I can see Jamie by the tree and he's making macabre jokes. How about you go and stand beneath Nikola and I'll go and lean up against the tree where Jamie is?"

Everlee took a deep breath. "Face off with the bogey."

"They do say the world is full of monsters with friendly faces."

"Whose they? And Nikola didn't have a friendly face, he had a big round face with bulging eyes. Bit like one of those frogs. Right. Let's take control of our bonkers brains."

Everlee stepped closer to the tree and then looked

straight up through the branches. "He's gone. Maybe he didn't like the frog analogy?"

I walked over to the trunk, trying to ignore Jamie, but as it got closer, the glinting was back. Jamie was wearing a necklace. It looked handmade, with a leather strap and an axe hanging from it with a circle at one end like a key with a blade in place of the teeth for the lock. A jewel hung in the centre of the circle, winking at me.

Everlee clapped her hands, snapping me out of my trance. "I think we should make this a daily routine."

"Yes, I think we should."

Everlee was looking up into the tree, a broad smile stretching across her face. I looked back at the trunk, but Jamie was gone. I wanted to know what the pendant meant—why I had remembered it. I needed to find out where Jamie got it. I followed Everlee back inside, squeezing Jamie's tooth between my finger and thumb, letting the sharp point poke into my skin. Scott would know where to look. He would know exactly how to find out about that pendant.

SIXTEEN

Scott

I HAD THE hangover to end all hangovers and vowed never to drink again as I dragged my sorry arse out of bed the next morning and blundered along the corridor to the bathroom. My head hurt like hell, and my lips were stuck to my gums. Not to mention the pain in my legs and buttocks from my nighttime pursuit of that wannabe kid-burglar.

"Oh, there you are." Leith appeared at the top of the stairs. "I was just coming to find you. I've made some breakfast. Nothing too fancy. I've got to get back to Freya; something's up with one of the twins. I reckon I've got enough time to help you look for that box before I go."

I paused outside Jamie's room. "let me have a quick shower. Down in five."

Leith headed back down the stairs. "Couple of fried eggs?"

"Yes, please. And try to keep the yolk runny."

"It will be brilliant," he called back.

He must have made a quick trip to the local shop. The smell of bacon wafting up from the kitchen made my stomach rumble.

Five minutes later, I was seated at the kitchen table tucking into perfectly executed fried eggs, fried toast, and crispy bacon. Leith had a deft hand in the kitchen when he put his mind to it. I worried for a long time that he'd never find a girl worthy of him. Then along came Freya. Two peas in a pod. He was a little late to fatherhood, but I had no doubt that being a dad would suit him, and with two more girls in the house, his kitchen skills could now be enjoyed by a bigger and even more adoring audience.

We ate breakfast in silence and gulped down two mugs of coffee, both deep in thought. I had that strange feeling in my stomach, the one you get right before a big presentation when you want to get it over with, and those last few minutes before you're in the spotlight seem to last forever.

I really wanted to find Jamie's puzzle box. I wanted it to fit the key we found in his time capsule. I even wanted it to contain the photographs and notes that the boy last night was talking about. But I also *didn't* want any of that because I didn't know what was in the photographs or what the notes were about. What if I didn't like what I found?

We left our dirty dishes by the sink, and Leith led the way up the stairs and into Jamie's bedroom. I inhaled deeply, searching for the smell of my son, but it had that unlived-in aroma, a musty, empty smell that no longer reminded me of Jamie. My boy's clothes still hung in the wardrobe, his endangered animal posters adorned the walls, his bedding lay scrunched on his bed. Blair went in every day just to feel close to him, to remember him, to lay on his bed and sit in his chair. To sob or scream.

I looked around but didn't know where to start.

Leith opened the wardrobe doors. "Right. I'll start this side. You get going over there. We'll meet in the middle. Be methodical. Tidy. That way we won't miss anything, and we'll be sure we did a thorough job."

I walked toward the bed that was pushed up against the far wall. "Have you ever wondered what it is that makes you such a great quality assurance director?"

Leith began to remove Jamie's clothes from the hangers, checking each item before carefully folding them and placing them in a neat pile in the middle of the room. "Sure, it's because I'm such a quality bloke!"

I lifted Jamie's mattress, leaning it up against the wall, to search under his bed. I pushed against the mattress to check there was nothing hidden inside, and then I pulled out the two storage boxes and emptied the contents onto the bed slats: shoes, paintings, gadgets, and unwanted birthday and Christmas presents. Nothing unusual or suspicious. I removed a few of the bed slats to double-check there was nothing tucked away in the corners under the bed. A small part of me was disappointed not to have found anything; another part of me was relieved.

"Wardrobes are clear," Leith announced. "I'm moving on to the desk area."

I looked back at the pile of clothes in the centre of the room and the empty wardrobe with the bare hangers pushed to one side on the rail. A lump formed in my throat and I couldn't swallow. Being in here didn't get any easier.

I reached up and opened a window. "I'll go and make us another coffee."

Leith paused by an open drawer. "Bit retro, your boy. I didn't think they'd bother with these when they have access to the internet." He pulled out a pornographic magazine and held it up to show me the picture of a naked model on the front page.

I shook my head and laughed. "I remember when you and I went through our top-shelf magazine phase. You always made me keep them in *my* room. Mum found them once. I tried to blame it on you, do you remember?"

"How could I forget; I couldn't look her in the eye for a month." Leith emptied the drawer then pulled it out of the dresser and placed it carefully to the side of the desk.

I took my time in the kitchen making the coffees. Rifling through Jamie's room was throwing me off balance. With every item and object came another memory, and I was struggling to hold it together.

"Scotty!" Leith had found something.

"Coming!" I took the stairs two at a time.

As I walked through the door, I saw Leith holding up a drawer. The end had been moved to make a false back two-thirds along, and a square hole had been cut into the ply-wood base behind it. I put the mugs on the desk and knelt to look into the gap where the drawer had been.

Leith moved out of my way. "I thought I'd let you do the honours."

I reached into the back of the gap and pulled out Jamie's puzzle box. It was an ornate wooden box with intricate carvings on the lid and an assortment of mechanisms on each face. I sat back on my heels and turned the box over in my hands.

Leith stood up and peered over my shoulder. "I've seen one of those before. In a film, I think. They're more difficult to open than you might think."

I tried to remember giving the box to Jamie or him asking for help to open it, but I had no memory of it. "I think I'll take it up to my study and have a play around, see if I can get it open. If not, I will use the magic power of Google."

Leith checked his watch. "I'm gonna get going. Freya's texted a few times now. I think she's starting to panic. I'm sure it's nothing. Suri is always getting coughs and seems to have a permanently snotty nose, but you know how she can get. If I leave now, I can be home before dark. She's already chewed my ear off for not taking a plane. I'd have been home quicker if I'd flown, and the flight would have cost less than the petrol, too. I just fancied a couple of days of peace in the car."

"You go." I could see he was anxious. "I totally get it. She'll feel better with you around. It's a hard gig being home alone with one baby, let alone two. And I know we didn't have our usual chat about you moving down south, but I still think you should. Get out of that little Scottish town you're shackled to and try something new. The weather's warmer here, too."

"You've rediscovered your inner bloodhound, I see." Leith moved to the doorway and then turned back. "Sorry to leave you with the cleanup. Let me know what you find in that box."

I stood up and gave my best friend a hug. "Thanks. I owe you."

"Next time, you're making breakfast." He disappeared down the stairs.

I heard him say goodbye to Minnie before he left. When the front door clicked shut, I made my way to the top of the house.

My office was in our sprawling attic room with its low beams and mismatched furniture: a heavy mahogany desk to accommodate my Mac, a cream leather armchair with an extendable footrest, a standing lamp with an antique tasselled pea-green shade, and a thick animal-print rug. Blair had decorated, painting the walls a cerulean blue and accessorising with patterned cushions in a kaleidoscope of colours. Retro-chic was her style, apparently. Who was I to quibble? It was fun, funky, and reminded me of her.

Normally, I love an investigation, especially one where there's a secret to be revealed. Given the circumstances, I wasn't so sure this time. I took the box up to my office, switched on the lamp, and sat in my armchair, turning the box in my hands. It was the same size as the tissue box holder I had bought for my mother last Christmas. At first, I thought it was a cube that I needed to get inside of, but on closer inspection, I could see that it was far more intricate and complex, like a 3D puzzle with a series of codes and locks. Jamie must have mastered it. How hard could it be?

Harder than it looked, as it turned out. It took me most of the day to crack the three codes, find the five hidden compartments, and work out in which order I needed to open each one. Then I had to search for the lock; there were eight hidden amongst a range of pin, magnetic, and cog mechanisms. I took a break to grab a coffee and a biscuit and to retrieve the key from the dish on the lounge mantlepiece. I returned to the office and tried the key in each of the eight locks, only to discover that it was the handle end of the key that opened another hidden mechanism, the key itself being a decoy.

Clever.

Jamie would have enjoyed observing my struggle, my frustration, and my failure. He would have scrutinised every move I made; he was patient like that. Along with his tarot reading and Minnie, his favourite pastime was painting, another testament to his patience and perseverance. He had an easel at the other end of my office where he would sit quietly painting whilst I worked, his beloved mutt laid out on my rug keeping him company.

He had been working on a portrait of me—well, the back of me—sitting at my desk. He was only halfway through a black-and-white drawing filled in with acrylics for only half my body.

"I'm going to paint your other half in a juxtaposition of complementary colours, Dad," he'd told me.

A surrealist in the making. Creative like his mum. She was teaching him photography, too. How's that for a combo—a creative, inquisitive spiritualist? Can't be too many parents who can say that about their teenage boys.

I was almost there. The box I now held was smaller and had wings, the outer layer of wood peeling away in sections at different points in the completion of the puzzles. The last mechanism was a sprung bolt that I could only release by turning a cog on the opposite side of the box to the left. A click signalled that the lid was open.

I paused for a minute before looking inside, nervous about what I was about to find. The lid revealed a shallow tray that housed a pack of tarot cards. When I lifted the cards, a thin seam at the back of the box caught my attention. I pressed above and below the seam. There was another click and a side panel popped open, housing a pocket-sized, wire-bound notepad, the type kids get in a party bag. This one had a multicoloured, spiral tie-dye pattern on the front.

I replaced the tarot cards and pulled out the notebook, resting the box on my lap and extending the leg rest on my armchair. I wanted to take this slow, see what the notebook contained with an open mind, and not jump to any conclusions. When I turned back the cover, the first thing I noticed was that it was, without a doubt, Jamie's handwriting. His cursive had a uniqueness to it, with overly elaborate swirls for the tails and extra-long stems for the tall letters as if every word was an opportunity to create a piece of micro-art.

The notebook made sense immediately. It held a record of the twelve boys murdered by Gunner Piper.

I knew Jamie was into his crime novels and had a healthy interest in my work when I was a crime reporter, but this notebook felt personal as if I had stumbled on something extremely private and incredibly dark. The notes were clear, logical, with bulleted lists as if they had been written for someone else to understand. Not the kind of notes an individual makes to remind themselves of something—no shorthand or doodles. I wondered if Jamie had wanted them to be found.

SEVENTEEN
Blair

I SAT UPRIGHT in the therapy chair, my feet planted firmly on the floor, hands in my lap. I still found these sessions a little awkward, knowing that Doctor Ortiz was recording and analysing everything I said.

"I met him once. On a sunny Monday morning a few months before Jamie was killed. I was wearing my favourite pair of Jimmy Choos and a new Valentino cape-sleeved mini-dress in cappuccino beige. I was on my way to a shoot for a top designer. I can't remember which one now. But I remember I had a really good feeling about the day."

Doctor Ortiz sat with his legs crossed, notebook in his lap, taking notes.

I closed my eyes, trying to picture every detail of my encounter with Gunner Piper. "The train was packed, but I'd squeezed into a window seat beside a large, disgruntled middle-aged man who had spread himself across both seats. I flipped open my laptop to check for emails. Two stops later, the man got up from his seat and another man slid in beside me. The second man wore jeans and a T-shirt, casual at best, with dirty trainers of no obvious brand. He stuck out like a sore thumb. His scrawny physique and scarred face made him look like a hit man from a second-rate gangster movie. I shuffled closer to the window and focussed on my screen."

Doctor Ortiz looked up. "How did the man make you feel?"

I crossed my arms over my body. "Uncomfortable. Embarrassed. I was busy tapping out an email on the laptop in a desperate attempt to find an available model with fashion experience to promote high-end sports clothing. Before I finished the email, though, the man beside me shifted in his seat, knocking my laptop, which made me fire off the email before I'd signed off. I swiped out of my inbox and a picture of Jamie flashed onto the screen, the one where he was reading Minnie's tarot cards for her. "Interesting fella," the man said. Fella. It sounded odd somehow. "Yes, he is interesting," I responded, looking up at him.

Doctor Ortiz sat listening. There was not a single sign that what I was telling him was anything out of the ordinary.

I shook my head. "I'll never forget his voice, that low menacing growl, or his fetid tobacco breath, or the scar across his right eye that gave him a lopsided squint. His lips were thin, nose bent as if it had been broken, skin pale. He made my skin crawl. I smiled at him, a quick polite smile, and turned back to the window, trying to avoid inhaling the stagnant pong that filled the space between us. The stench was quite distinct, with a heavy, nutty aroma. There was something about the smell, something familiar, that bothered me, an odour I had a faint whiff of from time to time at home."

Doctor Ortiz wrote something in his notes. "Do you think you might have added details to the description of the man or the meeting as a result of everything that has happened since? The pictures in the news, for example, or the things you have read about him?"

I pushed my hair off my face and rested my arms above my head. "Yes, I guess. But he made enough of an impression that day to make me go home and tell Scott."

The doctor made a note of this. "What was Scott's reaction?"

"He had a big story at work, so he wasn't very interested, said there are always weirdos on the train."

"So, the man called Jamie 'fella.' Then what happened?"

"There was a familiarity to his voice. A warmth that you don't usually get from a stranger. "The best ones are those unusual ones, don't ya think?" he said, twisting my laptop toward him to get a better look at the photograph of Jamie. "Stand out in a crowd, don't they?" It was unnerving. I remember it sent a shiver down the back of my neck. I felt violated. Shocked that a stranger would manhandle my laptop and touch my belongings, especially with such grubby hands. "I'm biased," I replied. "He is my son, after all." I pulled the screen back toward me and hoped he'd get off at the next stop."

I sat up and rested my hands on the soft cushion of the seat. "I remember people watching us, probably quietly relieved they weren't in my shoes. 'You a photographer then?' he asked, nodding toward my camera bag. 'I am,' I replied. I squeezed my feet together to keep a firm grip on the case. I thought he might have seen the case and was planning on stealing it."

"The train ride seemed like it was going on forever. I was watching out for every stop. Counting them down. The man shifted closer to me, smiling, his teeth yellow. He had a few missing. He tapped my laptop screen with a filthy fingernail. His stink was overwhelming, a tang of fusty body odour mixed in with the breath. His hands were mucky, with torn fingernails and cuts. And his manner was disturbing. I wanted to scream for help, but I was embarrassed. And afraid. "Reckon that's a big hound. How much does he weigh then?" he asked. I replied, 'Eighty-two kilos,' my voice tight and hoarse. He whistled, which drew attention from other passengers. I could feel their eyes on me, pitying me for landing the creepy guy on the train. I focussed on my laptop screen hoping for a reply to my message so that I had an excuse to ignore him."

Doctor Ortiz uncrossed his legs and let the notepad rest on his knees. "He doesn't sound like someone you could ignore. Or forget."

"No. Not at all." I held each side of the chair and rocked gently back and forth to try to shake the uncomfortable feeling the memory was giving me. "The train began to slow, so I snapped the screen shut and tucked my laptop away in my backpack. 'Mine's the next stop,' I said. I got up and pushed my way toward the exit. 'Really?' the man said as I shuffled past him, his knees knocking against my shins. I was shaking when I got off the train and carried on shaking as I waited for the next train, hoping that he hadn't spotted me doubling back on the stairs as his train trundled away."

"The next train was quieter. I got a seat in an empty bay. I pulled out my Chanel perfume and sprayed some onto my neck and wrists, inhaling the sweet scent to try to get his stench off me. I never saw him again. Not until…you know.

The police showed us photographs first. Then he was all over the news, on the television. Gunner Piper. The Pied Piper of Peasedale. Like some character out of a movie. He wasn't the villain in a storybook; he was real. And my son was real, and he took my boy away from me."

I dug my fingers into the chair.

Doctor Ortiz took a deep breath. "Did you recognise the man when you first saw the pictures of him after Jamie's death?"

I dabbed away the sweat that had formed on my upper lip. "Yes, I did. But I didn't tell the police. I didn't say anything to Scott again. I wanted to forget about it. Forget the whole thing."

Ortiz got to his feet, poured a glass of water from a jug on his desk, and handed it to me. "I think we'll stop for today. I think you've done so well, Blair. You must keep sharing in group therapy, and the next time we speak, I'd like to talk about what you'll need to put in place when you go home. That will include finding a weekly group for you and Scott to attend together, some couples therapy, maybe some time away from home, a weekend break or a visit to family. At some point, you are going to need to share all of this with your husband."

I sipped the water. "Was it my fault that Jamie died? Did Jamie die because Gunner Piper saw that picture of him on my screen? Or did he already know Jamie then?"

Doctor Ortiz shook his head. "I can't answer that. Perhaps no one except Gunnar can. I suggest you talk about this with Scott. The two of you knew Jamie better than anyone. What does your gut tell you?"

I finished my water and got to my feet. My gut was telling me that the boy who had been following me would have the answers.

Doctor Ortiz opened the door for me. "I'll see you again on Thursday."

I forced a smile as I left the room. "Thank you."

I headed to the garden. I needed some fresh air and space. The therapy sessions were making a huge difference in how I was feeling. It was like someone had opened the lid of the box I had shut myself in, and I could finally stretch my limbs and angle my face to the sun. I wanted to talk to Scott so badly. I wanted to tell him everything I could remember about Jamie, all the stuff I had kept secret, too afraid to share. I wanted to find out what the key opened, why I kept getting visions of that necklace Jamie was wearing, and what my son was hiding.

Because he *was* hiding something. I was sure of it.

EIGHTEEN

Scott

I FLICKED THROUGH the notebook first, scanning the pages. The writing was hurried, messy. The names of the boys were at the top with details scribbled in a list below. There were no dates. No timeline. Some details were scribbled out and corrected.

Seb caught my eye. The notes read:

Seb Coles
1st
12
Blue zip top
White trainers
Football phone case
Ear
2 toes
Cried

Sebastian Lucian Coles was the missing boy I had reported on eight years ago. When his body was identified as one of Gunner's thirteen victims, I was shaken up. I thought it was my fault Jamie was taken. Because of the article I wrote. A kind of payback from the killer for covering the story.

147

These notes change everything. Jamie knew details about Gunner's other victims. He'd had made a record of those details. I had to find out why.

The notes were clear enough. Seb was the first victim. He was twelve years old when he went missing. I wanted to check the details in the notebook against the missing person reports for each of the boys and their forensic autopsy reports. I wanted to see if they were wearing the clothes that Jamie had described in his notes on the day they went missing. If the body parts on the pages matched the missing parts in the pathologist's reports. I wanted to know, for sure, if my son knew what those boys were wearing when they were taken by Gunner Piper and if he knew what Gunner had done to them. Had he seen them on the day they had been killed? Had he seen their bodies after? Jamie would only have been seven when Seb was taken, so he must have got this information from somewhere or someone else.

I pulled off my jumper and dropped it onto the floor beside me. My whole body felt clammy. I wiped my hands against my jeans and began tapping away on the keypad. There were benefits to being a seasoned reporter with well-connected friends, including some who were shady, in positions of power and responsibility.

I stayed up most of that first night, the notebook opened on the desk in front of me as I requested the coroner's reports for all twelve victims, found photographs of the boys, and began to print news articles. I decided not to include Jamie in any of my investigations. Blair and I had agreed not to find out the details of his murder. The stories in the press were harrowing enough, detailing the horrific mutilation and abuse the boys had been subjected to at the hands of Gunner Piper. Neither of us could face reading the repugnant specifics of our son's last few hours. Besides, his name wasn't in this notebook.

I got up to make a coffee at some point in the night and tripped over Jamie's puzzle box, which was sitting at the foot of my armchair. The tarot cards spilled out onto the rug. I imagined Jamie peering over his easel at me, saying, "You playing a solo game of fifty-two-card pickup there, Dad?"

When I got onto my hands and knees to collect the tarot deck cards, I discovered some photographs among them, the kind you get from a pocket-sized instant printer. Sitting back on my heels, I sifted through the shots. They were teenager snaps: girls posing against graffiti-covered walls, perhaps in an underpass or a skatepark, boys smoking spliffs, a lad in a black hoodie hiding his face, the old ruins by the river, kids at the school gates. In the background of one of the pictures was a face I recognised—a boy, laughing.

It was Leon. One of the twelve. Another decaying battered corpse dug up at the same time Jamie's body was discovered. Did Jamie know him? Were they friends? Or did they just hang out together in the same crowd? I found pictures of some of the other boys, too, often in the background as if they were in the shot by accident, caught unawares.

For the first time in my life, I questioned my instincts and evaluations of the evidence in front of me. My perspective was so biased, I was in danger of interpreting anything I found in completely the wrong way. I texted Leith. He replied almost immediately, up in the early hours trying to coax his daughters to sleep with bottles and song apparently. I didn't rate his chances with the singing.

He was on a flight from Edinburgh first thing, and I picked him up from Heathrow late morning. I took the notebook and the photographs for him to look at in the car.

"I say we take a visit to some of the places in these pictures. See if any of the kids knew Jamie or remember seeing him with anyone else. Might get some kinda clue about the lad that your burglar was running errands for."

"And how, Sherlock, do we locate those skateparks and hangouts exactly? He hasn't written the address on the back of the photographs, you know."

"I'll have you know I'm a whizz with Google Earth. You can tell me where all the boys were from and get us a rough search area, and then I'll comb Google Earth for skateparks and you can identify all the underpasses and may well go bog-eyed looking at pictures until we find a match."

"It'll take hours."

"I'm happy to go with your suggestion."

"We'll need coffee and sustenance." I pulled into a well-stocked service station and loaded us up with food, coffee, and sugary snacks.

When we got back to the house, Leith glued himself to his laptop, relentless in his searching, and by midafternoon we had a handful of matches for our efforts. Interestingly, all of the locations were close to train stations. We'd made that connection early, which sped up our searches. After my fourth coffee and the same number of trips to the bathroom, I decided we needed to get out of the house and in the car.

Leith grabbed Minnie's lead as we pulled on our coats.

"Might as well take the hound. Kids love a big, soft mutt, and she's a showstopper so she's bound to attract attention."

Much of our detective work paid off. Several of the photographs were taken at one of the skateparks we'd earmarked, and we also found the underpass from the pictures. Graffiti all looks the same until you need to match it to the background of a photograph. We showed some of the kids a snap of Jamie and one of Devin, but none of them recognised either. Matching the locations to some of the pictures felt like a win, but as we headed back to the car, I felt disheartened. I was no nearer to finding the boy who sent Kevin.

Leith shut Minnie in the boot and looked back. "Maybe we're too early. Teenagers like to gather after dark, don't they? Let's head back to the first skatepark. It's where several of the pictures were taken. The light has started to fade, and it'll be dusk when we get there. We can sit tight and see if we recognise anyone."

It was a long shot. "I guess we have nothing to lose. Unless, of course, someone reports two dodgy-looking blokes with a Great Dane spying on teenagers."

"The teenagers are more likely to be doing something they shouldn't than us. Don't you remember being that age?"

"I certainly remember you at that age."

An hour into our stakeout, Leith was sure he recognised one of the girls. He leapt out of the car, grabbed Minnie, and marched over to the group of young people lingering at the edge of the ramps. I decided to stay put. I figured that the only thing more unnerving than a middle-aged man with a giant dog engaging some innocent teens was another middle-aged man chasing after them.

They chatted for a good five minutes. When Leith got back in the car, his face was lit up.

"Ha! Bingo, dear Watson. It was the girl from the photograph. I showed it to her. She remembered a kid with red curly hair who talked about his Great Dane. She knew what had happened to Jamie. They all did. Sounds like it's freaked them out. I'm lucky they talked to me. Must be my friendly Scottish demeanour."

"And?"

"And, my bosom buddy, they remembered another boy with Jamie. Older. Taller. Didn't say much, but he'd handed around some weed."

"Could it have been one of the twelve?"

"Nope. They confirmed he wasn't one of the faces on the news. But, get this: Sometimes, they saw the boy on his own, too. They thought he was a bit strange, so they avoided him."

Driving back to the house, we tossed this information back and forth. We hadn't made a breakthrough, with nothing concrete, but we had locations and reports of another boy with Jamie. It seemed safe to infer that the burglar was sent to find Jamie's notebook and photographs and that the boy who sent him knew Jamie. My gut was telling me that he had something to do with Jamie's death, with all the boys' deaths.

If I was going to find him then Kevin was my link.

NINETEEN

Blair

I WAS FIRST into breakfast and was back in my room before eight-thirty, packing my bag. I couldn't believe I'd been here for only two weeks. I felt like a new person. More myself than I'd felt in a long time. Scott was visiting, and I hoped he would take me home. I had done all the therapy I could take and was keen to be back in my own bed, ready to talk openly with my husband. I wanted to tell him about the other boy, the one in the black hoodie. The one who was always hanging around. I wanted to tell Scott that I had tried to ask Jamie about his friends, that I had shown an interest and attempted to draw out information about where our son was and who he was with, but that Jamie had always been so evasive, so tight-lipped. I wanted to tell Scott that Jamie's death wasn't my fault, and it wasn't his either.

I stuffed my clothes into my case, along with my wash bag, books, and shoes, zipped it up, and placed it by the door, ready to go. I just had to get through the morning activities, group therapy, a final chat with Dr Ortiz, and an art class. It would be a breeze.

As if on cue, the nurse knocked on my door. "Come in."

"Good morning, Blair. Are you ready for group therapy?" The nurse held the door open, suggesting the question was really a command.

"Yes. Ready. Let's get this over with." I trooped past the nurse and led the way along the corridor.

The room was the same as before, the cosy cohorts sitting in the same seats.

I sat patiently, listening to the others in the group talking about their loved ones, those who had died, their regrets, the unanswered questions that kept them imprisoned by their grief. So much of it was familiar—the torturing thoughts, the guilt, the anger, the inability to see a life beyond the pain.

In only two weeks, Dr Ortiz had opened my eyes, my heart, and my memories. It had been an unlocking. I too had unanswered questions. My son's death had been such a shock that I hadn't seen anything beyond my own broken soul, but now I could. I could see Scott and his pain, and I could see my son, too, a boy I didn't truly know.

A part of me wanted to stay here and get to know these people better. Keep listening to their struggles, keep sharing my own journey with them, and spend more time with Everlee. I could see a way past the trauma. I could see that there could be more to come if I let it—if Scott and I worked at it together and helped each other. But first, I needed to find out who Jamie really was, who he spent his time with, what he did, and perhaps even why he died.

Finally, it was my turn to talk, and the words tumbled out of my mouth like an avalanche. "I've been having nightmares about the man on the train. I was stuck on those dreams, thinking that they were the key to unlocking whatever it was that was stopping me from dealing with

Jamie's death. As I was talking things through with Doctor Ortiz, I realised that the nightmares were just a smoke screen blocking my memories. The ones I didn't want to acknowledge were memories of my son and his friend. Those memories are coming to me now much more clearly. It rained the other day. Hard, heavy rain from a dark sky. Watching the rain reminded me of something I had hidden away. About the abbey ruins where I used to take Jamie as a little boy. We'd picnic and climb the trees and play hide-and-seek among the stones and the broken-down walls."

I sat forward, my energy holding my audience captive. "I went to the abbey again when Jamie was older. I'd followed him and his friend, the boy I'd seen hanging around outside our gate, always waiting for Jamie just far enough away that I could never see his face. I followed them on a wet day when it was easy to see Minnie's footprints in the mud. They had their hoods up to shield their faces from the rain, and the sploshing of the water under their feet drowned out any sound I was making behind them."

Being able to share this with other people, to let the words free, to say out loud the things that had been eating at me for so long, felt cathartic, invigorating even. "The boys went to the old abbey ruins and sat smoking weed in a sheltered corner; I could smell it. I couldn't get close enough to hear what they were talking about, but after a while, another boy joined them. He was smaller, with a blue puffer jacket. The jacket had a broken zipper on one pocket, a tear on the left shoulder, and blood on the collar. The details about the jacket came later, but now it all fits together. He was one of the boys. Jordan. The jacket was Jordan's. That day, in the ruins, Jamie met one of the other victims. They knew each other. Jamie knew Jordan. The truth has been there, in the back of my mind, for so long, but I've been afraid of it. Afraid of sharing it with Scott. Afraid of what it would do to us and what he would think of me for keeping it from him."

Nigel took off his glasses and tucked them into his top pocket. "You've come a long way since your first session, Blair. We can all see that you have opened up and things are beginning to seem much clearer for you."

I sat back in my chair and sighed, looking around the room and smiling at my therapy comrades. "They are. They really are. I never wanted to have counselling or therapy. I couldn't think of anything worse than sitting in a group like this and talking about all the stuff that was going on in my head, but it's been amazing. You are all amazing and brave, and I am so thankful to have shared this journey with you all. Christ, listen to me. I'll be signing myself up for *Oprah* next and laying myself bare on global television. Seriously, though, thank you. It's been edifying."

Nigel stood up and placed his clipboard on his chair. "Well, on that note, it's time to bring this session to a close. I'll see most of you again on Friday."

I hugged each member of my group as they left, wishing them luck and bidding them farewell. I had already exchanged contact details with Everlee. I had finally made a friend who might just be in it for the long haul.

Nigel took me to one side. "Are you sure you want to go home? You still have a long way to go. You must make sure you find a local group, keep talking."

"I will, Nigel. I promise. I've achieved more in the last two weeks than I have in the last six months. I had no idea how easy it would be to talk once I started. Like writing an essay at school, when you have to get that first paragraph down and kick-start the flow. I needed to listen to everyone else open up and find the courage to do the same, and I have you and this place to thank for that."

We hugged our goodbyes, and I left the room with a lightness in my body that I hadn't felt in a long time. One step closer to Scott and home. Next stop, Dr Ortiz.

"SO, BLAIR," DR Ortiz began as he sat back in his beige, striped bucket chair. "We've covered a lot of ground in these sessions about Jamie's killer, the time you encountered him on the train, and the boy, Jamie's friend, with the black hoodie."

There was a pattern to counselling, a familiar rhythm: question, answer, repeat back, pause. This routine had formed the flesh and bones of my meetings with Dr Ortiz from the day I arrived. I had done a great job of responding to his questions consistently, acknowledging facts I had been trying so hard to deny and putting my feelings into words. I had learned a lot about the process of talk therapy.

Today, there was a different vibe in the room. Dr Ortiz did not have his notebook, he was lounging in his chair, and he had made eye contact with me for most of the initial chat. Something was going on.

"We've talked about your son, his death, your feelings

about the murderer, and your relationship with Scott. You've found some stability with the medication, I understand, and your sleep is improved. But I sense that you are holding back, that there is something you are trying to hide. Am I right?"

I could have guessed that he'd delve deeper. "Could we open a window?" I asked. "It feels a bit suffocating in here."

"Suffocating?"

It was a bad word choice. Ortiz loved words with hidden meanings, and he also loved pauses when he was in control of them. He fidgeted in his chair, stroking the back of his head where the hair was shortest. He wore his hair shaved at the back and sides leaving a flop of light brown wavy hair on top. Jamie called that a fade. Why did Ortiz always get that chair anyway? Plonking himself down in it before I even got into the room, leaving me to close the door and sit down on the hard, plastic chair.

"Why don't I ever get the good seat?"

"Would you like it?"

He wasn't as good-looking as Scott, but there was something about him.

"I just wanted to know if there was a reason in terms of our roles, doctor and patient, or if you just preferred that seat?"

"I just like to be comfortable when I'm sitting down all day. Are you avoiding my question?"

"Can we do this outside? You know, walk around whilst we talk. I think I'd find it easier, less stifling, in the fresh air."

"What a good idea."

His first name was Lance, but I didn't like that as much

as Ortiz, so I called him by his surname. I didn't think he minded; besides, I was determined to keep to the doctor-patient relationship, having seen how easily the other patients were growing roots in this place.

The doctor followed me out of the consult room, letting me hold the door open for him and walking beside me as we headed to the garden. It was a bright day, the clouds stretched out like cotton balls, forming a veil under the blue sky. The air was clean, with the smell of fresh-cut grass.

I walked alongside the doctor as he took the stone pathway that led in a loop around the outskirts of the hospital. He didn't speak, using his psychiatrist's pause to its full potential, leaving a gaping silence hanging in the air. Now was the time for disclosure, for the answer to his question. It was my last reveal before leaving, and I owed it to him to be open and frank.

"It's not that I'm trying to hide anything—more that I am afraid to reveal it, to acknowledge it."

Ortiz continued walking; his head tilted to the side as he listened. "What do you think might happen if you say the thing you are hiding?"

"It'll change how I feel about my son, it'll crush Scott, it'll ruin our lives if it ever made it in the press."

"And if you don't say it?"

"It'll eat me up inside, and I'll never be free of it."

"These sessions are confidential, Blair, it's just you and me."

I was leaving today and had no plans to return. I had come here after nearly killing myself charging out onto a busy road, chasing after an unknown boy who I could very well have imagined and who may or may not have something to do with my son's death. I had been hurt. Much as I longed to be with my son, getting myself killed and leaving Scott behind was not what I wanted. I had to see this process through and get my head straight. Face the questions and the grief.

"It's about the boy, the one in the hoodie." I pinched the skin on my palm, trying to find the right words.

"Go on."

My breathing quickened, and a lump clogged my gullet. I couldn't say it, not yet. I took a breath.

"Describe what you're seeing, Blair," said Ortiz.

It was confusing to begin with, a jumble of memories, of the man on the train, Jamie and the boy in the hoodie at the ruins, the bodies of the victims flashing on a television screen. Slowly, the images formed a more coherent timeline, beginning with the change in my son's behaviour.

"Jamie was always a solitary boy," I began. "Not because he couldn't make friends—he was never bullied—but because he liked his own company. He was in many ways like his father, with an investigative brain intent on finding the truth, content with his lot, not one to follow the crowd. The first sign of change was when he announced he was stopping football."

"Football?" Dr Ortiz asked.

"He announced it on the way to his last match. The final game of the season, just after his eleventh birthday. He told us it would be his farewell performance and that he wanted a dog and was going to learn to read the Tarot. Scott asked how he'd get fresh air and exercise if he gave up sports, and he said that was where the dog came in."

Dr Ortiz chuckled. He had children who were now teenagers. "Jamie was clearly a very determined young man."

"He was. He scored three goals in that game, won man of the match, and secured the team's winning position in the league for the season. A week later, we brought Minnie home and Jamie owned a set of Tarot cards, which he kept in an antique puzzle box hidden in his bedroom. He walked Minnie and practised with his Tarot cards every day, me and Scott receiving weekly readings and instructions for his Dane's behaviour training."

"Doesn't sound like you had much to concern yourself with. We've gone through this before, haven't we?"

"There's more. Stuff I haven't shared. Jamie began reading crime novels, talking about serial killers over dinner, reciting statistics on missing persons and unsolved murders. Scott had covered a story about a missing boy, Sebastian Coles, which Jamie quizzed his father about incessantly. Scott told him that he was not a detective, just a reporter, and he only knew what the police told him, but Jamie was relentless."

"So, he had a fascination with missing persons?"

"The questions kept coming and coming, and then they stopped. Just like that. Sebastian's remains were discovered when they found Jamie's body. It really spooked Scott for a while; he was convinced that it was his fault Jamie was taken, that it had something to do with the story he wrote. The police didn't agree—just a coincidence, they said."

The doctor took a deep breath. "You don't agree. You think that there was a link. That somehow Jamie's investigations led him to his killer."

I stopped walking and started to shake.

Ortiz rested a hand on my shoulder. "Would you like a break? Or a glass of water?"

"No. No. I need to tell you this. About the same time that Jamie stopped playing football, a lad started appearing at the gate. The boy I've talked about before, the one wearing the black hoodie, always dressed the same, always with his hood up so it was impossible for me to see his face. That's when Jamie started to change, coming home late, stinking of weed, sometimes drunk. He stopped talking to us. Scott put it down to hormones. I followed Jamie and this other boy to the ruins. Jordan was there, too. When they dug up that poor boy's jacket, I was convinced that Jamie had something to do with it all. He was somehow involved. Now the press has labelled Jamie an accomplice, and I feel like *I* did that. I jinxed him. Now that it's been put out there, I realise how ridiculous it sounds. How unlike Jamie that would be."

"He doesn't sound like a boy who would be drawn into something like this."

"I agree. It's ludicrous. He'd never be that boy. But then I wonder if I really knew him. If I was too busy to see who he was. I'm afraid. Afraid that I'll find out he was involved with his killer—helped him somehow to bury the bodies, hide the truth, or worse. I don't want to think it. I wish I wouldn't think it. My sweet boy wasn't like that. He was good and kind and honest. He wouldn't do something so awful unless he was forced. That thought breaks my heart. That he was so terrified, he was forced into doing dreadful things, and maybe he was killed because he wanted to stop.

Because I wasn't able to make it all go away."

"And have you ever talked to Scott about this?"

"I've tried. I think he hates me for even considering that Jamie might be involved somehow."

I needed to keep walking. Ortiz wandered along with me, both of us looking ahead.

"If you don't talk about this with Scott, if you only share it with me, what do you think will happen?"

"I'll be back here in a few months, still twisting it all around in my head until I can't function, and Scott and I will drift even further apart. Or worse, I'll go searching for the answers and do something stupid again."

"Then you need to find a way to really talk to him." He looked at his watch. "Time we were getting back. I do understand why you are keen to go home today, but I want to see you back here every fortnight. You and Everlee have been brave and achieved a lot, but you still have a long way to go. Find a weekly group to go to with your husband. You have all the contacts, and you must keep talking."

"I will. I promise."

We walked back inside in silence and said our goodbyes outside his office. The session had run over, so I hurried to the studio for art class. It was the last activity on the schedule before Scott arrived, and I couldn't wait to see him. I had refused his requests to visit due to a fear that I would lose my resolve and beg him to take me home sooner. I knew that the second I saw him, I would be desperate to leave, to sit in the car beside him as he drove me home, to be back in our lounge drinking coffee and talking about the last few weeks.

I was ready to persuade him to help me find out the truth about Jamie.

TWENTY

Scott

I HAD A few hours left before picking up Blair from the clinic. She had some therapy sessions booked in the morning, so we had agreed I would arrive at lunchtime. I had woken early, taken Minnie for a dawn walk around the park, finished my breakfast before nine, cleaned the house, and finally headed to the office.

Having spent the best part of last week trying to verify what was written in that notebook, I was now trying to work out why it existed. I had put together a board of the boys killed by Gunner, along with details of the clothes they were wearing when they went missing, which I had gleaned from police reports and statements from parents and friends. They matched the descriptions in the notes, suggesting that if Jamie was the author of these notes then he had either been with the boys when they were taken or knew someone who had. Considering that Gunner Piper's killing spree had lasted for almost a decade and Jamie was fifteen when he was killed, the latter seemed the most likely. Maybe he was drawn in later with some of the more recent murders, but I just couldn't get my head around that. No, Jamie must have found out all this information secondhand, and along with the information we got from the teenagers at the skatepark, this boy Jamie hung around with seemed an obvious candidate. It made sense that he was the boy Kevin was running errands for, the same boy Blair and Frank had seen lingering outside our gate. Unless there was more than one other boy.

Certainly, it was clear that the mysterious boy who had sent Kevin to retrieve the notebook was involved and knew Jamie. That made him a threat but also the key to finding out what was really going on with Jamie and why he died. So, this morning, I wanted to look for Kevin.

I did a quick search on social media and the local schools' websites, hoping he would pop up. So far, the searches were coming up empty, and I was getting jittery about seeing Blair. I was finding it hard to concentrate. It had been two weeks since I drove Blair to the clinic, the longest time we had been apart in the last thirty years. We'd talked on the phone, but Blair hadn't wanted me to visit. In that time, I had faced down the paparazzi with Frank at my side, had a visit from Leith, chased a burglar, and found Jamie's puzzle box. We had a lot to talk about. I had butterflies in my stomach wondering if Blair had experienced the same level of transformation that I did—if the therapy and the time away had opened her eyes as much as it had mine—and if things would feel different between us.

My head wasn't really focussed on finding Kevin right now. It was only eleven, but I couldn't wait any longer. I locked the back door, shut Minnie in the kitchen, and scooped up my keys from the hallway dresser. The postman had been by, a pile of letters and the newspaper sitting on the mat, still partly wedged into the letterbox. Bending down to pick up the post, I saw the headline on the front page:

Local Boy Found Dead in Thadley River

I reached for the wall to steady myself as I read the article and saw a picture of the boy. Devin. I couldn't believe it. I was looking at a picture of the wannabe kid-burglar I had chased the night Leith had stayed. I sat back on my heels and read the article. The body had been found by a dog walker in the early hours of the previous day. The boy, Devin Begun, had been missing since the night I dragged him from the river. I guess Kevin was the best alias he could come up with under pressure. No wonder I couldn't locate him.

The boy was found naked, wedged in among some reeds on the bank of Thadley River by the abbey ruins. It was a chance discovery by the dog owner, who had jumped the wire fencing that cordoned off the crumbling abbey because his mutt had chased a deer and got stuck on the wrong side of the barrier. Not an anonymous call like the one that led to Jamie's body. Devin could have rotted away in that river until his bones sank to the bottom, never to be found. A shiver ran through my body as I continued reading. There were signs of a struggle—marks and bruising—and the police were treating it as a murder. They didn't find Devin's clothes.

I pulled out my phone, took a picture of the front page, and sent it to Leith. Then I called him.

"Scotty! What's up?"

"I sent you a picture. Look at it."

There was a pause. He was scanning the article. Speed reading, picking out some of the words and saying them aloud.

"Holy crap! That's the boy, isn't it?"

"It is. What do we do? Should I tell the police what happened?"

"Mate, I don't know. Yeah, you should, of course."

He didn't sound convinced.

"But?"

"But…it sounds like we were the last people to see him. You dragged him out of that river. You were in contact with him, so there might be stuff transferred, you know, bits of material or DNA."

"He was naked. They didn't find his clothes."

"The murderer was obviously trying to get rid of any evidence that would incriminate him."

"Or us. Me. What if it's about the box?"

"Shit. Shit, mate. You don't want all that getting out. I mean, crap, it could help the police with this boy's death. It wouldn't look good for you, though."

"I need to think. I'll sit on it for a bit. I'm supposed to be picking up Blair today. What should I tell her?"

"Take a breath. See how she is. Maybe you can talk to her about it."

"And send her straight back in there? No way. This stays between you and me. I'll call you later."

"Okay. I need to get my head round it, too."

I hung up, stuffed the newspaper into the dresser drawer, and left the house.

How I survived the drive to the clinic, I have no idea. My head was replaying the night of the failed burglary, the boy, everything he said. I didn't remember seeing anyone else that evening. I didn't spot anyone by the river.

I was honked at twice when I failed to signal and nearly drove into the back of a van at some red lights. By the time I pulled into the clinic car park, I looked like I'd just run a marathon. I stood outside for a few minutes to let the breeze cool me down, although there wasn't a lot I could do about the sweat patches under my arms. I parked Devin and tried to focus on Blair.

The receptionist directed me to the studio where she was finishing an art therapy class. Despite being an extremely talented and creative photographer, my wife's drawing and painting abilities didn't really go beyond stick men and preschool monster drawings. If the aim of this place was to placate her demons, I wasn't sure art therapy would be the way to go.

Attempting not to disturb the class, I snuck in quietly and tiptoed around the easels until I found Blair. She was wearing one of my shirts and some loose grey trousers. Her feet were bare and her hair was bundled into a messy bun, those gorgeous auburn curls breaking free like sparks from a fire.

"I missed you," I whispered into her ear.

She jumped and spun around, flinging her arms around my neck and kissing me hard on the lips. My body instantly relaxed, and I kissed her back. As I suspected, things between us were not the same; they felt so much better.

"You'll have to stand there and keep quiet while I finish my painting. You shouldn't disturb an artist at work, you know."

I took a step back and let Blair continue with her art. The other women in the group looked around and smiled at me. I smiled back and mouthed a silent hello to each of them.

Blair sat back down at her easel and pondered the empty canvas in front of her.

"You haven't started yet?" I was sure the receptionist said the class would be finishing soon.

"I've been here half an hour already. I can't decide what to paint."

As noted, painting was not her forte. She much preferred hiding behind the lens of a camera.

"There are no rules today," the therapist said, coming up beside her and throwing me a sweet grin. "Just go ahead and paint whatever comes out, Blair."

I chuckled. "Crikey, is that wise advice considering where we are?"

Blair flashed me one of her looks.

I took a step back. "Sorry. Ignore me. You go for it, honey."

Blair squirted some black paint onto her palette then white on top. "It's surprisingly therapeutic. You should try it sometime. Maybe we could join an art class—sculpture maybe?"

"Maybe." Hobbies were not things Blair and I did; we were always too busy with work, Jamie, family, the house. "I've always fancied having a go at using a pottery wheel."

If it was a fresh start Blair and I were after, which meant I needed to start something new. We needed to change the way we did things. Needed to put each other first more often. I could do that. An image of Devin splashing around in the river flashed into my mind. A fresh new start required closure of the past, but the past looked like it was coming back to bite us.

Blair ran her hands over the canvas on the easel, smoothing it out. "Right, here goes."

She picked up a flat brush and gently pulled the fine bristles between her finger and thumb. Then, swirling the brush into the paint to partially mix the black and white, she began. She swept long strokes across the top of the canvas to create a sky. She clearly had a picture in her mind of the sky she was trying to represent, the grey and black creating heavy clouds and a darkness that unnerved me.

She swapped her brush for a bigger one with thick, wiry bristles. She mixed up a lighter grey and splashed it all over the canvas. So far, it was only grey. A whole canvas of grey. She hated grey. Endless, life-draining grey. She soaked the canvas in paint, letting the grey drip from its edges onto the floor.

I put my hand to my chin in mock contemplation. "Wow, grey, awesome, you've really captured a sense of doom and gloom."

"I haven't finished." She turned and glared at me and then smiled.

"You could try for that modern art style, like in the Tate gallery, where someone slashes a canvas and calls it 'Doom Infinitum: Humanity's Grip On The Earth.'"

Blair squirted more black onto her palette.

"How are we getting on over here?" the art therapist asked, swooping in over Blair's left shoulder, the bohemian woman's long blonde hair as unruly as her gangly limbs.

"Fine," Blair replied. "I've only just started."

"And what is it you have started with?" the therapist asked.

"Grey," I said, stepping next to the therapist and looking over Blair's other shoulder. "She's started with grey. Isn't it obvious? Misery on the page. She's really delving deep with this activity."

"It's the sky." Blair gently elbowed me in the ribs.

"Interesting," said the therapist.

"Why?" Blair asked.

The therapist smiled. "Well, you could have picked a sunny yellow sky, a clear blue sky, or a thundery sky filled with lightning. Why did you choose a grey sky?"

"I thought this was painting, not talking," said Blair.

"Quite right, Blair, you keep going," the therapist said, trotting away.

"You saw her off quickly. I'm excited to see where this is going." I took another step back.

Blair cleaned off her thick brush in the cup of water on the easel stand and chose some bright yellow paint, which she added to her palette. Carefully, she dabbed the yellow in the very top right corner of her painting with the thin brush, a speck barely visible through the thick, dark clouds. That yellow speck of light was the only part of the painting with any colour.

The therapist returned with a spare easel, a clean canvas, an empty palette, and a stool. "Scott, isn't it? How about you join in? Follow your wife's lead and paint whatever comes into your head."

"No, thank you. Not my thing."

Blair dropped her paintbrush onto her palette. "I'm not

continuing unless you join in."

There would be nothing to gain from arguing with her.

Squirting a variety of colours onto my palette, I began. It was fun. More fun than I expected it would be. I'd go as far as to say that I understood why kids had such big smiles on their faces when they were painting. I also understood my son a little better. He was often drawing pictures or up in the office painting. I also understood why it was a useful tool for therapy. I could put on the canvas whatever I chose, and only I knew what it meant. I could express everything that was in my head and my heart with shapes and lines and colours without judgement or explanation. I let myself go. It was liberating.

The activity also made me feel closer to Blair. We were sharing a common goal, to create a piece of art, and we were totally engrossed and being ourselves on the canvas. Her dark, angry picture worried me, but it was also a relief to see her get this stuff out of her head for the world—or at least the group, the therapist, and me—to see. I gave the process my full attention and respected the experience by leaving my feelings exposed on the canvas, too. I was in this moment with my wife, and it felt like we were connecting in a way that we hadn't in a long time.

By the end of the class, her picture had a huge black monster with sharp white teeth and grey drool, a black figure hiding in the monster's shadow, and a face stretched and twisted into an ugly scream with an axe pendant hanging from its neck. Sitting back on her stool, she admired her creation.

"Crikey," I said, taking in the finished piece. "I think

you're going to need to talk me through that sometime."

"It's a release of what was knotted up inside me. Because of all the help I've had in here, I am able to set all the fear and guilt and anger free. Now I need to learn to accept it and live with it."

She had come a long way. I was impressed. I had a hunch that the acceptance part would require some more work, and to live with it I needed to be on that journey, too. Finding out about this mysterious boy, whom I suspected killed Devin, might be the key to answering the questions about Jamie that were stopping us from letting go and moving forward. Acceptance would surely come when we had all the answers to our boy's death.

Blair looked across at my picture. "What have you painted?"

I twisted my easel around. I had splattered colours haphazardly to create a burning castle-type structure, with two figures falling from the windows, bright lightning striking the turrets, and orange flames rising from the top of the battlements and raging out of the windows.

"Wow!" Blair said. "It reminds me of one of Jamie's tarot cards. Especially the tower. Looks like I'm not the only one who belongs here."

I shrugged. "Busted. I remembered the picture from Jamie's pack of cards and thought it was a fitting representation of us since we lost him."

I wasn't sure if mentioning Jamie was appropriate at this point, but the painting seemed to have unlocked something.

"When did you see his tarot cards?" Blair asked. "I didn't think you paid any attention when he was giving you a reading."

I felt the heat rising in my body, my face flushing.

She inhaled a sharp breath. "Oh my god! You found his puzzle box. Did the key fit? What was inside? Were his things from the time capsule in there? What about the letter he wrote?"

The rest of those in the class were busy cleaning their brushes and palettes, pegging their creations to a string stretched across the room, and packing away their chairs and easels. Blair and I sat facing each other, our stands creating a barrier between us and the rest of the class. She looked at me expectantly. I couldn't lie to her. Not now. We had made a breakthrough, and shutting down now would destroy that.

"Yes, I found the box, and yes, the key did open it. There was no letter, no keepsakes from the capsule, but there were photographs and notes. I've spent most of the last week trying to make sense of them."

"I'd like to see them as soon as we get home."

"Well then, we'd better go and get your bag."

We cleared away our paints and easels, and I carefully carried our paintings to the car, collecting Blair's belongings en route and pausing several times for farewells.

As we drove away from the clinic, a sense of foreboding replaced the feeling of freedom that I had felt in the art studio. I had told Blair about the box, and we were going home to look at it together and decide what to do next, but I hadn't told her about Devi—the kid-burglar, the boy who paid Devin to search Jamie's room—or Devin's untimely death.

That conversation would be like opening Pandora's box.

We would have to decide whether we were going to tell the police or keep my encounter with Devin a secret. I had no doubt that Blair would want to find that other boy, whatever the consequences might be, and that meant putting ourselves in danger.

Were we ready for that?

TWENTY-ONE

Blair

I PUT THE photographs on the coffee table. "Look at all this. I had no idea he was doing this. Writing all this stuff down. He didn't say anything to me. Oh, Scott, I wish he'd shared it with us. We've all kept so much to ourselves. Haven't talked. Didn't talk. Not properly. We let him down. All this was going on in his world, in his head, and we had no knowledge of it. Do you think he hated us for that? For letting him down? I want to find out what it all means."

Scott placed the notebook beside the photographs and pulled me into a tight embrace. "He didn't hate us, honey, he loved us. He got caught up in something bad that he clearly couldn't get out of. Look, we don't have to deal with it all now. We don't have to make a plan or find answers or search for anything. We can just sit with this for a while. Let it register and sink in."

Sitting back and letting everything sink in without properly talking led us here in the first place. Inaction was our downfall. At the clinic, sharing everything that I was holding in had felt safe. Talking with Dr Ortiz had been easier than I expected. Being back home frightened me. What if I couldn't talk to Scott in the same way? What if he didn't understand? Then there were all the memories. The clinic had been a blank canvas. Nothing around to derail me. I needed to talk things through with Scott. I needed to connect with my husband and feel secure again.

I took Scott's hand in mine and interlocked fingers. "I looked into some of the groups and therapies locally for bereaved parents. There's a retreat next weekend. I know it's short notice, but these last few weeks have been so great, so helpful, that I thought maybe we could go together. Kick-start the therapy thing, spend some time with people who understand how we feel."

The look on his face made me smile. I felt like I'd just given him the best Christmas present ever. In those first weeks after Jamie died, he had begged me to see someone, talk about my feelings, go on a retreat with him. Not for him but for me. Eventually, he had shut down, but I knew that he'd stored away all those leaflets for therapists and retreats. He would never give up on me.

He kissed my forehead. "If it's anything like that art class then I'm in. We've avoided the tough conversations for long enough. That puzzle box has been a wake-up call."

I let myself sink into his arms. I was so pleased that he was open to a retreat and group therapy. I loved that he joined in with the art class and found benefit from it. I felt vindicated that he accepted there was something more to find out about Jamie. But it also felt too easy, too sudden. Scott was not a man who changed tack at a moment's notice. He was holding something back, which I hoped the retreat would reveal.

"I missed you so much," I said, holding him tight.

Scott buried his face in my thick curls. "I missed you,

too."

We had a takeaway curry on trays in the lounge while streaming a comedy film. Neither of us spoke again that evening, about the puzzle box or our son, and we both slept peacefully in each other arms, our son's beloved Dane snoring at the end of the bed.

Over the next few days, we eased our way back to some semblance of a routine, starting with breakfast and a long walk with Minnie. Scott talked about Frank and Leith and finding the puzzle box, and I described my experiences at the clinic. I was nervous about telling Scott too much at once, and we skirted around the big conversations: the other boy, Jamie's secrets, the implications of the photographs and the notebook. Mostly, I told Scott how therapy worked and what I had achieved with Ortiz.

Jamie remained the elephant in the room, and I hoped that the upcoming retreat would oil the wheels for some candid discussions.

At the end of that first week back, Scott decided to head into the office for a few hours. He had been working from home, but his frequent checking up on me and the constant trips into the lounge to look again at the contents of Jamie's puzzle box were clearly distracting him.

"I'm not getting as much done as I need, and my deadline is fast approaching," he announced, coming down the stairs with his briefcase in his hand.

I was in the hallway organising the stack of leaflets that had piled up in the dresser drawer. I kept one leaflet for each of the various groups, counsellors, or retreats that I thought Scott and I might be interested in. I had never seen any of these services advertised before Jamie died. It was the same after I had that car accident a few years ago and started getting cold calls and junk mail from accident claim companies.

I looked up and smiled at Scott. "See you later."

"I'll only be a few hours. Wil you be alright for the afternoon? I'll be back by six." He took my face in his hands and kissed me tenderly on the lips. "Call me if you need anything or want me to come home."

After all these years, he could still make me feel like I was the most important person in his world. "I'll be fine. I promise. I might fiddle about in the darkroom. I want to find just the right photograph of Jamie to put on the wall at the bottom of the stairs."

Scott gave Minnie a pat on the head, and the soppy mutt jumped up, rested her paws on Scott's shoulders, and returned the farewell with a full-face lick. After the door clicked shut, I wandered back to the kitchen and made myself a cup of tea before settling down on the sofa in the lounge with the photographs and notebook laid out on the coffee table.

I decided to begin with the photographs; the details in the notebook were overwhelming, and I didn't feel comfortable with much of what Jamie had recorded or researched. I wanted to take that part slowly.

One photograph had caught a boy in the background covering his face, a hood pulled up over his head. Hanging from his neck was a pendant similar to the one I had seen around Jamie's neck, the one that kept glinting at me whenever his phantasm appeared. This pendant was hanging from a black leather cord, the same as Jamie's, but instead of an axe shaped like a key, this one was a triangle of swords with a gem suspended from the centre.

The only images I had of the necklace Jamie was wearing were the one in my head and the painting that I had left at the clinic. I must have seen him wearing it at some point to have the memory stored away. The police didn't find a necklace on his body or in the shack, and Scott would have told me if it was in his puzzle box. I had quietly taken pictures of Jamie in the last few years, catching him unawares, his teenage mentality unable to bear the idea of posing for a photograph. Maybe I had managed to snap a picture with him wearing the pendant.

I tidied away the photographs and notebook into the drawer of the coffee table, rinsed my mug in the sink, left it on the drainer, and grabbed my cosy teal waterfall cardigan from the hook behind the back door. I hooked the door open so that Minnie could wander in and out of the garden, and then I walked across the lawn to my darkroom.

Once inside, the gentle amber glow of the safelight gave me just enough illumination to find my way around. I set about cleaning and checking my equipment and processing pictures of Jamie, some in colour, some black and white, using different levels of exposure and a variety of filters to adjust the contrast. I figured I would enjoy myself while I looked for that pendant, and maybe I would find the picture I wanted to hang in the hallway at the same time.

Photography had been a joy for me since I was a teenager, when my father bought me a camera for my thirteenth birthday, and although I loved using the camera, taking the shots, and being creative, nothing gave me more pleasure than seeing my pictures appear like magic on the photographic paper in the quiet of my darkroom, playing around with the images to reveal the essence and emotion of the subject. I adored vibrant colours and quirky finishes, so fashion suited me well, but I also loved to capture people, the detail of their faces and the feelings hidden behind their eyes.

Looking at the pictures of Jamie as I hung them to dry, I began to wonder if I had ever really known my boy. Had I seen *him*, or had I seen what I wanted to see? I decided to make some prints of Jamie as honestly as I could—no filters, no change in exposure, just him, as he was, and what I found was a solitude behind his eyes, a lack of focus that I hadn't picked up on before. His eyes were always looking somewhere else, somewhere far away, detached from the present.

There was a light tap at the door. "Are you coming out of there tonight? I'm getting hungry out here."

I was so absorbed in the photographs, in my need to know my son, that I hadn't registered Minnie's insane barking at the arrival of Scott's car or the sound of tyres crunching over our gravel drive. "Coming now. Sorry. Lost track of the time."

"I'll get the dinner started. There'll be a glass of wine waiting for you in the kitchen."

I had one last scan of the photographs for any sign of that pendant. One picture caught my eye. I had clipped it up and paid little attention to it, thinking I had taken it at a bad angle, a shaft of sunlight cutting across Jamie's face and torso. I looked again and realised that it wasn't sunlight, not exactly. The source of the bright streak was something around Jamie's neck that had caught the sun's rays at just the right, or wrong, angle. I pulled the photo from the clip, closed down the darkroom, and joined Scott in the kitchen ten minutes later.

Sitting at the kitchen table, I placed the photo on the tabletop beside me and took a large sip of my wine. "Did you have a productive afternoon?"

Scott was chopping vegetables, a wok and stir-fry sauce at the ready, and a pan of water on the hob heating up for the noodles. "I did. I reckon I'll be done by tomorrow, so we can go on this retreat without my dragging any work along."

I laughed. "Wow. A whole new you."

Scott tossed his neatly chopped veg into the wok with a satisfying sizzle. "I'm going to alter my focus in life. Adjust my priorities. You and me come first."

I liked this new Scott: attentive, loving, present. I hoped it would last. When we first got together as teenagers, we were each other's whole world, and it remained that way until our mid-twenties, until work and ambition took over. Then we became two separate people at the top of our careers with deadlines and responsibilities, snatching time for our relationship amid tight schedules, meetings, client dinners, and drinks with colleagues. Everything seemed to happen all at once. Jamie arrived before we were ready to compromise for a child, still both hellbent on climbing the ladders of success. Our sweet boy didn't stand a chance. We never went down the route of getting a live-in nanny, but there was a child minder in the house, early starts to get to breakfast club, and last-minute pickups with our little boy often the last to leave. That familiar feeling of guilt sank into the pit of my stomach, weighing me down.

Scott dropped the noodles into the boiling water, added the sauce to the wok, and tossed in the king prawns. "So, what have you been doing?"

"I've spent the day in my darkroom. In one of the photographs from the puzzle box, I saw a boy wearing a distinctive necklace. In the clinic, I kept having visions of Jamie wearing something similar."

"Like the one you painted in art class?"

"Yes."

"I'm glad you mentioned it because I thought I recognised it. I had meant to say something sooner, but then we moved on to my finding the puzzle box."

"I've been searching through photographs of Jamie to see if I could find a picture of him wearing it. I'm not sure what the relevance of it is, but it just seems important somehow. I found this." I held up the picture for Scott to look at. "It's not exactly what I was hoping for."

"I think I might be able to shed some light on it. I bought one of your Christmas presents from that little jewellery shop in town, the one down the alleyway where you get your dresses taken in. The quirky shop beside it, with the fairy statues and skull candleholders, had those necklaces hanging in the window. It's a pretty distinctive shop if you take a few minutes to look inside. Let's eat, and then we'll do a little research."

I ate fast. The idea of finding out something about our son that might be relevant to this other boy had me fired up. Scott was going to help me uncover the truth, and I knew he wouldn't stop until he knew everything.

TWENTY-TWO
Scott

DINNER THAT NIGHT was the quickest meal Blair and I had ever shared. It took minutes to cook and minutes to eat. Blair and I had something tangible that we wanted to investigate, something that might lead us closer to the answers we were searching for. We were supposed to be reconnecting, communicating our feelings, dealing with our grief. Instead, thoughts were rampaging through my mind at breakneck speed about this other boy and where we were headed, what we were risking, and whether it would be safer for us just to take all of this to the police and let them take it from here. Yet all we had was a necklace, a shop, a boy in a photograph, and a secret about a drowned boy that I wasn't ready to share.

A breeze from the utility room gave me goose bumps.

I got up and shut the back door. "Sorry, girl, you're going to have to ask to go out from now on. It's too cold to be leaving doors open."

Blair fastened her chunky knit cardigan with its big wood buttons while I loaded the dishwasher. We made coffee together, a fluid dance around each other getting the mugs, switching on the coffee machine, and taking the milk from the fridge, a familiar and comforting dance that we had performed hundreds of times. Blair carried the coffees on a tray into the lounge as I followed with my laptop.

Lifting the screen, my hand shook. That niggle about not liking what I was about to discover reared its head. I ignored it and searched for jewellery shops in town and up popped Stranger Things, a quirky gift shop claiming that everything in the store was handmade by Thadley residents. A look on maps showed its location down the alley, just as I remembered, right next to the jewellery shop where I'd bought Blair's earrings and bracelet.

"That's the shop. We'll need to go in and have a chat with the owner. I think we should go first thing tomorrow. We should take with us a picture of Jamie, that photo of the boy with the triangle-of-swords necklace, and a sketch of Jamie's pendant. What do you think?"

Blair started clicking through the gallery on the screen, and I knew what she was searching for. "Looking for those necklaces?"

Every few photos she enlarged on the screen and then continued scrolling. "I don't want it to be a waste of time. A dead end. I just want to be sure, that's all."

I sipped my coffee and kept an eye on the screen as Blair scoured through the images.

"There!" Blair zoomed in and pointed to a picture of the inside of the shop. In the corner of the picture was a glass cabinet laden with necklaces hanging from the bottom of its shelves.

I put down my mug and leant in to get a better look. "They look exactly like the one that boy is wearing."

Blair nodded. "Yes, they do. Okay, we'll go tomorrow.

I'm not going to sleep a wink now." She paused, with that faraway look in her eyes that told me she wanted to say something but wasn't sure how it would land.

I rested my hand on top of hers. "Go on."

"It's the same boy who's following us, isn't it? The boy by the gate, the necklace, the shop, Jamie."

"One step at a time."

I shut the laptop and picked up the remote control. "The coffee won't help. How about we watch a film? Try and distract ourselves."

Blair snuggled up beside me, lifting her legs onto the sofa. "We can give it a go."

By the time the final credits rolled, Blair was fast asleep on my lap. I nudged her awake and we dragged ourselves upstairs, peeled off our clothes, and flopped into bed without cleaning our teeth. I was out like a light and didn't come to until Blair pulled open the curtains to let the morning sun filter into the room. Perching on the edge of the bed, she handed me a cup of tea. "I figured we should get going early. You were out cold, so I walked Minnie around the park and grabbed some croissants from the bakery. See you downstairs in ten minutes?"

I sat up, leant back against our luxurious padded headboard—one of my favourite pieces of furniture—drank my tea, and rolled my shoulders. Blair was a different woman since going to the clinic. Present. Energised. I hoped it was going to last. I can't pretend I wasn't apprehensive about pushing her to her limits and losing her again. So far, I hadn't seen any signs of her talking to Jamie.

After a quick shower, I joined Blair in the kitchen for

coffee and a croissant, gave Minnie a brief morning hello, and then we set off for town on foot. It was a bold choice, walking through the park, with memories of Jamie hitting us left, right, and centre. Going to the swings and other play equipment were pretty much a daily activity in those primary school years, then we moved to the river and tried our hand at fishing and finding frog spawn. There was the obligatory tree climbing, with plenty of trees suitable for the task, and the bike rides, picnics, and walks around the lakes with Minnie.

Blair squeezed my hand tight and let the tears silently flow. Neither of us needed to speak—couldn't—but we took turns pausing, smiling, and wiping our tears away. Jamie was amazing in every way, and having him in our lives was a privilege—one we took too much for granted—and missing him hurt like hell.

I couldn't help but glance about for the stalker who Blair had been so adamant was hanging about outside our house. Frank had seen him, too. Blair was putting the pieces together, and I knew she was right. I was getting jittery; the river had brought the image of Devin back into my mind, and it only took a moment for me to add him to our puzzle and realise that the person we were searching for was anything but a friend of Jamie's. I had that itch at the back of my neck that we were being watched.

Striding down the gravel track into town, Blair cleared her throat, obviously shaking off the tsunami of emotions that had engulfed her on our walk. "Shall we get coffee?"

"Yes, we shall." I needed the caffeine hit.

The coffee shop in town was busy, the hiss of the machines and chatter of customers bringing me back to the here and now. That comforting smell of coffee and cake and the warmth of the interior were like a big hug. Standing in line, Blair put her arms around my waist and leant her head against my chest. I kissed the top of her head. We felt like a team again.

Armed with our large mochas, we wended out along the high street until we reached the alleyway that led to Stranger Things. It was only nine in the morning. A cool breeze nipped at my skin. Blair and I cradled our takeout mugs and headed down the alley.

Blair paused outside the jewellery shop. "What are we going to say when we get inside."

"Don't worry, I'll do the talking."

A bell jingled as we opened the door and went inside Stranger Things. The owner certainly chose a fitting name. Everything looked bespoke: carvings, statues, cushions, knitted items, jewellery, woodwork, glass-blown trinkets, stained glass. It was a tribute to the crafty hobbyists of Thadley, and they had skills in abundance. Also in the shop were furniture, toys, household items, decorative items, and gifts. It would be hard to leave without taking something home. Blair was drawn from one section to another, nose-deep in the wonder of the treasures.

A man stood behind the counter at the far end, engrossed in a task involving a soldering iron. He was a man past retirement age who had gained rather than lost in his later years a belly, uncontrollable nasal hair, several chins, and rosacea. I cleared my throat and approached. He looked up and smiled, laugh lines and wrinkles making him look like a human-Shar Pei cross.

"How can I help you?" He had a warm, gruff voice that instantly put me at ease.

Blair appeared by my side. I placed my coffee mug on the counter and reached into my pocket for the photographs.

The shop owner bent down and switched off his soldering iron, swiping the small tray that he had been working on to his left. "Not here to shop, I sense."

He was going to make this easy for me. I smiled and shook my head. "I'm Scott, and this is my wife Blair. We are the parents of one of the victims of the Pied Piper of Peasedale."

The man nodded. "Yes. I read all about that. A monster. How dreadful for you both. How can I help?"

I laid the photographs on the counter. "Our son was wearing a necklace that we think he purchased in your shop." I pointed to the picture of Jamie and the sketch Blair had made of the necklace she kept imagining. "We also found some photographs in our son's bedroom and noticed that one of his…" I swallowed. "A boy he was with was wearing a similar necklace. It's a long shot, but we were hoping that you might recognise the pendants and perhaps even the boy. Jamie was fifteen and not all that transparent about his friends."

"Well now, I'd tell you that nothing good comes out of digging up the past, but you don't want to hear that, and I don't want to know why you want to find the other boy. Still, I'm happy to tell you what I know."

I let my shoulders drop a little. "Thank you."

Blair took my hand.

The man lifted the picture of the boy with the pendant of swords. "I made that necklace. Been making them for years. You've got the right place, that's for sure. The boy wearing it is more complicated."

"Complicated?"

"He worked for me for a time. His mother had done the rounds in town to find him some work to keep him out of trouble. I didn't really need anyone, but I gave him some weekend shifts. He was awkward, not a big talker. Seemed to do alright at the start, polite enough with the customers, but then things started going missing. I know exactly what's in this shop and where. I asked the lad about the missing items and, as you can imagine, I got a mouthful of abuse. He smashed a few things, and he never came back."

Blair squeezed my hand and looked at me and then back to the shopkeeper. "So, you know his name and where he lives?"

"I do. Giving you that information wouldn't be right, but I guess if I had his details written down and you happened to find the piece of paper discarded in the shop, there's not a lot I can do about that. My advice is to go to the police and leave the lad alone. I reckon I got off lightly."

He took a slip of paper from a drawer under the counter and a pen from a pot by the till and wrote down the boy's details. "We'll forget this conversation every happened, shall we? I haven't bought into the CCTV thing, so your visit is between us."

He handed back the photo with the slip of paper, and Blair scooped up the sketch and the picture of Jamie.

The man slid his tray back across the counter and

switched on his soldering iron. "Good luck with it, and I hope you find what you're looking for."

Blair and I took our mugs and said thank you in unison.

Outside the shop, we looked at the slip of paper. The boy's name was Mason. The address was local, just on the other side of town.

TWENTY-THREE

Blair

P ART OF ME wanted to head straight to Mason's house and bang on the door until he answered, but another part of me was afraid that if we bulldozed our way into his life, he'd clam up and shut the door in our faces. Or worse. After all, we found him because of a necklace that he stole, and the shop owner looked worried for us.

This required careful handling, a woman's touch. Scott was an imposing man, tall, and well-built with thick, curly black hair. With his reporter hat on, he could be bullish and relentless, qualities that an older teenager may find daunting. A mother, pleading for information about her dead son, was a much safer proposition.

Scott and I walked back through the park. On the way into town, I had lost myself in my memories, the grief overwhelming me as I relived a hundred moments I had spent with Jamie: playing hide-and-seek in the woods, kicking a ball on the grass, laughing in the sunshine, carrying his bag as we trudged back from school on a rainy day.

On the journey home, I thought only of Mason and what we knew of him. He was probably our stalker, a thief, angry and aggressive, a boy who may have been involved with a serial killer. What does he know about Jamie? What will he tell me? What if he runs or tries to hurt us? I need answers from him; my whole body is aching to find out why my son had to die and why he was different from the others.

Scott was marching, and I could sense the determination in every step. "I'm not sure about this, Blair. I'm not sure what we are getting ourselves involved in. We could be walking into a whole lot of trouble, putting our lives at risk. If this Mason finds out we're looking for him and gets scared, well, we don't know what he'll do. It is worth it? Nothing he has to say will bring Jamie back."

Scott was thinking out loud. I had quietly decided that I would go to Mason's house alone, as one of us would be less intimidating than both. I just had to convince Scott that it was the right thing to do. Or not tell him at all, which would be wrong because we were supposed to be communicating and working together. I'd just tell him afterward.

The wind picked up as the day darkened. My hair blew across my face, the trees that lined the footpath rustled, and leaves drifted down around us. We were the only people in that section of the park and I felt exposed, the breeze a sign that the weather was turning. Finding out about Mason made me think of the boy I'd seen hanging about in the park and outside our gate. What if they were the same boy? The idea made me even more determined to go and find him.

I hooked my arm into Scott's and marched along with him, something inside telling me not to look back. "You've got that deadline to meet, haven't you?"

"I'll have to take it with me on the weekend. This is far more important."

"It would be a shame to go on the retreat with you thinking about work. It's taken us all these months to finally get to a place where we are both willing to talk openly about Jamie, and you're going to take work with you."

He ran his hand through his hair and sighed. "You're right. It's a stupid idea. Perhaps we should reschedule the retreat. Decide what we are going to do about Mason first and then our heads will be clear for each other."

This conversation was going in entirely the wrong direction. "Haven't we been putting *us* off for long enough? I feel so much clearer after the retreat. I'd hate to take a backward step. We can park Mason for a few days. Christ, he's been living across town from us all these months, I hardly think he's going anywhere anytime soon."

We crossed the road, and Scott opened the front gate. "I know I'm rushing ahead and being impatient. I've been static for so long over Jamie that now we have some momentum and I don't want to lose it, but a weekend won't do any harm. I do want to fix *us*. I want to talk, and I want to spend some time with you working through our grief. Let it out instead of bottling it all up."

I slid my arm around his waist, and we walked around to the back door. "Good, that's settled then. You go to work and hit that deadline, and I'll pack for our weekend away."

"Deal."

We were greeted with nuzzling and licking from Minnie, nearly knocking us off our feet as we took off our shoes. Half an hour later, I packed Scott off to work and made myself a cheese sandwich. I had no intention of leaving Mason until after our weekend. I checked the friend locator app on my phone to make sure Scott was well on his way to work before leaving the house. The weather hadn't deteriorated, so I decided to walk across town, the fresh air giving me time to collect my thoughts and calm my nerves.

Instead of following the tree-lined footpath, I took the most direct route straight across the open grassy area and around the big pond. There were plenty of dog walkers and parents with young children milling about and playing by the water. Town was busier too, a continuous rumble of car engines drowning out any conversations from passers-by. I had that alone-in-a-crowd feeling as I snaked my way off the high street and into the residential area on the north side of town.

Mason and his family lived on an estate amid rows of tightly packed terraced houses. The green open spaces of the park were out of sight, and the narrow roads of the estate were flanked by parked cars. Many of the houses were in disrepair, unloved and in need of a good cleaning. Some had made an effort, decorating their small front entrances with potted plants and freshly painted doors, but these houses stood out. Many had mismatched curtains or none at all, flaking paintwork around the windows, glass that was cloudy at best, and overgrown patches of grass behind rusted or rickety gates. A multitude of items were cluttered outside the houses ranging from kids' toys and bikes to an old mattress and a burnt-out cooker.

I began to feel out of place as if I didn't belong here and wouldn't be welcomed. I knew I should turn back, that I was making a mistake, but I had to know what Mason knew. I needed him to tell me about Jamie.

The front of his house, 34 Creekside Lane, was one of

the more cared-for frontages. The small square of grass was cut, the uneven paving slabs were moss-free, the windows were clean, and the door had been painted a pretty pale shade of green. There was no doorbell, just a knocker on the front, a dragon's head with the ring of the knocker in its mouth.

I rapped the knocker four times, firmly. If I was doing this, I had to do it with conviction. If I appeared nervous then I'd make him nervous. A muffled voice from behind the door called out "Coming!" and a few seconds later, the door opened. Standing before me was a tall slim woman with cropped blonde hair. She was wearing a yellow T-shirt, oversized dungarees, and fluffy zebra slippers.

She lifted a pair of clear rectangular glasses off her nose and wedged them on top of her head. "Hi!"

My smile wobbled, nerves getting the better of me. "Hello, I'm Blair. I live across town. I was hoping to find Mason."

The woman looked back up the stairs. "He's not here. Can I help?"

"I wanted to ask him about a necklace. I understand he used to work at a shop called Stranger Things." I was making a mess of this conversation right from the start and could feel myself redden at my own stupidity.

The woman crossed her arms. "I don't know anything about a necklace, I'm afraid, or his work. He's eighteen now, and he comes and goes as he pleases. Is he in trouble?"

I wasn't going to get anywhere asking direct questions with zero context. I needed to be open and honest with this woman—give her my story so that she had something to invest in. "No, not at all. I'm sorry I'm not making myself very clear. I'm assuming that Mason is your son?"

"He is." She sighed, and I could see by her stiff stance and pursed lips that she wanted this conversation to end.

"I had a son. His name was Jamie. He was killed by Gunner Piper."

The woman's face loosened, and she dropped her arms. "Oh my god, the serial killer who murdered all those boys and buried them in the woods?"

"Yes. Him." A lump formed in my throat.

"How terrible for you."

There was an uncomfortable pause. Usually at this point, I would break down and flee, finding a quiet place to hide, losing myself in my memories and hallucinations. The clinic taught me to stay focussed, be in the moment, sit with the painful feelings and move through them.

"Jamie was a bit of a lone wolf—independent, cagey, unconventional perhaps. He didn't have friends. None that we knew of, at least. Well, until now. You see, I'm a photographer and I've been putting together an album of Jamie, and I found a photograph of a boy wearing a necklace similar to one Jamie used to wear."

I showed the woman the picture of the boy in the photograph wearing the necklace. She took the photo and looked at it for a while. "Strange picture. More like a snapshot of a group of kids taken without them knowing. Is this one your boy?" She pointed to the boy in the forefront of the photograph.

I shook my head. I wasn't about to disclose Scott's discovery of Jamie's puzzle box or its contents, so I had to think on my feet. "I was in town a few years ago and happened to see Jamie heading for the skatepark and, like I said, he never invited friends over so I followed him. I'm not proud of that, but I wanted to see what he was up to. My default is taking photographs, so I snapped away, hiding behind my phone, watching him for a while. I hadn't paid much attention to the pictures until recently."

"That's Mason, alright, always hiding under that hood."

Mason. A boy always hidden under a black hoodie. Our stalker.

The woman thrust the photograph back at me. "So, how did you get from that necklace to my front door?"

God, I hoped I sounded genuine. "My husband bought me some jewellery last Christmas from the jewellers on the alleyway in town, and he remembered seeing Stranger Things. Said it was the type of shop where you'd find necklaces like these. It was a long shot, but we went to the shop and asked about the necklace, showed the shop owner this picture and a sketch I'd made of the one Jamie used to wear. He recognised your son. Said his name was Mason and that he used to work for him."

"And he just handed over our address, did he?"

I had two ways to go: lie and make something up that was bound to sound contrived or tell the truth and land the shop owner in it. I hoped he would understand.

I clenched my jaw. "Ah. Kind of. He was angry at the way Mason left the shop and was sorry for us, I guess. He meant no harm."

The woman shrugged. "Yeah, he's a nice old guy. I approached him about a job for Mason and he gave him a chance when no one else would."

There was a noise from inside the house.

The woman snapped her head around and looked back up the stairs. "That damn cat keeps getting itself shut in the cupboards—can't get out and then pees, the little bugger."

It didn't sound like a cat; it sounded like a door slamming. The woman put her hand on the doorframe and leant toward me.

"My name's Suzannah. You seem like a nice lady, and I know what you are going through. I lost my daughter nine years ago. I don't know what you are hoping to get from Mason, but I can assure you that you will be disappointed."

"I want to know if Jamie ever told Mason anything about Gunner Piper."

Suzannah blew out a big breath. "Look, it's just been the two of us for a while now. Mason's dad was never in the picture, and his stepdad left nine years ago. I do my best, but I work full-time, so Mason has to fend for himself quite a bit. I don't know all that much about what he gets up to, but we rub along together. How about you show me a picture of your boy and I'll tell you if I've ever seen him?"

Fumbling in my shoulder bag, I fished out the picture of Jamie I carried with me, which shows him sitting on the bench at the bottom of the garden, Minnie at his feet, the sun catching his auburn curls and igniting them.

Suzannah's face tightened when she looked at Jamie's image.

Another sound from upstairs made Suzannah flinch. "I'd better get back to work. My boss hates it if I'm not available to answer the phone at a moment's notice."

I turned and left, disappointed and frustrated at the same time. Mason did know Jamie, that was certain. Suzannah had recognised him from the photograph, which meant Jamie had been to their home. It wasn't what I was hoping for from the visit, and now I'd have to tell Scott that I went to the house without him and it got me nowhere.

I rushed back through the park hoping the darkening sky would wait until I got home before letting loose. It didn't, and when I got back, I peeled off my wet clothes in the utility room and enjoyed a long hot shower. The walk, the visit, and the wet finish had taken up most of the afternoon, and I didn't have to wait long for Scott to get home.

I heard the ruffle of his coat as he hung it on his thumbs-up hook by the front door. We had each chosen a different, fun hand-designed coat hook—mine was an 'okay' gesture and Jamie had chosen a 'rock on' one. Scott's keys jingled as they dropped into the tray on the pale blue sideboard that I upcycled, his shoes scuffing the floor as if he had wriggled them off with the shoehorn, and then I heard the soft plod of his socked feet wander toward the lounge, the sound ending when he reached the thick pile carpet.

I took him a cup of tea and sat beside him on the sofa. "Did you get everything done?"

He sipped his tea. "Yep. All good to go for the weekend." He put his hand on my thigh. "Some time away, together. I can't wait. How did you get on with the packing?"

"Ah. The packing. Well, I didn't exactly do any packing."

He put his tea on the coffee table and turned to face me. "Please don't tell me you went out and got another tattoo."

I laughed. "No. Although you might prefer it if I had. I went to Mason's house."

"You what? I thought we were parking that until after the weekend. It could have been dangerous, Blair, and if anything had happened to you, I would have had no idea where you were."

"I wanted you to get that article finished. His mother, Suzannah, answered the door and said Mason wasn't home., although I think she was lying. She did confirm that it is Mason in the photograph—'hiding behind his hood' was the phrase she used. I think he is our stalker. She also recognised Jamie from a photograph I showed her, not that she said as much, but I could tell from her reaction. Jamie must have been to their house."

"This isn't a game, Blair. You're not Poirot. You are never to go there again without me."

Scott headed upstairs to take a shower. "Can you check the doors are locked? I'll be down for dinner in ten minutes."

Scott's reaction made my heart race. I locked the door and then returned to the lounge and peeped around the side of the curtain. The light was fading outside, but I couldn't see anyone by the gate.

Perhaps going on this retreat was a mistake.

TWENTY-FOUR

Scott

WE LEFT MINNIE in the expert care of Frank, who collected all of her stuff—bed, bowls, food, and toys—and brought them to his house. He returned for the blanket that we put over our bed for the nights that Minnie decided downstairs was too lonely.

I followed Frank out the back door and around the house to his side gate, Minnie trotting along beside us. "You know where the key is, and you've got her collar and lead, haven't you?"

"I've got it all organised. I'll pop into your house each day, turn a few lights on, make it look lived in. You two go and have fun, relax, enjoy each other's company."

"Will do, Frank. See you on Monday." I patted Minnie on the head and turned to leave, hoping that she'd be a model guest and that Frank would enjoy having her so much that he'd offer to have her again.

Heading up the motorway to our grief retreat, with music and liquorice my trusty travel companions, I thought about Mason. We knew that he had lost his job because he was caught stealing. We knew that he knew Jamie. That same dreadful thought about Mason and Devin sat in the pit of my stomach, an idea that seemed to be gathering weight with every discovery we made—the idea that Mason was the boy who sent Devin to retrieve the puzzle box. It was very likely that whoever sent Devin to burgle our house also drowned him in the river. Blair could have had a lucky escape, and the last thing I wanted was for her to head over to his house again and find herself in a situation that put her life at risk. The possible consequences of meeting this boy buzzed around in my head like a bee in a jar.

I certainly wasn't ready to show Blair the newspaper article about Devin or disclose the encounter Leith and I had had with him. Not yet. Blair was much stronger, but I reckoned that it would take all of her energy and effort to get through this weekend, and I didn't need to throw in any more curveballs.

The last thing I needed right now was a weekend of camping and crying, but I'd promised Blair I would go, so I dutifully drove to a remote location in Dartmoor for a Grief Retreat with other parents of murdered children.

It was organised by SAMM, the Support After Murder and Manslaughter charity. One of the other couples, Seb's parents, had tried to encourage Blair and I to go on one of these weekends a number of times before, regaling the benefits of talking to other parents in a similar situation, but Blair was her usual resistant self, telling me what a waste of time it would be, how depressing it would be to hear all of those horrid stories and see all those strangers sobbing. I couldn't quite believe what a U-turn she had taken at the clinic. I guess it was easier to take advice from professionals.

After looking through all the leaflets that I had squirreled away in the dresser, I had been quite keen to go on one of the Good Grief Project weekends, their motto of "by the bereaved for the bereaved' really striking a chord, but Blair was insistent that we should be with parents who had lost children in a similar way to us—children taken violently, cruelly, at the hands of another human being—and SAMM's retreats came with a recommendation.

The location of the retreat was not a surprise, the roads leading to the woodland hideaway narrowing to a single gravel track until the trees loomed over a rutted path interwoven with knobbly roots whilst branches scraped at the polished paintwork of my car. We were most certainly in the thick of a forest. I parked alongside a row of other vehicles outside a mossy cabin. It felt more like a horror movie than a haven of healing.

I pulled out my phone to check for any last-minute work calls or a text from Frank, but there was no service.

"Hey there," a voice called out. A tall, bearded man waved from the door of the cabin. "No need for that here. No service. Might as well leave it in the car or bring it inside and store it in a locker."

Blair waved to the tanned, hardy-looking man. "He looks friendly."

We grabbed our backpacks and bedding and followed the man inside, opting for the locker after a brief, whispered conversation and deciding that leaving valuables in the car was too much of a risk even though we were in the middle of nowhere.

"Scott and Blair, isn't it?" the man said. "I'm Trey."

His name matched his American twang and his easygoing demeanour.

He shook our hands and gave us a warm and lingering smile. "Let's get you settled in and then you can join the others for dinner. They're all here; you're the last. An eager bunch this weekend."

I didn't know how to respond, so I said nothing. Eager and Grief Retreat didn't sound especially compatible or enticing. The accommodations did go some way to allaying my fears as we were led to a rustic log cabin that housed a single room with a double bed, sofa, log burner, and a compact shower room with toilet and sink. It was cosy, clean, and uncluttered and, as Blair and I laid out our bedding, I felt my shoulders relax.

"Simple's great, don't you think?" said Trey. "All that jumble of home and work gets in the way. Out here, you'll be free to focus on your heart and your spirit."

Following Trey through the trees felt a bit like following a pagan priest to the sacrificial stone. The woods were eerily silent, and the canopy left little room for the moonlight to filter through. He handed Blair and me a torch and carried one himself. I decided to keep my beam focussed on the path ahead, not wanting to illuminate anything unnerving like a galumphing wild bear or a ravenous Harpy. And yes, I knew there were no bears in the woods, or Harpies, but darkness can play tricks on the mind. I swallowed back several shrieks as sticks cracked and leaves rustled around us. Blair hung on tight to my hand and bumped shoulders with me a few times when Trey left a pause long enough for our imaginations to get the better of us.

Eventually, we came to a small clearing, lit by a roaring fire, a group of ten or so people sitting on logs around it.

The heat was a joy. The evening was getting nippy, and I'd left my beanie and gloves in my bag. Blair zipped up her puffer jacket and reached for a blanket from a pile on the ground as we approached the group.

"There we go, my friends." Trey gestured to two free logs and we sat down, greeting the women on either side of us and nodding our hellos to the rest of the group.

"Here, this'll help," the woman to my right said, handing me a can of beer. "Don't worry, we don't take our clothes off for the dancing until after dinner."

I spluttered my first mouthful, and the woman laughed.

"Lorey," she said, holding out a hand.

I shook it. "Scott. I'd have worn my best pants if I'd known."

"They don't do meat, by the way, but I've got a stash of pork scratchings in my bag if you need a hit."

"My favourite," I said.

It had been a while since I'd made new friends. Blair was chatting away with the woman beside her as if they had known each other for years. Seeing her interacting freely with another human being besides me was a pleasure, and I felt relieved and reassured that the progress she made in the clinic was not a temporary state. I saw glimpses of the Blair I married: the lively, talkative girl who whisked me into her whirlwind and never let me back down. My feisty, fiery, and passionate auburn-haired ball-breaker. I'd called her that in one of our anniversary cards once after she'd given one of the dads on the school playground a grilling about his son's unkind remarks to Jamie when he'd gone to school wearing odd socks.

"I'm not sure I came properly prepared," I said to Lorey. "Not the boy scout type."

"You'll be fine; Trey and his wife do all the work."

"Have you been before?"

"This is my fifth weekend."

"Oh, I see, you're an addict."

Lorey laughed. "There you go; now you're getting into the swing of it."

A plate of food was handed along to Lorey, which handed to me, I passed to Blair, and then she handed to Sara, whose husband Ren was sitting beside her. Sara informed us that the plate was made from biodegradable palm leaf; the food, which smelled delicious, was a sweet potato lasagne with cashew cheese sauce. The drive had made me hungry, my liquorice-and-lemonade-fuelled sugar rush and Blair's packed lunch long gone, and I polished off two large palm leaf platefuls of meat-free stew in under five minutes.

Blair looked across and smiled as I scraped my plate clean. "Delicious, isn't it? Maybe the food here will finally win us round to going vegan. Jamie often said we should do more to try and save the planet."

The rest of the evening was spent sitting by the fire, drinking hot chocolate, and listening to Trey telling us about the retreat and what to expect over the next two days. Blair snuggled up to me, wrapping a blanket around our legs and resting her head on my shoulder. Not only did I eat well that first evening and enjoy sitting around a bonfire in the depths of a dark forest with a group of strangers, but I also slept well, the heat from the bonfire keeping me warm as we staggered back to our cabin and curled up in the cosy bed.

Day one began far too early, literally at dawn—4:47 by my watch. The cold wake-up shower—Trey didn't mention the lack of hot water—was sufficiently refreshing to ensure that any thoughts of home were swiftly shivered out of me. I jogged to the fire and ate several plates of scrambled tofu on toast; the outdoor lifestyle had obviously ramped up my appetite. Blair was already there when I arrived—I guess she hadn't slept as well as I had—and the remainder of our group filtered in quickly.

To my surprise and delight, we began the day with a walk, a two-hour hike to be more precise, through the forest and down into a valley, where we snaked alongside a river and then trudged back up to a high ridge overlooking the countryside.

There was little conversation, most of us deep in thought, I suspected about our children. I spent the majority of the trek reliving all the best moments I'd had with Jamie: those warm cuddles, the infectious giggling, pushing the swing, cheering at the side of the football pitch, our walks with Minnie, holidays, amusement parks, film night.

It was only near the end of the walk, heading back through the thickets, that *he* returned to my thoughts. *His* filthy shack was located in the woods, the boys buried haphazardly in the same area, dirt covering Jamie's body, lodged in the crevices of his mangled face, wedged under his fingernails—of the fingers still attached—and matted into his curls.

"I'm sensing a dark mood," Blair said, walking up beside me as we neared the clearing.

"I was thinking about…" I trailed off. I couldn't say his

name just now.

Blair locked her arm around mine, slowing me down until we were at the back of the group. "Do you recognise any of the couples?"

I had only seen everyone around the fire the night before, half of them obscured by the flames, and this morning, I was so intent on eating I barely lifted my head from the plate before Trey announced our hike and we were collecting water and snacks and being herded off through the woods.

"I don't think so." I looked at the back of everyone's heads to check that I wasn't missing anything obvious. "Should I?"

"Sebastian's parents are here."

"Sebastian?" It only took me a second to register what Blair was telling me. "Seb? Good god! Seb. The first of Gunner's victims. The missing boy I wrote the article about. What are the odds of that?"

Blair took a deep breath. "Pretty high, I reckon. We are on a retreat with parents of murdered children, and Jamie was one of thirteen. I didn't recognise them straightaway; it's not like we spent time with any of them."

"Do you think they recognised us?"

"They did. Carla came and spoke to me this morning. Said she and her husband didn't believe what was being said about Jamie. We hugged. It felt good actually."

"Her husband's called Craig, isn't he?"

"He is."

"What do we say to them?"

"I don't know. I guess we'll find out."

I paused to put a little distance between us and the

group. "You're not going to mention the puzzle box, are you? I think we should keep quiet about those photographs and the notebook."

Blair squeezed my arm. "I agree. Don't worry, it'll be fine."

There was nothing fine about Seb's parents being here. I could feel heat rising through my body as I thought about the details in those pages and what they intimated. Jamie had details about Seb's death. He knew someone who had been there when it happened. Maybe Jamie had known where Seb's body was buried. Having found the notebook and photographs, I didn't know how on earth I was going to look these two people in the eye. With all this speculation about Jamie being an accomplice in the media, I felt like I held the key to his condemnation or his reprieve. Carla may have told Blair that they didn't believe any of it, but that was only because there wasn't any concrete evidence. At least not yet.

What was I even thinking? Jamie was seven when Seb was taken. There was no way that Jamie was involved in Seb's death. The notes were just that—notes, taken from someone else's account of events—and having those notes didn't make our son guilty of anything.

Blair took my hand, and we walked quietly back to the camp. Trey got the fire going, and we all collected sticks and logs to burn whilst his wife, Cindy, made us lunch.

The fire was the talking spot, the focal point of the weekend, and its warmth and glow somehow loosened our bodies and unbound our emotions. As we sat again in a circle, on the same logs as the night before, the true horror of our situations spilled out. One by one, we shared our stories, describing how our precious children were taken from us by monsters, the details of each death seared into the memories of everyone there. Mostly, there was anger, guilt, and regret.

"Kit was stabbed by a kid high on meth. They didn't even know each other. Just wrong place, wrong time," said Ren.

Sara squeezed his knee as he broke down. "It's only been three months, and neither of us can go into his bedroom yet."

"Judith was eleven. Her uncle raped and then drowned her. Her father, Tom, found her facedown in the bath. He hung himself a week later," said Lorey, twisting a strand of hair around her finger.

"Our Mickey got into the wrong crowd, thievin', graffiti, nickin' wallets from old ladies. Coppers were round our house like moths to a flame. We thought he'd end up in the nick, not in the ground," said Phil, a big, soft brute of a man. "Got shot, the little bugger; couldn't pay his dues when he started selling drugs for a local dealer. Carol won't talk about Mickey; she's lookin' after the other four as if he never existed. Won't let the others out of her sight."

"Andrew was strangled by our neighbour," said Mandy, a smart, polite woman who shook the entire weekend.

Her husband, Sora, hung onto her as if she would crumble to dust at any moment. "We had no idea we were living next to a man like him," Sora said. "He'd been on the register for nine years. It was a friend of Andrew's who told us that he had been invited into the house. The friend had refused to go, thought the neighbour was creepy, but Andrew was a trusting boy, and the neighbour had always been friendly and polite. The police found his body in a bin bag in his shed."

Then Carla spoke, and the words sent a chill down my spine. It was a story so familiar, it was almost impossible to hear.

"Seb was a rascal but a lovable one. He was a good boy, did well at school, had friends, but then he changed. He was only a year and a bit into secondary school, still so young and innocent. Became obsessed with being liked by the cool crowd. Started buying clothes with labels, hoodies, and joggers. Craig was constantly at him to smarten up. He stopped playing sports, hung out with a different group of boys, and started to shut us out. We tried confiscating the weed and the cigarettes that we found in his bag, we grounded him, we even took him away for weekends to give him space from the new friends, but nothing worked. Then one day, he didn't come home from school, and we never saw him again. Not until they pulled his remains from a hole in the ground nearly nine years later, a decayed husk that neither of us recognised. He had been killed by Gunner Piper, who was nicknamed the Pied Piper of Peasedale. They found the remains of thirteen boys in the woods that day. We have Blair and Scott's boy to thank for finding him. If it wasn't for Jamie sending that emergency message from his phone, the boys would have stayed buried and undiscovered."

I felt sick hearing the name Gunner Piper and listening to her description of her son's body, but most of all, I felt sick at the mention of new friends. Unsavoury friends. Friends who might have led Seb astray or worse. Was that what happened to Jamie? Was he led to his death by an unsavoury boy, or did my son become one of those unsavoury boys who parents tried to keep their children away from? Blair sat on our log, rigid. Her nails dug into the back of my hand. We didn't even dare look at each other.

I excused myself from the group and hid behind a tree, far enough away to be out of sight and, more importantly, out of earshot of the conversations. I needed a moment to take a breath.

"You okay there, Scott?" Trey came to my rescue with a hug and a strong black coffee. "Lot to take in, huh? The group's taken a coffee break, so I thought we could have a walk."

"I'm so sorry. It's just, you know, I wasn't expecting this," I said.

"No need to be sorry, Scott. We're all here to help each other. Cindy and I, too. We were where you are a decade ago."

A decade. Ten whole years of carrying around their grief. I wasn't sure I was strong enough to make it that far.

Trey put a hand on my shoulder. "It does get easier if you get the right support. That's why we need each other." He walked with me for a few, encouraging me to drink the coffee and take some deep breaths.

When I sat back down, Blair reached for my hand.

"How're you feeling, Scott?" Trey said, loud enough to involve the group.

"Sorry," I said. "Sorry about that."

"No apology necessary. Why don't you share how you're feeling?"

The words came more easily than I expected. "I feel angry. I don't want to belong here. I don't want this to be happening to me, to us. But it is. It has. All these children, these monsters, it's so wrong." I began to cry, something I had only ever done in front of Blair and my mother, and now I couldn't control my sobbing.

"I want to rip the limbs right off the body of the man who killed my son and watch him beg for mercy. I want him to be consumed by fire and burn to ashes. I want to scream so loud the whole world can hear me. Jesus fucking Christ, I just want my boy back. My boy. My sweet, funny boy, who was so close to being a man. I want him to have the future that I promised him when he first came into this world."

Blair knelt beside me and hugged me tight. We hadn't held each other like that for a long time, not given each other any real affection. For a while, I blubbered like a toddler, and the rest of the group hugged and sobbed right along with me. This was turning out to be every bit the kind of retreat that you imagine when you hear 'Grief Retreat for Parents of Murdered Children.' And I needed it. I needed every second of this weekend. I needed to be with these people, who understood. It was not so much a retreat for me but a surrender. I needed to give up, to give in, to stop trying to move forward.

Following the pre-lunch sob-fest, there was a sense of release among the group, as if the experience had been cathartic. Everyone seemed to have bonded, and there was a comradeship that was almost tangible. In the afternoon, we were taken to the river for canoeing and encouraged to spend our time with someone we didn't know. Before I had a chance to look around for a friendly face, Craig hustled me into the first canoe, and when everyone was afloat, we tucked in line behind Trey and Ren. Unsurprisingly, Carla and Blair had paired up. I didn't know if this was by Blair's design or Carla's, but I had an uneasy feeling about our couplings.

"So, what's home life look like?" Craig asked as we found our rhythm and glided along the waterway at a swift pace.

"Now?" I asked.

"Yes, now."

"Me, Blair, and our Great Dane, Minnie."

"A Great Dane. That's a brave choice."

"It was Jamie's choice. We agreed he could have a pet as long as he took full responsibility for it. He did, and he adored her. It helps having her around the house. She gives me a focus, a reason to get up and get going."

Craig slowed his rowing. "So, how are things with you and Blair?"

"Great," I said, pulling on the oars a little harder. "Blair's back in her darkroom, and I'm sinking my teeth into a new story at work. How about you and Carla?"

Craig pulled his oars into the boat and sighed. "Honestly? Improving slowly but still tough. It's like we're walking through treacle and can't see a way out. Our lives were so geared toward Seb. Carla was a full-time mum, the class rep, a member of the PTA. She was the cricket coach in the summer, ran the café at the rugby club home games, and was a dedicated Cub Scout leader. When Seb started secondary school, she trained to be a Duke of Edinburgh volunteer. Then he went missing and we spent eight years searching for him. Every day. It consumed us. She can't face going back into a school or working with children again, and she doesn't know what to do that feels worthwhile."

I wanted to keep pulling on my oars, drive us to the bank, and end the weekend here, but I knew I couldn't do that. I knew I would be failing Blair and myself if I didn't at least try. Whatever those photographs and that notebook meant, our son was still a victim, just like Seb and all the other boys. Still, it played on my conscience like a little Jiminy Cricket hopping around on my shoulder, reminding me to tell the truth and do the right thing. But what was the right thing? Giving the police the puzzle box? Telling them about Devin? And who would I be doing the right thing for? Me? Blair? Carla and Craig? Then there was Jamie to think about. He wouldn't be a victim anymore, and where would that line of investigation end up? The best I could do right now was to face my grief and focus on healing.

I stopped rowing. "'Great' was probably too strong a word for how Blair and I are doing. She's recently spent a few weeks in a clinic. She was talking to a phantasm of our son on a bunch of pills, and the two of us were drifting apart. This weekend is the first step on our journey of healing together since Jamie died. Blair lost herself and withdrew, while I tried to plough on and ignore how I felt. We haven't really been living, just staying alive."

Craig took a swig of water from the bottle he had tucked away on the floor of the canoe. "We never saw you or Blair at any of the meetings. You never replied to the emails. The other parents set up a group with a counsellor, and we've met up with them a bunch of times. Carla said she tried to reach out to Blair but never got a response."

"We weren't ready. Blair wasn't. She couldn't accept Jamie's death. I guess I couldn't either. But we're here now, finally ready to face it and talk and build a new life. What about you, Craig? How have you handled it all?"

"I was angry. Raging. Wound up like a jack-in-a-box. Drank too much. Eventually, Carla forced me to see someone, told me she'd leave if I didn't. Not too many relationships survive murdered children, apparently—too difficult to support someone else when you're in bits yourself. My boss was great and gave me as much time off as I needed. Keeping sober and sane is still a daily battle." He looked behind him. "We should catch up with the group."

The rest of our group was a long way up the river. It looked like they had all stopped. I noticed one of the canoes heading back our way. "Looks like they've sent the rescue team out for us."

I took up my oars, and Craig and I began to pull in sync, falling into a steady rhythm, Craig looking over his shoulder and giving instructions on direction.

We met up with Trey and Ren, who escorted us along the river until we reached the others. For the next hour, we stayed close to the pack and enjoyed our surroundings, discussing the tranquil beauty of the river, the variety of wildlife in the forest—specifically, the myriad noises that filled the forest at dusk—and how much we were appreciating the peace and quiet of the rustic retreat.

With the landing in sight, Craig and I picked up the pace. Any sport is an opportunity for a bit of healthy competition, and I saw no reason why canoeing on a Grief Retreat should be exempt. We snuck out in front and the race was on. Trey and Ren picked up their pace first and soon the only thing on anyone's mind was the win. Carla and Blair put in a valiant effort, but it was Lorey and Sora who gave us a run for our money—and we would have taken them if Craig and I hadn't lost our rhythm, tangled our oars, and capsized. There was no way we were getting back in—too slippery, too wobbly, and we couldn't stop laughing—so instead, we assumed positions on either side of the boat and swam it home.

"I see you two have had a refreshing dip," Trey said, helping us up onto the bank with the canoe.

Craig shivered. "Refreshing is one way of putting it."

"I don't suppose there's any chance of a *hot* shower, is there?" I asked.

The rest of the group laughed at that.

"Get on some dry clothes, and we'll have the fire roaring for you when you get back," said Trey.

Blair came over to me. "I'll just help put the boats away, then I'll catch you up."

"No need," I said. "I'll be quick. I won't be lingering in the shower, and the wood burner will take a while to get going, so my warmest option is the fire."

I moved in to give her a hug, but she stepped back, shaking her head. "Oh no, you don't. Wait for me, though, I want to come back to the cabin. Walk slowly."

She glanced back at the group. Something was up. I got the feeling that her trip on the river with Carla didn't go too well.

TWENTY-FIVE

Blair

I HELPED CARLA haul the canoe onto dry land then quickly rushed off after Scott. I wanted to get as far away from Carla and Craig as I could.

"That was fast," Scott said as I trotted up beside him.

I took his hand, linking my fingers into his. "I couldn't get away quick enough."

Scott's skin was cold and rubbery, and his shoes squelched with each step he took. "I thought you and Carla had bonded. You know, hugged it out and found a connection?"

"So did I. You and Craig certainly looked cosy in each other's company."

Scott started to march, and I could see his body shivering. "He's a good guy. Honest. Open. I like him. They've not had an easy time of it, either."

Twigs caught on my clothes and scraped my neck as Scott dragged me through the trees, taking the most direct—and least accessible—route to our cabin. "Well, I feel like I just had a grilling, as if Carla was interrogating me, accusing Jamie. All that stuff she said about it being thanks to Jamie that they finally found Seb's body was rubbish, all for show." I grabbed a branch that was sticking out of a tree right at my eye level just ahead, snapping it free of the trunk and throwing it on the ground.

"She whittled on about how Jamie was the last, how he had managed to call for help when the others hadn't, and how there was no sign of sexual abuse—as if this was all new news to me. She made it sound like he was different from the others, special, lucky even, for dying quickly from a single stab wound." A low branch snagged on the lace of my boot, and when I tried to yank my boot free, the branch split away from the tree and remained attached to my lace. "Well, I reminded her that Jamie had been bound to that board like all the others, been beaten, had fingers and toes chopped off, that it must have been terrifying and agonising, and he no doubt screamed for his parents to save him just like their son must have."

I stopped and grappled with the stuck branch, managing to pry it off by standing on the free end with my other foot. When I turned to Scott, he held me by my shoulders. I could feel my body shaking, my pulse throbbing in my neck. There was concern in his eyes, but he had nothing to worry about; I didn't feel as if I was going to fall apart or lose my mind. On the contrary, saying everything out loud was liberating, exhilarating almost. Like a dam being broken, my emotions were finally being let loose, and I was able to express the anger I had been suppressing for so long. My fists clenched, and I could feel my blood pressure hitting a crisis point. I took some deep breaths. "How dare she! How dare she make me feel like my son was somehow less of a victim."

Tears began streaming down my cheeks as Scott pulled me into an embrace and held me tight, rubbing the top of my back with the palm of his right hand. I huffed out some angry breaths and let my body sink into his chest, my arms wrapping tight around him.

He kissed the top of my head and then rested his cheek on the same spot. "This place is drawing out all those raw emotions that we've kept locked away. I guess it's the same for Carla and Craig. We never joined in with their counselling group or made contact, so I suppose they put two and two together and got five. Started to question why we were absent, what we had to hide, and maybe even wondering if we were afraid to come to the meetings. Human beings have a habit of turning a shadow into a monster and creating a story from a whisper."

"You'd know all about that." I looked into my husband's face for a reaction.

Scott grinned. "I have always based my articles on concrete, evidence-based information, I'll have you know. Watertight eyewitnesses and trustworthy sources."

"It helps that you are on very good terms with some high-ranking police officers and a couple of loose-lipped desk clerks."

Scott laughed. "It does. Now let's get back because I'm freezing." He released his hold on me and held out his elbow. I smiled and took a deep breath before linking my elbow with his. Then we walked back through the woods, arm in arm.

Back in the cabin, I sat on the end of the bed whilst Scott peeled off his wet clothes, rinsed himself off in the shower, and wrapped himself in both of the towels.

I removed my wet trainers and socks and wiggled my

numb toes. "I didn't say anything to Carla about the puzzle box or the other boy."

"Good." Scott rubbed his hair dry and flung the towel on the bed. "I think we should keep that to ourselves. We don't want to stir up a hornet's nest, especially as it sounds like the other parents are looking for a fall guy."

I watched Scott dry himself off, quietly admiring the toned figure he had cultivated during those cathartic and gruelling workouts in the garage gym. "I don't blame them, you know. I don't understand why those boys went off with a stranger, an older man. It's not as if parents and schools haven't gone on and on about stranger danger—never accept sweets, never get in a car, and so on. Gunner Piper wasn't even a friendly-looking man with that ugly scar and those bloodshot eyes."

Scott secured the towel around his waist and walked over to me, leaning forward and placing his hands on my hips. "Everyone wants to blame someone. I've seen it so many times. Incapable of finding fault in their own friend or relative, they have to point the finger elsewhere."

I placed my hands on my husband's chest, enjoying the feel of the fine, curly hairs brushing against the skin between my fingers. "But do you think they could be right to blame Jamie? Do you think he was dragged into Gunner's world somehow? That it was his fault some of the other boys died?"

Scott shook his head. "Absolutely not. No way. All those boys, ours included, were killed by a sick, twisted man. A coward. And if our son had anything to do with it, he would have been forced into it. No question. And as far as Carla and Craig are concerned, we know as much as they do."

Scott's hand swept under my jumper and T-shirt and settled against the skin around my waist. "How about we make the most of this weekend and properly reconnect?"

The thought of enjoying sex with Scott still made me feel guilty, and yet my body ached for his touch. "I don't know, Scott, it's been so long. My head's not really in the right place."

"Will our heads ever be in the right place?" He kissed me slowly on the lips.

I didn't move, didn't push him away. He kissed me again and I responded, running my fingers through his thick, soft hair, inhaling the delicate scent of his clean, wet skin. The spark between us was still there.

Lowering his head, he began to kiss my neck, his hands moving up under my T-shirt. I could feel the heat rising in my body, my breathing deepening with the arousal of his touch. He pushed me back onto the bed and laid himself on top of me, and I wrapped my legs around him, feeling him hard against me. He lifted my arms above my head and pushed my sweater and T-shirt up over my head in one clean movement. It helped that I had lost some weight in this last year and all my clothes were a little loose.

"Have you been practising that move?" I said as he held my hands above my head and continued to kiss my neck and shoulders.

That familiar tingle of anticipation prickled my skin when Scott ran his hands down my arms to my breasts, and I arched my back in response to his fingers peeling off my bra. I had missed this, missed my husband's touch, the feel of his skin against mine, the warmth and desire in his kisses. He was a generous, attentive lover who had never failed to please me in the bedroom, and that chilly afternoon in our log cabin was no exception. Our mutual climax came quickly.

As much as I wanted to linger in Scott's embrace and hide away in our woodland refuge for the rest of the evening, I was conscious that the group would be gathered around the fire wondering where we were.

I slid out of bed. "We should get back to the group."

Scott reluctantly sat up and pulled on his underwear. "We should."

Hurrying to dress, embarrassed about the reception we would receive turning up for the evening rendezvous late, I glanced over at Scott. "Do you remember our night in that abandoned bus by the lake? When we drank far too much cider? We'd only had sex a few times, but you made up that corny analogy about food."

He turned to face me, shuffling himself into his jeans. "Do I remember? That was a profound moment for me. The formation of the type of lover I wanted to become. Not a quick-heat-microwave-meal lover but a man who treats sex like an intricately prepared home-cooked meal, when the enjoyment of the final dish is made even more pleasurable as a result of the time and care taken to prepare it. It's a promise I've tried to live by ever since."

I picked up my T-shirt and sweater from the floor and slipped them over my head. "Oh, you remembered it almost word for word. I'm still unsure how I feel about being compared to a meal, although I do think you've made a valiant effort to uphold your promise these last two-and-a-bit decades."

Scott grinned with delight. "I'm glad you felt satiated."

I shook my head and threw a pillow at him. "Never use the word satiated when talking about sex ever again!"

We grabbed our insulated, waterproof outdoor coats and headed out into the woods. Approaching the group, the low rumble of chatter and the glow of the fire was a welcome contrast to the eerily silent, impenetrable forest. By the time we sat down, the light had faded and the evening dinner was ready to be served. Carla and Craig had sat down between Trey and Ren on the far side of the fire and were obviously trying to avoid us.

"I've worked up a bit of an appetite after all of today's activity," Scott whispered into my ear as I handed him a plate of food.

I stroked his thigh. "Me too."

Dinner was a more sedate affair than our last meal, the conversation mostly focussing on the canoeing and the serenity of our surroundings. Before we were all given the green light to return to our cabins for a well-earned night's sleep, Trey had one more activity for us to complete. I wasn't sure I had the strength for any more emotional revelations or poking around in my memories, but I sat tight, holding Scott's hand, telling myself that I had to make the most of this retreat and see the whole process through to the end.

With Cindy handing around slips of paper and pencils, Trey stood up to explain the task. "I'd like to finish this evening by giving you all a chance to throw away something that is holding you back. It could be a regret, a secret, a difficult memory, an argument, or a missed opportunity. Something that you keep coming back to, that you never had the opportunity to resolve with your child. For Cindy and me, it was the day before our daughter was killed. She had been feeling unwell and had asked to stay out of school the next day. I had a busy day of work planned and Cindy had clients booked in, so we were both unwilling to cancel our itinerary for Lucy. The regret stayed with us for a long time."

I could fill an entire notepad and still only have scratched the surface of regrets and missed opportunities with Jamie. As for secrets, well, I was still hoping to get to the bottom of those.

Cindy soon sat down beside Trey, pen and paper at the ready. "Cindy and I still do this every year, and no doubt will continue to do so. Grief is a lifelong journey. I want you all to write down that regret, that missed opportunity, or that secret you are unable to share. Write it down in as much detail as you like and how you feel about it. Then I want you to scrunch up that piece of paper and throw it into the fire. Discard it. It is not helping you. You can let it go. Cindy gave you several sheets of paper in case you find it hard to get it down on your first attempt."

For a while, no one moved. The group sat poised, pencils and paper at the ready, deep in thought. Slowly, memories were written down, paper torn up, and new sheets begun. I looked up several times and caught Carla looking across at me and Scott or whispering to Craig. She looked agitated as if she wasn't focussing on the task at all. Scott was too busy writing down his regret to notice, but they were making me feel uncomfortable. If Carla had something else she wanted to say to me, I'd rather she just come out and say it, although this wasn't the time or place. Maybe we'd get to clear the air

When everyone had finished, sitting like a group of schoolchildren with completed exam papers gripped between our fingers, Trey stood up.

He scrunched up his piece of paper and threw it into the fire. "Now, let it go."

Most of the group followed Trey's example, hurling their scrunched-up sheets into the flames. Scott lit his on the corner and let it burn slowly. I whispered a silent sorry to my slip of paper and dropped it onto the glowing embers at the edge of the fire so that I could see its ashes after the flames had devoured it.

Carla and Craig made a swift and obvious exit as soon as the last of the regrets had been burned. The rest of us sat for some quiet contemplation before wandering back to our cabins, faces flushed with heat from the smouldering logs, legs and arms aching from the canoeing.

I fell into step behind Scott as he flicked on his head torch and led us back to the cabin, this time along the cleared trail rather than through the knotted undergrowth. "Did you notice Craig and Carla? She was being a bit odd. Kept staring across at us."

Scott lifted his head to shine the beam toward the cabin then dropped it back to the ground ahead of him. "Yep, I noticed, and they scarpered as soon as we were all done with the task."

"They were all over us at the start of this weekend, crowbarring their way into our canoes, and now it feels like they're ignoring us."

Scott stopped walking. "I agree. I felt a different vibe

from Carl tonight, and Carla couldn't even look at me when she left the fire. Why don't we go and see what's wrong? Ask them directly? I don't think I could bear leaving with the idea that they have something against us and we haven't had a chance to put it right."

"If our conversation in the canoe was anything to go on, I'd say that the thing they are holding against us is Jamie and the idea that he was somehow involved with Gunner Piper." I took a big breath and shook out the tension from my shoulders. "I was angry earlier, but now I want to resolve it, set them right. Otherwise, it'll drive me crazy, knowing they think Jamie was less of a victim than their son with absolutely no evidence to support that viewpoint."

I couldn't see Scott's face properly because of the torch shining from his forehead, but I could feel the tension emanating from him, so much so that he didn't move or speak.

I reached out and touched his arm. "I promise I won't go crazy. Crazier. Come on, let's go and talk to Carla and Craig while I'm feeling brave."

I zipped my jacket all the way up to my neck and took Scott's hand. Craig and Carla's cabin was not far from ours. Some small stakes painted yellow dotted the paths between each lodging, showing us the way. Their cabin was called 'Pine.' Ours was named 'Oak.' Apt, I thought, as pines are easily combustible because of their high resin content, and oak trees are hardy and long-lived but not shade-tolerant. Certainly, Carla looked like she was close to combustion when she was in our presence earlier, and Scott and I were not about to be left in the dark as to the reasons why.

We stepped up to the door of Pine cabin, and Scott switched off his head torch. It was dark in the woods; the only illumination came from their small cabin window, a flickering orange glow from the wood burner inside. One night was not enough to acclimatise to the nighttime noises, and as we waited for Craig or Carla to come to the door, the cracks and crunches from nearby undergrowth seemed to grow louder and louder.

There was a low rumble of conversation from inside the cabin and then the door swung open and Craig stood in the doorway, a coat pulled over his pyjamas, his feet bare. Normally a stocky, round-faced man with thick blonde hair, tonight Craig's face seemed drawn, his eyes hollow, his hair wispy and unkempt. He had clearly been arguing because his eyes were hard and his lips pursed tight. He took a furtive glance back into the cabin then stepped forward, pulling the door half-closed behind him, the smell of wood smoke and coffee wafting out with a warm puff of air.

I cleared my throat. "Sorry to disturb you, Craig, but Scott and I were concerned about you both. Having had some intimate conversations with you and Carla about our boys today, we were worried that we had upset you in some way."

I was channelling my earlier anger, hoping that I wasn't overdoing the empathy I was feigning. If anything, I felt like they—or Carla, at least—owed me an apology, but finding out what was going on with them took precedence over my earlier rage.

I think Scott picked up on my conflicting emotions as he quickly took over. "We noticed that you were focussing on us at the fireplace this evening and wondered if we could help in some way. What we don't want is to leave here feeling worse than we arrived, and we are getting the impression that you and your wife are holding something back that is relevant to us. We'd like to clear the air if that's possible."

Craig cricked his neck and then clenched his jaw. "Look, you two being here has caused us some problems. Stuff we thought we'd put to one side has reared its ugly head. Let's just get tomorrow over and done with, shall we? Then we can go back to our own realities and try and put this behind us."

He turned to go back inside. I looked at Scott, and he shook his head, signalling me to leave it alone. I wasn't about to let Carla talk to me the way she did in that boat and then give me the cold shoulder. No way.

I stuck out my foot against the cabin door. "Don't do that, Craig. It isn't fair. I understand that Carla has questions about Jamie's involvement with Gunner Piper and that she has been swayed by the media accusations about him being some kind of accomplice. Our son's death wasn't like the others, but there is no evidence that Jamie was anything more than a victim, one who managed to make an emergency call before he was killed. Whatever it is she has decided about him, it isn't true. He was a seven-year-old boy when Seb went missing. He couldn't possibly be involved."

Craig gripped the door with one hand and the doorframe with the other and looked from me to Scott and back again. "Before Seb died, he told his mum that he met a boy whose sister had died. Something about her body being found in a log pile. It sounded far-fetched, and Carla thought it was the boys making up stories. When Seb went missing, we told the police. They confirmed that a girl's body had been found a year earlier in a log pile in the area and that the little girl had a brother. They told us that they asked the boy about Seb, and he didn't recognise him. They said a lot of the kids knew about this boy and what had happened to his sister. I'm only telling you this because one of the regrets Carla had all those years ago was that we never pushed harder about this boy Seb spoke of. Now our son's body has been found, and there's all this talk of an accomplice. It's made Carla think again about the boy with the sister found in the log pile. We've been arguing because she wanted to ask you about it. She wanted to ask if Jamie had ever mentioned anything similar. None of the other parents had, and I didn't want to go stirring things up. None of it will bring Seb back, so what's the point?"

Wow. I wasn't expecting that. I swallowed hard, remembering the conversation I had with Suzannah about her losing a daughter, a sister to Mason, nine years ago. I concentrated on my breathing, hoping that the heat that had engulfed me and the shock of their revelation wasn't obvious on my face.

I thought we were going there to listen to another rant about Jamie being different from the others or questions about why we didn't want to meet with the other parents. I didn't think they were going to offer up information. Maybe I'd misread Carla; maybe her intention in the boat wasn't accusatory but inquisitive. The mention of another boy was making me nervous, and I was keenly aware that Scott and I had secrets that we were withholding from the police, secrets about Jamie that may or may not be relevant to the deaths of thirteen boys.

I unzipped the top of my jacket. "I'm sorry, Carla doesn't want to talk to us right now. Jamie didn't say anything about another boy and certainly nothing about a boy whose sister had died. I guess if the police told you it was a dead end, there's not a lot else to be done."

I slipped my hand into Scott's and held tight, a wave of lightheadedness making me feel unsteady on my feet. They knew about Mason—had an idea, at least—and that meant it was only a matter of time before Mason was dragged into the investigation along with his friendship with Jamie.

Scott pulled off his beanie and ran his fingers through his hair. "As you know, I've been a crime reporter for years. I wrote a piece about your son when he went missing, although I'm sure you didn't pay much attention to the names at the bottom of the articles, only what was written about your son. I'm sorry I didn't mention that earlier. In my experience, if the police have ended a line of inquiry, it's because there isn't anything to find."

He said it with such authority that for a second, even I believed him, but we both knew that he was just trying to reassure Craig and steer him away from the idea of another boy and an accomplice.

I lifted my leg away from the base of the door. "I appreciate you sharing that with us, Craig, and I do hope we'll have a chance to speak to Carla again before the weekend comes to a close."

Craig nodded and closed the door. Scott flicked on his head torch, and we trudged to our cabin. I had a strange feeling in my stomach; I felt sick and scared.

When we were far enough away from Craig and Carla's cabin to be out of earshot, I paused. "Suzannah said that she lost a daughter nine years ago."

Scott turned and faced me, clicking off his head torch. "What? Mason had a sister who died?"

"It means that Mason met Seb. Mason is the missing link."

Lights from the cabins danced among the trees as a heavy silence hung in the air.

"Whoa! Slow down, Miss Marple. It is certainly a coincidence, and the timing is spot-on, but we don't know that for sure."

"He's been stalking us, he gave Jamie a necklace he stole from a shop he worked in, and he lost a sister a decade ago—and that fact links him to Seb. Come on, Scott, you're the investigative reporter."

"Maybe we shouldn't be trying to find out anything else. Maybe this is a sign that we're in too deep and need to involve the police."

There was a loud creak farther ahead in the trees and some rustling of branches overhead that made me jump. I was reminded of Peasedale Forest, our run for the car, and the look of panic in Scott's face. Whatever was going on with Mason, Scott and I had thrown ourselves headfirst into finding out the truth, and there was no going back now.

"We need to find out how Mason and Jamie were involved with Gunner Piper and what those notes mean before the police get involved. We need to minimise the damage, protect our son's reputation, and make sure everyone knows the truth before it's warped and sullied by the media."

Scott switched his torch back on. "Let's get back."

It felt like Scott was holding back, keeping something from me. Perhaps he was worrying about me, how I was coping with all this. He clearly didn't want to talk about it anymore tonight, so I followed him home in silence.

Arriving outside our cabin, we kicked our boots against the side wall to knock off the loose earth and debris before heading inside. Scott lit the wood burner, and we stood and watched it spit and crackle, standing close to absorb the heat as it warmed up. Neither of us spoke.

When the chill had left the room and we could feel the heat radiating from the burner, we changed for bed and snuggled up under the duvet in our pyjamas and socks.

Scott rolled onto his side and scooped his arm around my waist. "I remember something about a missing girl in our neck of the woods about ten years ago. It was the stepdad who killed her, I think."

I yawned. I remembered something about a dead girl too, but I couldn't think about that now. I was too tired, too overwhelmed, and had started to wish I had never pushed Scott into coming on this retreat.

"I'm glad I brought my thickest PJs," I said, pulling the duvet up to my chin.

As I lay in bed beside Scott, I thought back to the day I first saw the police officers at our door, moments before the belly of our world was about to be ripped out. I was about to find out something that I didn't want to know but had to hear.

I shivered. Here we were again.

TWENTY-SIX

Scott

A S WE TROOPED off to the fire for our last day of the retreat, Blair and I were both deep in thought. We had showered quickly, dressed in silence, and packed our bags before we left the cabin. I got the impression that Blair was as keen as I was to get home, and after last night's conversation with Carl, my head was buzzing with questions about Mason. A boy with a trauma in his past and a violent stepfather. A boy who the other kids knew of but avoided. A young man who probably sent Devin to our house to find Jamie's puzzle box and then pushed him into the river. That kid has accomplice written all over him.

Most of this, of course, was between me and Blair, although it was time I told her about Devin. If we were going to work this out together then she needed to know everything.

The police, on the other hand, had no evidence that there was an accomplice. They didn't have the notebook or photographs. They had no idea Devin came to burgle our home before being drowned in the river. They followed up on the information Carla and Craig gave them and it led them nowhere. Gunner Piper was behind bars and dishing out details of his crimes like he was a celebrity, but he'd made no mention of an accomplice. The speculation in the media was just that—speculation. Sensationalist reporting to keep the story of the Pied Piper of Peasedale in the forefront of the news to sell papers, and I knew that better than anyone. No one knew anything concrete relating to an accomplice except for me and Blair, and that's how it was going to stay.

I pulled on my beanie and wandered with Blair through the trees toward the warmth of the fire. Blair leant her head against my shoulder and slipped her arm around my waist. I lifted my arm around her shoulders. There was a closeness between us that I thought we had lost, and it made me feel hopeful for the future, our future, together. Whatever it was Trey had done, it had worked. We had found each other again. Our shoulders were looser, our hearts a little more open.

Wending our way through the trees to our meeting point, the crackling blaze of the fire lured us in, another delicious meal ready and waiting: sausages, bacon, tomatoes, scrambled eggs, and beans. It tasted magnificent, and taking the time to enjoy a decent breakfast was something I'd take home from this weekend. Starting the day slowly and properly, fuelling my body, and spending the first meal of the day really talking to Blair.

The group's morning conversation was a discussion of day-to-day life carrying grief: the difficulties of staying focussed; the struggle to perform basic daily functions like eating, washing, and mundane communications; the constant niggle of 'what if' that eats away at you minute by minute; the relentless struggle to focus on the now and not the past. Things, it turns out, that Blair and I had both been wrestling with but not spoken about. That would change going forward. We made a promise to each other to say when we were struggling and to help each other out—taking turns to lift each other up and share our energy—when we had it while letting ourselves be carried when we needed it.

Craig and Carla had not turned up for breakfast. At first, I assumed they had decided to sleep in and were running late. Cindy was also absent. I looked across at Blair and noticed that she had barely touched her food and had started to wring her hands. I reached over and placed my hand on hers. She looked up at me and I knew what she was thinking because I was thinking the same. Did Craig and Carla leave?

Cindy arrived just as Trey told us to get ourselves together for our final activity, which was caving. Nothing too strenuous, Trey had promised yesterday, just some gentle adventure—a boat ride, a zip wire, and a little climbing. Apparently, none of the spaces were small, and we would all be kitted out with helmets and given plenty of instruction. Cindy bent down and whispered something to Trey.

Trey stood up. "Carla isn't feeling up to the activity today, but Craig will join us shortly, so we'll leave in just a few minutes."

Craig appeared in a fluster, wrestling with the zip on his coat. He grabbed a water bottle from Cindy and marched straight up to me and Blair. Trey and the rest of the group set off, and the three of us tucked in at the back.

"I'm sorry Carla isn't feeling up to the caving this morning," I said, breaking the loaded silence.

Craig ran his hand through his hair and stared at the

ground. "She's not ill—just too knotted up to face you both. She believed the papers and was quite set on the idea that your boy was somehow involved. Clutching to the idea that Seb was lured to his death by a kid rather than an evil-looking monster. It's because she blames herself, of course. That she didn't teach him to run a mile at the sight of Gunner Piper. And, somehow, she's got it into her head that the only way your Jamie made that call is that he had some relationship with Gunner Piper, he was allowed to keep his phone, something went wrong, and Gunner turned on him. I don't know, it makes it easier for her to think that Seb was helpless rather than imagine that another boy, a stronger one, was perhaps able to fight back and make a call. God, I'm sorry to go on like this about your Jamie. I'm just trying to explain what's happening in Carla's head."

Craig pulled out his water bottle and took a huge gulp. Blair squeezed my hand, the look in her eyes pleading with me to end the conversation.

"I can assure you that if there was an accomplice, the police would have found some evidence. That emergency call Jamie made didn't help him, and now the media have twisted it into something sinister and ugly and we're paying the price."

Craig tucked his bottle in his pocket, his pace laboured as we snaked our way up a steep incline. "Yeah, it sucks. I'm really sorry we said anything. Your head can take you to some dark places if you let it."

"Yeah. We understand that, don't we, honey?" I put my hand against Blair's lower back to help her up through the forest behind Craig.

"It's been a lot," she said, reaching for a tree as her foot slipped on a rock. I could sense she was on high alert and feeling increasingly uncomfortable with the direction of our conversation.

"Thing is," Craig continued, "there's so much we'll never know. It's hard switching that off in your mind. Did you know that one of the parents used a contact in the police force to look into online grooming to see if that's how Gunner got to the boys? Turned out none of the lads used their social media accounts leading up to their disappearances. Wherever it was that Gunner Piper met our sons, it was out of sight, away from people, and undetected by CCTV. Like we said at the start of this weekend, if it wasn't for Jamie sending that emergency call, the boys might never have been found. I'm just sorry no one could get to your boy on time."

Our ascent through the forest had steered us to the barred-up entrance of an old mine. We were met by an instructor and given helmets and a safety briefing. The tension seemed to ramp up a notch as we took turns crouching and stepping through the opening of the damp, murky abandoned mine shaft. It was wet underfoot and pitch-black up ahead, only the head torches providing illumination. As we made our way farther into the mine, the passage behind was lost to a shadowy void. We all walked in silence, admiring the dappled rock and seeping mineral deposits flashing into view as we moved our heads about.

We came to a large opening that revealed a flooded cave and an inflatable raft.

"Split into two groups and get yourselves into a life jacket," Trey announced as he and the instructor placed oars onto the boat and held it steady.

Blair grabbed two life jackets, slipping hers on with great haste and then helping me with mine. She and I were the first to fasten ourselves.

She looked behind us and then pulled me toward the boat. "Quick, let's get on first."

Craig was grappling with the clips on his jacket. The fastening was not going his way on this excursion. I knew that Blair was trying to create some distance between him and us, so I hopped into the boat beside her and we pushed off with the first group, leaving Craig waiting for the second launch.

Off the boat on the far bank of the flooded cave, Blair moved away from the group and perched on a rock.

I followed and sat beside her. "You okay, honey?"

She nodded. "I remember it. It came back to me on the way to the cave. A little girl who was killed. It was when Jamie was at primary school. I wouldn't let him out of my sight for months."

"The details came flooding back to me last night, too. The stepdad was taken in for questioning, and then it all went quiet. Mason would have been nine or ten."

Blair shuffled closer to me on the rock. "I want to look it up on the way home. There must be some information about it. I'll do a Google search."

I was thinking exactly the same thing. "I reckon I can do better than a Google search. How about you drive while I'll work my investigative journalism magic? I reckon I can get the newspaper articles by the time we get home."

The second wave of our group had disembarked from the

boat, and we were ushered onward through the old mine. Blair and I stuck close together and stayed amongst the group so that we couldn't be singled out by Craig for any more conversation. We had both had our fill of revelations.

The final zip wire was a blast as we traversed another flooded cave, the crystal-clear water illuminated by submerged arctic blue spotlights. It was an eerie and exhilarating experience, which had everyone animatedly regaling the excitement of our final adventure as we headed out of the last tunnel and back down to camp to gather our belongings.

Our weekend ended with brief but heartfelt farewells, and we had the opportunity to thank Trey and Cindy for all their hard work and support and, of course, the delicious food. We were both glad that Carla and Craig decided to sneak away quietly. I knew that this would not be our last Grief Retreat, and I hoped that the next would be a chance to really move forward as a couple and remember only the best of our son.

Driving home, Blair sang along to some of her favourite tunes while I tapped away on my laptop. By the time she pulled into our driveway, I had read out loud all of the articles I found on the murdered girl. It was nine-and-a-half years ago. She was five, a year younger than Jamie at the time. Her name was Lily Bosko. My memory had served me well as the stepdad had indeed been taken in and questioned, then later released. As is often the case, the investigation dragged on, and media attention waned. Accidental death seemed to be the final judgement. The articles published several months after her body was found were unclear as to the cause of death. A head injury of questionable cause, a fall, possibly a blow to the head during or just before she was trapped in the log pile.

Back home, Blair made coffee while I emptied our bags and set the washing machine going, then we sat at the kitchen table and stared at a picture of Lily, which I had pulled up on my laptop screen.

Blair held her mug in both hands and blew on the steaming liquid inside. "Well, we know that Seb's account of a little girl being killed and found in a log pile was true."

I angled the screen toward me to get a better look at the picture.

Blair sipped her coffee with a loud slurp. "Is there a picture of her family? None of the articles mention a brother."

I flipped through the articles. "She went to the local nursery. Lived with her mother and stepdad. Here's a picture."

I spun the screen around to face Blair. She looked intently at it for a few seconds then drew the screen closer. "That's Suzannah. I mean, it's nine years ago, her hair is different, and she's aged, but it's her."

"Really? Are you sure it's her?" I pulled the screen back to look at the image of the mother. "If Suzannah is the mother, then Mason is the brother."

I had an uncomfortable feeling in my stomach. It sounded like the only friend Jamie had was a troubled young man. It was time for me to tell Blair about the attempted break-in and share the fate of the kid burglar.

TWENTY-SEVEN

Blair

I SLEPT SO well after two days of outdoor activities that the warmth and comfort of my bed made it hard to leave the following morning. By the time I dragged myself up and plodded my way into the kitchen, I saw the back door was open and Scott's walking boots were sitting on the mat, a coating of mud around the soles. Minnie was lounging in her basket, her food bowl on the floor and empty. The smell of fresh toast and coffee filled the kitchen. Scott was standing by the worktop with his back to me.

"Morning."

He turned. "Oh. Hey. How did you sleep?"

I stretched and twisted my head from side to side. "Great. It was so cosy. And no socks."

I sat at the table, and Scott bought over a steaming mug of milky coffee, resting it on one of our recycled plastic coasters, a gift from Scott and Jamie after one of their boys' camping weekends. A newspaper was open on the kitchen table; the headline was about a local boy found dead in the river.

"I see that you've taken Minnie for a walk and picked up the paper."

"Yes. Kind of." Scott poured me a glass of orange juice.

"There's something I need to share with you."

I took a slice of toast from the rack and spread on some butter and Marmite. "Has this got something to do with Lily and Mason by any chance?" I pulled the newspaper toward me and scanned the text. The boy in the article was called Devin, and he lived on the same street as Suzannah and Mason.

Scott sat down opposite me, his mug resting on the table in front of him, not on his coaster. "It's a recent edition. Remember I told you that Leith came to visit while you were in the clinic and we went out for the evening?"

I took a bite of toast. "Mm-hmm."

Scott ran his fingers through his hair, which was often a sign he was struggling to communicate something. I put my toast on the plate and gave him my full attention.

"Well, we got home late, a bit drunk, and surprised a burglar."

"A burglar?" My heartbeat did a loop the loop.

Scott pointed to the picture of Devin at the top of the article. "A kid. That kid. Devin. I chased him to the river, and by the time Leith caught up with me, I was dragging Devin out of the water. He was young and scared and said he had been paid to steal something from Jamie's room. A box. We let Devin go, and the next day we searched Jamie's room and found the puzzle box. This article appeared on the front page of the paper six days later."

I stared at the picture of the kid, a school photograph, his wiry black hair roughly combed, a shy smile, a frayed shirt collar. "Why didn't you tell me?"

Scott reached across the table and held my hand. "Because you were just out of the clinic. I didn't know if you could handle it. I'm not sure if I'm handling it, to be honest."

My body began to tingle, and I could feel a nervous energy building up inside me as I reread the words "Local Boy Drowned."

Minnie plodded over and rested her head in Scott's lap. He lifted his hand from mine and patted her on the head. "Someone paid Devin to burgle our house, and it seems possible, probable, that the same someone drowned him in the river. Clearly, the police have no idea about the burglary or Devin's movements around the time he died; otherwise, they would have been round here asking questions."

"Why didn't you go to the police after you caught Devin trying to break into our house?"

"Because Devin was frightened and young and sorry. Because he was looking for something of Jamie's, and I wanted to find it first. Because I didn't want the police combing through Jamie's things again. I didn't want more police and more reporters and the whole media shitshow that comes with it."

I rested my hands on the paper. "So, now we have a box containing some incriminating photographs and notes that belonged to our son which we are keeping a secret even though it's relevant to the recent murder of a young boy. That's withholding evidence, isn't it? Obstructing a police investigation? If they find out about the box and your run-in with Devin then we're in trouble, not to mention how it looks for Jamie."

"Yes. Exactly. The question is, what do we do about it?

We could find out what it means for Jamie and prove that he had nothing to do with Gunner Piper and then hand over the notes and photographs and tell the police the truth. Then again, we could just burn the photos and notes and forget about my run-in with Devin ever happened."

"Could we? I don't think so."

"No, me either."

Scott sighed and cricked his neck, a sign he was prepping for an uncomfortable reality check. He did exactly the same thing just before he told me my mother's cancer had spread.

"Or?"

"Or we do the sensible thing and come clean. Let the police deal with Mason. He's a messed-up kid who will be facing some terrible accusations about Devin and Gunner's victims."

"And a messed-up kid would say anything to the police to save his own arse, including throwing our son under the bus."

"What if Jamie was involved?"

"Do you think our son was some sort of accomplice to a serial killer? In league with Mason?"

"No. God, Blair, I've never thought that. Do you?"

I couldn't answer that question. I wished I was as sure as Scott of our son's innocence. I knew I only had myself to blame for not paying enough attention. If Jamie was in any way involved with Gunner Piper's crimes then I had to bear some of the responsibility. Jamie was my son. I raised him. I let him down.

I took a breath and paused for a minute. Scott's elbows rested on the table, and his head was in his hands. He was conflicted.

I pressed my palms into the table and looked at Scott. "Jamie got that information about the boys from someone, right? We are assuming it was Mason, which makes It is very likely that Mason led Jamie to his death. I want to know the whole truth about how and why my son died. Why he was different from the other boys, and if he was in any way involved, I want to know before someone else finds out and tells the world."

Scott lifted his head. "Mason wanted Jamie's box, and he was prepared to drown Devin to keep his identity hidden. That makes him dangerous, honey. I can't lose you, too."

I reached for one of Scott's hands and held it in both of mine. "It's too late for honesty now. Perverting the course of justice is a criminal offence. We could go to prison. No one knows we have the box. I don't want Jamie's name to be dragged through the mud, at least not until we know the truth about those notes and photographs and Mason and the part our son played in all of this."

"If Mason was Gunner's accomplice, don't you want him to go to prison? Face the consequences of what he's done?"

"Yes, I do. But first, I want the truth. Then I want justice."

I took a big swig of my coffee and squeezed my shoulder blades together to release some tension. "We need to get face to face with Mason."

"Okay. Listen, let's let all this settle in. I've just given you the news about Devin, and we've only been back from the retreat for one night. We reconnected while we were away, you gained some strength, and we both found a little respite from our grief. I don't want to lose all of that with a decision made in haste and desperation."

I smiled at my unsettled husband and kissed the back of his hand. "I know just what we need. Somewhere where we can relax and drown out all our jumbled thoughts for a few hours. The market is on in town today. How about a mooch around, and we can chat about Suzannah and Mason as we go?"

"Sounds like a plan."

"We could even cycle in if you'd like."

"Great idea. We haven't cycled anywhere in ages."

I wrestled a backpack out of the cupboard under the stairs, toppling the hoover and knocking my head on a hook as I backed out. We had ignored the inside of the house for as long as we had ignored the outside, so I made a mental note to reorganise the cupboard as soon as we got back from the market.

I sat on a chair in the kitchen to fold my trousers around my ankles before pulling my socks over the top.

Scott walked in, his hands filthy with grease. "You could just put on a more sensible style of trousers for the bike ride instead of doing that trouser-sock thing that your parents always made you do."

I smiled. "I like the trouser-sock thing. What happened to your hands?"

Scott turned on the tap at the kitchen sink and lathered his hands with soap. "Your bike had two flat tyres, and the chain had come off mine. I almost gave up. Jamie's is in perfect order, so I could have taken that, but I was determined to get mine going. I've had that bike for fifteen years now, and it hasn't let me down yet."

I stood up and handed my husband the nailbrush. "You say that every time you get the thing out. I don't know why you don't just buy yourself a new one, a bike with more than three gears. You're not as young as you were, you know."

Scott scrubbed at the grease until most of it was gone and then dried his hands on a dish towel. I tutted and took the towel into the utility room, where I filled the sink with warm water and detergent and left the towel to soak.

"Right, are we ready?" Scott appeared in the utility room with his trousers tucked into his socks.

I laughed. "Oh, you ridiculous man!"

"I think it's very his 'n' hers."

"Come on. Let's go and have a his 'n' hers time at the market." I gave Scott a gentle shove toward the back door. "We'll use *his* money to buy *her* some treats."

In the backpack, I had two water bottles, two bike locks, a spare inner tube, a metal tyre lever, some hand sanitizer, and a hand towel.

"I'll take the bag." Scott took the bag from me and pulled the pack onto his back.

We secured our helmets and adjusted the straps, making sure they were a snug fit.

I swung my leg over my bike and positioned my foot so it was ready for pushing off. "Jamie would be so embarrassed of us right now."

Scott was poised for takeoff. "There was a time when he loved to go bike riding with us, and he was the one telling us to put our helmets on and tighten the straps."

"Do you remember the time he clipped his so tight, he

caught his chin skin in the clasp? He screamed. I thought Frank might appear and call social services."

"I remember. He had a black bruise on his chin for a week."

"He told his teacher that I'd done it."

"Did he?"

"Don't you remember? Mr Lavigne pulled me aside at pickup to ask what happened. Jamie never admitted that he did it to himself. I can only imagine what the teachers said about me in the staff room."

"I have no doubt they saw right through his fib. Teachers have seen far more kids growing up than parents have. I'm sure they'd heard it all before."

Together, we kicked off the ground and wobbled our way along the road toward the bridge and the park beyond. After a few minutes, we found our cycling legs and were gliding side by side along the dirt path through the trees that led around the park to the edge of town. Scott slowed as we travelled beside the river, staring at the gently flowing water that rippled on the surface with the breeze.

I slowed down to keep pace with Scott. I looked over at the river and stopped. Scott stopped beside me. Beyond the overgrown bank was the murky water. It looked black on this grey day. Black and deep, ready to swallow up anything that fell into it, the tangle of rushes and weeds at the edge like tendrils waiting to pull something under.

"Was that where they found Devin's body?" I imagined the boy's naked body floating facedown, bobbing against the muddy bank.

"It was farther along. Near the old mill on the other side

of that rusty barbed wire." I pointed back down the river. "It was just back there that Leith and I caught up with Devin, on the other side where the bank slopes down to that sandy patch. He was so scared, poor kid. I wish I'd marched him home, dried him out, and called the police then and there, or his parents, at least. Maybe things would have turned out differently for him, but the idea of Jamie having a secret after all that stuff in the media about him being an accomplice clouded my judgement. Plus, Leith and I were drunk and not thinking straight. I dunno, I feel responsible and irresponsible!"

We turned away from the river and got back on our bikes. The ride through the woods was quiet, with only a few dog walkers about, but as Scott and I approached the town, we could hear the hustle and bustle of the market. There was a bike rack outside the supermarket on the edge of town, and the market was a ten-minute walk into the centre. I pulled out the bike locks and Scott secured the bikes to each other and the rack, making sure all four wheels were also secured to the frames and the rack.

"Can't be too careful," he said, tucking the keys into the zipped pocket of his cycling jacket.

"Because there'll be a queue of people lining up to steal your slightly rusted, unfashionable boneshaker." I reached down to release my trousers from my socks. "Will you be leaving your trousers tucked in, or would you like me to fix those for you?"

Scott looked down at his socks. "I'll only have to roll them up into the socks again later. Besides, socks are usually hidden away, and today I think mine would like some exposure."

I laughed. "Which is why you chose the Spock socks with ears?"

"Jamie wouldn't have bought them for me if he hadn't wanted me to show them off."

I shook my head and then linked my arm into Scott's. As we wandered into town, the streets were busier and busier.

"I haven't been into town since my run-in with that driver."

"How's the head? No headaches for a while?"

"Feels okay. No permanent damage."

A whirring, skidding sound crept up on us, and a boy on a skateboard whizzed past, knocking against my shoulder.

"Hey, careful!" I shouted as I fell into Scott.

Scott caught me and held me steady. "Bloody skateboards. What's he doing racing along at that speed in these crowds? You okay?"

I stood tall and took a deep breath. "Fine. Did you see his face?"

"He was wearing a hoodie. Come on, we won't let a lad on a skateboard ruin our day."

An uneasy feeling crawled over my skin.

I shook it off and linked arms with Scott. "Right. Let's go."

We snaked our way through myriad lanes lined with food stalls, the smells intoxicating, and, giving into temptation, we bought freshly baked bread, exotic fruits, and jars of spicy oriental sauces. Lingering by a driftwood sculpture stall whilst Scott admired the intricately carved animals on display, I thought I saw someone watching me from the other side of the stand. I nipped through the intersection between the adjoining units and around the back to see who was standing behind it, but when I emerged between the two kiosks, all I found was a bustle of people and more stalls.

"Where are you running off to?" Scott appeared beside me.

"I thought I saw someone staring at me." I slipped my hand into Scott's and we wandered along. I thought I had seen the boy with the skateboard watching, but I didn't want to spoil the day by being paranoid, and it was possible I had imagined it. It certainly wouldn't be the first time my mind had gotten the better of me.

"Oh, look at those!" Scott pulled me toward a long stall with a garden scene backdrop and a range of potted plants. "Brilliant! I might get one for Leith for his next birthday. Or perhaps for your dad."

Among the plants were garden gnomes of all shapes and sizes. Not ordinary garden gnomes—the ones that hold fishing rods and push wheelbarrows and, um, some of these garden gnomes were X-rated and wholly inappropriate.

Scott picked up one with its trousers around its ankles that looked as if it was having a pee. "What do you think of this one?"

I bent down and scooped up a biker gnome with its middle finger up. "This one's more Leith."

"These are the ones for my parents. I can just see my mother's face when I hand them to her." He held up a pair of naked gnomes wearing only sunglasses, all their little gnome bits out on display.

I laughed and handed mine to the stallholder. Scott

handed over his nude pair and one that looked as if it had face-planted with its bottom on display and a bottle of wine in its hand.

After Scott paid, I took the bag from the seller and wrestled it into his pack. "This is fun. What shall we buy next?"

Nearing the end of the row of stalls, I pulled against Scott's arm and stopped. "Look."

Scott looked ahead, trying to decipher what it was that I had seen. "What am I looking at?"

"That boy. He's just standing there. Staring at us."

It was ten in the morning, and the market frenzy was showing no sign of abating. People shuffled along the street, weaving past each other. Scott was straining his neck to find the boy I had seen.

"There." I pointed. "By the jewellery stall on the left."

How could he not see him? The boy was looking right at us.

"Nope. I can't see a boy. Are you sure you're not imagining it?"

I squeezed Scott's arm as the boy disappeared into the crowd. "I don't know. Maybe. When I was seeing Jamie, he was always closer. Nearby. Talking to me."

"Let's find a café and have a break. This mooching, shopping lark is quite exhausting."

"You love mooching and shopping. You've already bought food and gnomes, and we've only been here half an hour. I've never seen a market beat you before."

Wherever we've been on holiday, if there was a market of any kind, Scott would want to be there as soon as it opened and would leave with arms laden with an array of items that we didn't need.

"You're right. I could buy pointless but funny gifts and quirky foodstuffs all day. I was thinking of you."

He had learned that if he wanted my company on a shopping trip, he had to keep me fuelled with coffee and cake, or my enthusiasm would quickly wane. "I'd love a coffee and a slice of chocolate cake, please."

"Coming right up."

He led me through the throng to our favourite coffee shop, which doubled as a chocolate shop. I noticed him checking behind him and looking around as we bumped through the crowds. The coffee shop was where we bought a special Easter bunny with Jamie's name on it every year. We hadn't done it last Easter—we gave Jamie money instead— but I decided that from next year on, I would get one for Scott with his name on it.

I settled at a table by the window so that I could watch the hubbub of the market. I loved to sit and observe the craziness of my fellow human beings, a silent movie of everyday life playing out on the other side of the glass. I found it comforting, the busyness of a town centre keeping my mind engaged, with so many stimuli to fill my senses, leaving little room for troubling thoughts to overshadow my attention.

Scott unclipped his backpack and lowered it to the floor. "I'll go and order two lattes and a slice of their gooiest chocolate cake."

"Great. And don't forget a fork."

"I never forget the fork."

I slid the backpack under the table between my legs. As I

255

sat upright, I noticed a figure standing on the other side of the window. I looked up to see a teenage boy with piercing blue eyes staring down at me through the glass. He was wearing a plain black hoodie with the hood up and grey jeans. He had a skateboard tucked under one arm. He lifted his head to peer into the café, then he looked back down at me. With his free hand, he held up a piece of paper, which he pushed against the glass. In thick black letters, it read, "LEAVE MY MUM ALONE."

I couldn't breathe. I stared at him. Unable to move or turn away. A shiver ran through my body. He was more man than boy, tall but wiry, with a mop of black hair. His skin was smooth, not yet at the regular-shaving stage of life, and that youthful look of surly unease in his eyes, the emotions of a boy fighting to fit into the stature of a man. He held my gaze, and I saw the side of his mouth twitch, a tiny grin. I wanted to scream, but fear welded me to my seat and cemented my mouth closed. The boy scrunched up the note and turned away. Gripping the edge of the table, I watched him melt into the swarm of shoppers.

My heart thumped so loudly in my ears that I didn't hear Scott's voice until he grasped my shoulder and gave me a shake. "Blair? Honey? What is it? What's wrong?"

I looked at my husband and then back to the window. The boy was gone, the scene as it was before. "It was him. Just there. Mason."

TWENTY-EIGHT

Scott

B LAIR'S EYES WERE wide and wild, her face pale, and I knew that something had happened. She stared through the window. I thought she was doing better, the hallucinations gone, her grip on reality restored, but sitting in front of me was the woman she had been before she went into the clinic. A look of torment and disconnection back on her face. Was she seeing things again? Was all this too much? Suzannah, Mason, Jamie's puzzle box, Devin. The last thing I wanted was to push her over the edge. Find ourselves right back at square one.

"BB, honey, talk to me."

Her breathing was shallow, skin pale, knuckles white from the hold she had on the table.

I put my hands on hers. "Look at me and breathe."

She loosened her pincer grip on the tabletop. Holding my gaze, she took two long, slow breaths.

"Have a sip of coffee." I pushed the tray toward her.

She lifted her mug and sipped. Her hands were trembling. Something had really shaken her up.

"Now, tell me what you saw, or what you think you saw."

She set the mug back on the tray, lifted her elbows onto

the table, and rested her neck in her hands. "Oh, I saw it alright. I very definitely saw it. Him. Mason. He just stood there on the other side of the glass, staring at me. He held up a piece of paper against the glass, and in big black letters, it read, 'LEAVE MY MUM ALONE.' Then I saw the tiniest smile. He was wearing a black hoodie and was holding a skateboard."

A shiver ran up the length of my torso. This didn't feel the same as the times she imagined seeing Jamie. The lost look she had on her face a few moments ago had vanished, and she was right there with me. Eyeballing me. What she saw was no hallucination.

I remembered the kid on the skateboard knocking into Blair as we arrived in town. "Christ, BB. He must have been following us around the market this whole time." I took the cake off the tray and put it in front of Blair and then slid the tray under my chair. "Eat some cake, calm down, and then start from the beginning."

Thoughts swirled in my head. Mason was following us, warning Blair to leave Suzannah alone. He was trying to intimidate Blair, frighten her. He knows we came looking for him.

Blair pushed the cake away to the middle of the table. "I've lost my appetite." She put a piece on the fork and held it up for me.

I took the fork and ate the chunk of cake, but it stuck in my throat. "Me too. I'll get a box so we can take it home. Try and drink some of the coffee at least."

"Don't bother with the box; the cake will only make me think about Mason. I feel a bit lightheaded."

I spooned some sugar into Blair's mug, and we sat and drank our coffees. Blair was shaky and pallid, and I needed to get her home without any more surprises. She was doing so well. Getting back to the robust, no-nonsense Blair I was used to. The retreat had been a success, even with the unexpected appearance of Craig and Carla. I was so proud of her. She was fighting for her sanity and for Jamie, and I loved her for it. I reached across for her hand as she sipped her coffee. The sugar was doing her good; she had some colour back in her cheeks.

Walking back to the edge of town, Blair held tight to my arm, her eyes flitting around in every direction.

"He's gone, BB. Done what he came to do. He'll be on his way home hoping he's scared us into silence."

Approaching the bike rack, my stomach flipped a three-sixty. I could see that our bicycles were unrideable; all four tyres appeared to be flat. For a brief moment, I thought that, perhaps, we had ridden over some especially sharp stones as we made our way along the dirt tracks that encircled the park leaving the bikes with four slow punctures, but deep down I knew that the tyres had been slashed.

Clearly, Blair had seen it too. "Oh, no way! You've got to be kidding!"

I placed an arm around her shoulders and looked around the car park. "He's certainly determined to make his point."

We reached the bikes. Each of the tyres had a deep slash; that would be four new inner tubes and tyres that I'd have to buy and then install.

Blair lifted one of the locks. "At least these held. You might as well get that new bike, seeing as you'll be going into the cycle shop anyway."

"Always a silver lining, huh?"

"No. Not always."

I pulled the key from my pocket and began unlocking the bikes. Blair tucked the locks into the backpack, and we wheeled the bikes out of the car park.

Blair looked back as we joined the tree-lined path through the woods. "My emergency inner tube was pointless."

I nodded. "Yep. Although the water bottles will be my lifeline in about ten minutes. This pack is heavy."

There was a rustle in the undergrowth to our left, and we both jumped. "Let's get home as quick as we can, shall we?"

Blair looked back again and paused. "Scott, look."

I stopped and twisted around, my hands still clutching the bike handlebars. "The cocky piece of shit!"

The lad was standing, staring at us, from the end of the path. His hood was pulled down over his head. He was holding his middle finger up at us. I dropped the bike and sprinted toward him, grappling with the clip on the chest strap that was keeping the pack firmly fixed onto my back. By the time I'd released the clasp and thrown off the bag, the boy was long gone and I was dripping with sweat and gasping for breath. I put my hands on my knees and sucked in air, glancing back at Blair to check if she was alright. She was statuesque, as I'd left her, still holding her bike, her upper body twisted in my direction.

As I picked up the bag, I heard a disappointing clank coming from inside. The gnomes were in pieces. "Bollocks!"

I clipped up the chest strap as I stomped back to Blair

and yanked my bike off the ground. "There's no way we are going back round to Suzannah's house. We are going to the police to tell them everything. That boy needs locking up as soon as possible."

Blair put a hand on my bike. I stopped and looked at her.

She rested a hand on my cheek. "What about the police intrusion, the questions, the press, how it all looks for Jamie?"

"We'll just have to live with whatever comes next, whatever the police find out from Mason, whatever lies he tells. The truth isn't worth risking our lives."

"I'm not sure I can do all of that again. The police. The reporters. Graffiti."

We plodded home, huffing with the effort of pushing our bikes. I'd be buying those solid rubber tyres from now on, the ones that don't puncture. How could Jamie get involved with a kid like Mason? A devious, menacing vandal. Jamie wasn't that kind of teenager. Surly, yes. Grumpy, certainly. But not threatening or destructive.

Blair must have read my thoughts. "Mason had a defiant look on his face outside the café. The same one Jamie had whenever I asked where he'd been. I can still see the disconnect in his eyes that day he called me a bitch after I'd waited three hours for him to come home for dinner. *Three hours* I'd sat in the kitchen. Messaging him. Getting no reply. I was furious when he finally got back. Told him he was grounded for a month. He threw his plate across the kitchen and called me a bitch, then he stormed out of the house and slammed the door."

We crossed the footbridge over the river a little way down from our house, waited for a break in the traffic to cross the road, and pushed the bikes along the road to our driveway. I lifted the latch and opened the gate, letting Blair go through before wheeling my bike in and closing the gate behind us. "I don't remember you telling me about that."

I hated the idea of Jamie behaving so appallingly to Blair. I would never have spoken to my mother in that way.

Blair walked ahead to the garage. "I didn't tell you. I knew you'd be angry. I was afraid Jamie would leave and never come home. In those last few months, he became so insolent, so determined. It felt like he was angry at me all the time."

I was always defending Jamie. Blaming Blair for causing the friction, for being too critical and poking into his life too much. I thought he was just being a normal teenager. I hadn't listened to her, and it made me feel guilty. Jamie had needed a father, guidance, conversation. He had too much space, too much time on his own.

After standing my bike in the rack, I hung our hats on the hooks along the garage wall and shook off the pack. "It wasn't Jamie's fault. Our boy got in with the wrong kid and look where it all ended up."

Blair wrestled her bike onto the rack, the flat tyre coming loose from the wheel and catching on the bar. She jammed it into the slot with a grunt.

As we left the garage, I heard a voice calling.

"Scott?"

Frank was walking down the drive toward us.

"Hi, Frank. Everything okay?"

"I saw that young lad again, just after you left on your bikes. Jumped your gate and ran around the side of the house. I shouted and chased him away, but the cocky stripling acted like he wanted me to see him. Gave a salute as he straddled the gate on his way out then sped off on a skateboard toward town."

"What? He was here? In our garden? Christ, thanks for seeing him off, Frank. Did you call the police?"

Frank shook his head. "Wasn't sure you wanted all that to start up again."

Blair stepped in close behind me and slipped her arm around my waist, her body right up against mine so I could feel her heart beating fast against my shoulder blade.

Frank looked at the house and then back at us. "I've been meaning to say that I've seen a bit of activity around your house. That boy hanging around again. I heard a commotion a week or so ago. Woke me up. I think it was you and your friend after a night out."

I got the sense he was letting me know that he saw something the night we chased Devin, but he wasn't about to spell it out. I wondered if he saw Devin trying to break in or just me and Leith in pursuit. And if he did see anything suspicious, had he worked out that the burglar was the boy who was found drowned in the river? He was a vigilant neighbour, and I doubted he missed much. I felt like we had built a good relationship, so I decided to dive in and meet this head-on.

"Leith and I surprised a burglar. I guess the dog and our security lights woke you up. We came home a little worse for wear and chased him away. Never caught up with him."

Frank nodded. "I saw the pair of you racing down your drive. I figured whatever was going on, you had it all in hand, so I decided not to interfere."

It was a relief to hear that Frank had chosen not to call the police. God knows where we'd be now if he had. They'd have searched the house, possibly found Jamie's puzzle box, and we would all be back in a whirlwind media frenzy having to answer more questions. Not to mention how it would have looked with Devin turning up dead several days later.

"Shame about that young boy drowned in the river."

Wily old Frank had worked it out. "Yes. Awful. I know exactly how devastated his parents must be."

"Look, Scott, whatever's going on—and I really don't want to get involved—but whatever it is, I think you need to be careful. I'd hate to see you or Blair in any trouble, and that boy I keep seeing makes me nervous. I'm more than happy to report any sightings of him to the police if you give me the go-ahead."

"No need, Frank. It's one of Jamie's old friends, and the burglary was just a kid chancing his luck. Didn't even make it inside, so no harm done."

"No problem, Scott."

We waved Frank off and watched him walk back through the gate and down his drive next door.

Blair let her arm drop away from my waist and looked back at our house. "Do you think Mason came back for the notes and photographs?"

"I reckon so. Thankfully, Frank was here to scare him away."

We closed up the garage and walked around to the back

door. As we passed the side of the house, I noticed some broken branches on the ground.

I paused and looked at the hedge. "Looks like something has had a fight with the hedge."

Blair reached her hand inside the hedge until the ends of the branches were poking into her cheeks. "There's something in there."

Backing away from the hedge, her arm outstretched, she pulled out a bundle of soggy clothes. I helped her pull the items apart, and we held up a teenager-sized pair of trousers and a T-shirt. Pairs of pants, socks, and trainers fell to the ground as the clothes unravelled. I recognised the T-shirt immediately.

"It's Devin's." I took it from Blair and held it open.

It was pale grey with a big black Nike swoosh on the front. The clothes were damp, and there was a brown stain on the front, which I assumed was blood.

Blair dropped the trousers. "I touched the clothes. My DNA will be on them. What should we do?"

I paused. Stared down at the pile. The night of the burglary flashed into my mind; I remembered Devin's terrified face as I dragged him out of the river. "What *should* we do, or what are we *going* to do?"

"What?"

"Well, we *should* call the police. But then I'd have to tell them about the burglary and somehow explain why I didn't tell them about Devin sooner. Which would of course incriminate me. Plus, his clothes are at our home, and you and I have touched them."

"Mason must have put them here. To frame us. Stop us

going to the police."

"I agree. Another attempt to get us to leave him alone."

I needed a minute to think. My heart was going like the clappers, and my throat was dry. I took a deep breath and imagined the call to the police, the cars outside the house, the reporters who would be hot on their heels, and the questions—so many questions. Blair and I were just getting ourselves together, back on track.

Blair was wringing her hands, looking around to see if we were being watched. "This is so dreadful, Scott. What are we going to do?"

I started folding up the clothes. "I don't know, honey. We need to keep it together so we can figure it all out. We need time. To think. Why don't you get a bag and we'll put them away in the garage for a while. These clothes are evidence of Devin's murder, and Mason will not want them finding their way into the hands of the police."

"We should just call the police, shouldn't we? I mean, what about Devin's parents? They'll want to know what happened. Why their boy died."

I was torn. What she was saying was right. Those poor parents. But in front of me was the woman I loved looking tortured and terrified.

I held her face and looked into her eyes. "Do you remember how things were the last time we were front and centre in a murder investigation?"

We let ourselves in through the back door and made a beeline for the back of the garage. Hiding incriminating evidence was a surreal and disturbing experience, and every nerve in my body sparked and fizzed with fear.

Blair opened the chest freezer. "How about in here?"

I shook my head. "First place I'd look."

"Oh god, this is such a bad idea. I really think we should just turn them in and come clean about the burglary."

I opened our cool box and then decided that was also too obvious. "I agree. Honesty is the best policy. But this isn't just about Devin's killer. It's about our family's safety. If we let the police take over, it'll become a manhunt for Mason. You, me, and Leith will be charged with withholding evidence, perverting the course of justice, tampering with evidence, and god knows what else! Any chance we had to uncover answers about our son will be lost, and the media will run amok. We'll be hated and slated and Jamie labelled a monster. We were victims the first time around; this will be something different entirely."

Blair walked over to the corner of the garage and pulled out the freestanding metal shelving unit. Behind it was what looked like a repaired hole. "How about in here?"

I helped Blair move the structure to see the hole more clearly. "How did that happen?"

"It was a few weeks after Jamie died. I often heard him rummaging around in the garage. I don't know what I thought he was doing, but I never asked him—he'd become so resistant to communication. I'd wanted to find anything around the house that might explain why he was killed, so I came in here and started searching. I noticed the scrapes on the floor where the shelves had been moved, so I pulled everything off and looked behind. There was this hole. It was stuffed with cigarettes, bags of weed, and packets of pills. I burnt most of it, just left a half-empty packet of cigarettes and one bag of weed inside, then I showed the police."

"How come I didn't know about this?"

"You did. I told you. You said it was probably there from the previous owners, who had raised three teenagers in this house."

I stood for a minute looking at the hole. "I said that? I guess that does sound like something I would have said. I don't remember seeing the hole."

"You didn't. I patched it up with a plasterboard repair patch and wall filler."

"So I see."

I turned and looked at my wife. Her eyes were wide and wild, and I could see the tears forming.

I took her by the shoulders and held her gaze. "I'm so sorry, Blair. Sorry that I didn't listen to you. Sorry that I didn't pay attention. I understand why you retreated into your head and had to talk to an imaginary Jamie instead. I really am so sorry."

Tears ran down her face. She slid her arms around my chest and cried into my shoulder. "It's okay. You were dealing with it all in your own way. At least you're listening now."

We stood there for a minute wrapped in each other's arms, repairing another broken part of our marriage. The rebuild was always going to be a slow process, but we were making progress, we were sharing. The trust was back. We just had to keep talking and stick together.

"So, how about we release a bit of pent-up aggression and take a hammer and chisel to that hole? Do you still have the patches and filler?"

"I do. They're in the cupboard under the workbench with all the painting stuff."

"Little Miss DIY. I'm impressed. You did a pretty neat job of the filler, too."

"I used one of those flat spatula tools."

Blair collected the tools, patches, and filler from the cupboard. I let her take the first swing at the wall, and half an hour later we'd stuffed the clothes through the hole into the cavity, redistributed the fibreglass insulation to hide the items inside, and resealed the gap with a repair patch. As Blair had done such a good job of plastering over the last patch, I cleared up the mess while she finished off. We pushed back the shelving unit and restacked the shelves to hide the repaired hole. As long as the police didn't come and search our house in the next few days, to give the plaster a chance to dry out and harden, the patched-up hole was the perfect hiding spot.

I tidied away the tools into the cupboard and brushed off my jumper. "I need a shower and a glass of wine."

"Me too. It's been a roller-coaster of a day, and I need to unwind."

As I stood in the shower cubicle, warm water washing away the evidence of our cover-up, I prayed that it was only the tension in Blair's body that would unravel and not her mind or the secret we were keeping about Devin.

TWENTY-NINE

Blair

I COULDN'T SLEEP. Everything had gotten out of hand. We didn't know what we were doing, neither of us wanting to make a decision one way or another about what to do next, and the tussle in my head between what was right and what was wrong was tying my insides in knots.

I nudged Scott with my elbow. "Are you awake?"

"Yeah." He rolled onto his side to face me.

It was dark, and I could only just make out the contours of his face.

I placed my hand on his cheek. "Let's give Mason one more try."

Scott put his hand on mine and started to protest. "No way. He's a loose cannon. It's not worth the risk, BB."

I lifted myself onto my elbow and reached back to switch on the bedside lamp. "Hear me out. Please. We have Devin's clothes, we found Jamie's puzzle box, and we have the necklaces, the shop owner, and Frank. Enough evidence to go to the police and get Mason picked up and charged with something—manslaughter, at least—if he says Devin was a mistake and crimes related to Gunner Piper—stalking, harassment. So, let's confront him with all that and see if we can't force a confession. Both of us, together. Safety in numbers—right?—with our wits about us, prepared for him to get violent."

"I don't know, Blair."

"It's that or straight to the police. I'm not living like this, with these secrets, those clothes stuffed into the wall of our garage, and Mason out there doing awful things, threatening us, knowing what happened to Jamie, and keeping us in the dark."

"Okay, okay." Scott sat up and pulled me into a hug, kissing the top of my head. "We'll go to see if we can get a face-to-face with Mason. I'm in charge. If I say we leave, we leave. If I say call the police, call. Understood?"

"Understood."

We sat for a while, the dawn light starting to peek past the edges of the curtains.

I swallowed, but my throat was dry. "Well, I'm not going to sleep now. I won't sleep till after we've seen Mason or given up and gone to the police."

"Me either. Let's make coffee and head over early. Mason's more likely to be home in the early morning, half-asleep and drowsy."

"I'll do coffee, you shower first, and we can take Minnie out before we go."

We met in the kitchen after gulping coffee, showering, and pulling on our coats and boots. It was a cold, drizzly day, but the chilly droplets focussed my mind as we skirted the pond with Minnie. I was going to be firm and direct with Mason. I would sound like I was in control and unafraid. I wanted to make him think that he was the one with everything to lose.

I sat nervously in the car waiting for Scott to lock up the house and garage. I hadn't slept a wink, my mind was all over the place, my hands were clammy, and my foot had taken to tapping vigorously against the footwell.

"Ready?" Scott asked as he slid into the driver's seat. "Let's see if we can make a bargain with the devil in exchange for the truth."

"Just go."

Scott put a hand on my thigh. "You don't have to do this if you don't want to."

"I'm not backing out now."

We sat quietly as we drove across town, the tension in the car palpable. Scott pulled into a space on the side of the road just around the corner from Creekside Lane. "What number was it?"

"Thirty-four."

I stepped out of the car and looked up and down the road. It was empty. I bent down and ducked my head back into the car. "Come on then."

"I'm just putting on my voice recorder and hiding it in my pocket."

Pushing my hands into the pockets of my pale-green zip hoodie, I followed Scott around the corner to 34 Creekside Lane. My heart was missing beats and flipping out, and we weren't even halfway up the road. An elderly neighbour appeared in his doorway a few houses down and nodded to us. I nodded back, realising that if anything happened, he had our descriptions. I knew then that our final destination today would be the police station, with or without knowing what really happened to our son.

Scott rapped the knocker. We gripped tight to each other's hands. There was rustling from behind the door, then the latch clicked and it swung open.

Suzannah stood in the entrance looking flushed and sweaty. "Oh, it's you. Um…"

Scott took the lead. "We need to talk to Mason right now."

Suzannah pushed some damp hair off her forehead. "Sorry, what's going on? He won't talk to you, and I don't think you should be here."

She tried to shut the door, but Scott jammed his foot in the way. "Either we talk to Mason or we go straight to the police with evidence that proves he has something to do with the death of Devin…"

"Shhh." Suzannah pulled open the door and ushered us inside. "You can't go making those sorts of accusations on my doorstep. Devin lived four doors down. The neighbours would stone my son in the street if they thought he had anything to do with that sweet boy's death."

Suzannah rushed along the corridor, glancing up the staircase as she shepherded us through the kitchen to a small, square garden with neat, flower-laden borders. Beside a small metal table were three matching chairs, all painted a glossy amethyst.

She pointed to the chairs. "Sit down. I'll see if I can get Mason down here and I'll bring tea. Do you want milk and sugar?"

Scott and I looked at each other. "Yes, please," we said in unison, although tea was the last thing I wanted right now.

It was all so surreal sitting in Suzannah's garden having

just threatened to go to the police and accuse her son of murder. God knows what was going through her head right now. Maybe she was giving Mason the heads-up and telling him to run. Maybe she had no intention of getting him and thought she could appease us and send us away. I could feel my nerves building and decided that a hit of sugar would help me focus.

Scott sat in the far seat facing the house. His eyes darted from one window to another, always flitting back to the open sliding door. At the end of the lawn was a small shed, painted in a bright sea blue, and a bench in the corner, painted yellow. Scattered among the flowerbeds were decorative butterflies and ladybirds on metal stakes. Along the fence hung a string of jam jar lights. It was an attractive space that felt loved and appreciated. A space that I imagined Suzannah spent a lot of time in.

Looking back at the house, I saw two upstairs windows, one small with obscured glass, which had to be the bathroom, and another with a black blind, half-open. Downstairs, the sliding patio doors led into the breakfast room, and there was a large window above the kitchen sink. There wasn't a blade of grass out of place or a single smear on any of the windows. I loved seeing spaces so full of character and charm, spaces where people had expressed themselves, and I loved colour. In different circumstances, I imagined that Suzannah and I could spend hours talking about and shopping for quirky and vibrant home furnishings, redesigning rooms, and letting our imaginations run riot.

She appeared with two mugs of tea and a plate of biscuits. "You okay out here? Is it warm enough?"

I took one of the mugs from Suzannah and sipped the hot, sweet liquid. Scott took the other and placed it on the table. "Is Mason coming?"

Suzannah smiled awkwardly. "He didn't come home last night. I've no idea where he goes. Maybe he'll be home later."

Scott got to his feet and marched through the open doorway. "MASON! MASON!"

Suzannah stood up. "That won't do any good. This isn't right. I think you should both leave. If you've had any incriminating evidence on my son then I don't know why you haven't already taken it to the police."

I was about to answer when Scott walked back outside. "Because we think your son was involved with Gunner Piper and knows something about our son's death. We want to give him a chance to tell us what happened to Jamie and thought we might come to some deal with the evidence we have."

Suzannah broke down, falling into one of the chairs and burying her face in her hands. "Please, don't do this. He's all I've got. Please. I'll have nothing left. I beg you, I can't watch him go to prison. If you leave, I'll make him tell me what you want to know. I'll get it out of him, and then I'll tell you."

We weren't about to go home and wait to see if Mason came clean to his mother. "Scott and I found something of Jamie's a few weeks ago. It was hidden in his bedroom. A box with a notebook and photographs inside."

Scott came and stood beside me and rested a hand on my

shoulder.

Suzannah looked up. "I tore myself apart with questions about how my little girl ended up in that log pile. After Lily died, Mason seemed lighter, happier. Then Breck left—he was Lily's real dad—and Mason started to come out of his shell, make friends at school, and became more independent. Instead of sadness, her death seemed to give him strength, and it made me feel afraid. For weeks after Lily died, Mason had a haunted look in his eyes. I know this sounds terrible, but I thought that he killed Lily. I talked to Breck about it, and he went storming off to the station. I didn't think Mason had killed her on purpose; I figured maybe they'd had a row or he was too heavy-handed with her."

A siren was going off in my head—a silent, deafening siren. I gulped some sweet tea, trying to stay focussed. "Did you confront Mason about it?"

"He was nine. Nine! How could I suggest such a thing to a nine-year-old—his own mother accusing him of killing his sister even though I did think it was by mistake? No, I couldn't ask him about it. If I was wrong, I would have done so much damage to our relationship. Besides, what if it *was* his fault? Then what? I didn't want him to be taken away from me. So, I buried it."

I sat dumbfounded, unable to process the information. Suzannah had just told me that she thought her son killed her daughter. His own sister? Suzannah took another biscuit, her hand quivering.

Scott tightened his hold on my shoulder. "Why are you telling us all this?"

"I know Mason. He's bad news. He's my son and I love

him, but he's not like other kids. Never has been. Your son hung around with him, and that means your son wasn't like other kids either. Neither of us knew our boys were friends because they kept their friendship secret, so something was going on with them, and I doubt it was something good. It was only a matter of time before somebody came knocking at my door with accusations about Mason."

I couldn't believe what I was hearing. I hadn't expected this and was thrown.

Scott shook his head. "No. Don't you dare tar our son with the same brush as yours. Mason dragged Jamie into something, and it's our boy who was dug up with all those others, not yours."

Suzannah stared out into the garden. "Mason was an angry boy. No dad, a stepdad he couldn't connect with, struggling to fit in at school. Lily was sweet and kind and adored. I don't believe Mason killed her deliberately, but he could be rough with her. He took out some of his negative feelings on her. She was an easy target, and she doted on him, always forgiving him when he hurt her or frightened her. I should have got him some help, some counselling. Breck was always going on and on about it. I thought Mason would grow out of it; I hoped the anger and jealousy and aggression would pass."

She sighed and then looked directly at me and Scott. "It takes courage to really see your own children. To see them for exactly what they are in the eyes of the world. At first, I made excuses for him, but after a while, I began to see the troubled, disaffected boy he was. Unpredictable, lacking empathy. His stepfather saw it, but not me. I have to take some of the blame. After all, he was just a child."

My stomach felt empty, my head light, and I began to think that coming here was a bad idea.

"So," Suzannah said, "tell me about that box."

I reached up for Scott's hand, his fingers digging too hard into my skin. "There were photographs of the boys who Gunner Piper killed and information about each boy."

Suzannah stiffened, her fingers tightening around her mug. "What kind of information?"

"Their names and ages. Specific details about clothing, their murders, the mutilations. Disturbing details."

Suzannah ran her hand through her hair, sections of her neat bob sticking out at right angles from her head. "I'm guessing you haven't shown any of this to the police?"

"No. You know firsthand how that goes. How they twist things, how they make them seem. Not to mention the press, relentless and unforgiving. Mason has been hanging around our house for months. We've seen him by the gate or in the park; our neighbour has noticed him a few times. He's also in some of the photographs, and Scott and I saw him yesterday at the market."

Suzannah glanced up at the window with the blind. I followed her gaze. The blind was pulled all the way down. She got to her feet. "I can't force Mason to do anything, and I know I can't keep ignoring what is going on with him. You go to the police. It's the right thing."

She got up and headed toward the door.

I stood up and caught hold of her arm. "Please let me talk to him. I need to find out what he knows. I need to know about my son."

Suzannah turned to face me, a look of pity in her eyes. "You think that knowing the truth will set you free. It won't. The truth will only make things worse."

I held tight to Suzannah's arm. "Mason tried to warn me off talking to you. Slashed our bike tyres. I remember seeing him once when Jamie was alive. I followed my son to the ruins. Mason was there. Our sons met one of the other victims. It was Jordan's blue jacket that first jogged my memory when it was plastered all over the news, torn and covered in dirt. Jordan was the boy at the ruins. The boy who was killed before Jamie. He went missing months before Jamie did."

Suzannah pulled away from me and hurried back into the house. "You have to leave. I need you to leave. Now."

I stopped in the kitchen, gripping the worktop with one hand.

Scott came in behind me and pulled me into him. "You know something, Suzannah. What? How was Mason involved in all this?"

Suzannah whipped her head around. "I don't know anything. I suspected, that's all. I followed Mason a few times. Just like you followed your son. I just wanted to know where he was going. I thought it might be about Lily. Maybe he was visiting her grave or going to the woods where she died. I followed him to your house and saw him with your son. Mason and I drifted on like that for years, in silence, keeping secrets, my suspicions brewing. Then all those boys were dug up in Peasedale. So far away, but your son was one of them, and I knew then that Mason was involved in some way. Mason became even angrier and more withdrawn. When that boy Devin was found in the river, Mason disappeared for a few days. I don't know what to think, but none of it is good."

I held tight to Scott as tears began to stream down my cheeks. "I want to talk to Mason. I want to know what happened to Jamie. I want to know if they were helping Gunner. I want to know why my son would do that. Jamie wasn't an evil boy. He was a good boy, a kind boy."

Heavy footsteps clunked on the stairs, and Suzannah whipped her head round toward the doorway into the hall. "Please, you've got to leave."

My body went rigid as Mason appeared in the doorway leading from the hall. I tried to pull air into my lungs, but it felt as if I was inhaling treacle. I felt lightheaded, hot, unsteady. Mason was a tall, skinny teenager. Without the hood, he looked fragile and pale, almost ghostly, a look of panic in his eyes.

"Hi," Mason said, seemingly not a spark of recognition. "You're Blair and Scott, huh?"

Scott pushed me behind him, and I could feel his whole body shaking. I felt as if I'd been struck in the stomach with a mallet. My free hand balled into a fist as I hung on to my sanity with all my strength, my thoughts turning loop the loops in my head. The tension in the room felt like a vice squeezing the air out of me.

Suzannah waved a hand at Mason. "Could you go upstairs for a bit? I'm just seeing them out."

Mason stood firm, staring at me. "He looked like you. Jamie. With all that red curly hair."

Scott stood tall, puffing out his chest. "Did you murder

your sister and lure all those boys for Gunner? Did you drag my son into it all? And Devin? Did you kill him, too, when he didn't get you the box? I'm going to call the police. Tell them everything."

"Shut up!" Mason shouted. "Shut the fuck up!"

Suzannah spun round to face her son. "Mason!"

"Don't listen to them, Mum."

My body was on fire, every nerve ending sparking and fizzing. My heart pounded in my ears. Mason lunged at the worktop and snatched a serrated kitchen knife from the magnetic rack by the hob. He held it out in front of him.

"Oh my god, Mason, what are you doing? Put that down." Suzannah reached out for the knife, but the boy sliced the air in front of her, and she stumbled backward.

I stepped back to get nearer to the kitchen table, reaching out for the back of a chair, pulling Scott back by his jumper. "You need to tell the truth, Mason, to your mum and to the police."

Mason jabbed the knife in our direction. "Shut up."

Scott held his hands up in front of him. "Are you the reason Jamie was murdered?"

Mason took a step forward, his arm straight out in front of him, the blade directed at Scott. "He was my friend. It wasn't my fault. It was Gunner's fault." He brandished the knife again.

Suzannah held her hand out in front of her, palm up. "Give me the knife, sweetheart, and we can talk. No one is going to call the police."

"Don't lie, Mum. I heard you tell them to go to the police. *I heard you.*"

Mason lunged forward.

Scott stepped toward him, his arms outstretched, shielding me.

Suzannah dived sideways toward her son, knocking Scott out of the path of the blade.

Mason's fist thumped against his mother's chest.

"No!" I grabbed Scott's arm, pulling it down so that I could see Suzannah.

The scene seemed to run in slow motion. Suzannah teetered for a second, staring at Mason. He stood statuesque, his arm straight out in front of him as if it was glued to his mother's ribs. Suzannah lurched sideways. I reached out for her as she sank backward, the knife sticking out of her body, the handle slipping out of Mason's hand as his mother fell.

Suzannah was heavy in my arms, and my legs gave way under the weight. We both dropped to the floor. I felt numb as I pressed my hand against the part of Suzannah's chest that was oozing blood. I looked up at Mason.

His eyes were wide, mouth agape. "I'm sorry. I didn't mean it. I'm sorry, Mum. I'm so sorry." He ran.

For a moment, I just knelt on the floor staring at the open patio doors. Mason had left a bloody handprint on one of the glass panes.

Suzannah moaned. "It hurts."

Blood was pooling on her stomach, soaking her shirt, dribbling to the floor. I pressed harder. Suzannah's head was tilted toward me, eyes open, holding my gaze. There was so much blood.

THIRTY

Scott

"BLAIR, ARE YOU okay?"

"Yes, I'm okay." Her voice was thin and high-pitched.

The scene before me was surreal. My wife was kneeling on the kitchen floor cradling Suzannah. A pool of blood had collected around Suzannah's torso, and Blair's hand was jammed against her side, soaked in blood.

I pulled my mobile out of my back pocket and dialled emergency services, garbled the address, and asked them to hurry. Then I knelt beside Blair and put my hands over hers to help stem the flow of blood from Suzannah's wound.

I looked down at Suzannah. "The ambulance is coming. You're going to be alright." I had no idea if that was true.

Blair and I were side by side, hovering over Suzannah, both focussed on trying to keep her blood in her body. We weren't winning. The blood was oozing through our fingers.

Our fingers were slipping, our hands inadequate for the task. "Find me a tea towel. Slip your hands out from under mine. I've got it from here."

Blair carefully slid her hands away and brought me a tea towel. I pressed it against the wound and continued to apply pressure. Suzannah was still conscious. I did my best to hold her together, smiling to reassure her even though inside I was screaming. For a moment, her face changed, and I saw Jamie lying before me, covered in blood, his eyes pleading, desperate. No one was there to hold him together, stop the blood from leaking from his body, tell him he would be okay. The only person there was the man who killed him, smiling as his life slipped away. I pressed harder on Suzannah's wound, determined to slow the bleeding.

I heard the faint sound of an ambulance siren.

Suzannah slid her hand on top of mine. "Find...my boy. Don't let him...do anything foolish. If you hadn't...come, this never would...have happened. Please. Help him. I followed Mason...to the station. The day before...your son died. I saw him...with other boys...too. Always ending up...at the station."

I looked at Blair.

She took a deep breath and pushed down onto the tea towel, nudging me out of the way. "Don't go. Don't you dare."

I looked down at Suzannah. "Hang in there."

She smiled at me. "Tell him...I love him."

The siren was getting louder. I ran out of the patio doors, through the back gate, and out onto the road.

I heard Blair in the background. *"Scott! No!"*

I was bigger and stronger than Mason. I could handle him. He was running scared, and I wasn't about to let him disappear or do himself harm. He was going to answer for what he'd done. All of it.

I could hear the ambulance screeching around the corner. I dashed across the street and off toward the park. The train station was a short distance beyond the green. I took it at a steady pace. Running out of steam after a two-minute sprint would waste more time than it saved. I jogged around the pond, out to the far side of the park, and along the pavements to the train station.

A train was pulling away as I arrived, and I prayed that I wasn't too late. I looked around the platform and then watched the entrance. This was my chance to find out what really happened to my son, find out what it was Jamie was doing that led to his death. The police explanation of "wrong place, wrong time' wasn't good enough. Jamie was not in the wrong place at the wrong time. He was not a victim of hapless circumstance, the unlucky boy a serial killer chose to follow on that particular day. No. He was involved. He'd gotten himself tangled up in something he couldn't get out of. I was going to beat the truth out of Mason if I had to and then hand him to the police myself.

Being so close to finding the answers was almost overwhelming. My heart was pounding, my head was about to explode, and my skin felt like a thousand ants were crawling over it. I perched on the edge of a station bench like a lizard on a desert dune, unable to keep my body parts still, shifting my weight, standing and sitting every time someone new appeared on the platform. The wait was agonising; minutes dragged, seconds seemed to repeat themselves. I'm sure that at one point the station clock started ticking backward. I'd missed him. Must have. Unless he was waiting for a specific train, but why would he do that when he was trying to get away?

Sweat was engulfing me, and I was covered in Suzannah's

blood, making me look less customer, more crazed axe murderer, and as trains came and went, so did the sideways glances from the steady flow of passengers. I needed a drink, something to wet my throat, which was now so dry that the insides of my cheeks were receding and my tongue had welded itself to the roof of my mouth. Where the hell was he? Did he see me and decide to take off?

I stood up, ready to head back to the park, when Mason walked casually onto the platform. The hood was pulled over his face, far enough to cast a shadow hiding his features, but the basic outline of a head, its angular bony protrusions, and some flecks of dark hair could be seen.

A train pulled into the station. The door opened, and people shuffled off. Mason was walking toward the train, toward me. My body froze. I wanted to rush at him, throw punches, yell and kick and shake him, but by the time my body was ready to respond to my brain, my target peeled back his hood and smiled at me.

I swallowed hard, the droplet of spittle that I managed to squeeze from my glands only serving as a glue to fix my mouth firmly shut. He looked like his mother. Same face and body structure, wide blue eyes, small straight features, a slim and willowy frame. The only difference was his black hair. He stopped a few feet in front of me, shoved his hands into his pockets, and stared at the floor, kicking a discarded takeaway coffee cup with his left foot.

"You've been waiting for me, huh?" he said. "Thought so."

His voice was steady, emotionless. He lifted his eyes to meet mine. His steely gaze matched his voice; so did his conceited expression. It made my stomach flip about. People jostled past us, rushing for the train.

The boy shrugged. "I'll take you somewhere if you'd like."

I should have grabbed him, wrestled him to the floor, and called 999, but I wanted to see whatever it was he wanted to show me.

"Sure."

He wanted to show me something, and I was not about to decline the chance to find answers to my son's death. I had so many questions. Mason could be violent; I'd seen what he had done to his own mother. But I was bigger, broader, than him. He didn't intimidate me. I was too angry to be afraid, and up close, Mason looked like a lost, lonely young man, one who was in an awful lot of trouble.

He shuffled from foot to foot. "Gotta take this one."

The Tannoy announced the train's destinations. The final stop was Peasedale. In that moment, everything made sense. Gunner Piper killed the boys in his shack deep in Peasedale Forest. None of the boys were from Peasedale, but they were all from towns along the train lines that ran through Peasedale. Gunner didn't pick up the boys and coax them into a vehicle. He waited for them to come to him. With Mason. No one had joined the dots between the boys and their hometowns. No one had connected the stations with the murders. Why would they? The other boys were dug up. All the evidence the police needed to confirm that Gunner murdered the boys was in that shack and in those woods, and Gunner was behind bars. The police had no incentive to go searching for an accomplice; it was the press that conjured up that story, a work of fiction driven by desperate parents and anonymous individuals inciting hate on social media platforms.

Mason walked past me, knocking into my shoulder. He boarded the train. I followed, standing by the door, clinging to the rail with both hands, my eyes fixed on him as the train pulled away. We were there, locked together in this strange union, the atmosphere electric as the train stopped and started to let passengers on and off. For two hours, Mason sat in a seat by the window looking out at the world rushing past as if he didn't have a care in the world. I stood, rooted to the spot, my hands welded to the rail, wondering what was next. I should have called the police, let them handle this, but I wanted to hear the truth from Mason myself before officers and lawyers and prison got in the way. I didn't listen to Blair, and I didn't ask Jamie enough about his life. Now I wanted to know what I had missed, what I hadn't seen, who my boy really was, and deep down, I wanted Mason to tell me that Jamie was good, that he wasn't involved with Gunner's crimes, that my son was innocent.

I paid little attention to the people on the train. Several times, I was jostled by passengers disembarking or pushing their way through to the seats, all the while keeping my eyes fixed on Mason as I tried to figure out what was going on, where he was taking me, and what revelations he would share with me. It felt like I was running a marathon, the finish line in sight, unsure if I had what it took to make it to the end. Sweat was dampening my T-shirt, but I dared not remove my sweater, fearing that Mason would disappear if I didn't keep watching him. He didn't look in my direction once.

When we reached Peasedale, Mason casually departed the train, strolling past me as if I was invisible, exiting the far end of the platform via a break in the fence. It was the first time in my life I had taken a train ride without purchasing a ticket. I stumbled along behind Mason like a zombie. I had no idea where he was taking me, but I didn't care; wherever we ended up, I needed to know what he knew.

He led me through thick, gorse-ridden undergrowth that grew to shoulder height, alongside a moss-slicked stream, and then deep into untamed woodland. We were in an area of secluded wasteland, dense and dark, only the distant sound of trains breaking the silence. The thick dark canopy of tangled bare branches blocked the daylight, leaving brambles, ferns, fungi, and moss to thrive.

Mason stopped beside a makeshift den, something a child would erect from fallen branches and twigs. As I approached, I sensed that what waited inside would be of no comfort to me and would bring me no peace. The tepee-style hideout was cramped; I had to crouch to get through the opening to the interior. There was a stump for a stool, a small stone circle with charred sticks and ashes inside, and remnants of cigarette packets and butts, beer cans, and food packaging—a teenager's haunt.

Photographs were pinned to the trunk of the tree. Of kids hanging out. Mostly headshots. Some of the faces were familiar. Hanging from the sticks that lined the interior from differing lengths of string were a variety of personal effects: watches, a ring, key rings, shoelaces, a belt, a tie, phone cases. All meticulously hung. All in differing states of damage and decay. Some stained with what could be old, dried blood. I recognised the items. Pictures of them under the photographs of the boys were stuck to my office wall. I saw Seb's football phone case.

Then I caught sight of Jamie's necklace, the gem in the circle of the axe glinting at me from the back of the den. I reached for it, my hand shaking, and pulled it from the line, the branch it was attached to snapping as it came loose. I tucked it into my pocket, not because I wanted to keep it but because I wanted Blair to see it. I wanted to give her the chance to decide what to do with it. After all, she'd conjured the pendant in her hallucinations, and it was the pendant that led us to Mason.

The hideout had a distinctive stench, a reek that will stay with me forever. An odour so pungent, so gross, that the very thought of it makes me retch. My body convulsed, and I swallowed back the bile that burned my throat.

"I kept something from each boy Gunner killed. In a box under my bed. Made this place after all the bodies were dug up. Like a memorial. I can tell you who they all come from, which items from which boys if you'd like." Mason tapped Jordan's mini-torch key ring to make it swing to and fro on its wire. He was like a child in a crib, a grin stretching across his face as his souvenir moved, swatting more of the hanging articles until the whole den seemed to sway. But he wasn't taunting me; he didn't look for my reaction. He just kept flicking his morbid mobile and smirking.

"Stop it!" I shouted. *"Stop it!"*

This young man was eighteen, yet he behaved like a surly preteen, with a disconnect in his eyes that disturbed me.

"What is this? What the fuck is all of this?" I said, crawling out of the den.

"A secret," Mason called out from inside. "My secret."

"Not anymore."

"You won't say anything," Mason said as he emerged, brushing away the dead leaves and twigs that were stuck to his clothes.

Bent double, with my hands on my knees, I lifted my head to look at him. His face was taut, his expression scrunched like a jack-in-the-box ready to pop.

I shook my head. "I won't."

I knew only too well how this would play out in the media, how we would be dragged through the mud, how this boy could turn my son into something vile in the world's eyes, his words holding more weight than a book of notes and hidden photographs, evidence that could so easily be interpreted in more than one way.

Mason perched on a log, snapping a branch into pieces. "He was my mate, your Jamie. We were friends."

I let my body sink to the ground and leant back against a tree. All I could do was listen.

"At least, that's what I thought. He told me about you being a reporter for a big newspaper. I told him about the boys I took to Gunner and said they were scary stories that I made up for fun to scare the kids at school. Jamie said he was making notes about the stories in some notebook like a detective. It was like a stupid game. He had no idea it was real, just thought I used the names and details of some of the boys we met to make it more exciting. Said he hid the notes in some poncey box. After all the bodies were dug up, I got scared of what was in those notes, so I sent Devin to go get the box. I figured he was smaller than me—he could get in through the window—and if he was caught, I told him to lie, say he was just tryin' his luck."

Mason sat opposite me, flicking dirt and poking at dead leaves with a piece of his twig.

"How did you know Gunner Piper?" I asked. "How did you ever get involved in this?"

Mason sucked in air through his teeth and then let out a big breath. "Guess I've nothing to lose telling you. Mum has suspected something ever since Lily died. I was playing in the woods with her, Lily. Climbing trees. We were way up high in this really big tree. Her foot slipped and she fell—hit her head on a branch as she went down. Her body was all crumpled on the ground. I climbed down, shook her, and shouted for help. She didn't move. I cried and called for Mum. No one came. It felt like I was screaming and crying for ages. Then Gunner appeared. He felt her neck. Looked at me. Said she was dead. He told me that everyone would blame me. He said I'd be taken away and put into care. I nearly shit my pants I was so scared. I didn't want to be taken away from Mum. I was nine, for fuck's sake, and I believed everything he told me. Gunner said he'd help me if I kept it a secret. Sent me off to find Mum and tell her that I'd lost Lily. He said that everything would be alright."

"So, you didn't kill your sister?"

Mason was quiet for a second or two. "Police thought it was my stepdad at first. He loved Lily so much. He never would have hurt her. When they didn't find anyone to blame, some of the older kids at school started saying I did it. I hated those kids."

"That explains what happened to Lily if it's the truth, but it doesn't explain how you ended up helping Gunner."

"I didn't think I'd see him again after that. I didn't for two years. When I was eleven, he started turning up on my way back from school. Driving me around in his truck. Giving me stuff: money, sweets, fags. He said as long as I was his secret friend, he'd keep quiet about Lily. Mum got used to my staying out late after school. Thought I was hanging out with new friends. Then Gunner started taking me to the cabin. He had a room I wasn't allowed inside. One day, he left me there alone, and I looked inside the room. There was a cage and a boy inside. Said his name was Seb. The room stank. Seb was naked, skinny. He looked bad. He wanted my help. Begged and cried. I was petrified. I panicked and shut the door, figuring I'd wait till I got home and then call the police, but Gunner came back and he could tell something was wrong. Seb was screaming for help. I thought Gunner was going to kill me, but he didn't. He killed Seb instead. Right in front of me. Then he made me bury the body. I knew I couldn't tell Mum, couldn't tell anyone, or I'd be next. He told me I had to make friends with other boys, dropping me off in different places with my pockets crammed full of stuff to give away. Once or twice a year, he'd tell me to bring a friend to the cabin. That was the deal; that's what I had to do to keep my secret about Lily and to stay alive."

I pushed sweat-soaked hair off my face and leant my head back against the bark of the tree. "You never told anyone?"

"I knew he'd do it to me if I did. I begged him to kill me

once. I couldn't take it anymore. He threatened to go to the police about Lily, said he'd hurt Mum, and then he beat me. Dunno how I got home; I was in such a mess. Told Mum I got into a fight at school and didn't want any fuss. She wanted to go down there and give the headmaster hell, but I said it would only make things worse for me. I pleaded with her to leave it alone, and we never spoke about it again."

My heart was leaping, no rhythm to its beat, just thumping away in my chest in response to my sporadic breathing. I was listening to the confession of a serial killer's accomplice, and I felt sorry for him. This eighteen-year-old young man lured my son to his death, and I felt fucking sorry for him. My pity made my head spin.

"And Jamie? Was he just another boy you lured to his death?"

"I'll show you. Come on."

I followed Mason along an overgrown track with a rusty wire fence that ran along both sides until it opened out onto a service station car park. I recognised it. I remembered seeing it on the news, police vehicles and news crews like a swarm of angry bees moving in and out of the tree line. I knew where Mason was taking me. We snaked our way through a dense, remorseless forest to the site of Gunner Piper's disgusting crimes. To the place where my son took his last breath. We could have been walking for an hour or a minute. Trudging through the thick forest in silence, the only soundtrack to our journey was the rustle of leaves from the canopy above and the snap of twigs underfoot. I kept my eyes on Mason, the black hood of his sweatshirt pulled up, his jeans hanging loosely around his hips, worn trainers grey with muck.

I wondered if they were the trainers he was wearing when he drowned Devin.

THIRTY-ONE

Blair

THE FLOW OF blood had begun to slow. The pool of red liquid that had seeped along the seams between the tiles and Suzannah's soaked shirt were giving off a sweet metallic scent. I heard the police and ambulance sirens loud and clear as they pulled up outside number thirty-four.

I let loose a little of the tension that was gripping my body and allowed myself to take a deep breath. "They're here, Suzannah. Not long now. You're going to be okay."

"Thank you." Suzannah's breathing was shallow, her lips tinged with blue around the edges.

"I'll come to the hospital. Wait till you're out of surgery. Call your family." I wondered whether Scott had found Mason.

"No." Suzannah winced as I took a big breath. "I'll be okay. My parents will come. You should be there for Scott."

The police appeared first, securing the area, making sure that Mason was not in the house. I knelt patiently beside Suzannah until the paramedics took over. Before I was put in a police car and taken to the station, I was asked for a description of Mason. The police had sent out their APBs, telling other officers to be on the lookout for a dangerous criminal or missing person. The police apparatus was whirring, and it would only be a matter of time before they caught up with Scott and Mason.

At the station, I gave my details and a statement to the police and surrendered my clothes as evidence. Officer Shah was on duty, and she took charge of me. She helped me wash up a bit, took me to a quiet room, found me fresh clothes, and bought me a coffee. I couldn't stop shaking, my thoughts flashing between the blood and Mason's face. I said as little as I could. Nothing about Gunner Piper. I briefly explained how I met Suzannah, that I found out Mason was a friend of Jamie's by following the necklace trail, and that I had asked the shop owner for his address. I told them I'd met Suzannah and we'd talked about Lily and Jamie, made a connection, and shared a little of our grief. I offered no explanation for Mason's violent outburst. I was vague, unclear, giving them as little as I could. Finally, Officer Shah drove me home.

I knew that she would be back. That the police would have more questions. That Scott and I would have to give them more answers. I hadn't mentioned that Scott was at the house, but at some point, I would have to explain why I'd kept quiet, why I hadn't shared with the police where he had gone, where Suzannah had sent him to look for Mason. I closed the door of the police car and smiled at Officer Shah. She waited for me to open the gate and walk up the drive, and I didn't look back when I heard the patrol car drive away.

The wind whipped about the drive, whistling, rustling the branches on the hedge that enclosed our driveway, stirring up the fallen leaves and twigs that were strewn across the gravel. I opened my front door and was met by a frenetic Minnie, the noise of the wind whipping around the garden unsettling her. The trousers and T-shirt the police had given me had stuck to my skin. There was dried blood under my fingernails. I glanced at my reflection in the hallway mirror. A smear of blood streaked my forehead, some hair stuck to it. I was pale, with a haunted look in my eyes, and I smelled of blood and sweat.

It had all happened so fast. Incomprehensibly fast. How could something so violent happen so unexpectedly? It felt like a nightmare, one I couldn't fully wake up from. I could picture Mason in the kitchen and recalled the knife, how he wielded it with false bravado. I could hear Suzannah's voice shouting her son's name. But when the blade sank into Suzannah's chest? That bit was gone. I couldn't remember it. Suzannah fell, and then there was blood. Scott was there, then he was gone.

I couldn't tell the police which way Mason ran. I couldn't tell them whether he stabbed his mother or whether Suzannah got in the way as he tried to stab me. I couldn't tell them whether *any* stabbing occurred because one minute Suzannah was standing up trying to reason with Mason and the next minute she was in my arms fighting for her life.

I couldn't get the image of Suzannah's body out of my head—her body covered in blood, sprawled out on the kitchen floor. I couldn't shake the uneasy feeling of that weird silence as we waited for the ambulance, my hands pressed against the tea towel, blood trickling out of Suzannah and onto the clean white tiles.

Minnie started sniffing and licking my hands.

I pushed her muzzle away. "Leave it, Minnie."

I padded into the kitchen and took a bin bag from under the sink and carried it with me upstairs into the bathroom. I stood inside the bin bag to wriggle off the trousers and my underwear, revealing clammy, red-stained skin. As I stepped into the shower, I decided that the towels and bath mat would have to be thrown away, too. I didn't want to keep anything that would remind me of this day.

The warm water ran scarlet as I washed Suzannah's blood from my body. I slumped down in the tub and sobbed. I didn't even know who I was crying for. Suzannah, of course. Jamie, no question. But mostly, the tears were for me, for the awfulness of everything, for the agony in my heart. I wanted to be sucked down the drain to disappear with all my pain.

After scrubbing myself clean several times, I pulled on fresh clothes and wandered back downstairs, carrying the bin bag through the kitchen and utility to the outside bin. As I was about to drop the bag into the bin, I heard something buzzing inside. My phone. I hadn't let go of it after Scott left. I must have dropped it into the bag as I got undressed upstairs.

I fumbled around for the handset and watched Scott's name flash on the screen then disappear. I tried calling back, but the phone went straight to voice mail. A voice message alert pinged up on the screen, so I played the message. Scott had found Mason, and they were going to The Shack. Mason had something to show him.

The Shack. That dilapidated hunting cabin deep in Peasedale Forest where Gunner Piper had taken the boys and then buried their bodies in deep graves, deep enough to evade the noses of curious wildlife. Except Jamie's body. He had been buried in a hurry. His grave was shallow. Easy for the police to spot. For the dogs to sniff out. My son's body had only been in the ground for a matter of hours. The earth was still damp with his blood. The smell of him was still tangy and pungent, unlike the musty, putrid stench of the other boys. I couldn't understand why the police hadn't destroyed The Shack. Instead, they had left it standing, strewn with police tape, ripe for ghoulish souvenir hunters to plunder. They offered excuses about a lack of resources, the fire risk in a forest, and the remote location making it difficult to get any sizeable equipment to it. They decided it was so dilapidated that it would soon fall apart and be swallowed by nature.

I couldn't just sit at home and wait for Scott. Couldn't drink tea and tap my fingers on the kitchen counter, wondering what was happening, what Mason was saying about my boy, worrying for my husband's safety. Scott and I were a team. We needed each other. I made a tall travel mug of sweet strong coffee, pulled on my coat and walking boots, and bundled Minnie into the car.

"Let's go find Scott, shall we?"

Minnie sat patiently on the back seat, her nose pressed to the window, as I sped along the motorway, sipping my coffee to keep focussed. The drive took only two and a half hours, and I hadn't paid any attention to the three cameras that flashed as I drove at a speed far beyond the legal limit, my thoughts flitting between Suzannah, Mason, and The Shack.

I had seen the ramshackle shack before, briefly, and I never wanted to go back. I didn't want to see the place where my son's life was so cruelly taken. Scott hadn't either. The police had collected their evidence, taken their photographs, and eventually, The Shack had been cleared out and left to rot. Pictures were in the media, and other people went to see it. Curious people.

The Shack was hidden deep within the one hundred and nine square miles of Peasedale Forest. There was no way I could remember how to find it. But, I had seen a map of its location on the news once when they pointed out a service station on the edge of town, a pylon, and a valley with a steep drop to a shallow stream. There was always the friend locator app on my phone that I could use to find Scott, too.

The service station sat neatly to the left of the road just beyond the Peasedale sign. I pulled into the garage and parked the car in a bay nearest the forest, the dense woodland creating a foreboding backdrop to the town.

The afternoon was ticking on, the daylight beginning to fade. I checked Scott's location on my phone, clocked the full battery, and tested the torch. The map showed my husband about a fifty-minute walk through the woods. How hard could it be? I'd be with him before it got dark.

Opening the passenger door, I let Minnie out, scooping up her lead and hanging it across my shoulders. A glance back at the garage and off I strode. After ten minutes, I spotted the pylon looming above me, its apex just visible above the canopy. I stepped into the clearing surrounding the pylon and looked along the line of cables to the next pylon before checking the map on my phone again. Scott was in the same place. He and Mason must be at The Shack. Still a forty-minute walk.

Minnie had spent the first couple of minutes of the walk racing through the trees at breakneck speed, leaping over fallen branches and dodging the trunks as if she were on an agility course time trial. Her burst of energy was fleeting, the weight of her huge frame quickly slowing her down and making her pant. Slotting in beside me, she continued the walk protectively by my side.

I had changed into loose trousers and a thin, short-sleeved shirt. I had pulled on walking boots and a light puffer coat as I left the house but had not considered the terrain in the forest. I wasn't expecting brambles and unruly bushes and vegetation with skin-lacerating barbs. Even Minnie, covered in hair and excited to be outside, whimpered her way through sections of thorny overgrown briar. Prickly, creepy-crawly, dense, and dark woodland was as far from my comfort zone as I could get.

The sun fell faster than I had expected, and the thick canopy overhead stole the last of the light. My stomach knotted up as I flicked on my phone torch.

I frequently checked the ground for signs of a person, hoping for some indication that Scott and Mason had also taken this route, although what exact signs of a person would be, I had no idea. The ground was too dry and scattered with leaves and twigs and moss for footprints, and if the undergrowth had been disturbed by feet, I had no clue how to recognise it.

It was a funny thing searching for someone in the thick of a forest. I started off full of enthusiasm and hope, but very quickly that hope turned to disappointment and despair. Walking silently. Looking around. Not seeing anything familiar. A heavy feeling settled in my body. What had I been thinking, heading into a forest alone, unsure of my destination, not a single person aware of my location? A bird fluttered from the canopy above, and Minnie barked into the blackness.

I could be here for days and never find my husband. Swiping my phone screen, the map with Scott's location flashed.

"Minnie. Come on, girl."

Minnie had started sniffing at the ground. Pawing at nothing in particular. I stopped and looked around. The image of a shallow grave flickered in and out of my mind. Then more graves. Bodies. Bones. That blue jacket with the bloodstains. A shoe. A hand missing a finger. A foot missing toes. A bludgeoned face with earth clogging the broken nose and mouth. Jamie's face.

"Minnie. Leave it."

I marched on, flinching as my clothes and skin were scraped and stabbed by low branches and thick ferns. The cool, late afternoon breeze made me shiver. My heart was crashing against my ribs, my breathing fast and shallow.

"Where are you going, Mum?"

I spun around. Shone the torch left and right. Minnie sat obediently beside me.

"Did you hear that, Minnie? Did you hear Jamie?"

Minnie whined.

"No. Of course you didn't. It was just a voice in my head. Let's keep going." Yes. That's all it was. Just my brain playing tricks. I had worked so hard to get rid of my son's phantasm, I wasn't about to let it creep back into my head now.

Something rustled in the trees, and I jumped. I kept my eyes forward, following the torch light. Shadows had a habit of taking on scary shapes. It was true what they said about nature coming to life after dark. The forest was waking up; animals were scurrying about. Minnie was on high alert, her ears up, nose in the air. A bat dive-bombed her, bold as brass. But the loudest noise was my breathing despite my efforts to stay silent and stealthy.

"Seriously, Mum, this is ridiculous."

I knew Jamie wasn't real. I knew it was my mind inventing him. I was afraid, that's all, but ignoring him was an added complication that I didn't need right now.

"It's a hike, that's all, same as Hadrian's Wall," I said into the black beyond.

"You hated that!"

I couldn't see him. My mind hadn't gone that far. Yet.

"I did it, though, didn't I?"

"Barely. Me and Dad carried your bags at the end, and on the last day you cried."

"My legs hurt, and I had blisters."

"Exactly."

My legs *were* feeling tired, and I *was* about to cry. Then I heard it. A voice. Up ahead. I picked up my pace, Minnie trotting along with me. There was a window. A light.

The Shack.

THIRTY-TWO

Scott

G UNNER PIPER'S CABIN was like a crumbling cottage from a forgotten era with no glass in its tiny windows, moss blanketing the broken roof planks, and the door hanging from a single rusty hinge. It was dark inside, but Mason quickly set about foraging under a loose floorboard in the large, cobwebbed room until he found, and lit, several pillar candles. The flames threw an eerie glow around the empty space. We stood in the middle of the room. An endless sea of thick knobbly tree trunks was visible beyond the windows, sufficient daylight still seeping through the small openings. Inside, the air was stagnant, a lingering stench making the room feel like it was closing in around us.

Somewhere in here, my son died. I could feel rage bubbling deep inside me like a parasite straining to take hold, to devour me, to wreak revenge.

Mason held out a lit candle and wandered around the room, circling me, his fingers running along the walls, until he reached the blackened fireplace. He brushed away dust from the cracked, slanting mantelpiece, leant back, and rested his elbow on it.

Staring across the room, Mason pointed to an area by the back wall. "I'd sit over there. Facing the fire. Gunner would make me add logs and stoke it, keep it going. The police took the poker. I was watching them. Hiding. There was an old sofa and a glass table. Gunner gave me drinks in cans and biscuits and let me smoke his cigarettes and his weed. He taught me how to play gin rummy. Hey! You listening to me?"

My eyes were staring at him, but my focus was internal, picturing Mason sitting in this hovel beside my son's killer. I wanted to scream. Not a high-pitched shriek, not a sobbing yelp, but a roar. I wanted to turn my insides out and shatter the walls. I wanted to make a sound so loud, so low, so terrible, that it would shake this place to dust. I gritted my teeth. Held my nerve. I couldn't fall apart. Not yet. Not until I knew everything.

I slowly turned my head around, following Mason's gaze to the back wall. I was just about able to distinguish a rectangular area on the floor where the wood was lighter, cleaner, where a piece of furniture would have been.

"I'm listening to every word."

Looking back at Mason, I watched his face light up as he recounted his tale. The young man seemed small in the light, wiry, fragile. Yet, somehow, the room had brought him to life. He stood taller. The story he told of a lost young boy with no father and an adored half-sister, ignored by his stepdad, was compelling. Certainly, I could see how the jealousy toward his sister had grown, how Mason's absent father and indifferent stepfather had left him feeling aban-doned and unworthy. But, there was something else under the surface. Something was not right about this awkward, tetchy young man who was trying so hard to make sense of his life, his family, and his choices.

"Tell me about Jamie. What happened to my son?"

Mason pushed his hood off his head, letting his hair fall forward, half-covering his eyes. "It was just me, at first. Then Gunner said I could bring a mate. To be the dealer. I told him I didn't have any friends. He said making friends was easy; you just had to give them something. So, he gave me sweets and fags and weed, and I started making friends. He said I should hang out by the skateparks or on the swings at the rec after dark. That I shouldn't use my real name in case my mum found out about the gifts and tried to stop me from seeing him. The boys all knew me as Jace. Never told any of them my real name. Mum never suspected a thing. Didn't even say anything when I came home drunk or stinking of dope."

How can a mother not notice if her son is drunk or high? Teenagers can be tricky, Christ, I know that, but parents should know their kids. Know where the hell they are and what the fuck they're doing. How could Suzannah not have seen that her son had changed? Not even realise he wasn't home? No, she knew. She'd followed him. She just didn't want to admit it. She didn't want to see the truth.

I thought about Blair, lost in her world of grief. She hadn't known where Jamie was or what he was doing, but she was guessing, trying to put the pieces together. And she was working it out alone because I had switched off. Zoned out. I shut her down when she voiced her concerns and brushed off his wayward behaviour, so she stopped trying to talk to me. I let her down.

I took a deep breath. I pictured Mason sitting on that

sofa, playing cards and smoking a joint. Did Jamie do the same? Had he sat on that sofa in this hovel playing cards with Mason? Jamie had changed years before he died, not months. Something felt wrong with this story about the boys. It didn't fit with our son, and Jamie wasn't kept and tortured like the other boys. It wasn't making sense.

I looked toward the closed door that led into the room where the boys were held and then back to Mason. "How old was he, Jamie, when you met him?"

Mason looked at me, eyes wide. "Don't you know?"

My body stiffened, and I felt as if my lungs were being squeezed tight. I was barely able to take a breath. I knew. I'd always known. "When he was eleven. When he gave up football. When he bottled up the boy he was into that time capsule. The boy he couldn't be anymore. Or didn't want to be. When I started to blame secondary school and hormones for our broken bond, our lack of communication, the arguments."

Mason dipped his finger in the melted wax at the top of the candle and watched it harden before peeling it off his skin. "Jamie didn't have friends either. Got picked on. I followed him home from school. Watched him sit in the park on his own."

I ran my fingers through my hair, my scalp moist with sweat. "Jamie told us he was with mates. I thought he had friends. I thought he was getting on okay. My god, I didn't know. I didn't see it. I should have stopped all this. Spent more time with him. Saved him from you. From Gunner."

I was struggling to process what this messed-up kid was telling me. The Jamie he was describing wasn't the boy I raised. He wasn't bullied. He wasn't weak. He made different choices than most boys his age, but he was happy with those choices. Was Mason just using Jamie to describe himself? Was he simply trying to share the blame with my son to ease his conscience?

I understood why Blair was in such pain, so troubled. She thought that she had seen it. Known more than me whilst I had ignored the signs, ignored Jamie, and ignored her. I hadn't wanted to accept that my son had become someone I didn't recognise. Someone I didn't know anymore. Deep down, I knew something was wrong. Things had changed, and I didn't do anything to help him.

Mason came up from behind me, the candle in his hand. "I can stop if you'd like. You can go home. Forget about me."

I turned. "No way. You don't just get to walk away from this. I have questions."

"Can we sit down then?" Mason pushed past me and sat on a wonky step that led up to the precariously hanging front door that was wedged open by a large rock.

Perched on the step with the candle in his lap, he ran his finger back and forth through the flame. I leant against the wall of the shack, rubbing my eyes with the heels of my hands to try to relieve the pressure of my hundred-mile-an-hour mind. The temperature had dropped, and I didn't have a jacket, goose bumps appearing on my arms as I shivered. The forest was eerily quiet, not even a tiny rustle of leaves or crunch of undergrowth, as if it, too, was waiting to hear what was coming next, what horrors it would witness tonight, what terrible truths were about to be laid bare.

Mason hovered his palm over the orange flame, slowly moving it lower. "Go on then. What questions?"

"If you met Jamie when he was eleven, it means you were friends for five years, right?"

"Right."

"So, I don't understand why he became a victim of Gunner's five years after you met him."

"Jamie wasn't like the other kids. He didn't really want the stuff I offered him. He wasn't into being cool, couldn't be bothered with fitting in. He was just interested in getting to know me. I wanted a friend. A proper friend. I needed one. We clicked, me and Jamie, and I didn't want to give him to Gunner. So, I didn't. I kept him away, kept him to myself. We'd hang out in the park or by the river or at the ruins. He said that you and his mum weren't around much. Weren't really there a lot. Busy with your careers. He said you probably weren't ready to have a kid when you did. Guess that's why he spent so much time with me."

My fists balled, and I shook my head. "That's not true. I was there. I loved him. He'd paint while I worked, he'd take pictures with Blair, he walked Minnie."

Mason stood up. Jittery.

He picked at one of the rotting posts that held up the remains of the porch canopy with one hand, holding the candle in the other. "I told Jamie about Gunner in the end, a few months before he died. Told him that all those stories I'd made up were true. He didn't believe me at first, thought it wasn't a very funny joke. So, I bought him here to prove it, show him I wasn't lying. I said he couldn't call the police or ever tell anyone, or Gunner would find him and kill him or hurt his mum. He asked if he could take pictures, but I said he shouldn't. Gunner turned up, which scared the shit out of me because I thought that would be it for Jamie, but he was clever, your Jamie, a real quick thinker. He said he'd help Gunner. That he'd do whatever it was I did. Gunner liked that. Told him he had brass balls. Made Jamie swear on his mum's life that he'd keep it secret. Gunner told him he'd visit his mum just so Jamie knew he meant it. A few weeks later, Gunner followed her onto a train and told Jamie about the picture of him and his dog on her laptop screen, so Jamie knew he was telling the truth. Jamie did anything Gunner wanted after that."

There was a crack from the woods. Mason's head snapped up.

THIRTY-THREE

Blair

I CLIPPED MINNIE to her to her lead as I stood among a tangle of tall ferns behind a crooked, hollow trunk. The trees surrounding the cottage swayed and whispered to me as I stared at the derelict shack huddled in the woods in front of me. A disused hunting cabin hidden in the dense ancient woodland for so long. Long enough to claim the lives of thirteen innocent boys.

The building stood dishevelled and shameful amid a confusion of moss and lichen-ridden ancient oaks and yews as if it was waiting for the ground to swallow it up and erase its terrible secrets. I wanted to leave, run from the woods, but I was stuck. Rooted to the spot. Unable to escape the horrors: the soiled table, the cage, fingernails embedded into rotting wood panels, all those awful details that seeped into the news articles that Scott had tried so hard to hide from me.

I didn't look across to where my son had been dug up. Didn't dare. I was shaking, goose bumps prickled my skin, and an uneasy feeling sat in the pit of my stomach. Mason and Scott were looking in my direction. I hadn't come here to hide. I had come for answers.

Mason sat hunched over a candle. "Who's there? Who are you?" He looked across at Scott. "Did you call the cops?"

Minnie let out a single loud bark.

Scott walked toward me. "Blair? Is that you?"

I stepped out from behind the tree and ran to Scott, dragging Minnie beside me. I was so relieved to have found him, to be with him. I sank into his embrace, my whole body shaking. "I couldn't just sit at home waiting. I needed to find you. Find him."

Scott's strong arms held me up, the warmth of his body making me feel safe.

Mason didn't move. He stood in the doorway to the shack staring at us. "I told you to leave my mum alone."

I turned to him. "Don't you want to know if your mother is alive?"

Mason punched the post beside him, a loud crack echoing around us as the wood split. "Is she? Tell me. I didn't mean to hurt her. I wasn't trying to hurt anyone. I just wanted you to shut up. You needed to stop talking. She didn't need to hear any of that stuff."

I was afraid of this boy, but at the same time I pitied him. He was a grown man and yet simultaneously a pathetic boy. I felt about him how you feel about a sad clown—angry and let down, but also curious.

"Your mother's alive. At least, she was when she went to the hospital in the ambulance. The paramedics said it looked worse than it was. They didn't think any major organs were damaged."

Mason pulled up his hood and lowered his head so that we couldn't see his face. "You should have left us alone. Then she wouldn't have got hurt."

"You should have left *us* alone. You were the one hanging around outside *our* house. It was you who followed *us*, threatened *us*, not the other way around. You sent Devin to steal our son's box with those notes and pictures."

Mason poured the wax from the candle onto the back of his hand, watched it dry, and slowly peeled it off. "They were Jamie's record of what I did for Gunner. What we did, I guess. It was easier to make friends when Jamie was around. We were like a double act. Jamie was laid back. Laughed a lot. Most of the time, we just hung out together, chatting, smoking, watching the other kids skate or joke around. I always knew when Gunner wanted me to bring someone. He'd hand me some money, all rolled up neat with an elastic band, and then he'd wait here till I turned up with a new kid."

Did he just say that he and Jamie were a double act? I didn't understand what Mason was saying. I couldn't have heard right. I looked at Scott and put my hand on his arm.

Scott's brow furrowed, and he slowly shook his head from side to side. "I thought you said that Jamie didn't meet Gunner until a few months before he died? That he was just your friend, that he didn't know what you were doing for Gunner until a few months before he died?"

Mason lifted his head and grinned. "That's the best bit. He didn't have a clue. We were just friends, making new friends, and once or twice a year I brought one of them here. Jamie and I moved around, didn't hang with the same groups for long, didn't want to be tied down to the same mates having to make plans and all that crap. We liked being floaters, in and out, picking and choosing where we went and what we did."

Jamie was the kind of kid who would have one close friend, like Scott and Leith, a long-term buddy rather than a pack of semi-friends. It made sense, and it also made me mad. My skin felt like it was crawling with maggots. I let go of Scott, and a shiver shook through my body.

I handed Minnie's lead to Scott and stepped closer to Mason. "Take off your hood and look at me. I want to see that you're listening. Those boys you brought here weren't your friends. You lured them to horrible, painful deaths, with months of disgusting torture. That's not making friends."

Mason shrugged. "They didn't know that."

"Christ! Can you hear yourself?" Scott grasped his hair as if he was trying to pull it out. I knew that feeling. The need to feel pain, just to be sure that what was happening was real.

Mason pushed back his hood, holding the candle up to his face. "At first, we'd just have a laugh, play cards, drink. Then it would get late, and we'd fall asleep. Well, the new kid would fall asleep. I'd just pretend. Didn't look when Gunner dragged him into the room. When the screaming started, I'd go to the creek, wait a while, then go home. When Gunner was done with him—weeks, months later—Gunner would make me bury the body and burn all their stuff, clothes, and whatever." His voice wobbled and came out in a croaked whisper. "They were so messed up; he'd beat their faces so bad, I didn't recognise them."

Significant trauma. That's what the officers had said when they first turned up, refusing to let us identify Jamie's body, his face so smashed up that it was unrecognisable.

I pictured Mason in the shack, pretending to be asleep,

knowing what was about to happen. Minnie was straining against her lead. Scott let her loose, and she inched toward Mason, growling at him.

Scott clapped his hands. "Minnie. Sit."

She did as she was told, sitting tall and rigid right in front of Mason, her glower fixed on him. Mason's eyes darted about, searching for an escape route. Minnie half-stood, Mason froze, and the obedient mutt sat back down.

I put my hand on Minnie's head to keep her calm. "If you were such good friends with Jamie, why didn't you come round our house? Why didn't Jamie introduce you to us? We were always asking to meet his friends."

Mason held my gaze, his eyes narrow, defiant. "Grownups never liked me. My dad didn't want to know me, my stepdad didn't like me, my grandparents never wanted to look after me; even the old guy in the shop didn't want me there.

Scott threw his hands in the air and shook his head. "You stole from him!"

"Not much. He was looking for a reason to get rid of me. Only gave me the job because he felt sorry for Mum."

A fox screamed from somewhere deeper in the forest, sending Minnie into a frenzied bark. I held tight to her collar until she settled. "You never gave us a chance. Maybe we could have helped."

"If you'd have met me, you would've told Jamie I was no good, not the kind of friend he needed."

"And we would have been right. If you had never made friends with him, Jamie would still be here now."

Mason looked between me and Scott. "What are you

going to do with me?"

I looked at Scott; he looked at me. What I *wanted* to do and what I *would* do were two very different things. "I don't know. We hadn't talked about what would happen if we caught up with you."

Mason backed up into the doorframe of the cabin. I could see that he was crumbling. Scott reached for my hand and squeezed it. There was electricity between the three of us. Mason was like a lit firework, ready to explode at any minute. Shifting from foot to foot. Getting desperate. I didn't know what Scott was thinking, but I wanted to lock this boy in that stinking room at the back of the cabin and leave him there to rot with the images of what happened to those boys tormenting him, his shouts for help lost to a vast, silent forest.

He kicked at the doorframe, eyes down. "Jamie wanted to go to the police. Said that's what he was going to do. But I stopped him. I knew Gunner would hurt my mum and you, and then he'd do what he did to those other boys to us."

I put my hand to my mouth as a single sob escaped.

Scott dropped my hand and pulled me close to him, wrapping his arm tight around my shoulders. I could tell that he wasn't finished with Mason.

This was the boy we had been searching for all this time. Gunner Piper's accomplice. Was his story the truth? How would I ever know? If it was, then my sweet son was dragged into something that he couldn't escape from. Something he couldn't tell me or Scott about. If we went to the police then Jamie would also be labelled an accomplice, and all that hate we had already been subjected to would be back, but this time it would be worse.

The last of the light faded, and a gust of wind puffed through the trees, shaking the branches above us. A bird shrieked. Something rustled the undergrowth nearby. Minnie's ears pricked up. Mason stood like a Stygian demon in the doorway, the candlelight bathing him in a ghostly glow, his face ashen, eyes bulging, fingers digging into the wax.

Everything about this encounter felt wrong, surreal, like a nightmare that wouldn't end. But it wasn't a nightmare, and it would come to an end eventually. Mason was real. What he said may or may not be the truth. He wasn't defending anyone or trying to avoid his part in what happened, but he was passing some of the blame onto Jamie. Was Jamie involved, or was Mason trying to stop us from going to the police? He seemed defeated, his story solid. He had accepted his part in Gunner's crimes and taken responsibility. He sounded genuine.

I had one more question that I needed an answer to. "Why did Jamie die? What went wrong?"

Mason's shoulders hunched, his chin dropping to his chest. "You've seen the notebook. Everything about the boys. All their names. All that stuff about them. Jamie said it was evidence. Couldn't stop talking about it. I told him about the souvenirs I kept, and he said they were evidence, too."

Scott's fists clenched. "Souvenirs? Jesus Christ! This isn't a day out at the fucking beach. Those 'souvenirs' belonged to boys you buried. Boys who were screaming in agony as they were tortured just feet away from you. On the other side of a door, goddammit. Do you even care? Can you even comprehend how fucked up that is? Do you understand what you did? What that meant for the families of those boys? For us?"

Mason lashed out, dropping the candle and kicking the door off its hinge. "Of course, I understand. My sister died, remember? I saw what that did to my mum."

Minnie started growling at Mason, her teeth bared.

Mason lunged at her. "Get it away, or I won't tell you anything else."

Scott reached for the dog, taking hold of her collar and clipping her back onto the lead. "If you knew how it felt, why did you let it happen to all those other boys?"

Mason's fists were clenched tight. He punched at the doorframe. Punched and punched until his knuckles bled. "Because I didn't have a choice. Because I was scared. Because he was nice to me. Because I didn't want my mum to find out what I'd done to Lily."

I pulled back my shoulders and took a deep breath. I had no sympathy for Mason. My heart was ice.

"You still didn't say why *my* boy died."

Mason lifted his chin and pulled himself upright, composing himself. "Jamie made me bring him back here. I didn't want to. Didn't want to risk it, but Jamie told me we had to take photographs of everything to prove that his notes were the truth so the police would believe him. He said if he got photos of the shack and the graves then he wouldn't tell the police about the souven…the things I kept. Said he'd make sure they knew I was a victim, too, that I'd done what Gunner wanted because I had no choice."

There's always a choice. But, I understood that fear could make the right choice almost impossible to make.

Mason was cradling his damaged knuckles. "When we got here, I thought we were alone, just me and Jamie. The fire wasn't lit, and Gunner's boots weren't by the door, so I figured he wasn't there. I hadn't brought someone to Gunner for a while, so I thought the chamber was locked and empty. We lit the fire, smoked a bit. We were talking about the notebook and Jamie was taking photographs. Jamie said he'd hidden his notes in that box. Put the box and the key somewhere me and Gunner would never find them. He said he wished he'd told the police at the beginning, after the first time he met Gunner. He was really cut up about it that night. Wanted out. Wanted it to stop. Wanted to take it all back."

My poor, sweet, son. Scott and I hadn't protected him from that monster and this twisted-up boy.

Mason picked at the candle wax, scraping at it with his nails. "Gunner was so angry. He'd heard everything. Came roaring out of the chamber, his face all scrunched, his scar red and raised. Jamie pissed himself, and I thought I was gonna have a heart attack I was so freaked out. Gunnner dragged Jamie by his hair into the room. Didn't even close the door. Tied him to the board. I didn't know what to do. I shouted at him to stop. To leave him alone. I didn't want him to kill Jamie. Jamie was my friend. I'd done everything Gunner told me to. I saw Jamie's phone on the table, so I grabbed it and sent the emergency SOS, but I knew nobody would get here on time."

Scott held out a hand and rested it on my upper arm. "We were sent a message saying that Jamie had called 999. He had put us on his phone as emergency contacts. We didn't see the message until we woke up the next morning. It tore us apart agonising over whether we could have got to him before he was killed if we'd seen the message sooner."

I stumbled back against Scott's body.

Mason folded his arms across his stomach. "I was going to leave. Run away so I didn't have to listen. But, I couldn't. I begged Gunner to kill me instead. He laughed at me. I ran at him, kicked and punched him. But, he hit me hard. He was too strong. I grabbed a knife from his table. Gunner said if I tried to hurt him, I'd only make it worse for Jamie. I knew I'd only get one chance. I'd only get to use the knife once. So, I stabbed him."

I lifted my head from Scott's chest and looked at Mason. "You want us to believe that you tried to stop Gunner Piper? That you stabbed Gunner Piper to try to save *our* son after you left all those other boys to die?"

Mason took a deep breath, staring at the floor and kicking at the dirt. "No. I didn't stab Gunner. I stabbed Jamie."

THIRTY-FOUR

Scott

I FELT LIKE I had been engulfed by a fireball. "*You killed Jamie?*"

My anger morphed into rage, and the parasite within took charge. Every muscle in my body tensed. I let go of Blair, and she sank to the floor beside Minnie.

Mason dropped the candle and sidestepped, his eyes wild, hands reaching behind him for the outside wall of the cabin. "I wanted it to stop. I wanted to help him. I wanted to save him from any more pain."

I lunged for Mason, but he leapt out of my reach. "*You killed Jamie!*"

Mason blundered toward the nearest tree trunk. "I ended his suffering. I stopped Gunner from hurting him even more."

Minnie howled.

Mason skirted around the tree. "You won't tell the police or my mum, will you? She's all I got left."

I ran toward Mason, stumbling off the porch step. "You'll be begging to tell her when I've finished with you."

My hands found the bark of the tree, but Mason ran off into the forest before I could get to him. I had never felt so alive, so focussed, as I did at that moment. Reaching Mason and tearing his limbs from his body was my only goal. I wanted to rip him to pieces, beat his head against a tree until it was pulp. I wanted him to pay for taking my son's life with his own.

I heard Blair's voice fade away as I ran.

"Scott! No!"

It was dark. The forest closed in around me, clawed at me. I could only see an outline of Mason as he sped off through the trees. The sliver of moon that peeped through the accumulating clouds provided little illumination. I ran mindlessly, following the sound of Mason's feet crunching the undergrowth. I was only minutes into the chase and already my legs and lungs were screaming.

The temperature had dropped, and the chilly evening breeze stung my airways as I gulped in oxygen. I was only going to catch up with Mason if he was unable to maintain his pace or if he tripped and fell. With my legs moving as fast as they could, I narrowly avoided colliding with the tangle of thick, crooked trunks that loomed before me. I dodged left and right, trying to keep my target in earshot. My eyes slowly adjusted to the lack of light, bringing Mason's silhouette into focus up ahead. He was pushing hard, bouncing off the trunks, stumbling as he ran. He was getting farther away.

A superhuman strength seemed to flow through my veins as my body accelerated, my legs slightly numb, my breathing deep and steady. When Mason changed direction, I pushed off the base of a tree and followed, pumping my arms and lengthening my stride. I always wondered how Minnie managed to weave through the woods in pursuit of a deer at such incredible speed, never crashing into a tree, but now I realised it was purely a matter of focus and resolute determination. My senses were ablaze, my reactions electric, and my mind consumed with the sole mission of capturing my prey.

A rumble of thunder bellowed around me, and a strong gust of wind shook the canopy above. A branch scratched my cheek, making me lurch sideways and nearly lose my balance. Mason's footfall was getting quieter, his shadowy figure pulling away from me. Delicate flecks of moisture dotted my face and arms. It had begun to rain.

I could feel my body slowing down. My mind was willing me to push harder, keep ploughing forward, but my muscles were against me. I reached for the trees, gasping for breath, using the trunks as my springboards. Up ahead, I saw Mason pause. His outline was bent over, arms resting against his knees. He was as exhausted as I was. I tumbled toward him, hoping his spirit was as broken as his body. He didn't move. As I approached, I heard him retching. I felt triumphant, almost euphoric. I'd run this surly sadistic young man into the ground. I stood tall and took a deep breath, ready to finish this. The chase had dissipated my anger and left only resignation. I'd take him to the police. Let them dish out his punishment. My son had already paid his dues.

Another boom of thunder rang out, and the clouds erupted, spitting out their rain with instant venom. The force of the water hit the dry branches and crisp undergrowth with an angry surge, filling the forest with a loud, crackling roar. I shivered, my eyes still on Mason's hunched figure. His head snapped up. I wiped rain from my eyes. He sprang into motion and disappeared.

My body jerked into action, and I ran again. This time,

there was no superhuman burst of activity, only pain. Within a minute, the terrain became slippery; the moss on the trunks was like slime as mud splashed up my legs and filled my trainers. The water weighed me down and took away any hope of clear vision.

I heard a faint cry up ahead. I couldn't see Mason anywhere. The rain pelted down.

I moved from tree to tree. *"Mason! Mason!"*

Something was wrong, I could sense it. Up ahead, the canopy appeared to drop abruptly as if the trees had been dwarfed. I moved forward slowly, my feet slipping on loose ground, and held onto the last tall tree in my field of vision. I had reached a slope. A steep slope. I edged forward and looked down. The trees thinned out, their trunks slimmer, curled, exposed roots clinging to the steep sides of a cavernous ravine. Water snaked downward in rivulets to the gully below, joining a fast-flowing stream that bubbled and swirled with the driving rain.

I peered down the bank. The dark and the rain made it difficult to see anything significant. I could just make out a dark mass near the edge of the water. Nothing specific. If it was a body, it had to be a mangled, filthy, motionless body. My heartbeat sped up. With the back of my hand, I wiped the rain from my eyes. I did, and I didn't, want the dark mass to be Mason. If it was Mason and he was dead, what would I do? If he was hurt, did he deserve my help?

I stood at the top of the incline, holding my breath, trying to decide if I would go down there or leave—give up the chase and let Mason disappear from my life without retribution. The rain was relentless, thunder bellowing overhead and sheet lightning creating an eerie, slow-motion strobe effect. With each flash, the crumpled image at the water's edge became clearer. A body. Limbs askew. Clothes soaked and slick with mud. The face sunk into the damp earth.

If it wasn't Mason then someone needed my help. If it was Mason then I'd have a choice to make. Whoever was down there, I had to get to them.

I tried using the tree trunks for anchors as I descended, but as soon as my feet sank into the unstable ground, any hope of staying upright vanished. After a few wobbly strides, an ungainly stumble, and a worrying lurch, I was on my rear careening down the slope in an avalanche of earth and undergrowth. The fall left me shaken. Below the loose earth were boulders and rocks, and I had several near misses with low branches. I had a nasty cut on my arm, and my wrist bent too far the wrong way. Unlike the body at my feet, however, at least I was still upright.

It was immediately clear that the body was Mason and that he had fallen foul of the tricky incline. I fell to my knees, pulling my phone from my pocket and shining the light onto his face. He was a mess. The light, the weather, and the location could not have been worse. I swept my phone torch over his body to get a full picture of his injuries: an open wound deep in his skull, an out-of-place shoulder, and a leg that resembled a badly pulled wishbone.

Mason wasn't getting out of this alive without my help.

THIRTY-FIVE

Blair

MINNIE BARKED IN the direction that Mason and Scott had run. I stood up, holding tight to her lead as she strained to get free.

"That way, is it? I hope you know where you're going." Jamie was standing in the entrance to the cottage, his hair a lanky matted mess with a large area clumped and stained red, blood oozing from his chest and dripping from his left hand where his little finger once was.

I stared at him, frozen to the spot. "You're not real. You're not there. It isn't you."

"It's the last place I was alive, Mum."

Minnie whined.

I looked down at the dog and patted her head. "Shhh, girl. It's alright. We'll go and find Scott."

I looked back at the cottage. Jamie was gone.

Taking a deep breath, I lifted my phone and switched on the torch. I scanned the forest. "They went this way. We won't catch them, so you'll have to sniff them out, okay? Just don't leave me behind."

I unclipped Minnie's lead. For a few seconds, the big mutt sniffed around the undergrowth, looking up, crying and sniffing some more. Then she took off into the woodland, nose to the ground.

I marched into the thicket behind her. "Hey, girl, wait for me."

As if things couldn't get any worse, the heavens opened and a storm surged in the sky above. Roaring thunder, sheet lightning, and skin-numbing rain descended on the forest. If there was a God up there, He was as angry with Mason as Scott and I were.

With the torch held out in front of me, I picked my way through the trees. My phone service faded and eventually disappeared as I walked farther into the forest, leaving me no way of knowing if I was going in a straight line or in circles. All I could do was listen and rely on Minnie, hoping that Scott kept up with Mason and Minnie could keep up with Scott. For all I knew, all of us could be moving farther apart and getting more lost by the minute.

Minnie returned, trotting beside me for a minute, sniffing feverishly before bounding off again. I did my best to follow, adjusting my trajectory whenever Minnie set off in a different direction. I was making slow progress and growing more and more convinced that I was knee-deep in disaster and sinking fast.

"*Scott! Scott!*"

It was dark, cold, and spooky. My own footsteps squelching in the undergrowth were scaring me. Where was Scott? How far had they gone? I thought I could hear movement up ahead, but I couldn't be sure. Was that a flash of light I glimpsed through the trees? What if I got so lost I could never find my way out of the forest?

"*Scott!*"

"Keep it together, Mum. Think of something nice to take your mind off the darkness. Minnie can find Dad."

I couldn't see Jamie, but I felt comforted hearing his voice. "I'm glad you're here. I know you're not really here, of course, but I'm still glad."

"Do you remember those bright pink swimmers you bought me and that day I played in the sprinkler?"

I remembered. Jamie was six, a huge smile on his face as he ran through the shower of cold water on a baking-hot summer's day. He was wearing his new neon-pink swim trunks that he insisted I buy him from the supermarket, along with a pair of white and lime-green goggles. He also had his fingerless cycling gloves on, which he wore day and night for a month after getting his first bike for a birthday present. He hadn't cared that the gloves were getting wet. He just ran back and forth through the water, screaming as the freezing spray hit his skin.

Minnie veered to the left, a scent catching her attention. I followed.

Jamie's voice sounded far away. "Better when you distract yourself, isn't it? Just keep following Minnie."

I remembered more about our happy summer's day. "It didn't end so well, that day with the sprinkler."

I had been watching Jamie from the lounger, which I had pulled out of the path of the sprinkler with strict instructions not to get Mummy wet. I should've joined in, laughed and screamed with him. Instead, I sat reading my book, the towel ready at my feet to wrap him up when he had finished playing. He ran over to me, shivering, shaking cold water all over me and my book. Instead of drying him off and holding him close, I threw the towel at him in anger, shouting about my soaked pages.

I stopped. I couldn't see Minnie. *"Minnie? Here, girl!"*

I was alone in the dark—cold, wet, and frightened. I wanted to go back to the shack, but as I turned around, I lost my bearings. Every direction looked the same: tall, dark trees stretching out into blackness.

"Minnie!"

I wished I could take this day back. I wished I had stayed at home and waited for Scott. I wished I had never found out about Mason or what he had done. I wished Scott had never discovered that puzzle box.

I wished I could take back the sprinkler day, too. Do it over, not give a shit about that stupid book. I wanted to squeeze my little boy tight, feel his cold damp cheeks against mine, and sit his little shivery body on my lap to rub him warm. I wanted to say sorry for shouting and spoiling his happy mood. I wanted to push the wet curls off his forehead and kiss his face all over a hundred times.

A roll of thunder and a flash of lightning brought Minnie charging back to me, and when the rain pummelled down even harder, the terrified doofus cowered at my side. "Where have you been? We're not going to find Scott like this. You have to sniff him out, remember? Come on."

Minnie reluctantly inhaled the sodden undergrowth, shaking vigorously whenever her coat became sodden and heavy. She didn't venture far, so I clipped on her lead and let her tug me in the right direction.

"Scott! Scott!"

My clothes were quickly soaked through, and the chill in

the air made my damp skin prickle with goose bumps. Shivering soon followed, and my sopping shoes made walking slow and cumbersome. The torch light only revealed a never-ending sea of moss-choked, bowed tree trunks, clusters of skin-slicing ferns, and murky, root-ridden, ankle-twisting earth.

"Scott! Where are you, Scott?"

The noise of the rain and the thunder were deafening. Flashes of lightning exploded inside the clouds, momentarily illuminating my surroundings, the ensuing darkness thrusting me into a blackness that took my breath away. The charge on my phone was less than ten percent. The torch did little to ease my fears and was ineffective in this weather, so I switched it off, deciding that waiting for Scott to call was futile, the battery sensibly saved for an emergency call should the need arise.

Minnie had clearly picked up the scent of something, a sudden rush of strength and energy driving her forward. Carefully navigating the increasingly treacherous trail, my faithful companion led us to the precipice of a lethal, muddy bank. If it wasn't for Minnie coming to an abrupt halt only inches before the drop, I would have surely tumbled to my death.

A flash.

Below, I could see a figure hunched over on the ground.

"Scott?" There was no way he was going to hear me through this storm, and I dared not use the last of my phone battery in case it was the only lifeline we had left.

Minnie howled and then leapt down the slope, yanking her lead from my hand before slipping and sliding away from me, an ungainly rear-ended descent plunging her to the edge of the rushing river below. The dog lay still for a moment before tentatively shuffling her limbs and lifting herself to a crouch, one leg raised off the ground.

A flash.

I let go of the tree I was clinging to and took a step down onto the slope. My foot slipped out from under me, and I pitched forward, reaching for the next tree trunk. I was out of control. Gravity and loose earth took control, sweeping me downward at an alarmingly increasing rate. My foot caught on a raised root, tossing me forward, a dangerous lunge keeping me upright. My limbs scraped against bark and branches. Twigs and debris poked into my arms and legs, snatching at my clothes, snagging and tearing the material.

Just as I thought I would make it down feetfirst, my head smacked into a rigid branch, knocking me to the ground. The impact winded me. I threw out my hands to slow my descent, but the sopping unstable terrain gave way beneath me. Spinning over and over, I felt as if I was in a tumble dryer. Pain shot through my leg as it crunched against something hard and jagged. Muck filled my nostrils as the wet dirt beneath me was tossed about. Finally, my back thudded against the earth, bringing my fall to an abrupt end. My head smacked against a solid object with such force that I thought my skull might split like a cracked egg.

I laid still for a minute, too afraid to move, worried I had broken a bone.

Jamie stood over me. "It's okay, Mum, I'm here."

THIRTY-SIX

Scott

I DON'T KNOW how long I'd sat with Mason trying to get him to respond to me. I was beginning to panic. What should I do next? Leave him and go for help? He could die out here alone. What if I couldn't find my way back to him? I could wait for the storm to ease and hope for reception on my phone or for someone to find us. Neither of those options seemed likely. I could try to carry him and hope he survived until I found a road or a house or flagged down a car, but moving someone with his injuries would no doubt do more harm than good.

I was about to take out my phone again to see if I could get service or by some miracle the location app was working when movement and noise from above caught my attention. I spun my head around in time to witness someone tumbling down the slope toward me, landing in a heap at the bottom. I rushed over. It was Blair—and standing feet away from where she landed, looking forlorn and in discomfort, was Minnie.

"Blair? Blair, honey, are you all right?"

Sheltering her face from the rain with my body, I took her face in my hands. Her eyes were open, and she was grimacing. Thank god. What the hell was she doing here?

I kissed her on the forehead and held her tight. "Why did you follow me? Why didn't you stay in The Shack?"

Blair felt for her head, moved her arms around, and then pushed off her elbows to a sitting position. "I couldn't stay in that awful place. I couldn't just wait for you. I didn't know what you were going to do. What Mason would do. I thought I saw him down here, on top of you, hurting you."

I helped her sit up. "He's the one who's hurt. Badly hurt."

Blair reached around the back of her head and winced. "Have you checked if he's alive?"

"He has a pulse. I couldn't tell if he was breathing. He's unconscious. Broken leg. Bad gash on his head. No way of telling how much blood there is. He won't make it if we leave him here."

Minnie hobbled over, one back leg barely making contact with the ground.

Blair put her arm around Minnie's neck and kissed her cheek. "Oh, my poor girl. Have you hurt your leg? She was the one who got me here. She sniffed you out and stayed with me."

I rubbed Minnie's neck and kissed her hard on the snout. "Thank you, Minnie. My special girl."

She licked the rain off my face.

I felt the lump on Blair's head and checked her arms and legs. "Does it hurt anywhere? Do you think you're okay?"

Blair stroked my cheek. "I'm alright. A few scrapes and bruises. It knocked the wind out of me, that's all. Let's decide what to do about Mason."

We crawled back to where Mason's body lay.

I squeezed his hand. "Mason? Can you hear me?"

He was still unresponsive. His eyes were closed. I put an ear to his mouth to listen for breath, but the wind and rain made it impossible to tell whether he was breathing. I rested a hand on his chest and sat patiently, but I couldn't detect a rise and fall. My hands were freezing and numb, my body aching and drained. I didn't need a dead boy on my hands and neither did Blair. I placed two fingers on each side of Mason's neck and willed there to be a pulse. There was.

Part of me hadn't wanted to find a pulse. Part of me wanted this to be over. Wanted Mason to pay for the lives of those boys he lured to their deaths. Pay for Jamie. But that wasn't the answer. Blair and I would be responsible for his death. For hunting him down and chasing after him. I didn't need that on my conscience and neither did she.

I had to try my best to save him. "I don't think we should move him."

He was unconscious—his leg was in pieces, literally— and I could feel a worrying hole in his skull. He wasn't going to last long out here. I'd have to go and find help, but how on earth would I find my way back in this weather? All I could hope was that if I followed the stream I'd get to the road and then a house.

Blair touched my shoulder and held my gaze. "I'll stay with him. You take Minnie. There's not much time."

I squeezed Blair's hand. "I'll be quick as I can."

Blair ran her finger down the worry line that creased my forehead, trying to ease my anxiety by smoothing it away. "We'll be fine."

Getting to my feet, I hurried along the bank of the tributary in the direction of the road. I moved as fast as I could, taking care to avoid risks. An injury right now would risk all of our lives. I flicked open my phone, but the battery had long since run out; the torch must have sapped it of its last bit of juice. I had no concept of the time. I could have been travelling for five minutes or thirty-five. The gully evened out, and the stream disappeared underground. Finally, I reached a road.

I hurried across the tarmac and up a long drive to the nearest house. I hoped that my appearance wouldn't cause the resident to slam the door in my face. I rang the doorbell and was quickly met by a young girl, maybe in her early teens. The look on her face told me I was a state. Before I could get a word out, she pointed her phone in my direction and snapped a picture. The door was duly slammed, and I heard her screaming for her father. I rang again.

A small, balding man appeared, glasses sitting on top of his head, a shirt untucked over smart trousers, top button undone. "Yes? Are you alright?"

"There's been an accident in the woods with a young boy. He's alive. Barely. Farther down the stream in the gully."

The man paused for a second, looked me up and down, then stepped aside. "You'd better come in."

THIRTY-SEVEN

Blair

THE RAIN WAS still coming down, harder now, filling the stream, dislodging leaves and twigs from the branches of the overhanging trees. Minnie lay patiently beside Mason, her head resting on the ground by his shoulder.

Mason opened his eyes. Blinked away the rain and slowly tilted his head toward me. I reached for my phone, flicking on the torch. Maybe I could tear off a piece of his T-shirt and wrap it around his head or tie it above the breaks in his leg to stem some bleeding, give him more time. I scanned his body with the torch. His clothes were filthy. The rain was persistent. Resting the phone on his chest, I tore at his top.

Mason cried out in pain as I joggled his body with each tug on the material. "Stop! Stop! Please, stop."

The young man sprawled out in front of me was helpless and fragile. His injuries were severe, the pain clearly unbearable. Wretched and terrified, Mason had seen things most people couldn't even imagine. I wondered what damage had been done. How would all this affect him? Would he become a monster like the man who moulded him? Would he make amends? What would his life become when all of this was out in the open? Scott and I hadn't even begun to explore Mason's part in Devin's death. What was the right thing to do? Gunner was in prison, his victims' bodies unearthed. What good would it do to drag this boy through the courts and the public eye? Yet, my sweet son was lured to the butcher's table by the young man in front of me and killed by a knife he wielded, albeit out of mercy not malice.

I took Mason's hand. "I won't ever forgive you for what you did, do you understand? Never. You can never make this right. Even if you told the police everything you told me. Even if you took all the blame and never mentioned Jamie."

Mason's eyes fixed on me. "I don't want my mum to find out. Ever. I want her to know that Lily's death was an accident. That I didn't mean it."

My body was so tense, I thought I might shatter into a hundred shards. What right did he have to ask anything of me? He certainly didn't get to spare his mother the truth. And what about the other boys? Their deaths weren't accidents. Neither, I suspected, was Devin's.

Mason squeezed my hand. "Please."

I circled his palm with my thumb as I used to with Jamie, the rain washing away my tears and drowning out my sobs. I didn't owe him anything. He owed me. He hadn't even said he was sorry for what he did to Jamie.

I looked down at his fingers. Some of Jamie's had been missing. Cut off by Gunner Piper while Mason stood by. Should I even believe what he had told us? Was he being honest or just trying to pass some blame onto Jamie? He had hidden the truth when the boys were dug up, stayed quiet, slinking away into the shadows. He didn't come forward, confess, ask for forgiveness, or plead his innocence. Had he been just a young boy manipulated by an evil killer? Or was that just his way of avoiding responsibility for his part in all of this?

Mason tried to pull his hand away. A flash of lightning. Something on his wrist caught my attention. I closed my fingers around his palm and pushed up his sleeve with my other hand. It was too dark to distinguish anything. I lifted the phone from his chest. Just before the battery drained away to nothing, I saw three words tattooed on the underside of his arm.

Lily. Jamie. Devin.

The image of Gunner Piper's arm flashed into my head, the one they had shown on the newscasts and in all the papers. The list of the boys' names: Seb. James. Theo. Noah. Tristan. Ralph. Stanley. Christopher. Nicholas. Jordan. William. Leon. Each boy he had killed. Jamie's name hadn't been on it. I had always assumed it was because Gunner had turned himself in before he'd made it to a tattooist or hadn't wanted to give himself away in case the tattoo artist recognised the names from the news reports.

I leant forward, supporting myself with one hand in the dirt beside Mason's head, the other hand with a pincer grip on his cheeks. I held his face, my nose inches from his. "You killed them. Lily. Jamie. Devin. You kept a record, just like Gunner."

Mason's eyes were barely open. The rain stopped, and a strange silence filled the gully. I felt for a pulse. He was alive. Just. I looked around at the black bleakness of our situation. We were alone in the dark, lost in a ravine in a thunderstorm. No one could see us. No one could hear us. No one would witness what passed between us.

I didn't want to live the rest of my life knowing Mason was out there somewhere: breathing, moving, laughing. Knowing he had been saved, had told his version of events, and was being kept safe and well in a prison cell, loved by his mother. He didn't deserve any of that. If Mason died out here in a tragic accident, maybe I could finally move on, knowing the world would be a better place. Maybe, somewhere down the line, I would save someone else's life if I made sure Mason never had the chance to rejoin society.

I squeezed Mason's nostrils between my finger and thumb and pressed my palm against his mouth.

"Don't do it, Mum. That's not who you are. It's not what we are."

Jamie was crouched on the other side of Mason.

I looked at my son, kneeling in the dirt yet untouched by the mud or the rain. "But he'll be alive and you're dead. It's not fair. He killed you."

"If he hadn't used that knife, Gunner would have killed me. Slowly. Painfully. Mason saved me from that, Mum."

I let go of Mason and sobbed. He hadn't moved. Hadn't struggled.

I reached for his neck to feel for a pulse. "He's still alive."

Jamie was standing a little way off. "He was just a sad, angry little boy when Gunner found him. He didn't ask for any of this. It was all Gunner's fault. Gunner is to blame. Gunner was the monster. Gunner poisoned him. Scared him. Threatened him. It was Gunner."

I would try and save him because that's what Jamie would want me to do, and if he was going to die, then I would be there with him, just as I wanted to be with Jamie.

I lifted Mason's hand. "I'm not going to leave you. Scott has gone for help. You'll be alright, and you'll see your mother again."

A few minutes later, a flash of lights swam around the far end of the gorge. Jumpy bright beams seeking us out. The rescue team had arrived. I didn't know what Scott had done, whether he had called the ambulance or the army, but in a blaze and bluster of activity, a pop-up canopy was erected and I was bustled away from Mason's body. Swamped by people and equipment. Paramedics and police swarmed as if they were emerging from an invisible hive.

Scott huddled me into a silver blanket and guided me alongside the stream to a police car that was waiting in a narrow lane a short walk away. I shivered uncontrollably, my trousers stuck to my legs, heavy with mud. Minnie was awkwardly slumped between the front footwell and passenger seat looking pathetic. The officer took brief statements, explained that we would need to come to the station the following day, and talked us through what would happen next. It was a blur, and I was only too aware of what lay ahead: the questions, the speculation, the media, and no doubt an uncomfortable conversation with Suzannah. The officer took us to our car at the service station and Scott drove us home.

THIRTY-EIGHT

Scott

I T WAS LUNCHTIME three days later when Mika and PC Shah drove up to the house. No lights flashing, driving an unmarked car. We'd given our statements, a hazy account of me following Mason to the shack, Blair coming to help me, and us losing him in the woods and discovering him at the bottom of the gorge. The police had left us alone for the last few days to rest and recuperate. That allowed us some time to try to process what had happened with Suzannah and Mason.

Mika had called to let us know that both of them were alive and would make a full recovery. I wasn't sure how I felt about that. About Mason surviving. I wondered what they would tell the police about Devin, about Gunner, about Lily. Would they tell the truth, lay all their secrets bare? Would Mason incriminate Jamie? Admit to his part in my son's death?

I headed through the garden to Blair's studio and knocked gently. "Mika's here with PC Shah. They'll want to talk to us both."

The handle clicked, and Blair opened the door. That haunted look had gone, and her curls seemed to have extra bounce.

She smiled at me and took my hand as we walked back through the garden. "Let's not mention the puzzle box, shall we?"

It was an unusually warm day for that time of year, the rays of sunshine catching Blair's red hair in just the right way to give her that magnificent glow as if her hair was aflame.

I took a deep breath. "Or the break-in."

"Agreed."

I paused and kissed the back of her hand. "We'll wait and see what Mason has told them."

"Absolutely."

Apart from her restless nights, Blair was more focussed, clearer. We were a team again. In the kitchen, she flicked on the kettle and set out a tray for coffee and biscuits. I went to the door.

The officers stood on the steps looking smart and efficient. "Hi, Mika, PC Shah. Come on in."

I shook both of their hands and led them into the lounge. Minnie plodded behind us and sat tall in front of PC Shah.

Our Dane was as dopey as a dog could be, but she knew exactly which human would give her the most attention. "Looks like you two are friends. Minnie thinks so, at least."

PC Shah smiled and let Minnie rub her head against her shoulder. "Dogs are great for diffusing tension."

Blair arrived with the tray of hot drinks and biscuits. "I've made pots of coffee and tea. Help yourselves."

We all busied ourselves with the mugs and biscuits for a few minutes as if we were all avoiding the conversation that we were about to have. Blair sat next to me on the sofa, and we shared a glance as we sipped our drinks.

Mika kicked things off. "I know you've given your statements, but I just wanted to follow up now that we have had a chance to talk to Suzannah and Mason."

He wasn't there with a warrant for our arrest or to search the house. I wasn't getting the impression that we had done anything wrong. If anything, the pair of them seemed a little sheepish, apologetic even.

Mika shifted in his chair. "We've managed to talk to Suzannah. She said that you, Blair, had visited her house, and that you talked about Lily and Jamie. Is that correct?"

Blair held her mug in her lap and kept eye contact with Mika. "Yes, that's right."

PC Shah had a notebook and pen in her hands and made no secret of taking notes. I didn't want to sound as if I was on the defensive, so I decided to dive in and head off any awkward questions with my own. "So, did Suzannah say why Mason attacked her?"

PC Shah looked up from her notepad, clocked our expressions, and then looked at Mika.

Mika nodded. "She couldn't remember what was said before Mason stabbed her. He came in and saw you and lashed out. She told us that she never had visitors round to the house and thinks that seeing you there must have unsettled him."

Suzannah was telling them as little as possible. "He sounds like he needs some help."

Mika cleared his throat. "Actually, he's going to be getting more than that. This will come out in the news soon enough, and we wanted to give you the heads-up. We talked to Mason after we'd seen Suzannah. He had a lot to say. He admitted to killing that young lad, Devin, a few weeks back. Said the boy had stolen money from him and he'd pushed him into the river and Devin couldn't swim. Said he burnt Devin's clothes trying to get rid of any DNA evidence."

Mason lied about the clothes, and he hadn't mentioned the notebook or the photographs. I reached across for Blair's hand. PC Shah shifted uncomfortably in the chair.

Mika took a deep breath. "There's something else."

I squeezed Blair's hand, readying myself for what Mika was about to add. It had to have something to do with Jamie or he wouldn't be here. Blair was silent, her hand clammy.

Mika cleared his throat. "Mason admitted to pushing his sister, Lily, out of the tree where she was found. They were arguing. Gunner Piper was there. He helped Mason bury Lily's body in the woodpile. Turns out that Piper had an accomplice, after all."

Blair gripped my hand tighter. "I knew it wasn't Jamie."

Mika leant forward and put a hand on top of PC Shah's notebook to stop her scribbling. "I'm sorry to have to be telling you all this. At least your boy's name will be out of the media and we will be encouraging the newspapers to write you both an apology."

If I hadn't already spoken to Mason, I would have questions. I didn't want Mika or PC Shah to leave our house with any doubts about our son's innocence or our ignorance. "So, Mason was Gunner's accomplice, the one who befriended our son and took him to that shack?"

Mika nodded solemnly. "Yes. I'm afraid so."

I sat for a minute, letting the silence hang heavy in the

air. I looked at Blair, and she looked at me.

Then I looked back at Mika. "And will he go to prison? For Lily and Devin and Jamie and all those other boys?"

Mika nodded. "He will. There will be a trial. Mason will cooperate. Plead guilty."

Mason may be saying that now, but when the reality of his situation kicks in, he could very well change his mind. Was he clever enough to tell some of the truth and keep silent about Jamie? What was one more murder charge? He had already confessed to killing his sister and Devin.

I sat uneasily in my seat, wondering if the half-truths would one day come back to bite us. We had hidden Devin's clothes in our garage wall. I had chased Devin to the river after he tried to break into our house. Neither Suzannah nor Mason had mentioned the puzzle box to the police. Mason hadn't admitted to killing Jamie. He probably thought he could convince the police that Lily and Devin's deaths were accidents. Crimes of passion maybe. Admitting to stabbing Jamie, albeit in a mercy killing, would be unnecessary, I guess, as Gunner Piper was already the assumed killer.

Mika stood up and placed his mug on the tray. "If you have any questions, please call us. We are here to help. Any more trouble with graffiti, let me know."

Blair and I escorted the officers to the front door. When we closed the door behind him, we stood in the hallway and held each other, silent tears spilling down our cheeks. Jamie was no accomplice, but he had gotten caught up in something he didn't know how to handle. His loyalty to his friend kept him from telling us. That loyalty cost him his life.

I was glad Mason would go to jail to live with the guilt

and shame of his actions. I wanted to tell him how much I hated him for what he did to Jamie. Not just for my son's death, the brutality of it, but for making friends with him. Involving him in Gunner Piper's crimes. Dragging my sweet boy into a darkness that he should never have been part of. He should have walked on by and ignored my lonely son sitting in the park. He could so easily have chosen another boy.

I wished he had, and I hated myself for wishing it.

THIRTY-NINE

Blair

A S WE STOOD in the hall, clinging to each other, Minnie leaning against us, a family missing a limb, I let the reality of our discoveries sink in. I thought of Suzannah, telling me that the truth would only make things worse. She was wrong. There wasn't anything worse than not having Jamie in my life. The worst had already happened. I had been clinging to the questions about Jamie's involvement with Gunner to avoid the black hole of my grief. The answers to how Jamie died only served to make me face my new reality. The one without my son.

When our tears ran dry, we plodded to the kitchen to make tea, returning to the lounge with two steaming mugs and a packet of chocolate fingers, Jamie's favourites.

I sat beside Scott, Minnie stretched out at my feet and devoured six biscuits. "We should talk about the puzzle box and Devin's clothes. I think we should burn them."

Scott slurped his hot tea.

"They're the only evidence of Jamie's involvement with Mason and Gunner and your run-in with Devin." I gripped my mug, waiting for Scott to respond.

This was the last piece of the puzzle. Without the clothes and the notes and the photographs, we had covered over all the cracks, hidden the last of the secrets, wiped the past clean, just as we had with the garage doors. No one would believe Mason now, regardless of whatever version of events he told. A boy who killed his sister and Devin. The Pied Piper of Peasedale's accomplice.

I set my mug on the tray, a surge of energy making my skin tingle. "Let's do it now. Make today our fresh start. The day we put it all behind us. The day we promise only to remember the best of our son."

Scott put his mug on the tray. He took a deep breath and slowly raised his eyes to meet mine. "I'm not sure that's the right thing to do."

It was. I knew it was. We had to get rid of everything so that all that remained was the happy memories of our sweet boy. My hands shook as I lifted Jamie's puzzle box from under the table and took the photographs from the drawer. This whole time, I had hoped that something would come to light proving, without doubt, my son's innocence. Ignorance even. I'd wanted to discover that Jamie had found out about all of the sordid information about the killings secondhand. In the end, Mason told me what I wanted to hear. Jamie was innocent. A victim. But it didn't matter now. It was over. Mason would confess everything in court and Jamie would be blameless and we would have destroyed all the evidence that could be misinterpreted by the police or twisted by the press.

I lifted the lid of the box to check the notebook was still inside. "We'll burn everything. No one ever needs to know all of this existed. Let's get the incinerator going and open up that hole one last time."

Scott squeezed my shoulder and dropped his chin onto my head. "None of it was our fault. Or Jamie's. I don't even think it was Mason's. We were all Gunner's victims. People will see that in time. I can't be held ransom to Mason for the rest of my life. I can't worry every day what he might say. We need to face the facts, BB. If we expect Mason to take responsibility for his part in the deaths of all those boys, including ours, then we need to take responsibility for Jamie's part."

I pushed Scott away and stood up. "Jamie didn't have a part, at least not one he knew about, and Mason wasn't a victim. What about Lily? Mason pushed his little sister to her death before he even met Gunner. Jamie was a victim, just like all those other boys. But not Mason. Gunner saw the evil in that boy and knew how to exploit it."

Scott slammed his hand onto the coffee table. "Enough, Blair. I've had enough. I want to tell the police everything we know. I want to show them the box, the notes, the photographs. I want to give them Devin's clothes and tell them about the investigating that Leith and I did. I want to let it all go and move on. I'm going to bash a hole in that wall again and take everything to the station."

I couldn't believe what he was saying. After all that we had suffered. The graffiti, Mason stalking us, terrifying us. The media branding our son as an accomplice. How could we possibly share everything? It would destroy us.

My chest tightened; I couldn't breathe. "No. Please don't. I can't. I won't survive it. I don't want the world to know those things."

A wave of nausea swept through me, threatening to bring

up the biscuits. Scott's mouth was tight and set, his brow creased and his eyes narrow. He was going to do this with or without me. Pressure built in my head and for a moment I thought I might pass out. What if I couldn't do this? What if it was too hard?

Scott got up and walked to the doorway. "Come on. We'll do it together. Whatever comes next, we'll face it standing side by side."

He was right, of course. I blamed myself and Scott for our neglect, for being too focussed on work, too unapproachable, too distant. If we had been there for our son more often, if I had paid more attention, maybe he would have made better choices, safer choices. Maybe he would have come to me for advice or help.

I wanted to move on. I wanted Scott and I to have a happy future. I took a deep breath and followed Scott to the garage, where, together, we bashed and battered the garage wall, stripping away our repairs and removing Devin's clothes. Scott phoned Mika at the station, letting him know that we were coming down, and I placed the puzzle box and the clothes into a box.

Sitting in the car with the box on my lap, I ran my fingers over the intricate carvings of my son's puzzle box and imagined Jamie hiding the notes and photographs. Was he afraid? Did he feel guilty? He didn't tell me because he was protecting me, and that broke my heart.

Scott sat beside me, his hands resting on the steering wheel. "There's something else. Something I want you to see before I hand it in."

I turned to look at him. His eyes shone, and I could see

tears welling up. "What is it?"

My jaw dropped open as he pulled a folded slip of paper out of his back pocket. I recognised it immediately. Scott's mother had bought Jamie a writing set on his eighth birthday so that he could write her letters. I took the folded sheet of paper from Scott's hand and opened it. It was Jamie's handwriting.

Scott cleared his throat, his voice coming out in a scratchy whisper. "It was in the box. It must have been the one Jamie put inside the time capsule."

"Why didn't you show me sooner?" I knew, of course. "Don't answer that. It's okay. I wasn't ready."

I unfolded the piece of paper and read the words.

Dear Diary

I am 11 right now. School's OK, I guess. Mum spends most of her time at work or in her darkroom these days. She's earning big bucks! More than dad. I know because I heard them arguing about it a few weeks ago. Dad's always off somewhere new to get the best headlines. I thought I might like to be a reporter like him, but I've decided I don't want to after all. I think I might like to be a detective. I'm a bit lonely so I'm going to ask for a dog. I've decided on a Great Dane.

I made a new friend the other day. He's a bit older than me. He wants us to be secret friends. I met him in the park. He's really cool. Not like the other boys at school who are always on their games machines or play-ing sport. He's like me. Into crime and investigation. He showed me pictures of this cool shack in the woods near his home that was full of weird instruments and a rusty cage. He thinks it was used as an old hunting cabin. He even found a finger in there. It was cold and wrinkled and gross. He said he'll take me one day. When I'm old enough to go on the train by myself.

I'm going to do some research and see what I can find out about the cabin. It's my new project. Maybe I'll even uncover an old crime or a dead body! I'm not going to tell mum and dad about it yet. You know what they're like, always worrying and fussing.

"They'd known each other for a long time. How did we not know? And the shack. He was so young. So innocent."

My tears fell onto the letter. I held it all the way to the station and then folded it and dropped it into the box. Mika met us in the police station car park and took the box. Scott asked if we could give voluntary statements. It was Mika and Officer Shah in the interview room, and they were quiet and sympathetic, letting me say everything I needed to, the tape recording it all. Before we left, Mika informed us that we would need to come in for further questioning. I'd take it day by day. There would be a trial for Mason. More media intrusion. It would be a lot, but Scott and I would hold tight to each other and find a way through.

As we walked out of the station, I grasped Scott's hand and dropped my head on his shoulder. "I'm glad we did that."

Scott ran his fingers through his hair and sighed. "Me too. It's a relief to let it all out."

Driving home, we fact-checked each other's statements, making sure we had both remembered everything. We knew the police would find the holes and question anything that one of us said and the other left out. But, we had nothing to hide anymore.

Back home, Scott left me in the hallway and went upstairs. "There's something I want to get. Back in a sec."

I waited patiently, Minnie sitting to attention beside me. Scott came back downstairs carrying the unfinished portrait Jamie had painted of the back of his head.

"What are you doing with that?" It wasn't finished, and I thought it was an appropriate representation of Jamie's unfinished life.

"I thought we could hang it in here." Scott held it up against the wall.

"Wait. I have something too. They could go next to each other." I disappeared to my darkroom and returned with a large, framed print of Jamie and Minnie sitting together in the garden, both of them wearing sunglasses.

"He'd hate us for putting these up," Scott said.

"He would." I looked up to the top of the stairs, but Jamie didn't appear.

Scott knocked in some picture hooks and hung the painting and the framed photograph. We stood for a minute in silence, and then I slid my arms around Scott's waist. "Perhaps we could have another baby. Jamie would like that, I think. We could learn from our mistakes. Be less interested in our careers and more interested in him or her."

"We'd be old. There's a term for it, isn't there? Geriatric parents?"

"We'd be there. Present. Involved. We'd be better."

Scott twisted round to face me, took my face in his

hands, and kissed me gently on the lips. "Shall we take a coffee onto the porch?"

He hadn't said no. I nodded. We loved Jamie and loved each other, and neither Gunner nor Mason had taken that away from us.

We made the coffees in tandem, a finely tuned ritual of our marriage, then sat outside on the love seat that Jamie had insisted we buy on one of our many trips to the garden centre. Minnie lay at the end of the garden, sprawled sideways, mouth open, legs stretched out, enjoying the sun's rays.

I thought of Jamie sitting on the swing in the park before Mason had come into his life. I didn't want to be reminded of that image every time I took a walk into town. I didn't want to see the river where Devin was drowned or sit in the coffee shop and have flashbacks of Mason looking in at me through the window. I didn't want to worry every time I opened the front door that it might be Suzannah wanting to talk.

Scott blew on his hot coffee. "What do you think about moving?"

I smiled. He'd always had a knack for reading my mind. "Yes, please. Can we? Let's go somewhere hot and quiet. I'll take pictures of happy tourists, and you can write those travel articles you always wanted to."

"We'll call an estate agent in the morning."

The End

Acknowledgements

First, and most importantly, I would like to thank you, reader, for choosing this book. I hope it delivered what you were searching for, be it an adventure, a feeling, an exploration or an escape. For me, writing The Other Boy offered all of these and I am so grateful to you for sharing in my dream of becoming a writer and making it a reality.

I began this journey alone, new to motherhood and in need of some respite from all the challenges a new baby brings. I wrote quietly for a decade, before seeking the help that I needed to create something worthy of your time and your engagement.

That help came first in the form of a master's degree at Winchester University and all the inspiring tutors and dedicated students that I had the pleasure of spending two years with. Thank you for making me believe that I was good enough to call myself a writer.

Then came the incredible stockpile of knowledge offered by Jericho Writers, hours of masterclasses, online and in person events and opportunities to put my writing in front of editors, agents and fellow writers. I feel so lucky to have found such a valuable resource, I have learnt so much and there is still so much left to discover.

Once the book was written, when I had toiled away at

my craft, I needed to entrust my story to a reader. How fortunate was I to find Shalini, a beta reader I sourced through Goodreads. Her feedback was everything I needed and more and I cannot thank her enough. She is the reason I kept submitting my work and the reason I have written the next book and the next.

Although I am alone in my study tapping away on my Mac, I am not alone in my life. To the family I share my days with, thank you for listening to all my ideas, for reading my words, for your honesty and for being patient when I just had to finish the chapter.

Finally, my truly heartfelt gratitude goes to Tule; to Jane, Sinclair, the team and all the other wonderful authors. What a family I landed in! Lucky, lucky me! A perfect publishing partnership, where I feel seen, heard and appreciated. The journey so far has been amazing and I look forward to all that we share in the future.

About the Author

Heidi Field was raised in the beautiful countryside of the South of England with her parents and her two sisters. In her twenties she was a freelance Sports Massage Therapist. She achieved a Degree in Zoology at the age of thirty and then went on to raise two boys and became the stepmother of three more young children. She still lives near her family home with her partner, their Great Dane and the children that have yet to fly the nest. In her early forties Heidi completed a Masters in Creative Writing at Winchester University. She entered the course hoping she would become a children's fantasy writer and left with a burning desire to write contemporary mysteries and thrillers. Heidi wanted to put relatable people in extraordinary situations, challenge them, push them to their limits and watch them fight for their sanity. The Other Boy is her first novel.

Thank you for reading

The Other Boy

If you enjoyed this book, you can find more from all our great authors at TulePublishing.com, or from your favorite online retailer.

TULE

www.ingramcontent.com/pod-product-compliance
Lightning Source LLC
Chambersburg PA
CBHW022349020726
47500CB00002B/188